THE ENAMEL EYE

Also by Pamela Hill:

The Enamel Eye

Pamela Hill

UNITED WRITERS
Cornwall

UNITED WRITERS PUBLICATIONS LTD
Ailsa, Castle Gate, Penzance, Cornwall.

British Library Cataloguing in Publication Data:
A catalogue record for this book is
available from the British Library.

ISBN 9781852001308

Printed in Great Britain by
United Writers Publications Ltd
Cornwall.

To my publishers.

CONTENTS

Part I

Chapter One

The general's portrait hung in the hall, and was the only graven image allowed in the house. It was a half-length, and the brilliant uniform coat and gleaming orders caught the sunlight today, as did the sword, on whose pommel the long-dead hand rested firmly. The face was firm also, beneath a greying thatch of dark hair. The small hazel eyes under their thick brows were perceptive, those of a commander on campaign. When, as now, the sun shone brightly enough on the lake water beyond the open portico, the ripples reflected themselves through the marble pillars and made it seem as though the figure in the portrait moved. Possibly this was why the general, whose bones were in the vault below in a handsome memorial tomb, kept them all in subjection although he had been dead ten years.

This was the Sabbath, with no work allowed; luncheon had been eaten cold, having been prepared the day before. The servants mostly walked decorously in pairs round the lake and the further wooded estate as far as the cottages. No courting was permitted, but the alternative was to sit and read the Bible downstairs in the servants' hall. Some of the older ones preferred to do this, or look as if they did while enjoying a quiet nap. It got you off your feet.

One thing was singular about the general's portrait. His leather scabbard hung correctly below, but the sword was missing. This fact had ceased to interest anyone except the general's grandson Edmund Corbell, aged nine. He still hoped to find it, having hunted several times in vain. To succeed would surely please

Papa for once, and Edmund had once more hauled himself up by the balusters, despite his short leg in the iron shoe he hated. Today he wasn't allowed to swim, as generally happened in afternoons no matter what the weather. The water bore him up and made him feel like other people. It had salt in it from the sea some miles distant, though nobody knew how it got there.

He reached the attics, which ran the full length of the house. Trunks were stored here and he had already explored three. Things there had brought back a past he couldn't remember, but had heard of; the dark undress uniform coats, smelling of cedarwood and sandalwood and camphor, to keep away silverfish and moth; trivia brought home long ago from the India campaigns and from Portugal, where the general had been on Wellesley's staff. Later he had been left with total responsibility after the French withdrawal. Vance the housekeeper's father had been killed there before she was born, under the general's orders carrying despatches to the port; he'd been sniped at by a Bonapartist supporter hidden beside a roadside rock. As a gesture of gratitude his widow, Vance's mother, had been made housekeeper here from between-maid, and Vance herself – her name was Peggy – had received an education beyond her place, and now was housekeeper in turn. There wasn't much she didn't know; at times Edmund wished she knew less. It was like having a constant all-seeing eye watching, ears hearing. Everybody at Lackmere obeyed Peggy Vance and sought her advice instead of Mama's. This was understandable, as since his own twisted birth Mama had lain on her chaise-longue, unable to walk. Papa said he, Edmund, was a child of sin and must never marry, and that he himself was being punished for having married Mama instead of obeying his father and becoming the husband of Cousin Mildred, which would have continued the line as she was descended from the first lord's second marriage. As it was, her son Alfred, who resembled an angel, should rightly inherit rather than Edmund, who must ensure this.

Edmund's mouth tightened, unlike that of a child. He loathed Alfred already, although they hadn't met. He recalled being carried in, when he was about four years old, to be seen by Cousin Mildred and her new husband, who was quite old and had surprising hair the colour of marmalade. He was a law lord. Cousin Mildred had sat with her narrow feet together in well-polished shoes, and at sight of Edmund had said, "Poor little fellow, what a tragedy," which hadn't made anyone feel better. Peggy Vance told him afterwards that he wasn't a child of sin at all, except his mother's, who had gone on tight-lacing when he was expected because she wanted to keep a narrow waist to waltz with Prince Albert at Windsor.

"She's paid," had stated Peggy, with what sounded like satisfaction. He wasn't sure why, but it had left him with the short leg and one shoulder so much higher than the other that his face, which resembled the general's, was sunk beneath it. One way and the other he would never be a soldier. Neither could Papa, because no reputable regiment would accept the son of a man who had resigned on the eve of Waterloo.

Why had it happened? Nobody would tell him. Papa had said he was on no account to ask. Papa had taken to religion instead, and resembled God. His dark eyes were burning with the power of the Spirit, who told him what to say at household prayers. They were over for today.

The general – Edmund couldn't stop thinking of him – had lived all the rest of his life here at Lackmere, seen by few. Perhaps he had often passed by the window where Edmund stood for moments now, looking out at the whole expanse of the lake. It was a long oval, about a mile from the boathouse end to the other, which was near the vault and the woods, all of it bounded by the high estate wall the first lord had built to stop the world looking in.

Today Edmund could see the little figures, far below, of the servants on their decorous Sabbath walk, like a trail of ants. Beyond, on the far side, was the shore where dry shrubs grew and behind that, the path where the donkey from the home farm came along daily with panniers of milk for the house and the cottages. Nobody else went across there much. The farm was down a slope and couldn't be seen, and the cottages were up the hill beyond the woods and couldn't be seen either, except in winter when the trees were bare. Most of the tenants who lived there were Peggy's relations. They came down on Fridays with their rents. Otherwise Papa sometimes drove up in the dog-cart by himself to visit them, if anything needed putting right.

It might please Papa, and lighten the deep lines running from nose to mouth, if the sword was found. Today, as usual, it wasn't.

He had almost come to the last of the trunks, and what he had found made the rest wait for another day. It had been buried deep under other things. Edmund replaced them, then opened the hard green package in its cracked wax cloth, hidden under the remains of a silver-and-white striped muslin dress that smelt of old roses. The package wasn't the sword, but it might be the pommel.

It wasn't. Instead it was the most beautiful thing he had ever seen in his life.

It was silver, and hadn't tarnished because of the wax. It was round in shape, with a handle folded over. He extended the handle and wound it, and the ghost of a tune sounded through the attic; one-two-three, one-two-three. Edmund listened till it came to an end, then wound it again, and it played again. While it played, he had looked at the rest; it was a musical-box, and he'd heard of them, but this was special, a present for someone. On top were bunched feathers and the motto *Ich Dien*. Round the side ran words in Latin. *Bellissima Jocosa, Bellissima Jocosa, Bellissima.* Most beautiful Jocosa: he'd seen the name before, on a tomb in the vault, next to the general's large white marble memorial one with all the carved flags and the names of his victories. They held a service of remembrance there every year. Most beautiful Jocosa; and here she was, at the end of the Latin words, smiling, a miniature in enamels. Her dark hair was curly, cropped short in a way they didn't wear it now, and she had green eyes that laughed wickedly. She was wearing the silver-and-white striped dress, and it showed right through. He'd never seen a woman through her clothes before. It was his first sight of breasts. Hers were two little snowy mounds, tipped with wild strawberries like the ones that grew up at the edge of the woods in summer. He wanted to laugh with her, to touch her as though she was flesh. He would take the box and portrait down and play the waltz to Mama.

He closed the trunk, wrapped the silver box up in the green waxed cloth, and holding it to himself limped out of the attics. Looking far below at the turn of the stairs, he saw Peggy Vance cross the hall. She would ask where he'd been and what that was he was carrying, and he wanted Mama to know first; nobody ever showed Mama anything or talked to her much.

He waited on the half-landing while the tall queenly figure of the housekeeper, with its broad strand of white hair twisted among the black, and the keys bunched at her apron, crossed the marble tiles. They made a pattern in black and white, like Peggy herself. She stopped before the general's portrait, found a chair and stood on it, and ran her finger across the top of the gilded frame to make sure the maids hadn't left any dust. Then she got off the chair and replaced it, and stood again before the portrait, regarding it eye to eye. After a moment she spoke, quietly but Edmund could hear.

"Remember me, you old bastard? Shouldn't think so; it might have been anyone, at the time."

She turned and went through a further door, and Edmund came down with his package. He knew something now that she didn't know he knew. Also, she'd been carrying out work on the Sabbath, standing on the chair and looking for dust. He wouldn't say anything, but was aware of a slight feeling of triumph. Dust blew in constantly from the gravel path at the lake's edge, which just left room for carriages to drive past to the stables. However, Vance should have seen to it last night, and spent today in godly reflection, and hadn't.

Peggy Vance had gone back to the older part of the house, to her housekeeper's room where nobody might enter uninvited. It contained few personal things as these were mostly upstairs, in her bedroom on the second floor near Master Edmund's schoolroom. All of that part of the house had beds in every room the way they used to do, and you had to walk through one to reach the next.

On the shelves down here were the housekeeping books, some in Ma's handwriting and some in her own. Ma had died six years ago of a blockage. It was as well, or there would have been two queens in one hive. The other ledgers contained prescriptions she, Peggy, had collected and written out. Part of her education had been that of a lady's maid, to know how to make up creams and unguents, soothing lotions for spots and cures for freckles and sunburn and worse things. As well, there were mixtures for clysters, depending on what you wanted. One was the famous black draught used on the Lackmere maids if they transgressed, but they got it by mouth with their noses held. The dire effects worked unstoppably on what was then counted as the culprit's day off. Word of Mrs Vance's draught, given first thing in the early hours, got round as soon as a girl was hired, and as a result, transgressions were few.

Peggy sat down in the wooden rocking-chair and picked up a piece of plain white knitting. It was to be a vest for her little daughter Margaret, who was also the general's. Margaret had been left from the first up at the cottages with the two old Tesson cousins in case she got to look like her real father and cause gossip. She hadn't; almost exactly the same age as Master Edmund, she resembled nobody in particular except herself, a quiet biddable little creature with brown hair and the dark Tesson eyes. She and young George, old George and Agnes's son born late, were fond of each other and it was most desirable that they marry later on. It would secure the old Tesson line, which otherwise might have died out. George and Agnes wouldn't have more children now. Agnes had been forty when young George was born.

The general's part in the matter had never been spoken of. Peggy's own Ma, who'd been in service here all her life except for the brief marriage to a young soldier, wouldn't believe the story. General Lord Corbell was by far too godly a man, had never looked at a woman since his wife died, and because he'd been found dead of a seizure at the time, Peggy needn't wickedly put the blame on him after sinning with Josiah Vance, as must have happened. She and Josiah must be married at once, although Peggy could have done better for herself. All that book-learning needn't give her ideas above herself by this time; after all, who could say what would happen now Mr Henry – he was fourth lord by then, with the general's having died – had married a bird-witted nobody instead of good plain rich reliable Cousin Mildred Musters, as the general had intended? Peggy was to have become her lady's maid, but with things as they evidently were, that wouldn't have lasted. The best that could be done was a marriage with Josiah, and it was to be hoped nobody would count their fingers when the child came to be born.

Josiah – she hadn't been certain about him one way or the other – had taken it badly when he found she wasn't a maiden, and had gone off to London to find work. He never came home. By the time Margaret was born the new Lady Corbell wanted Peggy, who was good at arranging hair, as her lady's maid anyway, and took her along when she and the fourth lord went to Court. The newborn Margaret was left at the cottages, which was safer from all points of view. Lady Corbell was in the family way herself already, but hadn't said so as she wanted a carefree season.

"Tighter, Vance, you fool. There was an inch more to spare yesterday."

"My lady, it'll hurt the baby."

She hadn't cared, and look at Master Edmund now. Mr Henry – his lordship, one got used to it – hadn't taken anything to do with his wife since seeing his heir. At the beginning, he would have given her the moon.

Corbells, in any case, weren't the true heirs; those were the Tessons. She, Peggy, was one. They'd been here since the Conquest. Peggy thought of it as her needles clacked. Tesson tombs were trodden into the ground in the old vault, flat and not rearing like the later Corbell ones. Often the inscriptions couldn't be read for age. Tessons had been squires of *lacù mare*, mentioned in Domesday Book. After the last squire, two centuries ago, gambled away his estates and his daughter to his creditor, the rich Huguenot moneylender who took his name from *corbeille*, a shopping-basket, the Tessons had become servants of the Corbells. That was a shameful tale, and the sight of gilded baskets in wrought iron on the lodge gates, and embroidered on the black velvet hangings of the master bed, didn't alter it. The first Tesson bride had been unwilling anyway, and must have felt she was in a coffin with her mean old husband. After her son was born she'd run off with a cousin. The first lord's revenge had been fearful.

Best not think of that. She, Peggy, had been brushing down the same black-and-gold curtains, very old they were even then, when the general had come in at her, half mad with the news that had been sent.

"My son has eloped with a penniless fool. Come here, girl."

His face had grown livid in the very act of taking her maidenhead. He was sixty by then. When she was able to free herself and heard him gasp, she knew he was dying. She'd fled for help, and when they came and saw him they sent for the doctor, although it was already too late. The doctor wrote a certificate to say General Lord Corbell had died of a seizure.

Peggy knew well enough why he'd taken the news of Mr

17

Henry's sudden marriage so badly. He had never been certain Mr Henry was his own son; you couldn't tell one way or the other from looking at him, tall and thin with dark eyes. To marry cousin Mildred would have set matters right and ensured that the Corbell line, which she belonged to, continued. This unknown bride had made everything worse, besides being the only time Mr Henry had dared disobey the general.

The funeral had been well attended, and now Mr Henry had erected the marble memorial with the flags down in the vault. After Master Edmund's terrible birth he'd taken nothing more to do with his bride, and was firmly determined to make it up to Cousin Mildred by letting her son inherit. Well, all of that would be seen in due course. She herself would never have mentioned that last encounter with the general, but it became impossible not to. Nobody much knew about Margaret, even now.

She finished the row. Nobody was left here either now who would tell her what she might or might not do on the Sabbath. She could do as she chose in that and every other way, just as if she were the lady of the manor herself, while the real one lay idle and helpless on her chaise-longue.

Chapter Two

Anna Corbell was lying as she always did now, slender ankles crossed beneath a crocheted afghan. She had turned her fair head, with its side-bunched ringlets, petulantly aside from the constant sight of her own cracked reflection on the wall. Corbell wouldn't let her have the Spanish looking-glass repaired. Evidently his father the general, from whom one could seldom escape although he had been dead ten years, had smashed the glass with the hilt of his sword on return from the war in the Peninsula, saying no woman should ever take pleasure in looking at her face in it again. The origins of this remark had never been explained to Anna, but thankfully she had never had to face the old curmudgeon and was uninterested in the workings of his mind. Either Corbell refused to allow the least act of his late father to remain unforgotten, or else – and this was more probable – he had deliberately hung it there as a punishment to her for all that had happened since.

To watch the change in her own appearance was depressing enough in any case. Her mouth had acquired a discontented droop. Her former roseal complexion had faded with being constantly confined indoors, without entertainment except for having the fire kept up, and having her hair washed frequently by the maids and dressed by Peggy Vance after being dried out on pillows stuffed with lavender.

The hair was all that was left of her former beauty, wrenched apart as her innards had been by Edmund's dreadful birth. She would never have consented to go through such an experience

19

again even had it been possible. As it was, Corbell avoided her. Snippets of gossip from Vance were all that remained, as nobody called now. Sometimes she could have the Court Circular read aloud if Corbell had parted with his newspaper. She wasn't interested in what else went on in the world. Her sole exercise of power came when she tugged at the bell-pull to summon the maids, even late at night. The smell of illness, of bedpans, of lavender had long become unnoticed. She didn't sleep well, and the days and nights passed somehow.

There were things she could remember, and turn over in her mind. She had been an exquisitely pretty young girl, fresh from school, when plain dull Mildred Musters, who'd been a fellow-pupil, invited her to stay while she made ready to marry her rich cousin Henry Corbell, son of a general who was also a lord. Anna made up her mind to try to marry Henry herself before she so much as met him. Mildred was extremely rich already, and could support a fortune-hunter instead. Also, Anna had a secret to hide; her father was in trade. If it was known, she could never hope for a good marriage.

Mildred was absorbed in domestic matters which would enable her to make Cousin Henry a good wife, as she told Anna he had never been allowed any freedom or pleasure but had been strictly brought up in order that he should not take after his mother. On that subject Mildred had refused to say any more.

One way and another, when Henry Corbell arrived Anna deliberately set her cap, or rather her tossing silver-fair ringlets, at him. He was tall, thin and grave-faced, with fiery dark eyes. On first setting them on Anna, he told her soon, he had thought she was like a little china shepherdess, so delicate that she would break if handled roughly. "Try me in the waltz," she said, laughing and showing kitten's teeth. The days went past, and soon she said to Mildred, "You play the piano while I teach Henry to waltz; he should not be married till he can do it." Mildred had sat down and thumped out what she could, while Anna, dimpling and offering her tiny waist, circled the room with Cousin Henry. By the end of the waltz, he was hers.

After that it had been a matter of deciding how to break the news to Mildred and, worse, to Henry's father. The only answer in the end had been to run away together, leaving notes for both parties. There was no need to explain to Anna's Dad; he'd said to leave him out and do the best for herself.

She persuaded Henry to take her to Court to be presented on her marriage. As the future Lady Corbell she would have been acceptable, but in fact she was so already; the general had died of rage on receiving the news. Henry had to go back at once to arrange the funeral, and sent Peggy Vance to attend Anna and see to her hair and gowns. She was beginning to enjoy a giddy season when it became evident that she was already in the state ladies are said to be who love their lords. It was too soon for convenience, and Anna kept quiet about it as long as possible. The Queen, after all, danced when in the same condition. Prince Albert had partnered Anna twice, and waltzed like a god might, but seemed to find her frivolous. He was so handsome, it was a pity he was so solemn.

Mildred had married in a year or two, to a much older husband Anna remembered from schooldays, as he was considered mildly eligible; he was a law lord, known to those who know such things as the Palomino Stud. He seemed to have settled down on Mildred's money. The pair made a visit of reconciliation to Lackmere when Edmund was three. Lord Sissington, Mildred's husband, had the most extraordinary hair, thick, curly and the colour of orange marmalade. It didn't go with his port-wine face. Edmund had been brought in, and Mildred, who always meant well, had said, "Poor little fellow, what a tragedy," and he was taken out. Since then, Mildred, who looked like a horse, had given birth to a son said to resemble an angel. They'd called him Alfred. He had his father's hair.

Memory was all she had left. Dad had died quietly, behind his grocery counter. By then, of course, Henry – Corbell by now – had found out about him. Other things mattered more. The birth – ahh . . .

A scratching came at the door, and her son entered. He was carrying something. Anna never liked to look at him. Since Corbell had done so he had ceased to have anything to do with her after that terrible first visit. "You have ruined our son with your folly. The sin was mine for marrying you and breaking faith. It killed my father, and now a hunchback and cripple is my heir. It is a mercy there can be no more. In any case I have done with you."

She remembered that Edmund was standing there, having

21

unwrapped his package. "What is it?" said Anna coldly. She really couldn't bear to look at him, but the contents were interesting; it was something made of silver, still bright.

"Look, Mama, I've found a musical-box. It plays a tune."

The waltz ground out stiffly, subdued by time. Tears began to run down Anna's face.

"I used to waltz," she said. "Play it again." He'd pleased her, he believed, although she was crying. He wound the handle once more, and didn't hear at first the door open or see Papa standing there, drawn face pale with anger. Edmund remembered, too late, that it was the Sabbath.

"I could hear that noise in the library," said Henry Corbell. "Stop it instantly."

Edmund wanted to explain that you couldn't stop it, it had to wind to the end. However, Lord Corbell had perceived the bunched feathers, the enamel portrait of the young woman. He strode forward and seized the musical-box, throwing it on the ground and stamping on it with his heel. The little tune died in a sad jangle. Anna began to scream in her harsh voice. For some reason connected with the distributions of Providence, pretty women are seldom given soft ones.

"Where did you find this?" Edmund's father asked. His voice was icy.

"In the – in the attic, Papa. In a trunk." He needn't have expected to keep it to himself. Papa was very angry. He ground the enamel portrait into cracked fragments. Everything had gone wrong.

"Pick up the pieces, then come with me. You had no business to be in the attics, or opening trunks. In future it is forbidden. You will visit me in the library tomorrow at eleven. Before that, this abomination must be sunk in the lake."

He, Edmund, would be caned tomorrow, trousers down as usual, bent over the walnut desk. It was a ceremony that couldn't take place on the Sabbath. He took time to wonder what an abomination was and why, apart from the wickedness of music on Sundays, the pretty little box with its Latin words was one. He would have to ask Peggy after all.

By noon on Monday Edmund, still sobbing, was lying on the bed on his face while Vance applied a soothing ointment she kept for such occasions and which was compounded of cold used tea leaves and calamine. Already the angry red weals on his bottom were cooling, although the humiliation remained. He had been able to explain to Peggy why it had had to happen, and her answer had been predictable.

"You should have asked me before showing it to anyone. I could have told you how his lordship would take it, suddenly like that. It'll be the first time he's seen his mother's face."

She stood back from the bed. "The general burned all her portraits when he brought her home after the war. She hadn't behaved very well while he was away, refused a voucher at Almack's and the rest of it. Feeling a bit better now, eh?"

So Bellissima Jocosa had been Papa's mother. That meant she was his own grandmother. The idea was strange. He couldn't think of her as old.

"She didn't live to be old," Peggy replied. "She died when your father was born, up in the west tower where he'd kept her since the scandal, or rather his finding out about it after coming back from abroad." She clamped her lips on what more she could have said about everything, and related how the general, arriving home from Portugal and finding his young wife spoken of as the Corbell Strumpet, had resigned his army commission, brought her back to Lackmere and flogged her like a recruit, smashed the mirror he'd sent her from Spain, and got his son on her without even waiting to be sure it wasn't some other's she'd kicked up her heels with; some officer from the Tsar's suite at Pulteney's, or that Lord Yarmouth. Prinny by then was past it, but they said Jocosa had been found on his knee while he played his cello. They said a great many things. It was the irony of fate that had the general waited nine months to see his grandson, he would have known his own features again.

She hadn't said nearly all of that to Master Edmund. "Tell me more about her," he said. He had almost forgotten his sore bottom.

Jocosa, Lady Corbell, had been a Tesson, born at the cottages. The general, promoted young to major, had passed by and seen her playing in the dust, a pretty child with tangled dark curls. Corbells till then had done as they might with Tesson women, but the third lord, as he became soon after, was a well-doing young man, unlike his father. He sent Jocosa to a young ladies'

23

seminary, intending to marry her when she was old enough.

"Oh, she learnt French and the Court curtsey, and how to preside at teatables, but none of it would rid her of her wild blood." She shouldn't have said as much; Ma had told her how great-aunt Sarah Tesson had had an affair with a pack-pedlar, which was where the green eyes came from. It wasn't spoken of.

They were married in the end, Jocosa and the general, as he was by then, between the India and Portugal wars. General Lord Corbell had hired a town house to give his bride a season after having her presented on her marriage, as she found Lackmere dull. When he had to go overseas he left old Connie Musters, who was part Corbell from the first lord's second marriage, with Jocosa as chaperone. What Jocosa didn't tell him in any letter she wrote was that old Connie had taken a heart attack sitting watching at a ball, and died in the coach on the way home. She wasn't replaced, which left Jocosa free.

To be fair, it was a long time for a young woman not to see her husband, even if he'd been more like a father to her. He would have given her anything in the world, but the war against Boney occupied him for the time. Letters took six weeks to go back and forth, and life in Regency London was anything but dull. Lord Yarmouth, with his red whiskers and black reputation, wasn't the only one who came calling. Her ladyship flirted with Lord Byron, like a great many; and Prinny, as already remembered, who by then was, however, past much. Then there was the Tsar and his suite at Pulteney's; oh, yes, the Russians. If the general hadn't been delayed in Spain it might have been less of a disaster, with a Moldavian colonel wearing a silk rose in his hat from Jocosa's garter. They said that was what the general recognised when he came home. However, that might be a tall story; one silk rose was much like another. Nevertheless the voucher was certainly not renewed for Almack's.

The end of it, when the general came home at last, could have been foreseen. Peggy could just remember having seen her ladyship once, within the year after she was brought home in disgrace. She herself had been almost too young to climb the tower stairs, but had followed Ma with the daily tray of food.

She would never forget that one sight. Lady Corbell was an unwieldy shape by then, heavy with child. Her head and face were covered by a thick black veil. She was sitting in a chair facing the window, and didn't turn her head. On the wall was the cracked Spanish mirror. There was a memory, still, of hearing, earlier, a long agonised outraged scream, not the kind you'd give merely for being beaten. Ma said not to ask any more. Now she, Peggy, had to stop Master Edmund asking.

"Mr Henry, that's my lord, was born soon, and her ladyship died then." The small coffin had been carried, after the funeral, down to the vault, where it lay now in a low stone tomb beside the general's grand beflagged one of white marble.

Edmund listened. At the end he said, "Peggy, what's fornication? Papa –" he winced for a moment, remembering his stinging weals – "said it's the sin most displeasing to God of them all, and that I was to remember it, but I don't know what it means."

"It means doing what you oughtn't, dear. You'll know when you're older." She replaced the top on the jar of tea-leaf ointment, and departed.

Edmund felt in his pocket, knowing a moment's triumph. There was still something Peggy didn't know, that nobody knew but himself. He had managed to keep one green enamel eye. It was there now, in his pocket; he could feel it with his fingers. It was full of laughter and invitation and wickedness. The rest of Bellissima Jocosa was in the lake. He'd rowed out a stern-faced Papa first thing this morning, before the caning in the library, and had been made to empty everything, the ruined musical-box and the fragments of enamel, over and watch it sadly spiralling down, shards and dust and bubbles of air, to the deep centre. They had rowed back in silence.

He might have recovered enough to swim out this afternoon, and call down to Bellissima Jocosa that he still had her other eye and would keep it as a talisman, and later on would have it set in a gold fob like the Palomino Stud had worn on his visit with Cousin Mildred. *Poor little fellow, what a tragedy.* He'd show them. Today was Monday, and by afternoons he could do as he liked.

b

Chapter Three

Peggy Vance, with the day's orders seen to, got on her walking-boots and went up to visit her daughter. Margaret was growing up fast, forward for her age.

Going up through the woods past the lake, she saw Master Edmund doing an overarm crawl in spite of his weals, making the long water splash silver in the sun. He had the kind of bullheaded courage, she thought, that had made his grandfather second only to Wellington. It was the greater tragedy that the general's career had had to end as it did, in ostracism and twenty arid years spent alone. Both he and Mr Henry had led the kind of buttoned-up existence that was bad for any man. Mr Henry had been beaten by his father often enough in the way of discipline, as all boys were; but for him in turn to beat Master Edmund as he did was wrong, considering the way he was. She saw again the twisted hunchbacked body, and the rising weals. It was as though the fourth lord was taking revenge on his father's likeness arriving too late. A bit of love was what both of them needed, but it wasn't hers to give. All of her heart, now the general was gone, was for Margaret and the Tesson future.

She remembered hearing of the curse uttered by the last squire on leaving Lackmere. He had cursed all of Corbell blood, even his future grandchildren. Certainly if the first Lord Corbell wasn't roasting in hell, nobody would be. He'd married Maria Tesson to keep her father, the same last squire, out of a debtor's prison. He himself had made his money by robbing an abbey of its jewels near Calais, then had hidden them in the lining of his round hat to cross the Channel at the time of the Revocation, when many Huguenots left the France of Louis XIV. Corbeille, as he called himself at first, had sold them profitably in London, then set up as a moneylender in a small way and then a large one. His fortune and title had come at last by advising Sir Robert Walpole, then in power, on no account to back the South Sea Bubble, which left half England bankrupt. Sir Robert had shown his gratitude.

All that was fair in its way, but Maria Tesson had been in love with her cousin Oliver, and engaged to marry him. She'd loathed her enforced marriage with the rich mean old basket-maker, and had eloped with Oliver Tesson after the birth of her son, whom she left with his father. The old Huguenot had taken three years to find the couple, happy together in a cottage in Kildare and again in debt. They had a daughter by then, a little thing about the age Peggy herself had been when she set eyes on Jocosa Corbell in the tower.

The first lord had planned his revenge. He had Oliver Tesson arrested for debt and for abducting his wife. Having had him thrown in prison he made sure hired bravoes were waiting when the prisoner at last came out. They threw Oliver Tesson in front of a carriage and drove it back and forth over him till he was dead. The watch found the body after some delay. Nobody was held to blame; such things happened.

By then, the first Lord Corbell had locked Maria up in the west tower and taken away her daughter, who by law was his. That was the devilish part. He failed to have the child educated and brought her up as a servant. When she was fifteen he took her to his bed. She bore him two children, a boy and a girl, knowing no better. After that the first lord married her to one of his footmen. His earlier son by Maria, later second lord, a profligate, had his will of their two daughters.

Maria by then was mad, locked up still, out of her mind between the death of her lover and the fate of their child. She didn't die soon enough, but died cursing Corbell. He saw his boy by the Tesson girl debauched, then paid him to seduce his sister, boasting that there would always be a pure strain of Tessons in his service. He was in his eighties by then, but before he died married a rich widow. That was where Cousin Mildred's line had come from, with the widow's money inherited separately from a former marriage.

Ma had been the great-grandchild of incest and proud of it. She had married a husband of Tesson descent by way of the footman. Peggy, therefore, was doubly a Tesson, and till lately the line had seemed secure. However, she herself would be having no children by Josiah, wherever he was, and Agnes had George and that was all. George and Margaret seemed the only hope. It was possible there had been too much inbreeding for fertility.

Now here she was, almost at the wicket gate through which poor Maria had eloped long ago with her cousin. It was little known of, and sunk in the high back wall. The road beyond led to the village, but it was quicker to go down by the lodge gate. Here, still within the grounds, was the pit. Nobody knew how deep it was or how it had come. It had been used from the beginning for rubble and night-soil, and brambles grew across so that not everyone knew it was there. Young George and Margaret were near it now, picking blackberries and putting them in a basket, and eating some.

"Be careful," Peggy called. It was pleasant to see them together, two rosy laughing faces stained with blackberry juice, fingers entwined over the basket's handle. Agnes saw to it that they slept in the same box bed, so that when anything happened between them it would be natural enough, and then they could marry. Come to think, it was more or less what the first lord had done with his children by way of Maria and Oliver. It was to be hoped the curse made against all of Corbell blood wouldn't prevail, as that last was dispersed among most of them now, with Margaret the general's daughter.

Peggy had a word with the children, then walked on to visit Agnes Tesson at the cottage. Agnes made tea in the brown pot, and they sat and talked like the old friends they were. "Margaret's going to be a good little housewife," said Agnes proudly. "She can use the flatiron without burning herself or whatever she's smoothing. Soon she'll cook a floury potato." That was the test of a well-taught bride.

How short the years of happiness were to be nobody could have foreseen. Six months after the marriage, young George was crushed between the wall and a lurching farm-cart. Margaret, sixteen by then, was left to bear his child. There was a moment's hope when a big fine boy, with dark hair, was born at last; but Margaret didn't want to live lacking George. It was that rather then the birth that killed her.

She waited to give me a Tesson, Peggy thought; then she went to be with George. She herself hadn't taken time truly to know her daughter.

At least there was a grandson. However, as time passed it became clear that all wasn't as it should be. Jemmy was slow in learning to speak, and never did manage more than a few simple words. He was an innocent, as they call them; happy in himself, loving to those who were kind to him, singing a strange tuneless song. He cried when anyone mocked him, and some, especially girls as he grew up, did. The curse had done its work; a cripple down at the house, an idiot up at the cottages. Jemmy would be the last Tesson.

Peggy Vance raised her fists to heaven and swore that it should not be so. In some way, in whatever way, she would see a Tesson heir from Jemmy before she died.

All that was long after Yolande O'Neill had come to Lackmere, to teach Master Edmund Spanish at the request of his father.

Chapter Four

"I desire that you will write to your acquaintance, Anna, and find a reliable governess who will teach Edmund Spanish. I have progressed as far with him in Latin as I may, and he seems proficient enough to use it as a base for other derived tongues. I intend to send him to manage the sugar plantations abroad when Mildred's son comes here to familiarise himself with estate matters on the land which will one day be his."

"I have small acquaintance left," said Anna plaintively. She hadn't listened to most of the speech. Henry always talked, when he talked to her at all, as if he had a message from on high. The sugar plantations in the West Indies, one of the first lord's ventures, brought in a substantial part of the Corbell income. As for Mildred's son Alfred, Henry refused to go back on his assumption that he owed the little angel the estate for having jilted his mother. Mildred's husband, retired now, was poorly and wouldn't last.

"You were moving in the highest circles at Windsor, were you not? Follow that up." He spoke cruelly as usual; she'd stopped letting it trouble her. She recalled a certain marchioness who had always been short of money, her husband having gambled away her dowry. One saw less of that kind of thing now since the Queen's marriage.

Anna sent for pen and paper, and wrote to the marchioness, offering suitable reimbursement if she could contrive to find a Spanish governess for Edmund. Almost certainly such a person would be a papist, which would not suit Henry at all. However, she would have done what he asked, not that there would be any gratitude from him.

The marchioness replied with a long and gushing letter. Of course she remembered dear Lady Corbell, and happened to know of just such a young woman as was required. Last year, she herself had contrived to have presented – such things had to be arranged – the elder daughter of a *tradesman* named *Smith*. He seemed to make a great deal of money, and had spared no expense in fitting Miss Betty out. His wife had, of course, asked for advice about the correct appearance for presentation, including the height of the feathers. While visiting their house accordingly, she herself had happened to see a pleasant dark-haired young woman come in leading the younger daughter, who sadly would never achieve presentation, being mentally afflicted. The governess had been remarkably successful with her, and seemed to be part Spanish and part Irish, her father having been wounded at Vimeiro.

Since then two things had happened. Betty Smith had decided after all to marry a friend of her brother's, who was with the Honourable East India Company, and had gone out there. (Smith said the whole thing had been a waste of *brass*.) Secondly, the afflicted younger girl had died, as such persons tended to do, at fourteen. Mrs Smith had grown so fond of Miss O'Neill, the governess, that she wanted her to stay on as lady-companion, but the young woman considered herself bound to return to her convent by the autumn. It might just be possible to engage her before she did so if the convent authorities were offered enough in compensation through oneself.

Anna sent the letter to Corbell in his library. He spent the days there compiling notes from his everlasting sermons, or else was to be found downstairs ordering the cementing over of certain Roman tiles he considered improper. Sacks of lime had for some days been carted along the path beyond the portico to the outer vault entrance, to save carrying them down the steep flight of inner stairs. Anna was sick of the faint, acrid smell of dust which drifted even through the joints of closed windows, making everything worse than it was already.

Corbell did not reply that day or the next. He'd probably decided not to proceed with the matter of a decidedly popish governess. Any by now who spoke French or Spanish were probably from convent finishing-schools begun by nuns who had fled the Terror late last century. Often Catholic supporters in England had given them country-houses in which to maintain themselves by teaching, and such schools had continued to flourish. If Corbell refused to deal with them, he could look for a governess himself.

However, on the third afternoon he appeared. Edmund as usual was out swimming.

"As there is a military connection from my late father's war, I am prepared to overlook this person's religious views provided she does not impart them to my son," he said. "You may write to request this young woman's references."

Edmund had been disturbed at first when he heard there was to be a governess. One of the few times he and Papa dealt well together were during Latin lessons if he worked hard enough. Now, it would be like having an extra Peggy watching everything, somebody he didn't know sleeping next door to the schoolroom and sharing meals with him there. It wouldn't be possible to be private, except in the lake.

He fingered Jocosa's enamel eye, still in his pocket. He'd kept it secretly for a long time now, almost two years, and whenever he swam out to the lake's centre he spoke to her.

However, as soon as he set eyes on Miss Yolande, he knew it would be quite all right.

Chapter Five

It was her eyes he noticed first. They were grey, like the lake on a day when the sun was low, then you noticed sundry little flecks and sparkles of colour, dark and light, in the moving water. They held a kind of laughter which was different from Jocosa's, in her inviting eye. He understood now why she wasn't spoken of.

He had learnt by this time what fornication meant. He'd asked Tom Walshe, the new boy in the kitchens, who seemed to know most things. Tom had been sharpening knives at the great sandstone wheel which you turned with a handle, and the whirring of blades against soft stone drowned his voice so that nobody else heard. He explained quite well, although he admitted he hadn't tried it yet himself. He also told Edmund the ugly short word people used as a rule. That was that, and there needn't have been any mystery; it was like what dogs did.

Miss Yolande's laughter was different, and gave out a kind of contentment, a sharing of kindness and joy. Her fringed lashes were black like her hair, which was the colour of a raven's wing and twisted in a low knot on her short white neck. When she bent her head a silver chain could just be seen above the high dark bodice of her plain gown. Whatever hung at the end of the chain was hidden in her plumpness – he still dared not think of breasts – above her tiny waist. Her hands and feet were tiny also, and when she moved it was like somebody about to dance. When he knew her better he said so.

"I was never allowed to dance, but I used to look through a telescope at the stars at night. They had one on the roof."

33

Her voice was soft and Irish, like her father's; her mother had been Spanish and had married El Capitano, as they'd called him, during the war. She and Edmund had begun to talk a great deal by then in Castilian. Its clicking rolling consonants and its likeness to Latin, which he'd already been taught by Papa, made him want to laugh. He had never been as happy. No doctor could straighten his crooked shoulder or make his short leg the same as the other, but it no longer mattered. Miss Yolande said it was what people were like inside that counted, and that he had a fine mind and must nourish it. All that had sounded stately in Castilian.

She slept next door to the schoolroom, beyond his own bedroom. Beyond that again, Peggy Vance slept. Vance didn't keep as constant a watch these days. She would send up meals to the schoolroom, where he and Miss Yolande ate together, and one of the maids would come upstairs to make the beds. Otherwise they were almost in their own private world. At nights Miss Yolande would brush her black hair loose, tying it with a piece of wool to fall over one shoulder, like a dark waterfall. That was the way they used to wear it at the court of Spain, she said; but she only did it because otherwise, it would be tangled in the morning. "Please come in and say goodnight to me when it looks like that," he said; they always spoke now in Castilian. When she did so, Edmund could see the soft shapes of her breasts move beneath her nightgown and bedgown. Once, when she bent over him and kissed his cheek, they touched him and he felt a shiver of delight. The only way he couldn't trust her was to tell her about that. He still remembered the caning about Jocosa's, and didn't want another.

Papa made frequent visits to the schoolroom at first, disapproving because Miss Yolande was a papist. Once he remarked on the silver chain.

"What is that you wear on the end of your chain, Miss O'Neill? If it is a Romish crucifix, it must be taken off. The terms of your appointment specified that no popish symbols were to be brought into the house. Nor is adornment of any kind suitable for a governess."

"It is a lock of my mother's hair, Lord Corbell," she said quietly.

She brought out from inside her bodice the object on the end of the silver chain. It was a locket made of amber, which seemed to trap the light and warmth of the sun, the warmth of her body. She turned it so that a plain glass panel showed at the back, with coiled against it a loop of black hair, the colour of her own.

Corbell said gruffly, "You may wear it outside your gown if you wish," turned on his heel and went out. After that he didn't appear at lessons as often, but sent word that if they wished to make use of the library they might do so at a time when he was not working there.

That meant they could borrow books of English and French and Latin poetry, and read Shakespeare's plays and sonnets and other books the second lord, who had acquired a taste for fine things abroad, had collected, brought home and shelved anyhow. One day, Edmund thought, he'd tidy the books and index them. Then he remembered he was to go to the West Indies and that Cousin Alfred, whom he already disliked, would be here instead with the books and the lake. He mentioned it once to Yolande. Rain was misting the windows, obscuring the lake. He didn't like not to be able to see it.

"But it will be yours, surely," he heard her say. "You will be fifth lord."

"Papa says I mustn't marry." He tended to forget, in her company, that he wasn't the same shape as other people.

"There is no reason why you should not, if you meet someone who would make you happy," Yolande replied. She was looking at a herbal, and her white finger traced the outline of a camomile leaf. Edmund blurted out what he had long wanted to say, but hadn't liked to.

"You would make me happy. Nobody else would, now. I know I'm ugly and twisted, but if you will wait till I'm old enough to marry you and come to the West Indies, or wherever I go, I'd like that." He knew the ending sounded lame. He would buy her everything she wanted; pretty gowns, hats, furs for cold weather.

She hadn't laughed, to make him feel foolish. "I have told you often that it does not matter what people look like, but what they are," she said. "Our dear Lord said that, but I am not supposed to talk to you about him. As for marrying you, I love you very much, but I'm too old for you and have promised to be a nun."

"I don't want you to be a nun. You would have to cut your

hair." Mama had said that; it was the kind of thing she knew.

"There will be other things," said Yolande.

He asked her then to let him row her out on the lake on a dry day. It was time she met Jocosa.

Papa must be satisfied at last, as he no longer visited the schoolroom. On afternoons when Edmund swam, Yolande did a kind thing; she went down and read the newspapers and talked to poor Mama. That Anna was chiefly interested in the Court Circular didn't make it any less kind.

Otherwise, they weren't always in the schoolroom or the library. Once he and Miss Yolande went out at night into the garden to look at the sky full of bright stars. She taught him their names in English and Castilian, having learned them at the convent telescope on the roof. One of the nuns had brought it with her. There was Orion the giant with his belt and his dog Sirius, and the Milky Way, which was a galaxy; Venus, low on the horizon, was not a star at all but a planet, at the same time the six-point star of Mary Magdalene and the Wasp Star of the Mayas, which decided fate. There were others that couldn't be seen from here, but had stories attached to all of them; strange names like Betelgeuse and Aldebaran and Cassiopeia and the Southern Cross. There was a scent of jasmine in the garden, and unseen rosemary and night-scented stock. He would always remember the scents when he thought of the stars. Whatever they talked about, Miss Yolande was kind. She never lost her temper, like Vance, or answered sharply. This kindness was something Edmund came to rely on, though he had never known it before; something to trust; warm, loving, like fur or velvet, to be stroked and enjoyed. It was impossible not to love Miss Yolande in return. Nobody could fail to except Papa, who was still uncivil to her when they met, but it happened seldom.

Chapter Six

Yolande O'Neill could remember Spain, though after El Capitano, her father, was wounded they left for England when she was four. She remembered the market, and the laden donkeys with great round loaves in panniers, and baby sucking-pigs hung up at the stalls, dark brown with having been smoked on hooks to make bacon. There had been trees with oranges growing bright on them, and the high brown sierras with snow on their tops still, although it was summer. She would always think of it as summer in Spain, because when they had been a year or more in England, the *madre* died of the damp and cold. Yolande could remember her dead face, and El Capitano crying over her like a woman. However, he knew he wouldn't live long himself, and told Yolande he was going to take her to his sister who was the prioress of a convent, and would see her educated. "You must not forget your Castilian, *querida*," he told her. "They will make use of that." They had all spoken it together, he and the *madre* and herself; now, she would have to remember it alone.

They had travelled by post-chaise, and she remembered El Capitano's labouring breaths as he limped up the hill beyond the narrow gate with her hand in his. There were laurel bushes, and a large red stone building high above. It had once belonged to a family, he told her, but now the Order owned it, and she must do her best to please them in every way, because he hadn't any money to leave with her as was usually done.

They were shown into the parlour, and a grille in the wall opened and there sat the prioress, her aunt, in spectacles like the saints in Spanish churches. An attendant nun stood behind her. They didn't smile.

"So this is Yolande," said the prioress. "You say she is six. We will take her so that she becomes a pupil-teacher first, then, if she has a vocation, a member of the Order after her novitiate." El Capitano then took Yolande up in his arms and kissed her for the last time, and put the locket with the *madre*'s hair round her neck, and limped out. She never saw him again, as he died soon. There was a requiem mass for him in the chapel of the convent, and by then the young lady pupils were back for the autumn term and they all came. Everyone was kind to Yolande, especially the nun with the telescope, and she was told to keep up her Spanish as it would make an extra subject to teach for special fees later on. As for the locket, she might wear it till she took her vows. By then, it was assumed she would take them. She had lessons with the other pupils but was not allowed to join them at dancing, when a master came in. She used to hear his fiddle playing, and tap her foot.

She grew up, and used to read a great deal by herself during the school holidays. The family whose house it had been left all their books, and these covered a great many subjects. During term, an early task was to lead the daily crocodile, as the pupils' walk was called, round the outer enclosure walls under the birch trees where in late summer, poppies bloomed. Their bright flowers reminded her of Spain.

In course of the crocodile, one year, she met Betty Smith. Betty's father was in trade and in the ordinary way she would not have been admitted, but Mr Smith made so much money by doing whatever he did that he was able to pay for all the extras, pianoforte and water-colours and Spanish. Betty was a parlour-boarder and had a room to herself instead of sleeping in the dormitory with the rest. She had a loud laugh and open manners, but Yolande liked her. One day in the crocodile they walked past a straying branch of a blossoming tree that belonged inside the enclosure, but had escaped over the wall and was setting fruit, still green.

"They won't ever let you learn about *that*," said Betty. "They'll make you believe babies are born under gooseberry bushes. You're too pretty to be a nun, shut away behind the enclosure wall for life. Why don't you take the permitted year and come out and teach my little sister Chrissie? She's not like other people and can't speak except to make noises, and won't ever go to school."

Yolande hadn't known about the permitted year, and for some reason couldn't get the fruiting branch out of her head. The end of it was that she found herself once again in the prioress's parlour in front of the opened grille, with her nails biting into her palms. The prioress didn't look pleased.

"We have spent a certain amount on your board and education. You should send a proportion of your salary to us here in course of the year. At the end we expect you to return, in time for your novitiate."

After that, she wouldn't be allowed to wear the *madre*'s locket. The thought shouldn't be uppermost in her mind, any more than that Betty had told her she was pretty. There weren't many mirrors, and when taking a bath you did so under a sheet of striped ticking with a hole for the head, and draped it ever the sides after undressing beneath it. Yolande had never seen her own body since Spain.

At the Smiths' it was different. Luxury was everywhere, and the bed she slept in was the softest she had ever known. Little Chrissie had hugged her at sight. She had strange slanting eyes and strange little thumbs, and as Betty said couldn't speak, but she could love. She loved Yolande so much, and liked drawing houses with her whose chimneys had smoke coming out, that at the end of the year she cried at the thought of goodbye, and Yolande was hired for another year, then a third. She sent money regularly to the convent, so they put up with it; only she didn't see much of the world, as daily walks with Chrissie were always accompanied by good Mrs Smith. "It wouldn't be right to leave you to go out alone, dear," as she put it. Meantime, Betty was about to be presented and the house was full of dressmakers' pins and appointments. Mr Smith was hardly ever at home, being too busy making his money, and when he did appear he used to laugh as loudly as Betty, with a great rattling of his porcelain teeth.

One day Betty cast a white muslin gown at Yolande. "It's too tight for me in the waist. You would look like a queen in it. Have it; I'll never wear it."

She made Yolande put it on and then look at herself in a long pier-glass. Her reflection astonished her.

The gown was plain, and her shoulders and neck rose from it, crowned with the dark hair. The *madre*'s locket showed clearly, making everything richer. She was like a different person, one she hadn't known about; one it was perhaps better not to know. She had been brought up not to think of her appearance, but of her immortal soul. This, now, was the figure of someone in the world; and she wasn't to be of the world, but a novice soon, intent on prayer.

She took off the dress, folded it away and kept it carefully. She didn't want to hurt Betty by not accepting it, but returned to wearing her accustomed dark one. It was shortly after that that she was perceived by the hired marchioness who was to arrange Betty's presentation, and who later wrote to Anna Corbell.

Betty, after all of it, married a friend of her brother's who was a clerk, like him, in the Honourable East India Company. She sailed off, but before that, Chrissie had died. Such little people didn't live beyond about fourteen. She died with her strange little hand in Yolande's, and both she and Mrs Smith were left feeling very sad. Mrs Smith wanted to keep Yolande on as a companion now Betty was gone, but Yolande's conscience smote her about the convent. To her surprise, however, the prioress was anxious that she should go and take up the post offered about Lord Corbell's little lame boy. A lord was a good advertisement for the school; at the end of a further year, Yolande must return.

Yolande loved Edmund as she had loved Chrissie. There was something in common between herself and lonely children. It was a signal honour to be shown Edmund's secret fragment of a green enamel eye.

At the same time, she didn't forget El Capitano. The annual date of his death was next month, and she must ask Lady Corbell if she might go down then and pray for him at the general's tomb in the vault. They couldn't object to that here; it would be quite private, and El Capitano had taken his wound where the general had also fought, at Vimeiro.

However, she must ask.

Chapter Seven

Edmund likewise had to obtain Mama's permission to row Miss Yolande out on the lake, as Papa wasn't in the library. It had turned quite cold, with a wind that ruffled the water. Miss Yolande wore her warm pelisse and bonnet, and her gloves. They went together down to the boathouse, and he helped her climb into the thwarts as the little boat rocked slightly, even in the shelter of the thatched roof. Edmund was proud of the boat; it was always kept carefully caulked and painted. He handled the oars expertly, and they shot out on to the open water. Bellissima Jocosa would be disturbed in the depths, rolled to and fro by the wind. He wanted to call out to her that they were coming, but didn't.

He rowed out to the deep centre, then shipped the oars and groped for the talisman in his pocket. Closing his fingers over it he held it up. Papa had said her name must never be spoken, but he had an urge to call out "Jocosa! Bellissima Jocosa!" She might answer. At times, when swimming, he'd fancied he heard her laughter, far below. He hadn't told that even to Miss Yolande.

The green eye gleamed in the dull daylight. The wind had dropped. Miss Yolande leaned out over the side of the boat and made the sign of the cross over the water. He saw her lips move and knew she was praying for Jocosa. On the way out she had pinched her gloved fingers in the way she had, and had once admitted she was saying secret prayers because she wasn't allowed to bring out her beads. Perhaps Jocosa would rest in peace now she was being prayed for, but he didn't think so.

"Lord Corbell is beckoning to us to go back," said Yolande suddenly. Edmund looked round and saw Papa back at the boathouse. He must have been watching. Edmund drew up the anchor and began to row back, the enamel eye safe again in his pocket. He hoped it hadn't been noticed. The wind rose against them and it took some time to get back. Papa still waited.

When they arrived at the jetty he was frowning. "You should not have taken Miss O'Neill out on so cold a day," he said. Edmund was relieved that that was all. He tried to explain that he'd asked Mama's leave.

"Your mother has no notion of the extremes of the weather, as she is never out in it. Tie up the boat."

Lord Corbell then helped Miss Yolande out, setting both hands about her waist and lifting her so that his cheek, a man's rough cheek, brushed hers. Put ashore, she hurried back to the house, not waiting for either of them.

What happened in the vault was a day or two later, on the anniversary of Miss Yolande's father's death. Lessons had continued as usual and they hadn't mentioned the matter of Jocosa. One day Yolande said Papa had agreed for the upper cellar door to be unlocked so that she could go down to pray for the souls of her father and the general in the vault. She'd asked Mama. "I shall want to be by myself," she said gently. "You go for your swim." She hadn't said, as others would have, that the steep inner stairs would be too much for his short leg, but he knew.

He decided to swim as usual, although it had begun to rain quite heavily. He never minded any kind of weather when he was in the lake. He watched Miss Yolande go down by herself, then went out.

As regarded swimming he always obeyed Papa's instructions implicitly, otherwise permission might be withdrawn. On no account were the servants to see his nakedness. Edmund preferred to conceal his misshapen body in any case.

This meant undressing in the boathouse, winding a towel round himself in the boat, then rowing out, beyond the place where trees obscured him while diving in over the side. He would swim several lengths, crawling, left and right, turning and floating on his back as it pleased him; so long as he was in the water, nakedness was concealed. At the end he would swim back to the boat, reach for the towel, wrap it again round himself while climbing in, row back, dry himself and dress in the shadows of the boathouse, and return to the house.

Today the rain slanted down in sheets, and nobody could have seen whatever he did. He anchored the boat, dived in, and played about in the water, rain sending his dark hair into his eyes; brushing it back, he saw Papa's tall figure, in caped greatcoat and beehive hat, striding towards the vault's outer entrance, his coat flapping with the rain. Edmund hoped he wouldn't interrupt Miss Yolande at her prayers; he might have forgotten, though it wasn't like him to forget, that he'd given permission for her to go down today by the inside stairs, over the tiles which had been cemented over, as Papa said they were improper. The cement would be dry by now, but lime always clung. Perhaps Papa wanted to make sure Miss Yolande had made the journey down the steep stairs safely. Edmund trod water; and saw his father take out the key for the outer door. If it hadn't been for the matter of nakedness, he would have left the lake and reminded Papa that Yolande was inside, praying, and had asked to be left alone.

He saw Lord Corbell go in, and became increasingly uneasy for reasons he couldn't name. He got back into the boat, and rowed quickly towards the boathouse. The rain drummed down, making it difficult to see, turning the surface of the lake into little dimpled spatterings. He put his clothes on without taking time to dry himself, threw the towel into the boat – they'd get it later – and hurried back as fast as his lame leg would allow him. By now, perhaps Yolande had finished her prayers and he was disturbing himself for nothing. However, she still wasn't back in the schoolroom.

He stood there at a loss. Should he go and fetch her? Papa might be angry, but for once it didn't signify. If he was in the vault with her, she wasn't being left alone as she'd asked. *She wasn't being left alone.*

He heard her footsteps then; light, hurrying, distressed. She came into the room and flung herself down against him, clinging to him tightly. She was sobbing and trembling; he'd never seen her like this, she was always calm. He could feel the wet trickling down his neck, and didn't like to touch her in case he made her

43

clothes wet as well, but something made him hold her all the same, tightly. Her head lay against him and he could see the white parting in her hair, and the white lime-marks on the soles of her little shoes where she'd run up through the cellar again by the steep stairs. She'd been frightened, hurt, altered; was no longer the person he knew.

"Miss Yolande, what is it? What has happened? What's wrong?" He longed to say it, yet felt that saying nothing was somehow best. He began to soothe her, as if she was a pony that has been slashed with a whip for the first time, a puppy that has been trodden on. At last he heard her speak, the words torn from her with a great shuddering. He heard what she said without at first understanding it, while the rain still beat against the windows.

"Oh, Edmund, I am no longer fit to be the bride of Christ."

He couldn't think what to say, except that he must keep holding her. She put him away, however, and rose to her feet, smiling a little.

"Forgive me,' she said. "I should not have upset you. I think I will go and lie down for a little while. You must have supper by yourself in the schoolroom for once. I hope you will not mind."

After she had gone a scratching came at the door; one of the maids. There was a message for Miss O'Neill from his lordship. It didn't require any answer.

"She is in her room," Edmund told the girl, and heard her go in. Her footsteps died away afterwards down the passage. He waited; the rain had grown wilder. It was beginning to grow dark.

Supper came up, for one. He must find out what was happening. He'd been in Miss Yolande's room once or twice before, and always knocked before entering. He did so now. There was no answer. Fearful, he went in.

She wasn't there. There was only what he knew about already, the small chest of drawers with the swing mirror and her hairbrushes, and the washstand table and her iron bed. Behind the door was a hook where her pelisse and bonnet hung. They'd been put back. She must have gone downstairs.

He did an unpardonable thing then. In the wastepaper basket, the note in Papa's writing lay, torn in two. He bent and retrieved it, put the pieces together and read them, then returned it as it had been. He would remember the words always:

44

Forgive me if you can. I have lived as a monk for twelve years. Will you dine with me tonight? There are certain things I must say to you before I leave for the north to go to my cousin. Word has come that her husband is dead, and I must see to her affairs and her son's and attend the funeral.

Pray come as I ask. I leave tomorrow. I swear that I will not touch you again without your leave.

H.C.

By some means Edmund was certain what must have happened in the vault. Tom Walshe had told him that time about fornication, and the ugly short word used instead. His father had come upon Yolande in the vault, held her down on Jocosa's tomb next the general's, and done to her what dogs did. An increasing rage and loathing came to him. She'd still made herself go down to have dinner with Papa. He himself didn't want any supper, thinking of what had happened.

Again he acted unpardonably. It was as though rightness was being corroded in him. He stole downstairs and concealed himself between two pillars that stood outside the dining-room door, making a little alcove where one could remain unseen. He knew he would be severely beaten if found, and didn't care. There was a place where the door joined the wall and he could hear what Papa was saying. What he had to say was another matter. Edmund didn't understand all of it.

He crept back upstairs. When he heard Yolande come up, hesitate and then look in to say goodnight, he pretended to be asleep. It was the first time he had ever deceived her.

Chapter Eight

Yolande undressed quickly and went and lay down in bed. She had loosened and tied her hair in its fall, but hadn't brushed it. She closed her eyes and tried to pray, but the prayers wouldn't come. Behind her eyelids still shone the yellow candle-flames in their sconces on tonight's long polished dining-table, with the food set out, but she hadn't eaten any. He had handed her a glass of wine. His tall gaunt figure might have been before her now. The hurt deep in her body still throbbed now she was alone again. His words still sounded in her ears.

"Do you suppose I have not wrestled with myself in prayer for long since I first saw you? I desired you from the first, as Jacob desired Rachel. God permitted him two wives, one he loved and one he did not. My marriage killed my father. It was the first time in my life I had disobeyed him."

She tried to think of Anna Corbell, who had given idle permission for her to go down to the vault, saying she'd ask Henry. What had happened was adultery. Such things ought to trouble her. As it was, what she felt for this man was pity. He was speaking now about his bitter childhood, when the father he revered was uncertain whether or not he was his son, and yet no regiment would receive him because he was so by law. "I turned to God," said the fourth lord. "God speaks to me daily. Your own religion contains the doctrine of atonement. Your body atoned today for my mother's sin, on her tomb. The law of Moses, the ancient laws of the pagan gods, all demand innocent blood."

He had begun to walk up and down; neither of them had sat.

There were no servants present. "You prayed for my mother, out on the lake with my son," said Corbell. "Had the general seen Edmund, twisted as he is, he would have known that I was his. He died unknowing."

He turned towards her then, hands outstretched. "I desire you," he said. "You can comfort me. Your convent, I believe, will not now take you back. What else is to become of you?"

He sounded confident, as if he had achieved a victory. She heard her own uncertain answer.

"I – I do not know. They may consider that I was unprepared. There will be conditions about such things."

"I may have given you a child, Yolande. That will not benefit their school's good name, or will they consider that your sacrifice has released Jocosa Corbell from purgatory?" He was mocking now; she resented it.

"It was adultery," she said quietly aloud.

"Do not fall back on dry laws. Jacob and Rachel had sons who were not cursed by God; they prospered, as would any children you bear me."

She could have answered that there is no tribe of Joseph, and that the tribe of Benjamin were denied brides at last and driven abroad. However, she was silent except to say that the convent had spent money on her and wanted it repaid as a member of the teaching Order.

"You may teach Edmund for as long as you choose. He is prospering under your instruction." He would write, he said, to his solicitor requesting a document from the convent with every penny they had ever spent on her from the beginning; board and education from the day El Capitano had left her with them at the age of six. On receipt of the sum, they must sign a statement that they would make no further demands on her. "You would be free. I would deny you nothing."

It wouldn't be freedom to have to depend on him, but she didn't say so. It was like standing above a precipice with an enemy approaching from behind; one was afraid to leap over, afraid to remain. Either way, there was fear that she had already fallen into sin. Everything had changed. She had been praying for El Capitano and the general at the marble tomb in the vault, and had become aware of a second presence. He must have been waiting there from the beginning. There had come a sudden

47

overwhelming nearness of rain-soaked tweed, a man's hard mouth on hers, a man's intent hands, then his hard member within her. It had happened, and nothing could alter that now.

Edmund would be glad if she stayed. She knew that, in the end, was the deciding factor. He loved her, and she loved him in return. If she left him he would be bereft. To be able to stay, watch and guide him, might be worth any sacrifice she could make; and she didn't hate Lord Corbell. If it was God's will that she bargain her body for Edmund's future, so be it, perhaps. To return to the convent seemed arid now. The money would help them. It would attract other novices, with dowries. Rightly or wrongly, she knew she was persuaded.

She looked in on Edmund. His smooth cheek lay against the pillow, his dark thatch of hair ruffled in sleep. Love for him made her heart beat more strongly. Lord Corbell was going away for a little while; she was to give him her decision when he returned.

In the dawn, she heard Corbell's carriage drive off. It would be easier now to live from day to day. She could perhaps, in time, influence him regarding Edmund. If he couldn't love Edmund as she did, he might still be brought to safeguard the boy's rights. The possibility strengthened her.

Corbell did not return that week or the next. Anna began to fear lest he bring the strict and godly Mildred and her son to live at Lackmere now Mildred was widowed. That would make her own position more intolerable than ever. Henry's neglect left her unaware of his intentions as a rule, but she knew, with the intuition all women have and which in her case had turned to a sour and vindictive suspicion, that something had taken place between her husband and Edmund's governess. It didn't trouble her; in its way, it was amusing. The papers were being read to her as usual, and the weather had turned extremely hot. However, Anna liked the heat. When Miss Yolande next came in she looked exhausted in the dark high-necked dress.

"Have you nothing cooler?" Anna asked. Even the windows had had to be opened, a rare concession. She still had them light the fire.

"Only a white muslin, not suitable for me."

"Wear it; there is nobody to cavil, and there is all summer to

48

get through."

By the time Yolande appeared in the white dress, there had been word from Corbell, asking Anna to inform Vance that he might be back very soon. She had not yet done so. She was aware of distinct envy of the young woman in muslin; at no time had she herself owned anything approaching that bosom. The low-cut gown set it off.

Edmund was in the garden among the scent of early roses. He couldn't swim today as he had fallen and sprained his wrist. He would be glad when Miss Yolande had finished reading to Mama. He wanted to tell her about something he'd found out, a star that pointed straight at Glastonbury.

She came out earlier than he expected, and he had never seen her look so beautiful. If he had both hands free, he'd like to put a rose in her hair. He forgot about the star.

"You look like a flower," he said in Spanish. He was less shy in that language. Her wide pale skirts made the petals, her narrow waist the stem. What showed above left him wordless. Her white revealed flesh was already warmed by the sun, like the ripe curves of a peach; but her eyes were sad. He asked why, still using the tongue she'd taught him; it made a bond between them, a secret nobody else knew. They'd been happy since Papa left; what had happened no longer mattered.

"I should not appear like this," Yolande said, "but perhaps it is what I am in my heart. Also," and her voice was lowered, as though anyone overhearing would understand, "I have had a terrible letter from my aunt the prioress, telling me my soul is lost. She may be right."

He didn't know quite what she meant, but took the hand she held out. Hers and his own were warm and damp with the heat. Yolande's other hand held the amber locket, which she'd taken off. There was a fine dew of sweat below her hairline and on her upper lip, and a dark line soaked under her arms through the thin muslin, before her full parts began. The sight made him want to share the dampness, the enervating heat, with her.

She sat down beside him, spreading her skirts, and they stared together at the roses. If he had two free hands and no sling, and if his water-colours weren't upstairs, he'd draw and then paint her

49

c

as she was now; hair blue-black in the sun, which drew other colours from it. The scent of roses was heavy on the air. Perhaps it was from this same garden that Bellissima Jocosa had had dried pot-pourri made long ago to be laid among her clothes, the silver-and-white dress he'd found in the trunk in the attic, other things. He had a memory, a ghost, of laughter and old roses. He found it was too hot to think. He stayed close to Yolande, feeling her warmth against his own.

Somebody was shooting in the distance. The little *plop* of bullets came, heard clearly with the lack of any wind.

Edmund continued in his dream. Then he felt Yolande leave go of his hand; saw her rise to her feet, with her face, neck and bosom all one growing blush, deeper than the roses. His father was standing between them and the sun, holding a brace of shot hares dangling limply by their feet. Their soft noses were gouted with blood, their eyes glazed over. In Papa's dark gaze was a searing agony, staring at Yolande in the low-necked muslin dress. An axe seemed to come down and sever past from present. He, Edmund, had become a child again, unable to fathom swift change. He made his mind focus instead on the strangeness of his father's shooting hares out of season.

The days passed, the warm weather ceasing as suddenly as it had begun. Miss Yolande was again wearing her dark high-necked dress. She seemed to have become formal and cold, a governess; as if his father's return had quenched the joy there had been between them. Lessons continued, but she no longer ate in the schoolroom. Edmund did his best and worked as well as he might, but his heart wasn't in it any longer.

He began to waken at night. At times he had become aware of a strange knocking not far off, like somebody driving a nail into a wall. It would stop after some time, then start again. He could have asked Peggy Vance about it, but didn't. These days he kept to himself.

The donkey at the home farm died. The milk churns now were fetched and returned by George Tesson daily, sometimes bringing young Margaret with him. She'd grown taller and had stopped looking like a child. They would begin courting in a year or two. Everything went for some people as expected. The nightly knocking was still unexplained.

He found out about it soon, and knew he hadn't really wanted to. One night he had to get up late to go along the passage to the new lavatory Papa had had installed. It had a pattern of small blue flowers in the porcelain, and the servants didn't use it. Edmund liked pulling the chain and watching the rush of water, his own lake water, swirling fussily round and round in the bowl, rinsing everything clean. Papa said pipes took it away so that it didn't go back into the lake.

He watched the phenomenon as usual, then came out to see Papa's tall figure, in its brocade dressing-gown, go into Miss Yolande's room.

The high cistern hissed behind him, refilling. Edmund shut himself inside the door till the sound should have subsided. Then he opened and closed it again silently, and made his way unheard past her room. The knocking had begun already, louder because it was nearer. It was Yolande's iron bed, creaking and knocking against the wall. There were other sounds he could hear now he was close outside; a man's avid gruntings, a woman's soft moaning. Presently there was silence and they began to talk together in low voices. He listened, pressed against the lintel of the door till he hurt himself, his bare feet – he hadn't put on his slippers – growing cold on the flags of the passage. He knew he must be gone before his father came out.

She spoke first. "Lord Corbell, pray be a little careful. If there should indeed be a child –"

"If there is a child I will protect you, never fear. How glorious your breasts are, like mounds of snow, sun-flushed at the peaks! I like to hold them, to mouth them. You are everything to me." There was a pause, then, "Again, Yolande."

It began again, the knocking. He'd always thought everything happened from the back. Dogs did it that way. The knocking subsided. Presently he heard his own name.

"I am certain Edmund knows. His manner to me is different. He no longer learns gladly; by now, it's a task." So she had noticed. That was something. He waited to hear his father's reply.

"He is of no consequence to us. He shall be sent to school when it's time, in the autumn."

She had given a cry. "Ah, you promised me – you said I might teach him, and that he will inherit what you can leave him. Other

51

children will be cruel."

"He will inherit as I promised you. I informed my cousin Mildred accordingly. However, he must learn to make his way in a world which is never easy. I myself have had to do so. You, on your side of our bargain, do not give yourself entirely; you withhold yourself, you are still thinking of him, a boy. You, your body and mind and soul, must become mine, and mine entirely. Your every thought must be mine, even as we are one flesh. Again."

Edmund left and got himself back to bed, pulling the covers over his ears. It took a long time to get warm He supposed that he slept.

Their comradeship had gone. She was still remote, almost cold, as if she was trying to withdraw into herself. One day she gave him a passage from Cervantes to translate, about the deluded knight who tilted at windmills. Don Quixote had loved some woman who wasn't really what he thought she was. Had she intended it as a message to him? They couldn't speak to one another about what was really happening any more.

He completed the task and left it for her; she wasn't always in the schoolroom now. After luncheon eaten alone he went down to the lake as usual, but didn't swim. Instead, he limped round to the further side where he'd seldom been; where gorse bushes reared and George had been down with Margaret earlier. He seized a branch of gorse and squeezed it, watching the blood spring up on his hand, feeling the sharp pain. He didn't know why he had had to hurt himself, or why it relieved him when he had.

Blood. There wasn't much grass growing here to wipe it off; the trodden path was bare and so were the places beneath the bushes. There was earth there and he clawed at it, staining and breaking his fingernails, at last holding a clod of it in his hand. This would be his earth, his. Yolande had sold herself so that he could inherit. Cousin Alfred wouldn't come here after all when Papa was dead.

He wished Papa was dead now. He admitted that he loathed him. What happened when he got back to the house made everything worse.

He appeared upstairs to find a maid throwing out sheets from

Miss Yolande's door as they always did for the laundry. Inside, Vance was rolling up the thin mattress. All of Yolande's things had gone; her hairbrushes, the bonnet and cloak behind the door, her slippers from below the only chair. He knew sudden fear that she'd left, and asked, blurting it out.

"She's gone downstairs," was all Peggy would say, adding that he would be up here on his own. That meant Papa had taken Yolande down to a grander bed, that had curtains and didn't creak and knock, and slept with her. He, Edmund, wouldn't be able to listen to what they were saying any more. He wouldn't know what was decided next about himself; that didn't matter.

Lessons continued after that. Yolande would come up to the schoolroom late and flushed, not having attended household prayers; she never had. Papa would visit her again afterwards, having preached with increasing certainty, still as though he were God. He had acquired a sleek, satisfied look. Edmund hated the new arrangement by which he was taken up beside Papa in the pony-trap to see to the tenants, as now he was to inherit the estate he ought to know about it; mending thatch, priming the pump, other things that had to be attended to. Edmund disliked being near enough to jolt against Papa in the cart at rough places on the path. He didn't like touching him. However, the welfare of the tenants was important and Papa was known to be a good landlord, acting as his own factor. If other business prevented the cottage visits, the tenants would come down on Fridays with their rents, and Papa received them sitting behind the walnut desk in the library. He jotted down the amounts in columns in a ledger and Edmund was made to inspect them afterwards. By then, the tenants had gone, walking back past the bramble-covered pit that was so deep it was bottomless. They'd pass it in the cart. Edmund had a fantasy wherein Papa fell in and down, down so far no one would ever find him. He, Edmund, would then be fifth lord.

As it was, he saw much less of Yolande.

Chapter Nine

One afternoon he decided again not to swim, but instead to play his organ. Papa had had it installed when he was smaller, to try to cure his short leg by using the foot-pedals, but it hadn't made any difference. He mostly used the manuals, and liked to play Bach and Handel, and, of course, hymns. He'd been taught at the time by the church organist, although they didn't attend church. He could play quite well.

He made his way along; the organ room was on the same floor as the schoolroom, but in the old part of the house, which this was, there were uneven floors and half-steps, and beds in every room which you went through before finding the next. Nobody in old days could have had much privacy.

He found the room, whose entry lacked a door as they all did, but at the other end there were stairs down to the lower floors. The pump to blow up and make the organ work was near the entry, and Edmund went down on both knees before noticing that the bench held clothes, a woman's; Yolande's. Her gown, stays and petticoat were laid over it, with her shoes placed together on the floor. His father's jacket and half-boots were nearby.

They were on the bed together behind the drawn curtains. He supposed they'd thought he was out swimming. At this time of day, Yolande usually read the paper to Mama. She'd been brought up here and made to undress instead. Her low, pleasurable moaning, that hurt him more than anything, came. Presently a further sound came from her he had never before heard or imagined; a deep cry of utmost surrender, like a mated female

54

animal. The great bed was trembling and quivering. It wasn't the one they slept in at nights.

He felt faint, then knew he must leave her some sign that he'd heard, that he knew she'd been made to do it. He reached towards her clothes; she had taken off the amber locket, and its chain lay gleaming within reach. Edmund, with surprisingly steady fingers, made three knots in the chain. Then he put the locket back, returned downstairs as he had come, and went straight to the boathouse to undress. To swim out naked would cleanse him. His father had been fornicating, committing the worst of sins. He wasn't God, after all. He was no better than the next person, than oneself.

Edmund swam till it was almost dark. After he dried and dressed himself and went in, he was told his lordship waited for him in the library.

It was the worst caning of his life. He was thrashed without mercy till he howled like a dog. He became incontinent, standing with his trousers round his ankles, piddling and with shit and blood flying in reply to the incessant, vicious blows of the cane. Suddenly, there came from him a spurting of milky fluid he hadn't before seen. It hit the front of the walnut desk and dribbled down to the floor. His humiliation and pain were complete. "You are a disgusting sight," he heard his father say. The blows stopped at last, and Lord Corbell rang the hand-bell for a servant to clean up the mess. That way, they'd all know. He, Edmund, was to go straight to his room, without supper. "Tomorrow, you will be sent elsewhere."

He didn't look at his father, or know it was the last time he would hear his voice. Had he known, it would have made no difference. The tall figure straddled his life, corroded his soul and Yolande's. Edmund limped his way out of the library, pulling up his trousers in degradation and shame. He didn't recall gaining his room, or washing himself. Soon he was lying face down on his bed, in the old way. He didn't know where his father would send him. It was probably to some tutor, to get ready for school. It didn't seem real. Nothing was real but pain.

This time, there was no Peggy Vance with tea-leaves. Nobody was to come near, and the door had been locked. He couldn't go to the lavatory, and when he could bear to had to use the pot, like a child. He had stopped sobbing long ago; it had grown dark. He was hungry, sick with remembered shame, and his bottom was still roaring with pain; tomorrow, he would have to sit in the carriage to the railway station. He'd never been on a train; the prospect didn't excite him at the moment. The future loomed, grey and bleak. There was to be the tutor, then school when he gained entry. He couldn't think as far ahead, only aware of his sore bottom, his empty stomach and the locked door. He'd never been locked in before; there was a feeling of indignity, like being in prison. Soon, at this rate, he might go there for some crime of rage against the world.

There had come a hushing sound of skirts outside; Yolande. He heard her calling through the door. At first he didn't want to answer. She let his father fuck her. She liked it. It wasn't because of him, Edmund, at all. He'd heard her moanings upstairs. He'd heard her cry out today. It was what hurt more than the cane; she'd liked it.

She was calling again, softly. "Edmund, listen to me. We don't have much time. He must not know I am here. He has sent a telegram and the answer has come. You are to leave tomorrow to go to the tutor."

He got up stiffly and limped to the door, sensing the warmth of her presence on the other side. Her cheek must be against the wood. She spoke quickly, as if to make sure everything was said that must be, as if it might be cut short.

"Edmund, your father was very angry when he saw the locket. I tried to hide it, but he noticed. I am not supposed to say goodbye before you go off, but I want to say that I love you with all my heart. Do not heed what happened today. That is of the body, which cannot help itself in such ways. The heart is quite other. You have had mine from the beginning. Him I pity, and I can comfort him, and perhaps that is what God intended me to do rather than making me a nun. I knew of nothing else before they let me out into the world. I didn't return to the convent in time, because I did not want to leave you. You were alone, and so once was he. He had a harsh childhood, and his marriage is ashes. My Church says I am wrong. Well, God will judge me. My love for you will endure always; remember the times when we looked at the flowers and the stars. Wherever you see the night sky, think of me. Those are the things that matter, not the rest; not what happened today.

56

"I will love you and pray for you always. He took away my rosary, but I still count the prayers on my ten fingers when he's within me. That is a secret between you and me. We have had our perfect time together; remember it, as I will. You have a fine mind; nourish it. The mind matters more than the body. As for the soul, that's different. There is not time to say more. Do not forget that I am thinking of you, as he may not let me write. He has repaid the convent, and so I owe him kindness, though never love except the love we must give to all God's creatures. My heart is yours always."

"I love you too," he said. "I won't ever love anyone else."

"Never say that; you must welcome love when it comes. Ah, he's calling and I must go, or you will be punished. I am not to be allowed to say goodbye to you. This is our goodbye, but if we never meet again till after death, heaven is made up only of love. Remember it, and pray for me as I will for you, as long as I shall live."

She had gone. He knelt on at the locked door, his cheek against it as hers had been on the other side. He heard the hushing of her skirts as she went away.

Chapter Ten

Next day, Henry Corbell sat complacently at his desk over the tenants' accounts. The floor and the walnut surface had been cleansed from yesterday's incident. He had heard, without feeling or regret, the carriage come to the door and take his son away; he never wanted to see Edmund again. Only Vance had been permitted to see him off at the door, with his yellow hair trunk packed and the crammer's telegram in the baggage. The reply had come without delay. Dr Slater, erstwhile of Trinity, would be pleased to take full charge of the Honourable Edmund Corbell for as long as his lordship chose, whether or not he attained school entry this year. As had been specified, Dr Slater accepted full responsibility in the matter.

Lord Corbell's expression grew bland. Chastising Edmund had, as usual, stimulated him, but till now there had been no cure but fleshly discipline and abstinence. Last night, on the contrary, he had again, as a result, achieved ultimate mastery of Yolande. For a time, as always, there had seemed a slight unwillingness in her, in its way resembling Anna's recalled coy hesitancies after leading him into direct disobedience to his father's orders. He was curing such things in Yolande by insistence on frequent intercourse, relying on her Irish generosity and her Spanish blood. If the initial hindrance had been the thought of a twisted boy, he'd overcome it, causing her total yielding. The sect did not permit incomplete relations, and that he was obeying its tenets pleased him. Now that he possessed her body he would correct her mind, gradually ridding it not only of Romish error but of

58

independent thought. She should become the perfect wife, submissive and unquestioning, seeing all things through his eyes. God's Spirit enlightened him before he preached, putting words in his mouth; Yolande, lying in his arms last night, her eyelids heavy with pending sleep, and again today on waking, cheeks still flushed, had increased the certainty he already had that he was the elect of God. It had been his cross not to become a soldier like his father, to have caused that father's death through disobedience; now, he could see God's will for him as a latter-day prophet, a second Jacob, strengthened by physical ties to earth while communing daily, nightly with heaven. In this satisfaction he could remain now Edmund was no longer near, to intrude as profoundly as had happened with the matter of the knotted chain.

He thought of the tutor, and smiled. Dr Slater would know well enough what *carte blanche* implied. Edmund's own revelation of physical development yesterday had been inconvenient. It was as well he was gone.

Slater the crammer had been meant for greater things. He had been the foremost graduate of Trinity year, thereafter taking up a prestigious post at a famous boys' school. He had been sacked after three terms. He now eked out a living in a humbler capacity. His unmarried sister, who had inherited money on her own account, supported and kept house for him. The pupils as a rule did not board. Edmund was to do so.

The fourth Lord Corbell was a respected figure and conscientious landlord, zealous for the welfare of his tenantry and his servants. Until recently there had been no whisper as to his moral rectitude. It would still not have occurred to him, or to most others, that in selecting the course he had to eliminate a younger male from the contest, he resembled a certain empress whose reputation had been putrid for centuries. She had caused the young rival for her husband's affections to be consigned to a brothel.

The carriage returned from the station, divested of its occupant. Lord Corbell went to the window to ensure this state of affairs, then stood for some time staring at the lake Edmund had loved. It was smooth, grey and empty beneath the sky.

Part II

Chapter One

"I say, it's got a portico," remarked Alfred, Lord Sissington, his marmalade curls blowing in the light spring wind as the open carriage drove them to Lackmere from the train. "No wonder Mama was peeved when Cousin Henry said I wasn't to get it after all. That was your stepmother, Crip, ha, ha. He and she stayed with Mama, you know, on their way up to Sutherland. *She* had the miscarriage there. Mama says she isn't a lady. Cousin Henry won't leave her alone. They had to leave, and let this, in the end, because of the scandal. County wouldn't call as soon after Cousin Anna's funeral, and nobody marries the governess."

The dark, bitter and hunched presence beside him did not answer. There was no way of stopping Angel Alf's flow of spite except by punching him on his elegant nose, and soon now he might. However, Papa had written to the Head to say that, to repay Cousin Mildred's hospitality to Edmund over the years, he might take Alfred to see Lackmere before the tenants moved in. It was the Easter holidays. Most of the staff were staying on.

It was Edmund's first sight of his lake for five years, and he let himself forget Alfred while his eyes feasted on it. He would swim this evening, if possible alone. Alf was afraid of water and his posturings would spoil it. It was bad enough at school, now he, Edmund, was a prefect, to have had Alf made his fag. No doubt the Head regarded them both with tender concern. Cousin Mildred had written in protest to ask if the boys might kindly be prevented from calling her son Sis. There had been reason; on first arrival, Alf's cherubic curves had been in hot demand in the dorm until somebody discovered that he liked it, when his value plummeted. Now, he had tautened to the shape of Adonis, but only the desperate took him on. Edmund himself had never touched him. This was a lasting grudge. "You won't even *whack* me, Crip." The large blue eyes, with their expression of spurious innocence, had been truly concerned. It had been worse at Cousin Mildred's, where they had shared a bed. Edmund had wrapped the blankets firmly round himself. "I don't like touching you, you little swine."

It was true enough, and now Alf evidently regarded Lackmere and the portico as liable to be his own one day after all. The miscarriage had been good news for him. Crip, of course, couldn't be expected to marry. All one need do was to wait.

It was more than a year since Edmund himself had been summoned to the Head's study. Nobody as a rule was sent for there unless there was trouble, and all he could think of was the failed black mass the boys who didn't attend communion classes had tried to have in the cellar. Alfred had known where to get black candles. It was the kind of thing he knew. However, the cat, the scapegoat, had refused to be hanged and had simply walked away in contempt. It couldn't be that, although he'd provided a Bible given by Papa, to be used upside down. "Your affectionate father, Henry Corbell" had remained readable despite what else had happened to it. However, the Head's expression was benign above his half-moon spectacles, and he was standing in front of his fire with a black-edged letter in his hand.

"It is bad news, Corbell, I fear. Your mother is dead. I am to inform you of it, also that as the funeral is already over you need not go home."

No. He never did go home. He could feel nothing at the news. Mama had been found dead on her chaise-longue, and the room now would be empty except for the cracked mirror. He stared at the bright fire and brass andirons in the Head's hearth. Mama had always liked to have her fire kept high.

Almost immediately after that, word had come that Papa and Yolande were married. They were beginning to turn into people he'd once known. He didn't go home for the holidays; other fellows sometimes asked him once they'd got used to his shape and the fact that he kept winning prizes. To bury himself in books and more books was the only way to stop remembering. None of the other fellows seemed to live anywhere near the sea, so he hadn't been able to swim since leaving Lackmere. Now, he couldn't wait to row out and dive in again. It might even cleanse him from the memory of the tutor.

That had been unspeakable. After the first shock and disgust he had developed a will of steel, picking the flawed scholar's brains beneath the bald pate in determination to attain school entry this year rather than next. As regarded having his body invaded he had remembered Yolande, who endured it also. At school they had left him alone after his first striking out with muscles still powerful from swimming; it was accepted that Crip, as they inevitably called him, kept himself to himself. Since becoming a prefect he had his own room; and then they'd inflicted Alf on him. Later, at Cousin Mildred's again, with the drawing-room dominated by a portrait of Alfred in a blue velvet suit aged four, the marmalade angel had renewed his invitations. Edmund's reply that time had been specific. "You keep to your side and I'll keep to mine. Otherwise I'll smash your face in."

"At least it'll still be on my shoulders, not under one of 'em." There had been silence, and Alfred had begun his eternal story of when a school housemaid called Martha had invited him to visit her upstairs. He'd had to spend the time under her bed instead of in it, squashed flat by a visiting housemaster. He'd made an anecdote round the phrase "Martha, thou art busied with many things" which still aroused a polite snigger from those inclined. Edmund wasn't, and liked still less the riposte which came now. "They say at school you won't do anything because you can't," finished Alfred triumphantly. "You ought to wear a turban and turned-up slippers."

They'd almost reached the portico. Edmund wondered if the general's portrait had been taken to Sutherland. It hadn't been; his own face looked down at him. The servants were staying on, and Peggy Vance would keep an eye. He'd hoped she would come out to meet them.

Peggy was, however, red-eyed, having lately buried her widowed daughter. Margaret had left a fine big boy; Master Edmund must see him. Did he know both Georges were dead as well? There had been a great many changes.

He was glad Peggy had a grandson, although it was sad about Margaret and young George; the older one could have expected to die soon. Agnes, his other grandmother, was looking after the baby; they'd called him Jemmy.

"I say, will someone see to my bags?" put in Alfred. He disliked being ignored. Someone came.

Edmund left Tom Walshe, who was still in service, to show Alfred over the house before supper while he himself went swimming. It was wonderful to be again alone and free, breasting the water. He found that his muscles responded in the old way, as if he'd never left. Coming out at last, dripping and content, he met Peggy, on her way up to see the baby. She was smiling; now there was a Tesson heir she had been able to shed some of her grief.

"You're grown a man, very near, Master Edmund," she said. As for that Lord Alfred, she'd sized him up at sight, best left out of the reckoning. He was going about playing a flute he'd brought along, having seen all he wanted to see. The mournful hooting had pursued her as she went out.

"Why did my father go to Scotland?" Edmund asked her. He'd always been direct. It was probable Alf's spiteful gossip had no foundation. Vance looked thoughtful.

"It was her new ladyship wasn't happy here, after your mother died. She wanted to get away. There was a time when his lordship meant to go with her to the West Indies, but she wasn't in good health, so he put in a manager there. They went to the north parts after that. That's all I can tell you."

Those parts, he believed, were Catholic still. It was possible Yolande had the consolations of her faith, but it wasn't like his father to give in to them. It was possible that by now, he could deny her nothing; perhaps he, Edmund, owed it to her that a manager had been sent to the sugar plantations instead of himself.

Alfred inflicted the Etruscan flute on him that evening. "It's what they used at funerals," he explained. "Remember that poem they made us read at school? The good Mrs Browning thought Pan had a penknife. All he had to notch the reed was what he always used to notch every passing nymph. He began in Syrinx at the bottom, and the biggest hole in a flute is where he started in her before she began to turn into wood. He tried again and again, going upwards, and the smallest hole at the top is *piccolo*."

He bowed, as though expecting applause. Edmund didn't give any. He'd heard Alf on the subject before and it was boring. Nevertheless the flute came with them in the boat next day, when it was discourteous not to take the guest out on the water. To his disquiet, Alfred began to play Jocosa's tune, heard that time long ago in the ruined musical-box.

"Stop that," he said. "How did you learn that tune?" It was eerie, hearing it again. The enamel eye was safe in his pocket. Jocosa herself was waiting, deep in the lake. He'd called to her yesterday.

"Everyone knows it. Old Prinny wrote it. He was extremely musical. Mama's companion Miss McVey used to play it on the piano."

"Don't play it here."

"I'll play what I like."

"Then I'm rowing back." He did so, hearing no sound but the splashing of the oars. Alfred was in the sulks, but brightened on landing.

"Mama remembers a Roman pavement here," he said. "Walshe didn't show it to me."

"He couldn't, because it's been cemented over. You can come down and see the place if you like. It's next to the tombs."

The cellar was unheated and chilly. Alfred turned himself into a satyr, sat down cross-legged, and began to play Jocosa's tune again. Edmund put his hands to his ears.

"Stop it, I said. You're calling up the dead."

Alf wouldn't stop, and Edmund seized the flute from him and tried to break it over his sound knee, but it wouldn't. "It's mine," said Alfred sullenly. "Give it back. I'll put it away."

He had been kicking at the cement, and in one place it was cracked. Alfred turned up a piece of flaking lime. Beneath were earth colours. "Leave that," said his host. "Come and see the tombs."

The thin daylight filtered through on them from the lancet window near the outer door. "We can go out by the lake," said Edmund, and turned the key.

"You're crazy about the lake. I want to see the woods and the folly. Mama told me it has a roof of pine cones."

They went out into the fresh air. To Edmund's surprise, Alfred elected to come in the boat with him again next day.

"You can take the oars presently if you like. I'm going to dive in from the centre."

He had stripped in the boathouse as usual, and dived in, feeling the cold water strike his body refreshingly. He began to swim overarm, forgetting Alfred at the rowlocks. It didn't matter. He swam off, again glad of solitude.

Alfred Sissington had been taken aback, a rare occurrence. Crip's naked body, revealed in the boathouse and again now, had revealed parts as enviable as Pan's own. It had always been assumed that he could never marry, being as he was. Now, some woman wouldn't mind his being as ugly as sin, with all his money and the title. Oneself could no longer take it for granted that this desirable estate would, in the end, become one's own. If the governess didn't have children, or even if she did, Crip might.

Alfred began to row with determination away from the centre. Crip was coming up from a close dive, hair wet as a water-spaniel's. He dived a second time. Alfred continued to row strongly, feeling the light wind behind him. He could say he felt so cold he couldn't wait for Edmund to come out, and knew he was a strong swimmer.

Edmund surfaced a second time to find his guest far distant. He hadn't thought of Alf as able to row. He knew at once that the whole thing had been intended, and why.

Four years out of practice made a difference after all. He felt himself struggling, breathing too quickly. He calmed himself, turned and floated on his back, taking time to rest, then turned and swam again towards the shore, ridding himself of frequent gulps of water.

He gained the shore in the end, and limped to dry land, naked. Alfred had stowed the boat and made his way back to the house. If asked, he would say Edmund had wanted to go on swimming. Otherwise, he would know nothing.

Confronted, he was careful not to show surprise. Edmund also was careful not to show that he knew. If they took out guns on this visit, he'd carry them himself.

The pair returned to school in due course, and went their separate ways. Edmund was still uncertain what his way was to be. His masters hoped for Cambridge. No doubt the Head would write to Papa. Edmund himself didn't much care what was to happen to him, although from what Vance had said he was not to be sent overseas to the plantation. That must have been Yolande's doing; as she'd promised, she was remembering him in her prayers, and at the end he, and not Alfred, would own Lackmere and the library and the lake.

Chapter Two

On leaving school, Edmund was permitted a year at Cambridge. He made few friends, as his appearance still made him unwilling to manifest himself except for lectures, when he occupied the rear benches. Otherwise he remained mostly in his rooms, reading. However, he made the acquaintance of the occupant of the next room, whose father was a stockbroker at Lloyds. When at the end of Hilary term he was handed a letter from his father's solicitors, he was glad of the advice of this neighbour.

Henry Corbell had made over to him the full rights of the West Indian sugar plantation. Its annual income, as the formal letter stated, should be enough to keep him, Edmund, in the state in which he no doubt desired to live and which would suit his position. He might either finish his degree, or travel, as he chose. A condition was that he must not live in England in his father's lifetime otherwise.

The chilly legal letter requested Mr Corbell to call at his convenience at the address in Middle Temple, where he might examine all relevant documents and sign the clause giving him outright ownership. Before doing so, Edmund asked the stockbroker's son to consult his father.

Any pricking of the thumbs he had had was proved right. "My pater says sell, but keep quiet," was the reply. Safe in their rooms, more was said. "The bottom hasn't dropped out of the market yet, not by a long way. You'll get a good price. This beet sugar they're growing in France hasn't been taken seriously yet, but it will cost less as freight charges will be smaller by a long way. It stands to reason a monopoly will come to an end; they always do."

At one point, Edmund remembered again, Lord Corbell had intended him to go out there, leaving the Lackmere estate with Alfred. Yolande had saved him from that. Limping up through the stress of Middle Temple to the small dark offices of one of its longest-established firms, Edmund resolved to make certain of his position. Was it possible that his father resented him enough to fob him off with a failing market overseas, while still considering Angel Alf his heir in all but the title? However, the firm's senior partner, looking at him over rimless spectacles, seemed kindlier than his letter and, as far as he might be, proved informative.

"When you were announced, it was like looking at your grandfather the general again," Mr Carey said. "I remember him when I was an articled clerk here. You resemble him greatly."

"Except for a straight back and legs of equal length." He couldn't resist the bitter gibe.

"Do not let that prevent you from living your life fully. You are fortunate in all other ways. The world's a more prosperous and a safer place than it was in my youth. Marry, and see your grandchildren reap the benefit of all this industry that's springing up now. I myself have been too greatly attached to my profession to trouble with a wife or children. Were I your age again I'd act differently." The thin white brows and bowed shoulders raised themselves in deprecation. Boxes of wills and scrolls of parchment had perhaps ceased to console.

"Does this document I have just signed permit me to sell outright?"

"It permits you to do exactly as you wish, except for residing in England while Lord Corbell lives, other than completing your degree if you desire to do so. Those are his instructions, and I cannot comment further."

"May I enquire for the health of my stepmother, and if there are other heirs?" He hadn't heard from Yolande; any letters she sent would have been stopped. Alfred would know if there had been children, but he wasn't going to ask there. Nothing of the kind had been in the papers.

"Not that I am aware of. You are the sole heir for whom provision has been made. I do not think I am betraying any confidence by saying so."

"Please keep me informed. I will send you directions as I acquire them. I intend to travel, to see great art. It interests me more than marriage or a degree."

"I envy you the prospect of Italy, Belgium, Holland and Spain," said Mr Carey, and they parted.

Before he left London, Edmund arranged to have his name listed at Lloyds. His chief investment, on the advice of his Cambridge friend's father, would be in French railways. The shares were still relatively cheap to buy, and the yield would grow. "The chief investor grows sugar beet," wrote the former fellow-student. He added that the Duc de Morny also travelled in a special train along the new and ever-increasing steel distances, taking his racehorses and his library.

Edmund had no such grandiose ambitions. Once his affairs were settled he took himself abroad. He would make first for Toledo to see the El Grecos, then elsewhere as the spirit moved. He could be glad, at least, that his father had equipped him with the Spanish language. He even hoped Henry Corbell was happy, if such a state was possible to him.

Chapter Three

Edmund visited countries other than Spain, but it was there that Yolande seemed near to him and he spent some years back and forth there. He knew she could barely remember the first four years of her life, but the very air of the strange harsh land was hers; and the clicking rolling consonants of her mother-tongue. He saw the great enclosed grid of the Escorial, where that other most private man, Philip II, had lived and died; the dusty way wound up past it, past a monastery, to the high sierras where snow on the tops in summer was as white as Yolande's flesh. The women in the cities walked like she did; ready to break out into some graceful, formal dance.

He stayed in Seville with a Jewish family where the grandfather was a goldsmith. That such people were compelled to live in semi-secret behind latticed sills angered him. In the half-dark of the narrow unknown street the old craftsman fashioned a gold fob, as Yolande had once suggested long ago, of Jocosa's enamel eye. Thereafter Edmund wore it on his watch-chain. It was a sign of freedom that he no longer had to finger it, hidden, in his pocket.

He walked in Granada's gardens, saw others heavy with roses, experienced the Alcázar; at times had a glimpse of half-seen veiled flesh as some woman threw down a single rose to a lover in the street; but never to himself. He was forever apart from such things; no girl would be interested in him, and he himself was still afraid at the thought of women's breasts. He studied the liquid fire, the spiritual large-eyed faces, of the Greek painter who had immortalised himself at Toledo; he saw Velasquez' little apricot-haired infanta painted in her stiff gowns with her maids and dwarfs. He came upon a sketch by Goya in a private collection, and never forgot it; it showed old and young women offering their children to Satan, as a black he-goat. Some of the children were alive, others dead, one decomposing. Rather than the painter's crumbling royalties, monstrous gods, shovel-hatted priests and the raucous life of his century, he remembered that. The spurious benevolence of Satan was like the innocence in the eyes of Alfred Sissington.

Perhaps he was seeing the world through a cracked lens, the mirror at home. He left his name with the Madrid embassy; he forced himself to attend a bullfight. The embassy procured him invitations in which it became clear that hopeful mothers of eligible young ladies would consider his fortune and his pending title as of more importance than his crooked spine and hunched shoulder, but he cared for none of them. As for the bullfight, it was winter and he wrapped himself in a cloak. His valet had lately asked permission to return to England, and Edmund's clothes were uncared for, his hair roughly cut. He sat on a bench among the crowd, hearing them shout expectant slogans as the posturing matador came in. On came the bulls, one after another, despatched with full etiquette, teased and driven to madness and wounded and slain. The blood ran into the sawdust and there was triumphant yelling, cushions thrown by opponents, the smells of blood and garlic and tawdry clothes, male sweat and women's cheap scent. The women yelled more loudly than the men, in the timbre from which Yolande's Irish blood had saved her. At last the final valiant bull lay dead, a dark heap of subsided flesh and bones, its eyes glazing over like those of the hares his father had shot out of season that time long ago. His father and Yolande would know peace now, among the silent distances.

He prepared to leave, to shoulder his way alone through the still crowd and limp towards the exit. He wouldn't attend another bullfight. He was free to go where he would, travel as he might, untrammelled as the wind. The thought of high mountains sustained him; he would leave Spain for a time, go to Switzerland. Somewhere on the way, he must find a valet.

As if in answer he felt a touch on his arm. A small creature who

73

might have been any age was standing there, ugly and pock-marked. His clothes were a beggar's, ill-fitting as if he was used to others. His hands and feet were enormous, perhaps the size of the man he ought to have been. The crowd was pouring past them to hail or revile the victor at the exit. Edmund and the little creature were alone.

"Señor, you are an Englishman." He spoke with an accent which might have been that of Mile End. "You was sorry for the poor bloody bulls, and so am I. I'm looking for work. I can do anything with hosses and most things with 'umans. Will you take me on?"

It was later revealed that the only name he knew he had was Fred.

Fred's age remained difficult to guess; he might have been fourteen or forty, but having been weaned on gin, as he put it, he had never grown much and his teeth weren't all they ought to be. His body was stunted like one of the dwarfs in a Velasquez painting, his legs bowed with rickets and horsemanship. They would show even if Fred were to be put into a reasonable suit of clothes. He had a puckish and disarming grin, despite the appalling teeth. Edmund took to him, cautiously.

It turned out that Fred had been born in London, at least he supposed so. He didn't know his mother's name, and she wouldn't have known his father's.

He had been left outside the door of an East End orphanage late one night wrapped in a bundle of rags, and next day when they opened up they'd taken him in. Later, after smallpox – "everybody got it" – they'd tried to force him to sweep chimneys under a master, being the right size for it; all of the orphans learned a trade. "I wasn't having none of that, havin' a fire lit under my arse so's I wouldn't climb down till the job was done. Them chimneys is stinking black hell. I knew I'd end in hell anyway, and I might as well see a bit of life first. I lit out on me own, holding hosses in the streets for the nobs, halfpenny an hour."

He had hired himself out for other purposes as well; as he put it, some like them the way he was. Sooner or later, by controlling with expertise a vicious horse nobody else could handle – he'd allus been able to do anything with hosses, some way – its equally vicious owner had taken him on and had used him, at first, for steeple-chasing.

"Wasn't my fault he lost out," Fred explained. "I used to win for 'im, but he owed brass right and left and never paid up." In the end his employer, whose unsavoury name Edmund knew already because his son and heir had been at school, was forced abroad, took Fred with him and, when times continued hard, finally sold him with unshared profit to a male brothel in Hamburg.

"Thirty pieces of silver, 'e said they guv," continued Fred picturesquely. "They don't like that kind of thing over 'ere, though, so I'm at a loose end, as it were."

It turned out that his most persistent client in Hamburg had been an elderly Spanish marquesa, married in youth to a still more elderly, and by that time impotent, marquès. The latter had kept her virtually locked up until, widowed at last, but no longer young, the reluctant nun had gone firmly on her travels. "She didn't 'arf make up for what she'd missed, I can tell yer. Wanted it both ways, that old faggot did. She brought me out of there and took me home with her. As I said some likes it one way, some the other. Then she died, and I'm in Spain on me uppers. Give me any kind of a job, guv, do."

He shoved back his hat, which faintly resembled the recent matador's, and scratched his bristly, shaven head for lice. The gesture moved Edmund to a final sympathy. "You can come back with me and have a bath, at least," he said. He would see how the little monster shaped as a valet.

They continued in company, he and Fred. It was evident that the latter would serve in his former, or any, capacity. Although Edmund did not take up this offer with immediate eagerness, he knew he still had no interest in women and had, by this time, natural needs; it would be a way of meeting them and of retaining his privacy, but the need for that made him hesitate.

Fred also proved knowledgeable in finding mild diversions of a satanic sort. These existed, if one knew where, precisely as in the days of Goya or, for that matter, those of Adam. Edmund became, if not a practical expert – he was never interested deeply enough – at least a dilettante. There was a certain amount of esoteric knowledge involved, and like all knowledge he enjoyed acquiring it.

To his own surprise, Edmund found that he had spent two years in Spain without attempting to travel further. The bizarre nature of the harsh country had intrigued him. In any case, why go anywhere else? There was one place where he could not go, one person he was not permitted to see; Yolande had become almost a phantom by now, existing whitely in memory.

Whatever he did, wherever he went, it was refreshing to get back to Fred's earthy comments while he was being shaved or dressed for some formal occasion. Dress here, like everything else, was one generation in arrears. Some old men still wore powder, and the coaches were antique. The bowing and scraping of diplomatic exchanges bored him. Switzerland beckoned. He and Fred set out.

They journeyed once more through Italy, again beholding the archaic smile of the Apollo of Veii, the Pompeian excavations, stripped chambers in northern towns, Rome itself. Then they made for the snowy Alpine passes of Hannibal and Charlemagne. At last he could marvel at the height of the villages seen from the valleys by night, their lamps higher from here than the stars. Once he heard music.

"It's from the inns. They sing at night after a day's climbing," said Fred, who had been here with the marquesa. However, it was unlike any music Edmund had ever heard. He could not rid himself of the feeling that it had been a message to him from Yolande. He must return to Madrid, to see if there were letters. It was true there had been none for years, but the certainty remained with him.

On arrival a letter awaited. It had been sent with urgency; it was from the solicitor at Middle Temple. The late Lord Corbell and his wife were both dead. It was essential that he, fifth lord, return at once.

How had she died? He was more greatly concerned with that than with his father's death or his own new position. He considered probabilities as if they concerned some being who was not himself. His father and Yolande had been married for ten years. Alfred's gossip had made it clear that childbirth would kill her. Had there been a child? He didn't care. Yolande was dead. He could still feel her presence about him. She had tried to reach him, that time among the Alpine stars.

Fred handled everything; baggage, fares, a carriage to the port. Corbell, fifth lord, no longer thought of life without him. On reaching London he went straight to Mr Carey's office, to find him surprisingly the same, like a specimen in a bottle. Remote from the rub of society, hedged in by the precisions of the law, such persons were like nuns, and didn't age. He himself knew he looked older.

"How did my father die?" One must ask that first. The old lawyer handed him a letter. It was in his father's sloping handwriting, and sealed.

"He prepared that to be given to you before filling his pockets with stones and walking into the lake at Lackmere," said Carey. "He could not live on after his wife's death in childbirth. There is a daughter." He failed to add that the body had not floated up for some days. There would be the inquest to face, and the delayed funerals.

Corbell stared down at the letter, but would not open it till he was alone. When he did, he knew his father had taken his final revenge by the manner of his dying. He did not know if he could bear to swim in the lake again; then realised that that was precisely what Henry Corbell had hoped for in a final bitter victory. They must have returned to Lackmere for the birth, assuming it might be a son. As it was, his own heir, allowing for the entail, until he married, was still Alfred Sissington.

He made his way back to Lackmere with a heavy heart. Fred sat opposite, wordless. Steam drifted past the windows, obscuring the flat, unforgotten country. Once home, and the pending inquest over, he must arrange for the separate forms of burial, those of a suicide and a papist.

On arrival, met by the carriage, he stared almost unseeing at the lake. On nearing the portico he saw a dark-haired little boy standing staring. His eyes were vacant, and he was singing a tuneless song. This must be Peggy Vance's grandson, and he seemed to be an idiot. Maria Tesson's curse hadn't spared anyone. He knew, from that time on the half-landing long ago, that Peggy's

77

dead daughter had been the general's. The malediction ran in all Corbell blood, and in his own.

After it was all over, and the coffins disposed in their tombs, he jerked his head towards the bed and Fred went and lay face down on it. This comfort was all that remained. He had visited the nursery, seen the dark curls of the baby girl who'd killed her mother. She had been asleep, with the bruise on her temple fading from the grip of forceps. When her eyes opened, no doubt they would be green. He didn't want to see more of her. Now he was home again he would shut himself in the library, with his books. Vance could see to everything else, as she had always done.

Lackmere. *Lacù mare*. It was in the Domesday Book. He supposed he should marry. All that must be in the future. For the present he had no feeling left, not even grief.

Chapter Four

When the stones had been finally laid over, he visited the vault. As always, the place was a dormitory of the dead, each bed being identical except for the carved names. The general and Jocosa, so different in life, lay side by side, no doubt indistinguishable now from one another. His father lay between both his wives; Anna Corbell, Yolande Corbell. There was just enough space between the latter tombs for his own twisted body to make its way through. He stood for a time, without much feeling now, by his father's. Henry Corbell's flesh, bloated by long immersion, would adhere for a short time only to the bones. The man feared for so long in childhood was mortal; and lay nearer his own mother Jocosa now than at any time since his birth.

Standing by the tombs, Edmund remembered how as a child he had thought of his father as God. Henry Corbell had ended as God to himself. His son began to feel sensation return in the form of a cold and abiding hatred. He felt it chill his own bones as though he were dead like the rest.

"The sin of fornication will not avail you now," he heard himself say aloud to the fourth lord's coffin. Yolande lay, at last, alone.

The echoes of his voice died away in the closed air of the vault. It crept about him like a thin fog. He touched Yolande's tomb, as one might touch a relic; then went out.

On his way back to the house he stumbled in the cellar on the crack Alfred had made long ago, and fell on his sound knee. He righted himself, cursing; then noticed the crumbling of the dried cement. Out of curiosity he delved further, and presently unearthed, scraping with his fingernails, a pagan symbol, fired centuries ago into the half-revealed tile.

There were others to be found; once the stuff had begun to shrink it could be lifted off in fragments. Lime was brittle when dry. He unearthed a second tile showing the dog Anubis, sacred to the Egyptians and adopted late by Rome. This floor might well have belonged to some villa of the period just before withdrawal of the legions from Britain.

It was then, filthy with white dust as he was, that he looked up and saw Peggy Vance, as usual silently and respectfully, present. He had no idea how long she had been watching. She was holding something between her hands; Yolande's amber locket, still on its chain.

"My lord, I took this from her ladyship's neck when she was dead. I thought it might have been her wish, and maybe yours, that little Miss Henrietta should have it when she's older. There was something inside it, my lord, but it isn't there now. She – my lady – took it out when she was in the last throes, and put it in her mouth; and after that she was calm. She said to me, I remember, before she died, that she'd been better served in such ways in Sutherland than anyone knew.

"I didn't speak, but kept my counsel, until now to yourself. I hope I haven't left it too long, but with the funerals and that I didn't like to trouble you."

"You did rightly," he told her, and added that she might leave the locket on his desk upstairs. His hands were still dusty with lime, his nails ragged. Later, he'd look at the locket for a long time before putting it away.

Vance was still speaking, twisting her freed hands in her apron. Her eyes, he thought, had faded a little; how old would she be now? No matter. She was the kind of faithful servant one didn't want to lose; he must see to it that she received more money.

"There's another thing, my lord. The rest of us was asking if you'd kindly continue to take household prayers, the way we was used to in his late lordship's time. It wasn't done for us while the house was let, and it's good for the maids, makes them mind their ways. It would be appreciated if you was to do it again. They asked me to say this, and I hope it's not a liberty."

A kind of wild laughter rose in him; he, Satan's pupil, Goya's

80

disciple, reading household prayers, his own twisted ungainly figure replacing that of his father, of an Old Testament prophet! Yet it was impossible to give a reason for refusing, and so he nodded, as though it was no great matter. Peggy then expressed regret at the present state of his clothes. "Send them down, my lord, and I'll brush and sponge them myself," she promised. "It's that nasty lime; I remember when it was put in by my late lord, to cover up the ungodly pavement."

"I intend to clear the pavement," the new lord said firmly. He would by no means be bound by every rule of the dead hand.

He went up to the library after changing his clothes and washing his hands free of dust. The locket lay there, its silver chain spread reverently lengthways, the great oval amber gleaming. He had in some way assumed it to be inseparable from Yolande herself, placed still about her neck in the coffin. He was uncertain whether he was disturbed or pleased to see it again. He supposed that, as Peggy Vance had said, Etta should properly have it in due course. Meantime, he opened it, finding the little inner clasp Yolande had once denied him. Behind the glass panel containing the lock of her mother's hair there was a flat circular space, pressed in the silver. It was empty, and on the inmost surface of all was the outline of a crucifix. There was no doubt what it had contained at the last; it was a pyx, for concealing a Romish host. No doubt the Highland servants his father employed had seen to it that Yolande was not totally deprived of her religion. Those were Catholic parts still, as he was aware.

He recalled reading somewhere that Mary Stuart, when in prison, had been sent a consecrated Host for use in danger of death, and had contrived to take it secretly on the scaffold. Well, a second dying woman had been consoled by that same means, at least. He put the locket in a drawer, out of sight. He had already read his father's last letter. *Lackmere, the ninth of August* – that was the day Henry Corbell had died. It had no heading:

I know that you are my son, as you resemble my father. Unfaithfulness was not among Anna's follies, evidently.

This is to tell you that I killed your mother. As you know, the marriage had for long been dust and ashes. Also, my dear love was with child by me. The child was later lost.

Anna did not suffer greatly. I held the afghan she always kept

81

to cover her ankles over her nose and mouth, then left and waited for news to be brought to me in the library. It was assumed she had died naturally. She had been a complaining invalid for long.

I could not have exposed Yolande to the censure of society, and we were married as soon as possible. If she guessed the reason for Anna's death she never said so. Otherwise there was complete trust between us. I knew that she was ill at ease in Lackmere after the death, and agreed to take her away. We had many years of peace and contentment among the green silences and the hills. The riches of her mind were made available to me. She never denied me her body, but after the miscarriage I had to limit my attentions to her, and did so for the sake of saving her life. By then it meant more to me than my own.

You were the cause of Yolande's death. I want you to know it, and to keep the knowledge as long as you live. One day we were walking together beside one of the long sea-lochs that thrust into the coastline of those parts. I noticed tears in her eyes, the first since the cruel letter her aunt the prioress had sent on news of our marriage. That woman will burn in hell alongside myself. I took my wife in my arms and asked her why she was sad.

"I can never see water without thinking of Edmund," she said. "He so loved to swim. I pray for him always."

She did not add, as would have been proper in her, that she prayed also for me, her husband. I had the certainty that for the moment, she no longer recalled my existence. I was filled with enraged jealousy of a kind I had not for long felt, though it used to consume me in the days when you, a boy, were her pupil and meant everything to her. I guided her instantly to a private place among the trees, which are sparse in that region. I asserted my rights on her forcefully, more so than I intended. The child who has lately killed her was conceived there, by that water.

I still hoped that it might prove a son who should become the true heir to Lackmere. I persuaded Yolande to return there with me in time for the birth. It was a long and terrible one. Forceps extracted the child, a girl, at last from her dead body. I looked on it once only. It resembles my evil mother. You may do with this child what you will.

I stayed for a long time beside Yolande in death, and knew I could not live on alone. My father the general had more strength than I.

82

The title is yours, the house and estate here and the one in Ireland, and the money. It was Yolande herself who persuaded me to do this on your behalf. God, as I believe, will ensure that if you marry, you will not prosper. It was my wish that your cousin Alfred Sissington should inherit, as I betrayed his mother when I married yours. Disobedience to a parent brings its own lack of fortune.

I regret nothing that I have done, nor the way in which I will now die. It is possible that Yolande's prayers may save me from hell. I lived in it for long after the general's death, which my act caused. Your physical state was my punishment.

This is all. I can pretend no affection for you, but you will live your life as you decide.

I remain your father, Henry Corbell.

Edmund tore the letter to shreds and put it in the back of the fire. Then he went out and walked by the lake, almost persuading himself that its glairy surface was caused by the decomposing flesh of the man who had drowned in it. He did not know if he could bear to swim in it again.

Chapter Five

The fifth lord found himself changing, hardening. He no longer had affection for anyone, except possibly Peggy. Intimacy with Fred had stopped since the return voyage, and would not be renewed, he decided; Fred had been given quarters in the coachhouse, reached by a wooden stair from the stable. He was happy looking after the horses. Sometimes he drove Corbell, sometimes not. What else he did with himself was his own concern.

Corbell himself had determined to imitate his father in one respect: being a responsible landlord. He visited the tenants' cottages frequently, acted as his own bailiff and received their rents monthly. He did not intend opening up to the outside world, and the gates remained locked unless he required them otherwise.

One day, he had already told himself, he would marry and get an heir, if only to deprive Alfred Sissington of the prospect; but there was no haste. Meantime, his chief pleasure was the library, of which he was now quite free. The departed tenants had been careful of it, and Corbell proceeded to rearrange the shelves and to index what he might, in addition to reading by the fire. Papa's desk sat where it always had, no longer an object to be feared; and he earned his own place at it.

The county called, leaving cards with the lodge-keeper. Corbell did not pay return visits. Apart from a disinclination for small-talk he was aware of his own appearance, and that no young woman could desire to marry him except for gain. When the time came, arrangements must be formal. He recalled, with an echo of pain no longer felt, his mother's voice saying only a fortune-hunter's daughter would consider him. She hadn't known he overheard her.

Then Alfred Sissington arrived, having presented himself at the back gate instead of asking for admission at the lodge. Corbell remained civil in face of this effrontery, while hoping the young man would break his neck one day in the pit; it wasn't far off, hidden still by brambles. What Alfred wanted, of course, was money; only a loan, he assured Crip, no more. Cousin Mildred must be beginning to see daylight as regarding her erstwhile cherub. Corbell advanced the sum, knowing well enough he would never see it more. Lord Sissington by now was leading the life of a young masher about town, and no doubt it was expensive.

Corbell, to prevent the danger of his own idleness, began to pass the days in another occupation; excavating the hidden pavement with care and skill till it was clear. He had read about the methods used last century in Naples, and used a small hammer and chisel as archaeologists did. The revealed symbols were uniquely phallic, without question evil from his sect's point of view, but he was rapidly shedding it; the tiles possessed a perverted beauty. He could picture Henry Corbell, pursemouthed, cementing over the evidences of ancient sin, not yet contemplating his own.

Yolande. Would her memory never leave him, the sound of her voice, the sight of the fiery torments of hell in his father's glance, that summer day in the garden, and the roses heavy with scent? It was about then he, a green boy, had asked her to marry him. What had happened instead filled him even yet with torment; her cry of ecstasy in the unknown silences near a long sea-loch, in the green and private place by the far water.

Etta was a child of water. Perhaps she would learn to swim in the lake. He himself was persuaded to go in again after some time. The fourth lord's death had happened in it; the fifth lord entered it again after the benison of a cleansing storm of rain which lasted days.

Looking through his father's ledger of notes on his sermons he came across a late entry which surprised him, although it was familiar already. Had Yolande begun, at the last, to persuade Henry Corbell to her own faith? It was possible; and might give rest to that tormented spirit.

Procul recedant somnia
Et noctium phantasmata.
Hostemque nostra comprime
Ne polluantur corpora.

So, let them rest in peace, despite the Corbell curse. It had already done its worst with himself.

Part III

Chapter One

The fact that the fifth Lord Corbell still remained a bachelor by his middle thirties aroused hope in some, especially as it was fairly certain that the cause was the presence of that extremely odd young deaf half-sister. It was known that there had been an accident with forceps at the sad birth of the Honourable Henrietta Corbell, and that part of her brain which affected the hearing had been permanently damaged. As a result, the deaf child had never been able to learn to speak. Those older persons who remembered the fourth lord, respected in his day, were saddened by the thought of the only descendants he had been able to leave; a cripple and a deaf-mute.

Kindly mothers of young families in the county had at first invited young Etta to other children's Christmas and birthday parties, and although swarthy, she was pretty, with green eyes and dark curly hair; but she behaved uncontrollably, not only shrieking harsh noises she could not herself hear, but pushing and even biting any fellow-guests who got in her way. She was soon left out of invitation-lists, and shortly any servants who talked beyond Lackmere walls said she'd been sent, by his present lordship her half-brother, to a school said to be very good at bringing on afflicted children to become acceptable members of society.

However, Miss Etta had been returned in a fortnight, with a note from the headmistress to the effect that she was unteachable, and a bad influence on other pupils. Miss Etta had kicked off her shoes in the carriage home, as she disliked wearing them. She could, evidently, swim and dive like a fish; and in this occupation she passed her days. His lordship, the servants said, had forbidden her to swim in the lake at the same time as himself. He seemed to be the only one able to do anything with her.

The regrettable truth was, the servants whispered, that Miss Etta swam *naked*. It was hardly decent, and a mercy visitors were few.

The fifth lord would in any case not have encouraged these. He was by nature increasingly reclusive, and apart from reading his father's household prayers to the gratified few – "It might be the old lord over again. We're all most grateful to your lordship" – and his recent elevation to Justice of the Peace, he preferred to be alone. He would sit reading all manner of things including ancient recipes, among which he found Peggy Vance's black draught she gave to maidservants in trouble instead of whipping them. He wasn't surprised if trouble was rare. The ingredients were, mostly, castor oil and black smut of rye, an abortifacient. Peggy held their noses to make sure it went down, first thing in the morning.

Meanwhile, one day a green-eyed child in a grey hodden gown had erupted in barefoot, and Corbell's peace was never again certain.

That time, a flustered nursemaid had appeared, saying she was sorry, but Miss Etta had got away by herself. "See that it does not happen again," he said coldly, and watched the child dragged away by one hand, looking back at him. She had the complexion of a young Moor, never the whiteness of her mother. It troubled him that her short hair was in a tangle and that she was dressed like a servant, and wore no shoes. He complained to Peggy, who said Miss Etta wouldn't wear shoes, or anything but the hodden. Peggy said it wasn't that they had not tried to clothe Miss Etta according to her station, but there was nothing to be done with her.

Next time it happened – there had to be a next time – he decided that the child must learn that to follow him about meant a smacked bottom. He turned the skimpy hodden up accordingly, administered justice with the flat of his hand, and was disturbed when she writhed agreeably, though emitting harsh cries she herself couldn't hear. Peggy came in.

"Thankful we are, my lord, that you're dealing with her. None of us dared lay a finger on her, being who she is."

"You may whip her when necessary. I do not want to be troubled with her."

Some time later they had brought him the maid who had tried. Her forearm was bruised and swollen, with the marks of teeth. It was pointless to expose the maids to hurt; he would have to deal with Etta himself.

He found the process intensely disturbing. He had not, while at school, taken advantage of his position as prefect to cane anyone, particularly Alfred; it was in fact a deprivation to that young gentleman not to be caned. Etta herself seemed to be another such; plainly she enjoyed it. Defeated and disgusted, Corbell reduced such attempts to the irreducible minimum. He had no wish to feel compelled to visit Fred every time he caned Etta. It had had to happen already on more than one occasion.

He was beginning to be physically wretched. It was seldom now, except when he swam or worked at the Roman pavement, that he could again be certain of peace.

The tiles themselves brought him continued discovery. Their evil was manifest, and the most powerful of all, set near the centre, was the rendering in earth-coloured firings of the dog-god Anubis, who weighed the hearts of the dead in company with Horus, god of the underworld and who – Corbell tried not to remember the analogy – had been born of the coupling, in their mother's womb, of his twin parents Isis and Osiris, brother and sister. Why remember that? Horus in any case was still covered over, if he was present at all. His eye, an ancient talisman, was absent. Perhaps he, Corbell, was wearing it on his watch-chain.

Chapter Two

To his annoyance, Alfred Sissington came down to the cellar without invitation one day; he was beginning to make himself known to the county, who found him a diversion, especially the new and slightly vulgar couple at The Towers, an excrescence lately built where a former charming ruin had stood. The Penhaligons were accepted, because they had a great deal of money however it had been made; somebody whispered boot polish. Eileen Penhaligon was showy, but hospitable, and contributed charity-bundles at Christmas. She liked to flirt with Alfie. Her husband, who was older and tolerant, let her; there were two little boys safely in the nursery, and geraniums were being planted in the drive. Alfred would sweep down this in a carriage not yet paid for, and make for Lackmere, which was not far distant except in degree.

Corbell, not as a rule conscious of his clothes, had taken to wearing workman's overalls to protect them from the pervasive lime-dust. The elegant sight of Alfred, dressed to kill, irritated him. The pavement was his private world, not yet ready for inspection.

"It's shaping up," Alfred remarked. "No wonder Cousin Henry covered it; it brings out the worst, what? Dare say it was late Roman, after they brought back notions from Egypt and Syria the old senators wouldn't have allowed in." He had not, after all, wasted his education entirely. "When it's clear, Crip, old boy, we must have a proper black mass down here; that one at school was a shambles. Black candles, a black cockerel with its throat cut, a scapegoat; leave all that to me." He added that Corbell ought to erect a black altar; thirteen stones, the devil's dozen. His talk was so expansive that Corbell listened despite himself; it would be a simple matter to erect an altar, if he felt so inclined.

He dusted his hands for the time, and went upstairs to inspect Alfred's new carriage. He was becoming interested in the prospect of driving himself in a similar equipage, if less flashy; it would get him out of Lackmere and away – he admitted it – from the proximity of Etta. He found her increasingly disturbing.

There was someone who was afraid of Etta; Peggy Vance's grandson young Jemmy. He had grown into a big strong boy, but with no more wit than a block of wood. At times he helped out down at the home farm. He wasn't afraid of animals, but the sight of Etta made him run off, crying like a child. She used to point and give vent to her harsh laughter. Peggy hadn't missed any of that. At the beginning, she'd hoped the young pair would play together. Miss Etta would pay, in the end, for her mockery of Jemmy. He was an innocent, and loveable. Miss Etta was neither. Vance watched and waited. She was in control of Lackmere, as much so as if she'd been its mistress. She still kept the general's portrait free of dust in the hall. It wasn't hard to guess what he would have thought of young Alfred Sissington; not army material, and that was the least of it.

Alfred continued to visit, at times to stay. Corbell was careful not to leave him alone in company with Etta; Lord Sissington's known nature as an adult made him unsafe company for a little girl. He was still a beautiful Adonis, the delight of ladies everywhere as long as they were not expected to venture their reputations by being left alone with him. Far-sighted mamas whisked, with promptitude, their daughters out of the way after the second waltz; young Lord Sissington would have to marry a great deal of money, as he spent it recklessly and had already racketed through his paternal inheritance on coming of age. He was irresponsible, untruthful, and untrustworthy, but had looks and charm.

He had already established a kind of comradeship with Etta under her half-brother's watchful eye; treating her like a child, tickling and chasing her, and making her laugh her harsh

93

unknowing laughter. This was harmless enough, and diverted the deaf child. Corbell proceeded with his purchase of carriage-horses, having at last found a pair to suit him with the knowledgeable advice of Fred. He could not resist driving them out alone as soon as they arrived and had been rested; drove them at speed along the flat country roads, finding the experience gave him infinitely greater pleasure than riding, where he had of necessity to use one short stirrup, jolting his spine. He nodded to passing acquaintance, but did not stop. Freedom was heady, and brought with it the continued pleasure of keeping himself to himself.

On one such occasion he returned, and having stabled the greys went back to the house. He was informed that Lord Sissington had arrived while he was out, and would stay for a day or two.

Corbell went in search of his self-invited guest. Halfway up the stairs he could hear the sound of a low, obscene giggling. It was coming from the attics, and with his painful limp he was unable to attain them quickly and without warning. When he flung open the ultimate door, it was to reveal Etta with Sissington, the pair close together, but to all appearance innocently. Etta was holding against herself the ruins of the striped white-and-silver dress, taken from the opened trunk, its lid still gaping. She began to pirouette, so that the frail folds whirled; a nostalgic scent of dried roses came. "I've been teaching her to waltz," Alfred explained, his blue eyes bland.

"You can't. She doesn't hear."

Etta went on whirling about by herself, the raised dust spiralling in the filtered sunbeams from the attic windows. Perhaps there had been no harm in it; but he didn't like their being up here alone. He ordered Etta downstairs, gesturing with one hand. He followed, with Alfred, more leisurely. It appeared that there was a reason for the visit.

"I say, Crip, old boy, I'm in a spot of trouble," Alfred explained. "Would you lend me a couple of thousand?" He added that it was quite a serious matter. Then he added, concerning Etta, "That little bitch knows more than you think, wherever she learnt it. I didn't start anything, old boy; she did."

The serious matter turned out to be blackmail, involving Alfred's relations with a cabinet minister; they had been

94

witnessed, and the witness was asking for money. Corbell was uncertain whether or not the other party in the case was being approached; but the one to deal with such situations was his lawyer. He wrote instructions, a firm letter was sent, and no more was heard of the matter. Alfred expressed himself as abjectly sorry; it would never happen again. "I'm glad I've got you to keep me straight, Ed," he announced mendaciously.

It was possible that he really was repentant, having had a fright. Corbell decided to indulge him in the matter of the satanic coven he had repeatedly requested should take place on the final excavation of the tiles. It was at any rate a more harmless diversion than certain varieties of aside with politicians.

Sissington himself was meticulous about the coven's details. A black cockerel must be provided from the home farm; it would have its throat cut, and the blood would drip into the chalice. Christmas, an event the sect did not in any case recognise, was approaching, and the ceremony would duly be held on Christmas Eve. The weather outside had turned intensely cold.

Corbell, with the assistance of a mason, used his own strong arms to erect the thirteen black marble slabs required for the temporary altar. It was sited just behind the Anubis tile, making the dog-god of central importance, second only to the devil himself. Corbell agreed to represent that personage. He would sit cross-legged, with a band round his head to which were attached stag's antlers. The whole business was a schoolboy game, the other participants trustworthy and unlikely to spread word of what was after all a jest: Walshe, by now valet, Fred himself, and Alfred and his flute to make up the infernal trinity. The scapegoat, an essential ingredient, was promised by Sissington. Corbell was not particularly interested; once all this was over he could again be left in peace. It would no doubt prove to be a sheep or calf, in derision of the Old Testament.

Towards midnight on Christmas Eve Corbell sat naked, except for the antlers, but a lit brazier kept him warm. Its light flung shadows on the walls of the cellar, grotesquely magnifying his shape as he sat cross-legged, in the ancient attitude of fertility. He reflected idly that there were various ways of personifying the devil; some schools of thought kissed the unhallowed arse.

However, this was an all-male concern and nobody taking part would be surprised at his own appearance; the valet, Fred, and Sissington all knew what he looked like already. He waited, and there came the sound of the Etruscan flute, nearing from the direction of the upper staircase.

Behind him waited the symbols, or some of them; the black cockerel with its feet tied, its bright gaze wary as if it knew what awaited it. Beside it was a loving-cup, borrowed from upstairs; it had been a bride-gift to some Corbell woman in the eighteenth century. The knife waited by it; shortly the bird's dark blood would drip into the chalice, to be mixed with wine. Alfred had, of course, provided black candles.

He watched them enter, prancing; Fred came first, bearing the anti-host, however it had been obtained, on a platter. Corbell was more interested in the vast size of Fred's parts, which he had not before seen; the little tiger had always been the pathic partner, the receptor, in their occasional relations. Behind him, Walshe, naked likewise, looked a trifle self-conscious, carrying the wine and, inverted, the leather-bound Bible donated by the late Henry Corbell. His son regarded its dilapidated presence without emotion. Sissington followed, playing an unearthly tune on his pipe; then last of all, the scapegoat, blindfold, laughing, and as by habit in the lake stark naked; Etta, following close behind Sissington, keeping her hand on his shoulder for guidance.

Corbell, outraged, rose to his feet. He tore the antlers from his head and cast them on the floor. He then seized Etta, carried her, passive in his arms, out of the damned cellar with its symbols, limping up the stone stairs again, stopping for nobody. Behind him he heard Alf's pouting disappointment find expression; he'd spoilt everything, how could they have the coven without the devil and the scapegoat?

Corbell pulled the linen bandage off Etta's head. She made no sound or resistance; her eyes had darkened, with wide pupils. It was possible she had seen nothing of what had been intended below. Once out of the cellar, she slid her arms round his neck and began to kiss him repeatedly all over his face.

Sissington had initiated her, without any doubt; using her as a boy, perhaps since before that time he'd caught them in the attic. Corbell set Etta face down across his sound knee, smacked her hard twice or thrice, knowing it probably gratified her; and gestured to her firmly to go to bed.

Far down, he could still hear the archaic sound of the Etruscan flute. They were continuing the ceremony in some fashion other than the one at first intended. Had Sissington expected him to endure that? A memory of the Goya horror seen in Spain came to him; the drawing of living and dead children, made in offering to a black he-goat; himself.

He went to bed, but it was too cold to sleep. The sounds from below had died, and the dark was less thick than it had been. It was Christmas Day. He became aware of a second presence in his room; Etta, in her thin nightgown, standing barefoot by the bed.

"Cold," she said. She was shivering, and he let down a corner of his blanket. She slid into bed with him, offering her buttocks in the old way of punishment. He could have taken her, if only for warmth; she was accustomed to it, evidently. He was angry, left the bed, went out to the stables and wrapped himself in a blanket, lying down beside the horses. He was profoundly disturbed and did not sleep.

He got up early and went out to stare at the lake, frozen under paling stars. Not even he could swim in it. As he stood there he saw a slim white woman's figure watching him from the other side. It could not be Etta. It must be Jocosa, chilled upwards by the ice. He would not warm her, would by no means deal with either of them; or were they in fact one?

He did not stop to reflect, but went down to the cellar. The brazier was almost out, and the cockerel, freed, was strutting about, crowing softly and leaving droppings across the floor. The wine was finished; they'd had their celebration of Christmas, evidently. He heard a man's throat cleared, and beheld Fred, who hadn't left. The little man caught the strutting bird expertly, holding it against himself.

"Like 'im plucked and roasted for the season, m'lord?"

He grinned, showing the disastrous teeth. Corbell felt less of a fool than he had.

"Do as you please, after driving Lord Sissington to an inn," he said. "He will not continue to occupy his room."

He had dealt with Alfred personally after that, telling him to take himself off and not return. "You spoilt it," was all Angel Alf said. "You spoilt the coven."

Corbell decided that he could no longer endure the sight of

97

e

Alfred, Etta, or even Lackmere as it had become. As soon as the so-called festive season was over he would go up to his club for a few days. It was time he met other humanity.

Meantime, Fred and the guest having gone, Corbell went down into the vault alone. To demolish the black altar and pile the stones up for removal challenged his strength and emptied his mind. He wouldn't permit such episodes again at Lackmere. The effect on himself was malefic, apart from anything.

Finally at his club, reading the papers, he saw a fortalice advertised for sale in Scotland. It was said to be in a ruinous state and to need extensive repair. Well, he could spend the time repairing it; the work on the pavement was done, and he needed occupation

The first sight of the place pleased him, a small grey pencil of a tower thrusting up among the green hills Yolande had known. It was built in a hollow with, in front, a jumble of drystone dyking which had once been a garden wall. There was a rounded hill behind which gave it shelter and which was called The Ghluin, the hassock. The place had once been a lookout tower for the coming of rival clans, and its walls were ancient enough to have arrow-slits. In front was a rowan tree, at that time of year blazing with berries. Edmund told himself afterwards that he had bought the place for the sake of the tree. Had it been ready to live in, he could cheerfully have stayed there without returning; there was peace in the quiet air, and no one to trouble him. He decided that he would not at any time bring even Fred up here. He could contrive with locally hired servants from the glens. They could be trusted to look after The Ghluin while he was away. It was part of their heritage, a reminder of the world they had almost been made to lose with the sheep-grazing horror of the last century.

He was particular that the character of the little tower itself should not be lost, and was fortunate in finding local craftsmen to whom the long-suppressed Highland way of life was dear and who had tradition in their bones.

He stayed, meantime, at the only inn, and talked often with the innkeeper, a dignified bearded clansman who had returned home from abroad. He had married late, to a wife who cooked well, and they had a young daughter who saw to the linen and kept it clean. Lacking interest in women as he did as a rule, Corbell watched with pleasure as young Mhairi trod the used linen in the burn. She brought it out at last white and spotless, wringing it expertly and spreading it on the sweet moorland grass and scented bog-myrtle to dry in the afternoon sun.

Mhairi was like her father, having the inherent dignity of the folk left here. He recalled how they had suffered over the past two centuries, decimated by evictions, the Stuart risings, the taking of their men afterwards for the army when regiments were raised for the English wars. Mhairi had a soft voice, soft young limbs and, thankfully, none of Etta's demands and shrill restlessness. He could stay watching her for a long time, he knew, but knew also that he must return home. Fred could be trusted to exercise and feed the greys, but there were other matters which needed his own attention.

One of them was Etta. Despite himself he could not help feeling responsible for her. What was to become of her? She was nubile by now, and had been troublesome enough in childhood. Marriage in the ordinary way of other girls was unlikely, and he recalled Alfred Sissington's unrepentant words; *That little bitch knows more then you think.* It would be impossible for her to meet her social equals; she would antagonise genteel society by now more than ever. Yet his own life was to be lived, and he should provide himself with a suitable wife and heir. He was still determined that Sissington must not inherit.

Returning to Lackmere, Etta's greeting was as usual; she flung herself on him, kissing him over and over. He made some excuse and went along to the stables, finding Fred rubbing down the greys. Corbell passed his hand over their sleek necks in appreciation; he'd missed them in the north. Fred had kept them in fine condition.

Fred, after all, belonged to no class. He could mix with anyone at Newmarket who recalled his jockey days. Nobody could call him an ordinary servant. He'd seen the world, could deal with any situation. He could control any horse, however vicious. He could perhaps control Etta.

The notion grew less alien the more Corbell thought of it. In the end, with an eye to the not too immediate future, he approached Fred himself. In a year or two, for a not inconsiderable sum down and board and keep for the rest of his life, would he marry Miss Etta?

Fred grinned, showing the carious teeth. "If you mean will I

99

leather the living daylights out of her if she don't behave – oh, she won't like it from me the way she does from you – and give anything she has in the oven a name if so, I can if you was to pay me a bit more." It was no worse, in prospect, than the late marquesa; and he could dictate his own terms. Nobody else would take on that hot little hellcat, deaf or not.

So it was arranged, if needed. Corbell thankfully returned to his fortalice, the building of which was beginning to fascinate him even more than the pavement had done; and there was nothing evil about The Ghluin. Its sole lack was a sheet of grey water.

For some years his life divided itself into two parts; in the north The Ghluin, in the south the galloping greys. The unchanging hills gave him lasting pleasures; taking off his low-crowned hat to acquaintances met on the road at home was shallower, more fleeting; he would never care greatly for company. However, he was known in the county, respected as his father had once been. He came and went. Fred cared well for the horses. Etta survived, swimming daily.

Once while north, a letter had come from Sissington, asking if he might visit once more. It was certainly better to be there while he did so. Corbell unwillingly said goodbye to the innkeeper and his family, promised to come back soon, and returned as he had come. He was almost unwilling to see the lake again, which struck him as curious. It had once meant all his waking life.

Etta's welcome was as before; she slid her thin arms round his neck, writhing against him. "Ed-die. Ed-die." She had little pricking breasts whose shape could be seen beneath her dress. He looked away.

Next day Sissington arrived. He looked older than his years, and the flesh beneath his eyes was already loose. Nevertheless he retained persuasive charm, knew it, and evidently hoped to use it to obtain money again if he could. It wasn't quite so bad this time, politics not being involved; but a young woman of High Church connections said he, Alfred, had got her in the family way, and he hadn't even touched her. "Her uncle's a bishop, and it'll put paid to any kind of career I might have had." He did not add what this might be.

"Why not marry her?" Corbell asked reasonably, thinking that if that happened, he himself must do likewise soon.

"She's married," said Alfred despairingly. "Her husband's a curate and he can't live up to her, and I – well, I comforted her a bit, if you must know. Money would keep it among ourselves."

For the sake of everyone concerned, Corbell knew he would pay. As for careers, it was unlikely that Alfred would become anything but a social butterfly, the powder on its wings already a trifle balding. His erstwhile doting mother was becoming increasingly tight-fisted. It was, he said, extremely difficult to keep up his position. Corbell guessed that a rich marriage was out of the question; even tradesmen would not be deceived, by now, into buying their daughters into this degraded title.

In the meantime, while discussing the matter of the bishop's niece, whose marriage was in plain fact finally annulled, the two cousins walked together in outward amity on the terrace Corbell had had built. It gave a view of the lake while one sat in comfort, near shelter if it rained. Unfortunately Etta had chosen to go in for her swim; it was possible that she knew Alfred had come. In full view of both men, exactly as she was, she rose from the water, flaunting herself. Corbell resolved to forbid her the lake for a week. Locked up accordingly, she would hammer at the door and yell, disturbing the whole house. However, Sissington was observing her with a connoisseur's eye.

"She's comin' on, like the pavement," he observed, his blue gaze brightening above its loose flesh. Corbell was more than ever thankful to have made the earlier understanding with Fred. He sent for Etta to the library and caned her, more out of principle than hope. When he had done she flung her arms about him and laid her head in his lap. If he had known, Vance had a less welcome punishment for her after certain kinds of misbehaviour; a curative douche and the black enema. It took three maids to hold Miss Etta down. Peggy had said nothing to his lordship; it would upset him, and he'd told her long ago to do with Miss Etta what she thought was needed. That had certainly been needed more than once.

Within a few days Corbell returned to The Ghluin. Its solitude and peace were becoming necessary to him, and there was no more of either to be found at home.

The little fortalice had been tastefully improved. The outside

101

walls were pointed, the drystone mended tidily by a craftsman who knew his skill. It was winter and the rowan was bare, but Corbell passed his time in finding furniture to suit the place at sales held now and then at former great houses, many of whose owners had gone away. Many more were abandoned, as The Ghluin had been, to decay and rooflessness. Next time he came, he told himself, it would be possible to move in at last.

Meantime, he stayed as usual, contentedly at the inn with Mhairi's parents. The young girl had matured, but very differently from Etta. She had the quality by now that he remembered and had loved in Yolande; a deep and gentle purity, a quality both of flesh and spirit. Corbell seldom addressed her, as Mhairi knew no English, and he would never master the soft ungovernable tongue of the Gael. Once or twice he heard Mhairi crooning in it as she trod her linen, oblivious of the coldness of the running water, of the nearness of his watching self. His crookedness did not seem to perturb her. This suited him well enough.

Again he was unaware of the passing of time. He began to plan his garden at The Ghluin, himself burning the bracken that had been allowed to creep in and multiply there. He left the earth dug ready for late spring; everything here was later than at home.

In April in the Highlands, after Culloden last century, women and children whose houses had been burned had died after nights of cold in the open.

He saw the post arrive one day without premonition; but it contained a letter in Peggy Vance's careful round writing. He opened it with a feeling of intrusion; would Lackmere never leave him in peace? It was a curious thought about the place he had once loved.

> *My lord,*
>
> *Forgive my troubling you, but Lord Alfred has taken to staying here a good deal, knowing you was away. It isn't my place to say anything to him, and as for Miss Etta, she does as she pleases. I've done what I may, but she's past heeding me or anyone. She remained his devoted servant, Margaret Vance.*

It was time to tear himself away from his peace, and go back. He travelled south at once.

Peggy was waiting at the door; she knew the times of trains. "My lord, if you was to go down to the boathouse this minute you'd find them at it. I didn't say you would be here, but it's time."

Corbell went to the tackroom, and took down the long-handled whip he used on the greys. He made his way, still in his travelling-clothes, down to the jetty and the boathouse. The recesses of the latter were in shadow under its roof. Inside the boat lay, quivering above darkened water, rocking with the coupling of the pair inside; Sissington, with Etta locked beneath him, man and woman together. Corbell felt a fury rise he did not know he possessed. He called out curtly, "Stop that. Come out of there, both of you. Come out at once, I say."

Sissington struggled to his feet, fastening himself; his degenerate face was flushed. Corbell jerked his head at him to get on shore. When he had done so he took him by the scruff, flogging him with the long whip till he lay screaming on the ground. When Corbell stopped for breath the excuses began, streaming out of the loose mouth, mingled with further gasps and howling.

"She was ready for it; why shouldn't I?"

"Will you marry her?"

"God, no. Ow, aow, Crip, don't hurt me any more, not any more, aow."

Corbell proceeded to hurt him considerably. Then he said, "Get out. You will not show your face again here in my lifetime."

"Oh, no, old boy – "

The whip flailed down, again and again. When at last he had done, and the weeping bundle of chastened flesh had limped off almost in his own lopsided fashion, Corbell brought himself to look into the boat. Etta still lay in there motionless, her green eyes wide and vague. Her thighs and their secret remained exposed. Could she not cover herself, at least? He heard himself shouting angrily, as though she could hear.

He was aware of an instant, appalling attraction. It had always been there, but he had never before admitted to its presence. Now, his sectarian upbringing rose, as it seldom did, to save him; he recalled reading in the Bible how a son of King David had lain with his sister Tamar and had been accursed and killed by their brothers. Of all ancient sins, incest was the most abhorred, and he loathed himself for what he now knew he felt, had felt unadmitted for long; for how long? Since her childhood? At any rate it must stop. He thought swiftly of Fred. Fred could deal with any matter. He could control his, Corbell's, half-sister, this little amoral whore, with Jocosa's blood strong in her from her father, and her green eyes looking out on a world she could never enter.

It would serve, because it must. If she could tolerate Alfred Sissington, who might well have got her pregnant, she could endure his, Corbell's, catamite. Fred had said he'd give anything a name; but no embryo of Sissington's would be permitted to endure in Etta. He'd get Peggy to administer the black draught at once.

He turned away, no longer permitting himself to look at the boat with its occupant. She was unrepentant; and had he lain down upon her now, she would have allowed him what she'd allowed Sissington. He need have no compassion for her.

In the near distance he saw Alfred's carriage drive away. He hoped that young man had had to be helped into it, and would not move with ease for some considerable time.

The marriage of Etta and Fred was no more than a hand-fasting, according to the permitted rules of the sect. However, Corbell had ensured that it was registered with the Anglican authorities, as the law required. In fact he had gone with Fred to acquire a special licence.

He had chosen the occasion to make the bride a present of her mother's amber locket, taking it from the drawer where it had long been kept and fastening it round Etta's neck himself. She stood passively, the warm stone gleaming against the new dress she had been bought for the occasion. He had tried to get her to understand the lock of hair at the back, but it was doubtful if she did so; at his touch she swung her body insinuatingly, so that the amber changed colours as she moved. She seemed pleased with the dress.

There were no witnesses except himself and Peggy Vance, and some of the household; he had left it to them to convey the news to the village and, if so, the county. The situation would come to be accepted in time; no doubt it would be assumed that Fred had

104

anticipated his rights. Little was known about Lord Corbell's odd half-sister by now except the rumoured fact of her deafness, and the memory of her impossible manners as a child. Most people assumed that there must be something further wrong as she was kept so closely at home, with never any invited company. Possibly she took fits. Few except the servants at Lackmere could have told anyone much about her, and they kept their counsel.

Corbell went to read for a quarter-hour alone. It had begun to rain, with the force of a strong prevailing southwesterly wind driving against the windows and drowning other sounds. Suddenly, above the storm, he heard a man's high scream.

He went out and towards Etta's room as fast as he might. Fred was already outside, standing in the passage, doubled up and clutching his genitals. His screams had died down and he was sobbing like a child.

"Aow Gawd. What she done to me, that bitch of hell. Kicked me in the balls over and over, never knew the like in all my natural, never felt the like, somebody else can try it with her. Aow Gawd. Gawd. I'll never touch her again, keep her away, keep her away from me. I'll never be the same as I were, never, never no more, aow, keep her away, keep her off of me." The last words died away in a long wail. Tears were streaming down Fred's face; he was probably the most revolting object ever seen, and Edmund nevertheless persuaded him to his own bed, made him lie down and promised him a sedative. Fred lay on his side, knees drawn up, still howling.

The sedative came, he drank it and grew quieter. Edmund by then was packing his own gear. That hellion, Etta, could do as she chose from now on; he himself had finished with her. He would take Fred to The Ghluin. They would leave together by the first train; Peggy would fetch the little tiger's gear from the stables. The greys – he remembered then – must regrettably be put up for sale; they wouldn't perform at peak on the rough roads of the north. All he himself wanted was to be away from Lackmere and its demons; even the lake meant only horror now. He hoped Etta would drown in it, and didn't want to be here to see or know.

He wanted no farewell to her either, and there was none; good Peggy Vance kept her locked up, and he could hear her clamour. "Whip her if you must, keep her under lock and key, dose her, do as you will," he had said. If Etta wouldn't behave as anything but a savage, she must be treated as one. Bedlam would be welcome to her. He heard Peggy speak.

"It takes three of us to hold her down, my lord, and a fourth to turn the lock."

"Well, you have enough for that," he said coldly, and left. Fred lay cowering on the carriage cushions, sobbing at every jolt of the wheel.

On the train at last, Fred grew slightly better, though by this time feverish; he would need nursing for some days. Edmund thought with relief of the gentle Highland folk at the inn. Fred cried when he heard the greys were to go, but nothing much at present affected him except the evident fixed belief that he would never be the same again. Corbell turned away from his care of Fred to the arrangements he had made with the new driver, the valet Walshe, to take the greys to Newmarket. Walshe had already begun to court the cook, and would probably therefore stay. Corbell felt that his own world had shattered overnight; but at least there was the prospect of being left in peace in the north.

Chapter Three

After they alighted from the train there was some delay. Fred still whimpered at the idea of sitting in the saddle, and it was necessary to hire a pony and cart in the back of which he lay, groaning at every jolt in the road. They made frequent inn-stops to rest him. The mountains began at last to be evident; Fred admitted he had never seen the like before, even in Spain. On one stop, climbing out, his huge hand suddenly gripped Corbell's with returned strength. "Gawd," he said again, "what's that? That up there on the hill."

It was a stag, royal with antlers displayed, its incomparable head clear and proud on the strong neck, its body poised in a cleft between two great frowning peaks. They enhanced its splendour rather than diminishing it. Tears suddenly began to run down Fred's cheeks.

"I'll never be the like of that again," he said. "No use to nobody, I'm not now, that way."

Corbell felt compassion, at the same time knowing himself an outlaw to society, Fred had been badly bruised, and clung to Corbell like the mother he had never known. It was in the natural way of comfort, by now on his own part, to resume their former relations. These were still more natural when at last they shared a bed below the eaves at the Highland inn.

Young Mhairi used to bring up their breakfast where they lay beneath the thatch; she was too innocent to see more than two gentlemen guests in bed, and used to give a little respectful bob, then leave them. "That was a nice bit," remarked Fred once. It was evident that he was nearly himself again.

They moved into the Ghluin, still smelling of fresh lime plaster as it was. The newly glazed and white-painted windows shone, and one could look out beyond at the hassock-shaped hill. Soon, Corbell thought, he would start work on the garden; it had again been freshly dug to his order in his absence. All should have been serene; yet perhaps the misery of his own state regarding Etta was less thoroughly slaked than Fred's; Fred had had no feeling for her one way or the other. She had merely been part of a bargain. Corbell himself was in deep perturbation of mind regarding her.

He had wanted peace more than anything, and had hope for it here. He could contrive without the sight of the lake, without swimming, or driving his horses; but his mind was still in torment. Perhaps it was for that reason, to blot out what lay in his mind, that he yielded to Fred otherwise, for the first time, at The Ghluin. The little man had come to him and said he felt much better; and, respectfully, wondered if his lordship would let him have a try for himself?

The memory of Dr Slater the crammer, buried deep, rose again for moments. However, Fred had asked humbly enough, and this would not be prolonged. Corbell permitted it.

Fred proved a superb lover. At first Corbell was astonished by his own reaction, his gradual delighted ecstasy; then an immense relief, a garnered pleasure, a residual languor which persisted and increased, as though they were not now together in the clear air of the north but in some exotic, intimate paradise. The suppressed recollection of that first night in the dorm at school, when he'd hit out at older boys who'd tried it in turn, as expected, lost any importance it had ever had in his mind. It was as though he had been ill for a long time and was convalescing, was finding himself. He was looked after, cherished as never before; he left all decisions to Fred. Fred had become Jove to him, he himself Ganymede; passive, obeying, unresisting, languid, content. His twisted body had become a minor god's, capable of infinite reception. Time had ceased.

Otherwise the ghillie and his wife, who had been installed by him earlier as caretakers at The Ghluin, able to shoot and maintain the game on the small estate while he was away, had welcomed them, having already been told to expect his lordship at any time. The savoury smell of venison stew would float up to where the lovers lay, above stairs on the small circular forecourt where once the women of the clan had sat sewing or spinning in summer beneath the upper tower. As the days passed this became Edmund's favourite place, alone or else with Fred, expertly caressing, foreseeing everything, allowing no need for thought or remembrance.

Fred had learnt already, with his quick ways, to catch brown trout in the burns. Edmund left that and the walking of the hills to so eager a learner, himself living for the moment, the hour of Fred's return. In a dream which excluded past and future, the present was bliss; catching sight at times of the ugly little man who purveyed it amused him. The possibilities aroused by his own full abandonment, his yielding, enthralled him totally. He had known and imagined nothing like it in all his life.

The first jarring note came when he heard Fred say, behind him, "Think what Etta's missing, eh?" Who Etta might be he had to recall; she was in another life, forgotten. He heard his own voice, peevish that Fred should remember anyone but himself.

"Go on, go on. Harder, harder."

"You don't 'arf ask for it, lordship. Pity we took as long." A touch of disrespect there; he shouldn't allow it, but couldn't withdraw; he was deep in enchantment. He heard himself whimpering a little, as if he was a child who'd been betrayed. Presently he forgot the matter.

The second interruption, the harsh bringing back to earth, came when the ghillie, Seumas, asked to have a word with himself, as they called Corbell here. The man's face was set and unfriendly. He said he and his wife were leaving. "We do not like what is happening here, and that is the truth of it," he announced, his blue eyes cold. He uttered a certain term in Gaelic; then turned and went.

Fred shrugged when he heard, and said it wasn't the first time he'd had to look after himself. "I can buy stuff for us both from the inn; there's pack-ponies comes there Tuesdays."

Corbell left him to deal with such matters, and continued in his dream as best he could; it occurred to him now and again that Fred ruled matters by this time and couldn't be done without. No other couple would come here, gossip no doubt having spread through the glens; well, let it. He found Fred could cook well enough; it was a parody of husband and wife, their roles reversed.

At times Edmund would stand naked in the tower, staring out at the hills and the budding rowan, and wonder that they still held their former peace.

He was determined to retain it. It occurred to him that he might take up sketching again as a pastime. He would go down daily, while it was fine, to the burn, where Mhairi would be treading and wringing her linen, white feet bare, skirts kilted up out of the water. It would be pleasant to sit in the heather and sketch her; the line of her neck, with the fair hair drawn back in a shining knot; her bosom, the already developed curves of womanhood. For the first time by now he understood women, the way they felt. He went down, and Mhairi heeded him little after the first shyness at being drawn at all; smiling, treading, wringing the linen. By summer, she would take it in her strong young arms and spread it out to dry on the fragrant bog-myrtle, ready by evening, dry and sweet-scented for folding away.

He drew her in all her attitudes, ignoring the biting Highland flies that came with summer. Fred, who brought him down a daily collation at midday, had a cure; he made a small ring of stones, and used to light a smoking fire of dry gorse wood; the stones kept it from spreading in the heather. Fred watched, tending the fire, clearing away the remains of the food. Corbell was at peace; soon the bright berries of the rowan would show once again.

He painted it as intended by early autumn, but was interrupted by the innkeeper who had come to him, his face grim. "What is it?" Corbell asked impatiently. The light would soon be gone; the days were already shorter at this time of the year.

Mhairi's father uttered an imprecation in Gaelic. "Your serving-man has ravished my daughter," he said. "We do not forget such things here. Tell the *beathach* to go if he values his life."

Later he heard more. Mhairi had been gathering the old pale broken-off wood that lay deep among the prickled whins, dry for the inn fires. The Sassenach servant had appeared and thrust her down. She had come home crying.

Corbell was too greatly stunned even to feel betrayal. The first thing he knew was that it would be wrong to offer money, as might have been done in England. "You yourself have no place here," said the innkeeper, and it was the speech of the Gael, who held nobody prouder than himself except his chief. Even the chief

110

in his time would not have been forgiven this.

"He shall go," Corbell promised, and, sick, degraded and betrayed, turned on Fred when he came back. "You must leave," he told the man. "They needed none of that here. Take your wages, and make your own way off."

"What of it? She's the barmaid, ain't she? Yer can do it to a barmaid, they expects it. Shoved her down in the gorse, I did, and pricked her like I was gorse myself, only better." He laughed. "Tits like pumpkins, she had, enough to fill both your hands. Showing her legs in the water every day like that, asking for it. I needed a 'oliday, didn't I? Can't say you didn't get your own money's worth, at that, can yer?"

"Get out of my sight. I have no wish to see you again."

Fred leered. "Can't get rid o' me that easy, lordship. I'm your bruvver-in-law, remember? Special licence and all."

He added, with insouciance, that he'd got Mhairi to like it in the end, they all did if you stayed up them long enough. He was like a strutting bantam, again reasserting his healed manhood. Corbell disguised his own deep outrage and betrayal; the ape Fred had now become mustn't guess. "Get out of here, at any rate," he said. "Go back to Lackmere if you must, but keep to the coach-quarters."

"You keep that Etta off of me."

"Etta will not come near you. Take your gear and go before the clan comes out for your blood; you are lucky to have had warning."

"Clan? There ain't none left. Polished off, they was, last cent'ry, gone for soldiers, a duchess kissed 'em to go." Nevertheless he accepted his wages and his train fare; he would be lucky, Corbell thought, if he got as far as the train.

He himself knew that he could no longer stay. The peace had gone. He could never face Mhairi again, or her parents. There was only one place to which to return, drawing him ineluctably; the lake, the unforgotten lake, which would surely even yet console him. These folk had been kindly to a stranger; but as they said, he had no place here. His place was, after all, at home.

He followed alone, leaving The Ghluin tower rearing untenanted; he had put it up for sale through an agent and knew he would not see it again. Nor had they allowed him to say farewell to Mhairi, or to leave any gift for her. He was bitterly aware of his own

111

neglect and blame. All he could do now was to leave these folk with their peace, and cease to disturb it.

It was strange to come home, less so to learn that Fred was by now again living calmly in his stable-quarters. The little tiger would survive anything. It was unlikely he would trouble Etta again, or she him. She herself was as foreseen; flinging, hugging, writhing, kissing, expectant. So disgusted was Corbell with the late matter and the way it had ended that he was as near as he had ever been to yielding to her; after all, why not? If he took her in the conventional way, any child she bore would be known as Fred's. That thought in itself revolted him. He knew he could never touch Fred again, that their former relations had come to an end. He himself would no doubt reach the state of sexual deprivation in which his father had remained for twelve years, with the same effect on his nature; making him stiff, narrow, unapproachable, tied to the tenets of his sect. That last Corbell would not permit himself; he began to examine these, then to abandon them. He would continue to take household prayers as the fourth lord had done, but that was all; the beliefs that had tried to make of him an outcast because of his physical state no longer mattered to him. He was as other men; except that fastidiousness forbade him to make use of the maids, or even one of the younger menservants. To control his urges was the only answer, for the time.

He devised a way to make Etta obey him. If she became out of control, he would tie her wrists to a bedpost and utter the word "Fred". That syllable quieted her at once. She knew nothing of what had happened except for her own deep loathing and fear. Nor did she know that Fred would on no account come near her, feeling similarly. It was an ironic situation that suited Corbell well enough.

He took to spending a good deal of his time in town, mostly alone in his club reading the newspapers. In this way he saw the account of Alfred Sissington's engagement to the Honourable Ione Pusey-Pound. A letter from Alfred himself was waiting on return to Lackmere.

Corbell made his savage resolution at once. The Honourable Ione's parents were penniless, her father an inveterate gambler, her mother an aristocrat, not of the first water. Alfred said he was in love, and apologised for his late behaviour with Etta. He hoped Corbell would agree to meet Ione and her parents as soon as was convenient to him. The letter ended with a naïve hope that Corbell would provide a modest advance on expectations, to enable him, Sissington, to maintain his bride in the manner to which she had been accustomed.

Corbell had, on his Newmarket visits, heard of the Pusey-Pounds. Since the days of The Ghluin, the too-short time in Elfland like Thomas the Rhymer, he could tell himself nothing but the truth. He was aware, now, that his intentions were dictated by spite and revenge; but why should he not take it for what life had so constantly done to him? He would still make as good a husband as Alfred to any presentable young woman. He would inspect the Honourable Ione as though she were a Newmarket mare, ascertaining, as far as it might be done, that she was both unmated and fertile; then marry her, providing himself with an heir who was at any rate not Alfred Sissington. There was after all no reason otherwise. The Pusey-Pounds were deep in debt, and the engagement to Alfred had probably only been considered by some mention of his expectations at one's own demise. Well, he himself was not dead yet. He could provide a wife with all she might require. This young woman was well born, as far as that went; she had no doubt been taught to behave before she was presented; she might even teach a few manners to Etta. The thought diverted Etta's harried half-brother. If Etta's tantrums continued troublesome, he would again threaten to turn her over to Fred. Fred himself, left sullen as Uranus in his stable-quarters except for probable forays now and again to the village, should learn to drive a horseless carriage, a basketwork Daimler like the Lord Lieutenant's own. The Honourable Ione – her pardon, Lady Corbell – could be escorted about in it, with or without his company, in a long dust-coat and a motoring veil. It only remained to inspect the young woman and pay off her parents.

His thoughts diverted him, as had not happened in years. It was again near morning, and he rose early and went for a swim before breakfast and before Etta should invade the lake. That was his own still; he deliberately circled the centre; both in her grave and her enamel fragments, Jocosa, now, might lie still. He was his own man, with money and a title; he would take a wife and deprive Sissington, who had after all once tried to drown him here; and that was only one aspect of pervasive evil which might now be driven out.

Chapter Four

Corbell made arrangements for the Pusey-Pounds to come with their daughter to luncheon, arriving by train and being met at the station by Fred, with the carriage. He himself stood behind the window-curtain and watched them arrive at the front entrance; a thin middle-aged woman in a black false front of hair curled like a poodle's, as was fashionable, beneath her toque; a seedy grey-haired man, his moustache still gallant, in plaid trousers and a bowler; and a queenly young woman with piled golden hair, who took great care of her pale skirts, and her pinned and modish hat, as she emerged from the carriage. Whatever she had looked like, he would have taken away Sissington's selected girl; and this one did not look too bad, though he had not yet heard the Honourable Ione speak.

When she did so, it was reasonable. While they were in prior talk before luncheon she remained properly silent, and her mother (Lady Leonora's second cousin was a duke, slightly off his head and confined, but the relationship lent clout) talked instead. The young lady smiled once, revealing fine teeth. He decided that she would do; eyes perhaps a trifle close together. Undoubtedly she would have attracted better proposals in her first season than Alfred Sissington's in her second, were it not for her sire's known and regrettable habit of backing consistent losers. With unerring lack of foresight he had run through all of Lady Leonora's moderate dowry in this way, and they had lived ever since on occasional mentions of the unavoidably absent duke. Despite his surname, Pusey-Pound had no High Church leanings whatever and was known to close acquaintance as Pussy.

What Corbell had not taken into account was that the Honourable Ione was as deeply in love as was possible to her nature. It had been more than a relief when Lord Sissington had proposed behind some potted palms at a recent subscription ball. He waltzed divinely, and they thought in the same way about most things, in other words not very profoundly. Dear Alfie had been perfectly honest with her; he had no money either, as what was left appeared to be tied up in his canny old mother's jointure in the north. "We can't very well wait till Mama snuffs it," Alfred had remarked in his elegant way, and told Ione about his expectations from an extremely rich, reclusive and deformed cousin whose fortune, with the title, he would one day inherit. "Poor Crip can never marry," he assured her with slight mendacity.

However, Lord Corbell was looking her over in a most speculative way below his heavy eyebrows, and Mama, who missed nothing at any time, watched approvingly.

At that moment, while they all four sipped madeira, there was an interruption, and there sidled into the room a most extraordinary young woman, with wild green eyes, tangled hair, and a pair of sheepskin slippers much too large for her evidently otherwise bare feet. She wore a grey flannel dress like a nightgown or – the Honourable Ione had been given certain brief cultural and historical instruction at a finishing school in Lisson Grove – like the *sanbenitos* worn by those about to perish in the flames of the Inquisition. Ione shivered a little, and Lord Corbell frowned.

"This is my half-sister Henrietta," he said. "Unfortunately she is deaf. Etta, go out." He pointed severely, but Lady Leonora, who had been awaiting some chance to seize this infinitely better-feathered bird in hand if only dear Ione could be taken out of earshot for a few moments, broke in.

"May she not perhaps take Ione for a short walk to see the lake before luncheon? We all admired it greatly on driving in." She smiled, revealing porcelain dentures, and Ione, who had been seated correctly upright like a well-trained pointer bitch, aware of Alfie's dear little keepsake (it was unpaid for) nestling securely on her fourth left finger, rose unwillingly. She didn't want to go anywhere at all with so odd a creature, but one didn't disobey Mama. The elders were left to continue the conversation by

116

themselves, although Pussy seemed absent-minded and contributed little. He was wondering why the devil Fred, whom he'd known well in his best days, had driven them in the carriage from the station. His wife, though, was concentrating fiercely on the matter in hand.

By the time Ione returned, she was no longer engaged to Alfred Sissington, the defects of whose character had been briefly dwelt on, but to his lordship himself. Such things are readily rearranged with enough worldly experience, but it was perhaps not quite time to break it to the dear child yet; wait till they got home. "There is more to marriage than waltzing, Ione," was how lady Leonora had decided to break the news. No doubt there would be a little tantrum to contend with, but a promised trip to Marshall & Snelgrove, to purchase becoming gowns and other items with some hope of having them paid for, had risen at once to mind. How fortunate that she had always contrived to see to it that the dear child was fitted with proper stays! They made all the difference.

Driving back to the train, such rearrangements had of course not yet been broached, and Pussy, who had hardly listened to the earlier conversation between his wife and their host as his mind was fixed on the performance of Firecracker in the twelve-fifteen, broke in.

"By God, that's Fred drivin' us again," he said. He jabbed the tiger in the back with his cane. "What the devil are you doin' here?" he demanded, adding that Fred was the best jockey he had ever seen ride, and could be makin' a better livin' by far at Newmarket and Goodwood.

Fred replied modestly that he had retired, and mostly kept to himself. Lady Leonora looked down her nose. One didn't hobnob with the servants.

On the train, with the hissing of steam drifting past the windows, the expected little tantrum was dealt with prematurely. "Think what it will mean to be rich, dearest, and all Papa's debts paid! We must not be selfish, must we? Look how careless you have been with your new gown only today; if it had not been for this offer of Lord Corbell's, we would be hard put to it to buy another, and there would be only the dark-blue bombazine for you to wear to everything."

"That creature pushed me into the water. It wasn't my fault, and I would rather marry Alfred." She sounded stubborn; this would never do.

"We will go shopping tomorrow," said Lady Leonora firmly. A vision of feather boas, hats weighed down with flowers, transparent nightwear in which to close one's eyes and think of England, the wedding dress itself – the ceremony would of course be very quiet, probably held in the drawing room at Lackmere, and naturally *no* honeymoon – would shortly console Ione; the child was not, as a rule, disobedient.

Pussy broke in, tactlessly, at that point to ask why Alf Sissington hadn't come with them today.

"Because he was not invited," replied his spouse sharply. She then instructed Ione to blow her nose and avoid making an exhibition of herself when they reappeared in public, at the main station.

They reached home safely in the end, to find Firecracker hadn't even been placed. "You see, it is essential for Ione to make a *good* marriage," pointed out Ione's mother in triumph. It would at least stave off the bailiffs when the announcement appeared in *The Times*.

She tried to recall the circumstances of the suicide, some years ago now, of Lord Corbell's father. The deaf girl's mother must be the second wife, said to have been a governess. It didn't signify. Ione had returned from her little walk looking rather angry, which raised some colour in her pale cheeks and became her. Her dress had got wet at the pleated satin hem. "Mama, I was *pushed* into the lake, and only managed to save myself by holding on to a branch. I fear this gown will not recover."

"Never mind, dear, we will buy you a replacement," Lady Leonora felt able to say now with some certainty. Lord Corbell had made it clear that once Pussy's debts were paid, he and she would be expected to reside in the South of France. The whole thing would be a relief, the best possible arrangement for everybody.

Back at Lackmere, Corbell himself, on the party's departure, had dragged himself upstairs with his awkward, lopsided gait, one hand gripping the dark carved wood of the familiar balusters. He gained the organ room, where he could be private, and flung himself down in a chair. The thing was done; he'd made a heartless and cynical speech to that harpy of a woman who would arrange everything, pointing out Alfred's inadequacies and how over the years he himself had determined to provide himself with an heir of his own when he encountered the right young woman. "However, I've been out of the world for some time, looking after my sister," he had put it; it was true enough. He stared at the known things he had gathered in here over the years, which comforted him; shelves of books of a lighter nature than those kept in the library downstairs, a few French novels, poetry and plays. There were framed drawings he had brought from Spain, although no Goyas. There were the familiar busts of Handel and Bach, sheet music, the Well-Tempered Clavichord he would still at times play; marriage needn't alter that, he could still escape up here, despite the long-ago awareness of what had happened in the bed; he never slept in here for that reason.

Marriage. He didn't really want it. There was no evading the matter now, however; he'd committed himself.

The door opened and Etta came in, hurrying across, subsiding and laying her head against his knee in the familiar way. He'd forgotten about her behaviour and that he ought to be angry.

"Ed-die. Not her. Not her, Ed-die."

How did she know what he intended? She was a witch. He put her gently from him. She'd taken a dislike to the Honourable Ione, from a world so different from her own; that was it. Perhaps the two young women could be persuaded to benefit one another in some way.

"Not her," persisted Etta. "Cow. White cow. No."

He almost laughed. He'd taken her once to the home farm to watch the cows being milked. He'd also taught her to lip-read a few words. The comparison with Ione was irreverent; the young woman had worn, as observed, properly fitting stays, but her bosom had been notable and a point in her favour, doubtless indicating fertility. A cow. "Go away," he told Etta, and ruffled her dark hair instead of punishing her. She should have another new dress as bridal attendant. He would send Alfred, without apology, an invitation to the wedding. Lady Leonora could be relied upon to see to matters otherwise.

Some days later a framed photograph of Ione arrived, taken especially at one of the new West End studios. Corbell put it on the mantel. Etta noticed it at once, seized it and threw it on the floor.

"No," she said. It was a word she knew, used often and meant many things.

He slapped her face that time, picked up the photograph and replaced it. Etta began to scream, the harsh sound scarring the day.

After she had gone he looked at the photographed face of his betrothed. It had no softness. The features were well-bred enough, the hair magnificent, the nose somewhat long, the eyes pale and, as he had already noted, too close together. Having ousted Alfred had ceased to cause triumph. However, there was no help for it now; he'd sent the ring, a handsome solitaire; the announcement was in the papers, and the wedding was to be in three weeks. The vicar had been informed and the banns read. In this case, a sectarian handfasting would not, of course, do. Whether the crazy duke would attend the ceremony Corbell had no idea, and it didn't matter one way or the other.

Sissington sent a bitter gift; a box of black candles. He wrote to decline the invitation to the wedding. Corbell hoped they would not encounter one another before it; he himself was anxious to spend some days in town, meantime, at his club, chiefly to avoid Etta. He must also visit his lawyer and arrange the marriage settlements.

Whilst in town, he also inspected Daimlers. It would be a diversion, and would replace his lost greys, to drive one about the countryside with his wife beside him. He delayed purchase, meantime, nevertheless; it would be an excuse for another trip to town. He would have to accustom himself to making excuses.

He returned at last to Lackmere on the day before his marriage. He had earlier left orders as to what was to be done next day. To cleanse himself from the train journey, and also because it was probably his last venture into freedom, he undressed after dinner and waded into the lake.

He spent a long time in the water. It had been a still evening, in the dark of the moon, so that the stars showed, by now, brilliant as diamonds against the black velvet of the sky. Their light was enough to bear witness that he was not, after all, alone. There was a second presence close by, growing closer, edging nearer. He had not seen or heard Etta come. Anger rose in him; this was his succuba, faceless and threatening, in half-darkness, the short wet hair covering her face. He swam rapidly away; she overtook him, thereafter matching his speed, writhing ever closer, like a fish or a water-snake. Her pale shape was like his own shadow, lit by the stars. She went wherever he went, sleekly swimming alongside like a spaniel or seal: diving when he dived, meeting him beneath the surface like a phantom, rising again to the surface when he rose. Nothing would shake her off; he heard himself cry out presently that she had broken her promise to leave him alone here at nights, must never swim here again, that he forbade it. Her mocking laughter floated across the water. They were near the cold, still centre by then; he felt her hair wipe itself against his body, flinging its short soaked length against his flesh. He wrenched away for the last time, speaking as though she could hear.

"Get away from me, you harlot. Leave me in peace." She would not; he saw her mouth open darkly in the starlight, emitting silent laughter. Words sounded, and he realised that they were his own, spoken without conscious will. *Bellissima Jocosa; bellissima, bellissima.* Her slim breasts touched him, her arms reached out towards him. He found himself within her, and yet they swam still; together, one flesh. *Bellissima.* It was the first time he had had a woman.

They swam back to the shallows together, still locked. He had felt the seed spill out of him into her. He was helpless, stranded without will, a mermaid's drowning sailor. Water and sweat poured off him as he again emptied himself in course of this strange, alien act. He was no longer himself; he was hers, had always been hers. *Bellissima.* She writhed agreeably.

"More," he heard her say. "More. Do it, Ed-die. More. Do it more."

At last, all strength drained from him, he found himself alone. He sank down into the shallow water. Now that she had gone he felt cold outrage rise. It hadn't been his doing. It must on no account happen again. Tomorrow was his wedding. Today.

He could not recall returning to the house, but woke later in bed, still weak as the water he had left. Daylight had come, inexorably; and he, Corbell, was a bridegroom. The ceremony was to be at noon.

Corbell's wedding day had in fact dawned moderately fine, which meant that the collation could be *al fresco* instead of having inquisitive guests making free of the house itself. Trestles were set out by the menservants in time for the afternoon. Snowy cloths were then spread on them by the maids already attired in their best caps, and Walshe and the cook, as usual in silent harmony, set out the dishes of cold meats and jellies, moulded cream blancmanges and neatly cut sandwiches and cakes at the last predictable moment. The flies were kept off, till after the ceremony, by laundered napkins bearing the Corbell device of a small flat shopping basket. Everything was as it should be; and the bride had arrived. Nothing seemed out of place.

Miss Etta, as after the matrimonial disaster with Fred she had continued to be known, had been forbidden to take her morning swim, which might otherwise well have happened. Corbell was told by a gratified Peggy that the new dress, bonnet and shoes in which Miss Etta was today to present herself had arrived in time from London. Lady Leonora had chosen everything of the kind by request, and they were no doubt both becoming and suitable. It would, Edmund had hoped, it some way modify and placate his half-sister. Now, he doubted it.

He still had a sense of unreality about last night; perhaps it hadn't happened, had been a dream. He awaited everything that was to come in a state of what was, almost, passive contemplation: by this time he could alter nothing. Carriages were already beginning to arrive through the rarely opened iron gates. Society had invaded Lackmere. Presently, seen from the upper windows, enormous feathered hats, like a sudden invasion of flamingoes, were parading themselves about the verges of the thankfully empty lake. He would have known no surprise had Etta as usual risen from it naked, in full view of all.

It was then that Corbell noted that Etta herself had not been seen for some time. Had she put on the new dress? he asked Peggy. Yes, the good servant answered, and the shoes and the little bonnet as well. That meant, at least, no trouble meantime. In any case Edmund, warily awaiting the arrival of his bride, decided memory could go to the devil. He was about to be married. Tonight he would fashion his heir, or at least commence to. Feeling nevertheless anything but bridally inclined, he had himself been shaved and dressed with particular care by Walshe. Fred, who had once unquestionably performed both services, never now came near the house.

The flamingoes altered course and became an increasing

progression of hour-glass figures trailing their upholstered satins and crêpes towards the drawing room. Corbell began to hope that perhaps Ione had decided to elope with Sissington; there seemed no sign of her, but the bride was, by tradition, not seen before the ceremony or it brought bad luck. The vicar arrived, and was perceived to fuss about socially before vanishing to vest himself in surplice and bands. It was a victory for the Establishment to have penetrated the oddly persisting, sectarian seclusion of Lackmere.

At last Corbell bowed to necessity – it was five minutes to the hour – and limped down to the drawing room, thronged by now with whaleboned satin hour-glasses and hats. There was to be no escape; Lady Leonora came in, prosperous in lilac, a hen who, despite everything, has laid her golden egg. The vicar had assumed an expression of gratified piety; and here came the bride.

Ione entered, expressionless and escorted by her father. There was no sign of Etta. Ione looked, Corbell had to admit, superb; she wore a close-fitting gown of plain white satin, and the long rope of pearls which had been his own wedding gift, selected by her mother and setting off, very suitably, the large solitaire diamond which no doubt more than made up for the enforced return of Alfred's keepsake in an empty tin of Eucryl tooth powder, through the post.

The vows were exchanged. Ione's controlled curves loomed as Corbell placed his plain gold ring on her large white fourth left finger. He felt jaded already, and consummation likewise loomed. Where the deuce was Etta?

As usual, Peggy knew. After the carriages had departed and the trestles were cleared, she asked if she might have a brief word. She was wearing an unexceptionable bonnet with jet beads, bought for the wedding. Her faded eyes regarded him from under its narrow brim. He noted again that she was growing old: as old as he felt.

"My lord, I know very well where Miss Etta's gone, and I doubt if she'll be back, or ought to be. Lord Sissington came in his carriage once they were all inside, and took her off in it. I didn't mention it till now, my lord, not to upset things. If I may make so bold, it's good riddance, and gives you a fresh start with her new ladyship. That's what I thought, and as you know I've always spoken my mind when I had to. I hope I've done right."

He supposed she had; at any rate it solved one difficulty, in a way.

Unusually, for he was not addicted to spirits, he poured himself brandy and drank it in a gulp. To picture Etta once again in Sissington's arms was an outrage, but it was, after all, tit for tat. It also freed him from any future obligation towards her; but he told himself reprehensibly that if Alfred had had to behave like Young Lochinvar, it would have been better to make off with the bride.

In proper course, by late evening and attired in his brocade dressing-gown and nightshirt, he entered the nuptial chamber. The four-poster in which generations of Corbells had been conceived and had, variously thereafter, died, bore the usual tester and counterpane emblazoned with gilded shopping-baskets. Ione, who had entertained the guests in a commendable manner while they remained on the premises, eating and drinking, lay now in bed in a state of ominous silence. Corbell realised that he had had very little conversation with her in any case, and did not now know what to say. Her golden hair, rather than being combed loose in bridal anticipation, had been put in a tidy plait fastened at one end with white wool. Her pale blue, close-set eyes glared angrily, reminding him of a crow he had once shot badly and had had to finish off. Crows' eyes were, surprisingly, this exact pale colour. It occurred to him that he and his bride disliked one another already. He hoped her mother had told her what had to happen next.

In the event, he himself was bewildered, as without the benefit of supporting stays there turned out to be a great deal of the Honourable Ione. He found himself fumbling between large released breasts, an ample stomach, and thighs like the Pillars of Hercules. She kept these closed, and he had to heave them apart like the late blocks of cold unyielding marble in the cellar. In fact he found himself unable to do full justice to the occasion; it was like being in bed with the Parthenon. In the summer dark he saw that she had closed her eyes and was no doubt, as was proper, thinking of England. He himself was struggling to penetrate what was in fact the toughest virginity since Pallas Athene's. Wrestling with it occupied his attention to the extent even of making him

124

forget Etta, at that same moment, no doubt, in Sissington's embrace.

If he had known, Ione was not thinking of England at all, but of Sissington; her lost Alfred, with his slim upright figure, his valiant bright moustache, almost military although he had never fired a shot in anger; and the little keepsake ring, which she resented having been made to return. Mama had purloined the letter he'd written to her, saying his heart was broken and he would never forget her. Her own heart was, naturally, broken as well; and what this monster they'd made her marry was doing was extremely painful.

Corbell became aware that there was a young woman disconsolate beneath him, and having achieved his object at last, tried to console her. She must, he explained, give him an heir; that apart, he'd leave her alone. "You may have all the money to spend that you need, anything in the world that you want to buy; you will make new friends here, everyone will want to know you." He explained that they wouldn't begin to call upon her for three weeks, it wasn't etiquette. Ione, recovering slightly, asked if after that she could perhaps arrange a boating party.

Corbell winced. "Perhaps later on," he said untruthfully. Whatever else she got up to, it must not include the lake. The lake was private. Tomorrow – he mustn't delay – he ought to go up to town to put matters right between Sissington and Etta. It was his plain duty, and one he must not shirk.

Almost suffocated by his bride's amplitudes, he finally climbed out of bed and went to his dressing-room. He slept for a few hours, then woke early and departed for town, taking a hackney straight to Sissington's lodging. He had instructed Peggy Vance to make his excuses, meantime, to the bride.

Ione herself, having passed a wretched night, saw Vance bring in her breakfast. "I'm to say that his lordship has been called urgently to town, my lady, but that I'm to show you over the house if you would like to see it, otherwise there's a fire lit in her late ladyship's sitting-room, and the newspapers."

She added that his lordship sent his apologies at having to leave as soon, but Miss Etta had run off yesterday with that Lord Alfred Sissington.

The new Lady Corbell opened her mouth and howled, forgetting her upbringing and that one didn't hobnob with servants. There seemed no help anywhere; Alfie had gone off with that creature who'd tried to push her in the lake, Papa and Mama had departed with indecent haste to the South of France immediately after the ceremony; and as for marriage, she loathed it. She hoped Lord Corbell would stay away as long as possible.

"There, dear, he won't be gone longer than he can help," said Peggy in well-meaning though absent fashion.

In fact he returned in time for Sunday, as he could hardly avoid the courtesy of escorting his bride to church for the first time. Ione, Lady Corbell, had the consolation of appearing, a prosperous great white stork, in a wide hat with feathers, and they occupied the honorary, generally vacant Corbell pew. Afterwards there was polite talk at the lychgate, respectful bobbings from the tenants, and the drive home behind Walshe's broad, unresponsive back. However, Corbell's mind had been elsewhere throughout, aware of his continued failure to find Etta. The little bitch had left him after two days, Alfred said. "Took her down to the old Ship and Bladebone, knowin' you'd come here, Crip: and, God, I fucked her. Kept me from thinkin' of you with Ione. No, I don't know which way she went, and what's more I don't care. That one's a born tart, like the Corbell Strumpet. She'll earn her living; don't trouble yourself. How is my lost Ione?" He achieved a sigh.

Corbell replied somewhat heartlessly that his bride was as well as could be expected. He would purchase a Daimler to entertain her. "You shouldn't have let my sister go," he said, rising. Sissington shrugged.

"You know damned well nobody can stop her. Perhaps you'd leave."

"I have no wish to stay. You are an utter scoundrel. My wife is well rid of you."

He left, and after a further useless search and the almost absent-minded selection of a motor, returned to his library, his lake, and his wife. There seemed no more to be done otherwise. There was only one thing that could have become of Etta, alone in London in a new gown and bonnet, without any money. The likelihood tormented him constantly.

*   *   *   *

One day before the arrival of the Daimler, and the correctly timed piling up of the calling-cards delivered from the lodge to her salver, Ione, in the absence of her husband, told her maid to fetch her outdoor things, as she was going for a walk. She was active by nature and enjoyed life in town, but was bored in the country, disliked increasingly the great silent house she hadn't asked for – they said there were actually tombs in one part – and the dreadfully dull dinners with Lord Corbell seated at one end of the long shining mahogany table and herself at the other, with no conversation worth pursuing. The nocturnal processes of marriage were by now likewise wordless, and still disliked. She might as well walk off her continuing depression.

The fresh air was certainly pleasant; she'd been feeling queasy. She found herself walking the same way as the day Etta Corbell had tried to push her into the lake; thankfully that wouldn't happen again. The lake itself was as dreary as everything else here, no life on its grey surface, not a swan or moorhen to be seen; no reeds, nothing. Everything in life seemed grey; and Ione sat down on a prone log near the trees, and cried. She was simply not feeling herself, and there was nobody to ask. Lady Corbell, sniffling dolefully, fished in her reticule for a handkerchief. It was only in romances that tears coursed becomingly down one's cheeks instead of down one's nose.

It was then that she became aware of the small, ugly presence of Fred the tiger, who'd driven her back to the train that time with Papa and Mama, after everything had been arranged without consulting her at all. Fred remarked that it was a fine day.

One didn't hobnob with servants. Ione tried to remember that adage and Mama's others, but she was sick and lonely and for once, nodded amiably and agreed. Thinking it over afterwards she admitted that the day hadn't been as fine as all that; it had been a mere prelude to Fred's announcement that he had a hot tip for the twelve-thirty on Monday, that was if her ladyship happened to be interested. The odds were twenty to one on a horse he'd been recommended, and last time the same horse had overcome mild difficulty at Tattenham Corner and still come in third. "If it hadn't been for that, I'd be richer than what I am," Fred concluded. He added again that it was, of course, just as her ladyship liked.

He was, however, talking to Pussy's daughter and knew it. Ione fished again in her reticule and carefully, for dearest Papa had given her only ten of them for her very own, counted out five golden sovereigns into Fred's eagerly awaiting palm. "Remember, the horse must win, or this is the last time," she said prudently, knowing already, from experience with Papa, that such a remark was superfluous.

Chapter Five

The weeks passed, with still no word of the Honourable Henrietta Corbell, dead or alive. However, Ione's state was rewarding; the wrestling with her virginity had after all induced conception on the first night. Corbell was grateful to her, and indulged her in every way except to permit the boating party; he said it would upset her condition. Nor must she use tight-lacing, which caused Ione deep resentment. "Look at what I am," Corbell countered. "Our son must have a straight spine."

He had been unable to develop any feeling for her other than gratitude about the coming child. Apart from driving the first Daimler – in his time he was to own three – he spent his days as he had done before his marriage, either in the library or in the water, weekly conducting tenants' affairs at the cottages or else from his father's memorable walnut desk, whereon the malachite paperweight still sat. He also attended to his recently acquired duties as Justice of the Peace.

The months passed. Corbell's hopes were shattered in proper course. In the presence of a briefly returned Lady Leonora from Cannes, Ione gave birth, with some difficulty and immense fuss, to a daughter. It was almost as though she hoped Sissington would succeed, he told himself bitterly; and now there must be a second attempt. Meanwhile the child, for no particular reason, was christened Joan. She was long, thin, plain and not very intelligent, and vaguely resembled her remote cousin Mildred Sissington.

Shortly, in the connubial bed with its heraldic shopping

baskets, Corbell tried again, but Ione was peevish; she'd had a bad time, she said, and didn't want others. So evident was the lack of their appearance as time passed that he began to suspect Peggy Vance and her black rye tisanes, but Peggy swore blind never to have given them to her ladyship, she wouldn't do such a thing in the circumstances. It began to seem as if Sissington, after all, would conquer; and, meantime, there was no word of Etta herself, despite continuing enquiry both by himself and paid agents.

Ione by this time, placidly accepted by the county and invited everywhere, was driven about a good deal in the carriage rather than the Daimler; Corbell preferred to drive that himself. It was tacitly agreed that he and she had their separate pursuits and interests; hers were sociable, his own concerned privacy at all costs. When Joan was small he tried to teach her swimming, but she had no aptitude for that or much else. She liked riding, and Corbell bought her a Shetland pony and then, by the time she was nine, a Welsh skewbald called Punch. Punch began to occupy Joan's every waking thought, and he could no longer ignore Ione's repeated statements that she could never hope to give their daughter a season unless she became civilised.

There was no escape. He must employ a governess. He would ensure that such a person was totally lacking in attraction.

Part IV

Chapter One

The middle-aged man with one hunched shoulder, his still thick hair greying slightly below and his body more solid than it had been, was seated at his walnut desk looking out on the lake where his father, more than thirty years ago now, had drowned himself. Beyond, Corbell's nine-year-old daughter Joan could be seen exercising her new pony, the second Welsh skewbald again called Punch. Joan's dark hair bobbed as she trotted Punch along the further shore where gorse grew, and where Corbell himself had lain long ago as a boy in agony of mind, having pricked his palm and clawed the earth. As he had foreseen then, it was his now, the Lackmere earth; but Sissington would still inherit unless Ione bore a son.

She had gone today into town, with Vance to escort her, on one of her twice-yearly visits to a gynaecologist in Harley Street. They were going to bring back, as well as the usual news that Ione had nothing wrong with her except that she ought to lose weight, the governess he'd decided on for Joan. She had progressed as far as Etta's flannel books and brief lessons from the local schoolmistress could take her, but apart from saddling and riding her pony and teaching it tricks, that was all she knew. She was still fairly plain and not very clever, and Ione continued to complain that she would never be able to give her a season unless something was done. Joan's fortune would be considerable, and with the new lack of conscience about marrying money since the American brides had arrived in society, ought to be made aware of her own assets lest she be taken advantage of. Adorning the local hunt wouldn't be enough. For that reason he had unwillingly gone in person to an agency in South Street which advertised governesses and preceptresses, and had interviewed its presiding ogress. Had she a candidate who excelled in mathematics? That would at least be a beginning. Corbell added that the person selected must be plain.

Mrs Udney, the proprietress of an institution begun by her mother-in-law back in the middle of the century, assured Lord Corbell that the person she had in mind, who would be free in the autumn, was extremely plain and had a considerable grasp of mathematics. Miss Smail should suit his lordship very well. One remembered, of course, the scandal about his lordship's father in complete silence. Nothing of the kind would happen this time. It was a pity about that extreme scoliosis; if upright, Lord Corbell would be personable despite his lame leg. In any case it was always rewarding to have a title on one's books.

The carriage with its three occupants would return from the station at any moment. Walshe was driving today. He'd progressed upwards from knife-machine days to turn his hand to several things; butler, driver, valet. Fred still saw to the horses, and generally drove Ione to church, putting her on to winners and losers. He, Corbell, settled up when required, otherwise didn't see Fred at all. There was still no word, would probably be none now, of Etta.

Corbell switched his mind away from all of that and rose from the desk, going to the library shelves; he didn't want to see the party arrive. Jemmy, Vance's grandson, a man now, had taken up his stance by the steps, as he always did when there was baggage to be carried upstairs. It gave purpose to his existence. His tall powerful dark-haired figure was like one's own should have been, but what mind he had only understood a few simple words, that was all. It was sad for Peggy.

Ione Corbell loathed her marriage. With Alfie she'd have been happy, even though they would have been always in debt; after all, she was used to that with Papa. Alfie and she had loved to dance together, to appear fashionably dressed in the right places and make friends; that was what life was for. Also, she would greatly have liked to learn lawn tennis, which was becoming popular for ladies. However, Corbell wouldn't hear of laying out a tennis court although there was plenty of room, or of allowing her to play elsewhere. He said overarm serves might interfere with conception or bring about a miscarriage. He thought of her, evidently, as a brood-mare. He'd compromised with a croquet lawn, and when it was fine Ione would ask acquaintance over, but the clacking of mallets disturbed Corbell in his precious library.

As for more children, she didn't want them. They said you forgot the pain of childbirth, but she certainly hadn't forgotten Joan's. Mama had come over from Cannes at the time, leaving Papa to enjoy himself for once at the new Longchamps race-course outside Paris. That was all Ione remembered, and the agony of bearing down for what turned out to be only a girl. If Joan had been the least interesting or pretty, it might have been worth it. Corbell had kept trying ever since, but she herself wasn't interested. She'd taken instead to sending for covered silver dishes of hot buttered toast between meals.

As for today, Eileen Penhaligon had come with them both ways on the train. Leaving lately at the last station but one, her brown hair had looked suspiciously ruffled beneath her hat. She'd left her, Ione, with Vance who of course stuck like glue, to go to Marshall & Snelgrove as usual after the Harley Street visit, saying she had promised to visit an old nurse in Paddington. It was more likely she had an assignation with Alfie at the Pineapple Rooms, and it wasn't fair. He visited The Towers from the Friday to Monday almost every week, but Corbell would never allow her to go there, or, in fact, anywhere without Vance trailing behind like a shadow. Vance was getting deaf, but that didn't signify.

Now, this frumpish governess had joined them on the train, conveyed from third by the stationmaster with apologies, as the main train uncoupled at the station before last. Ione had pretended not to know who the creature was, and had stared out of the window at the drifting steam.

She supposed Corbell would want to know what the specialist said. He'd said the same as usual. He'd given Vance a letter and not herself, so Vance could see to it. She, Ione, wanted to get out of her stays and lie down before dinner.

The party arrived at the portico, and Ione rustled down from the berline, leaving Walshe to hand the Marshall & Snelgrove box, with a new hat in it, to Vance's afflicted grandson. She then swept up the steps to the house and missed what happened.

Vance had climbed out next. The new governess, in silence, followed. Jemmy knew enough to take Miss Smail's ark-shaped hamper to carry it up, but first he did an unexpected thing; he kissed Miss Smail on the cheek, directly below her spectacles. The gesture was not lost on Peggy. He'd never done such a thing before. Nobody said anything, however, and they all went in past the general's portrait and upstairs.

Chapter Two

Vance sent Jemmy downstairs after leaving Miss Smail's baggage. She was pleased that he had shown confidence in approaching what was, after all, still a young woman. The girls up at the cottages mocked him and ran away, and so he was shy as a rule. However, he was a man now, and it came naturally to recall her vow that some woman should give him a child, a Tesson. She had hardly looked at the governess on the train after a first glance, which had told her what everybody else would know; nothing had ever happened to Miss Smail, nor was it likely to. But she hadn't recoiled from the kiss. No doubt it had taken her by surprise.

Having shown the new governess her room, with the familiar jug and ewer and commode, Vance added that there was a lavatory along the passage the servants didn't use and that when Miss Smail had refreshed herself his lordship would see her in the smaller drawing room downstairs, second left. Having made social distinctions clear – governesses thought themselves a cut above servants, but they were still paid – she followed Jemmy down, for the first time remembering an episode which had taken place when he was fourteen. At least it had left him aware of his considerable assets.

One of the maids known as Holy Flo read her Bible on Sundays more than anybody. This had led Peggy, without further proof, to suspect her as randy. Flo was too sly to be caught until one day, at the cottages, she'd been found alone with Jemmy, teaching him to play with what it wasn't proper even to show. It hadn't gone beyond using their fingers to bring him on, but Vance had fetched Holy Flo a good slap across the face and when she got her back down to the house, left her disinclined to sit down for a fair two days after fetching out, as she seldom did, the rod in pickle. Things hadn't gone far enough for the black dose. Flo was warned that if she ever went near Jemmy again, she'd be sent away without a character. She was a good worker, and for that reason had been kept on still. She sneaked up to the wicket on her days off, but hadn't dared trouble Jemmy a second time. As for him, it had shown him what might happen one day; Agnes said he played with himself under the blanket in the box bed at nights, but that was natural.

There it was, and in any case Holy Flo wouldn't have been a suitable mother for a Tesson; it might not even be Jemmy's child. Until today, with this governess, there had been nothing and nobody. She'd keep an eye; there were ways and means. Miss Smail was skinny, short-sighted and flat as a board. Jemmy must see something in her others didn't, and had said so in the only way he could.

Chapter Three

Corbell interviewed the governess in what had once been Anna's room. It still held the chaise-longue, the cracked mirror and a few gilt chairs. He invited Miss Smail to sit down on one. Her glance behind the spectacles was as usual directed downwards, and the first thing she noticed was the green enamel eye, hanging in its fob from Lord Corbell's watch-chain. It affected her strangely; she wondered why he wore it. Lady Corbell's eyes, noted on the train, had been pale blue. It was tragic for Lord Corbell to be so lame.

Miss Smail gradually brought herself to look upwards, and found herself gazing at the portrayed face already glimpsed in uniform hanging in the hall, but now displaced well under one shoulder. The whole experience, including the kiss from that afflicted young porter or footman who'd taken up her baggage, was by no means what she had been accustomed to. Miss Smail scuttled back into herself like a hermit crab, and answered in monosyllables.

Mrs Udney had assured Lord Corbell that Miss Smail was extremely plain. Now, looking at her, he could not but agree. Not only did her Christian name, Mercy, breathe thoughts of calico for the heathen, but she was the living epitome of all Mrs Udney had guaranteed. Miss Smail's dun-coloured dress, correctly devoid of trimming, sat on her small flat body like the reproach it was. Her features were unremarkable. On her nose perched ugly metal-rimmed spectacles with thick lenses. Behind these, Miss Smail's myopic and almost lashless glance was directed forever downwards, as if afraid of what it might otherwise perceive. Corbell himself had never set eyes on anyone as nearly non-existent, as if Miss Smail's chief end in life consisted in effacing herself. Nevertheless she was equable enough, even smug, regarding her own attainments. He pointed out that Joan's handwriting needed particular attention.

"I excel in correctness, Lord Corbell. She shall be taught reason and precision of thought, which will reflect themselves in her writing as well as in other matters."

So much for that. She answered other questions in her flat, toneless little voice, hardly moving lips that must have been kept firmly compressed since childhood; the mouth itself reminded him of a resolutely closed sea-anemone or, with less propriety, a little tight pink anus. Her chin receded slightly above her thin neck. He had certainly never in his life set eyes on anyone as lacking in attraction.

"How old are you, Miss Smail?" It was no doubt impertinent to ask, but he had decided that he wanted to know. Miss Smail flushed slightly, the colour coming up becomingly beneath her admittedly delicate skin.

"I am twenty-six years old, Lord Corbell." She looked more in ways, less so in others. He wondered idly about her past life; undoubtedly nothing had ever happened in it.

"Have you parents, relations?" She must, he thought, have arrived on the planet by parthenogenesis. It was impossible to picture any bodily passion that could have evolved a Miss Smail.

"My parents were missionaries. They died of cholera in India when I was quite young. Charitable persons saw me educated. I became a pupil-teacher when I was sixteen, and, after my probationary period, was enabled to register with Mrs Udney, who has found me several appointments. I have copies of my references if you care to inspect them, Lord Corbell."

Feeling slightly put in his place, he sent for Peggy to escort the new governess to the schoolroom to meet Joan. Peggy reported later – servants never approved of governesses – that the young person seemed very pleased indeed to have a room of her own. Last time, she'd said, it had been only a cubicle curtained off from the nursery where the children slept. As for the blue-flowered lavatory along the passage, she had seemed awestruck by permission to use it.

Miss Smail's room contained, as Edmund well knew, the bare necessities of living: the iron bedstead Yolande had in the first place been given, identical to that used by the housemaids; a washstand with ewer, jug and commode; a chest of drawers with swing mirror; a hook behind the door for her outdoor things. He found himself picturing Miss Smail unpacking. There wouldn't be much in the hamper, perhaps a hairbrush to tidy her dull light-brown hair after the journey and pin it up again in its tight little spinster's bun. She would have taken off her travelling-cloak and bonnet – her clothes seemed to belong to a past generation – and had perhaps made discreet use of the chamber-pot instead of going along the passage quite yet. Corbell found himself picturing this operation, lacking as it would any rustle of feminine petticoats. Miss Smail would wear a plain linen or cotton chemise beneath her cheap, adequate gown.

He thought of her little closed prim mouth and envisaged its unwary opening, a relaxed anemone almost, under persuasion, emitting fronds. He then thought of possible means of persuasion. The fertility of his own imagination intrigued him.

Miss Smail had, the agency's letter repeated, a particular talent for mathematics. One did not lightly disturb the principle of Archimedes or ravish Pythagoras' theorem unprepared. Seduction along the lines of the Law of Moments might, however, by its very nature, prove both diverting and successful.

He was, in fact, already assailed by a curious sensation which he recognised as lust.

Meantime, he left Miss Smail with Joan. The child had never been easy to teach; even Etta's cat that sat on the mat had been assimilated with greater ease in its day. The humdrum occupation paid dividends under Miss Smail, however, over the next few weeks, and the child liked her; no doubt so colourless a personality gave Joan confidence on their improving botanical walks. As a reward for his daughter, whose spelling and writing had already also improved, likewise with certain ulterior motives, he bought Joan a superior pony to ride in afternoons, safely watched over by Walshe. That meant Miss Smail was left with time on her hands. Corbell assured her that she was welcome, if she chose, to make use of his library. He began to feel increasingly like Mr Rochester.

Miss Smail flushed pink all over her unexceptionable little face, but merely replied that she felt most gratified by Lord Corbell's offer. It was some time before she ventured to avail herself of it, however, and he found himself growing surprisingly impatient.

Time passed, and Corbell found himself increasingly unable to concentrate on his reading in the library, which as a rule shut all else out. He could hear the placid clack of croquet mallets from the lawn he had permitted Ione to have laid some years ago. He still hoped, following the specialist's report, for results from his continued visits to the nuptial couch. These continued to embarrass both himself and Ione, and brought neither pleasure nor reward.

Chapter Four

Lessons for Joan continued, and were allowed to do so uneventfully for some time. It even began to seem that the child was progressing a little in all ways, though it was as well she would never have to earn her living. After a few weeks, when her pupil was out on the new pony, inevitably yet again called Punch, Mercy Smail brought herself shyly to accept Lord Corbell's invitation to make use of his library. She had read *Jane Eyre*, but lacked the imagination to put herself in the heroine's place; her own mind was strictly literal.

She could see from the door that Lord Corbell's library was truly magnificent, and very comfortable, with a leather armchair drawn up beside the blazing hearth. Miss Smail had not wanted to intrude, and had hoped on this occasion that her employer was elsewhere. However, he was present, seated behind a large and imposing desk on which reposed a bright green malachite paperweight. He was working on some papers, the dark greying head beneath the hunched shoulder, which so aroused her pity, bent over them. He raised his head and smiled.

"No, no, my dear Miss Smail, on no account withdraw. Permit me to show you, as best I can, where things are to be found. They are not in order by any means. To assemble them is the work of a lifetime."

He rose, still smiling. It made a difference, Mercy thought, to the habitual sadness of his face. It was a tragedy to be so lacking in symmetry.

He had a great many books of unusual interest; some must be

143

of great value, and some were so old that bookworms, mostly heard of nowadays only as a joke, really had eaten holes right through. One great volume was a herbal, with hand-painted illustrations. "I myself paint a little," said Lord Corbell. "I used to make botanical drawings and floral diagrams. Do you understand those, Miss Smail?"

Miss Smail understood them, as he had surmised she would; also most other subjects he raised. By the time Joan came back to the house for schoolroom tea, flushed and happy from her ride, the little governess had decided that Joan's father was extremely affable, most approachable; the feeling of his hand under her elbow, guiding her to certain shelves, had been reassuring and pleasant. She hoped that she might return tomorrow afternoon, if it was permitted. She had, she admitted, enjoyed herself.

As the days passed, and her visits grew less tentative, Corbell accustomed Miss Smail still further to his touch. It was no more, at first, than the guiding hand, a slight, almost accidental pressure on her arm within its sleeve, even her flat breast within its repressive, and unnecessary, controls. He had decided that it must be this very flatness which enticed him, differing as it did from Ione's unleashed vastnesses. Otherwise, talk with Miss Smail was itself not dull; she was knowledgeable, certainly, but lacked humour. Possibly nobody who had any could endure her profession, with the humiliations it entailed. Corbell did not ask himself whether or not Yolande had possessed it. She had had beauty and kindness; that was enough.

He was also amused by Miss Smail's petty snobberies. She addressed him as Lord Corbell, as social equals did; never your lordship or my lord, like the servants and tenants. The intent to remain a cut above the domestics made her somewhat over-genteel; he looked forward to divesting her of gentility; of virginity, of the very lack of knowledge concerning the one subject in which he might well educate her. He was determined to have her. He had never before nourished dishonourable intentions, and found these surprisingly entertaining.

Miss Smail's meals took place in the schoolroom with Joan. Ione showed no signs of inviting the governess downstairs, and in fact ignored her existence totally. She was at present occupied with collecting garments for Christmas charity bundles, together with Lady Penhaligon.

Corbell suggested shortly that Miss Smail might like to help him with cataloguing and indexing the library books. Her intelligence, he told her, needed more in the way of occupation than the unremitting teaching of Joan. Miss Smail proved willing; she began to appear in afternoons, while Joan was riding, eyes still fixed on the ground behind her everlasting spectacles. Corbell's fingers itched to take these off. One day he assured her that they terrified him, and Miss Smail blushed, giving her little tight, prudent smile. Joy was evidently suspect to her, perhaps till now unknown.

"Lord Corbell, I fear I am useless without them. I am excessively short-sighted."

He had assumed as much; reached out and deliberately took them off, allowing his finger to stray across her cheek. The blush deepened; she began to tremble. "Please –"

Seduction would be easy, he decided; but not yet. They had been listing a book on astronomy, and Corbell made a point of mentioning the legend of the Milky Way. "Juno – Hera – was not notably a fecund goddess," he observed. "Her spurted milk must have been a rarity, not enough for a son like Heracles. Amphitrite, however, who loathed her spouse Poseidon, bore him Triton, blowing forever on his horn. There ought perhaps to be signs in the sea. Your own little hands, you know, resemble starfish."

Miss Smail had turned a beetroot red, and her mouth, which had begun to loosen somewhat of late, resumed its former strictness.

"I do not approve of myth, Lord Corbell. I prefer the investigative discussion of scientific fact." Her voice trembled, but was firm.

"Then let us discuss Leonardo da Vinci, and whether or not he was wasting his time by designing aeroplanes when he ought to have been painting."

He had, at least, discovered that she had relatively little knowledge of biology: the subject disturbed her. He would lead her, in due course, towards the Law of Moments instead, but meantime asked impersonally if he might sketch her arms and hands. "They are those of a mathematician," he assured her, not having entirely made the notion up.

145

g

Miss Smail agreed that he might sketch her, although such an experience had never come her way before. There seemed no harm in it that she could foresee, though for instants, just now, she imagined that Lord Corbell was behaving with the impropriety against which Mrs Udney warned all her young ladies, without exactly specifying what it might be. Mercy Smail herself had never had to encounter it. She told herself she was being uncharitable, and must be obliging to Lord Corbell, who was taking so much trouble to make her feel at home. No doubt he was lonely, and still looked sad except when he was smiling, as now. Mercy continued to pray for him each night, which meant that she thought about him increasingly.

Chapter Five

Ione was being driven by Corbell in the Daimler to a morning party at Eileen Penhaligon's. She disliked motoring, fashionable as it had become. It was impossible to be elegant, clad forever in a long dust-coat and protective veil; nobody, as Eileen had pointed out, wore feathers any more. If her husband, beside her, had been less taciturn things would be improved, but as always Corbell maintained complete silence, with his coat collar turned up towards the accustomed beehive hat he wore when driving. Today was Thursday, so Walshe was not with them in case anything broke down; instead, Fred sat behind in his chauffeur's cap; ready to leap out quickly and repair a puncture or, equally well, leap in again after using the starting-handle. She herself had something to ask Fred, but there was no opportunity at present.

Beyond the trees and the surrounding wall as they passed the limits of the estate, she could see Joan's new pony, grazing; the child would be with that governess at this hour. She herself wasn't permitted to ride, didn't want to walk, and so was unable to take any exercise except for croquet. Without that she would be mountainous by now; and Corbell still wouldn't permit her tight-lacing, always hoping for results which didn't follow. He had come in again last night and had taken his rights, as they were called, absently and, as usual, without saying anything. There was, after all, nothing left to say.

She was excruciatingly bored, and told herself she had been so ever since she was married. Eileen Penhaligon's mother would want to talk about gardening, in which she, Ione, couldn't summon up any interest, although the roses at Lackmere in summer were deservedly famous. No, there was nothing left of what had once been her life; and since Alfred had eloped with that extraordinary half-sister of Corbell's one hadn't heard any more.

There were only the horses left; and they either won or else they lost. She particularly wanted to ask Fred about this latest bet, as if she'd lost again it would be necessary to inform Corbell, and he would be coldly angry. They had, of course, made him a Justice of the Peace some years ago, which as dear Mama would have said took him out of himself, and she had hoped for a little social life to accrue thereby, but it mostly seemed to take place, such as it was, on the bench. Just now, he and Fred would drive on there, transact whatever they had to see to, and return later to pick her up. Then there would be luncheon, eaten as usual in silence; and the rest of the day to fill in somehow.

They reached Penhaligon Towers, and drove gallantly up the drive towards the new and vulgar house which boasted a myriad pepper-pot turrets in red sandstone, always a difficult medium to render aristocratic. As if to atone, there was a small pillared porch in something lighter below, round which other motors waited. The drive itself blazed, unfortunately by contrast, with geraniums. The Daimler drew to a halt, and Fred leaped out to hand Ione down. Corbell's hand remained on the attachment, whatever it might be, that kept the engine running; starting again was complicated. She said quickly to Fred in a low voice, "Win or lose?"

"Lose. Try again Friday." He would send round further word, she knew. He never came near the house as a rule, and he and Corbell never seemed to address one another. No doubt it was merely one more aspect of her husband's customary ungraciousness.

"My dear Miss Smail, it is a relief to be back in my library. The more I see of the human race the less I like it. Let us discuss one fact, or rather law, which has always interested me and concerning which you can undoubtedly instruct me. I refer to the Law of Moments. There is a certain point beyond which my limited understanding cannot go."

Corbell held forth for some time over the force about a point, the product of that force and its distance from the line of action. He made himself sound faintly bewildered.

Miss Smail gave the matter her full attention. Almost severely, as if he had not been attending when he was first taught, she replied that the same reasoning must apply to any quantity which could be represented by a direct line. This being exactly what Corbell wanted, he picked her up without ceremony and perched her on his knee. "Varignon's theorem," he murmured. Miss Smail, pink as a peony, protested, her voice grown suddenly weak.

"This is surely a little improper, Lord Corbell. Perhaps some other method –"

"The conterminous sides of a parallelogram represent a velocity and its change. Do you agree, Miss Smail?"

"Oh – I – Yes, oh –"

"I am demonstrating the use of the fulcrum, Miss Smail. Am I likely to ask you to do anything improper? Remember your place, I beg."

Moving her backwards, continuing ruthlessly to talk physics, he was able to observe that Miss Smail, within her skimpy chemise, wore, as he had hoped might be the case, old-fashioned drawers of an initial type designed to save laundry, being merely two cloth legs fastened round the waist by a tape. He had a moment's tantalising vision of the small helpless mound of the exposed mons veneris, invitingly downed with light-brown hair.

"The sum of the moments of two forces about any point in their plane equals the moment of their resultant about the same point, is it not so? Permit me to ascertain the position of O, Miss Smail."

He did so, at the same time recalling the famous clubman who for the rest of his days had kept, withered and long dry, a certain coveted virginity on the end of his finger. He contrived a certain amount of havoc, though no more, at point O. Miss Smail, from her inescapable position at the centre of the experiment, could no longer, in the nature of things, be thinking purely of mathematics.

"I cannot permit this to continue any longer, Lord Corbell; oh – oh, pray –"

"Prayer is for once unavailing, my dear Miss Smail; it will by no means solve our problem."

Owing to a certain to-ing and fro-ing involved in demonstrating the theorem, there happened at this moment what he had hoped would happen, namely that her spectacles fell off. Thereafter she was wax in his hands. He could have deflowered her then and there, but did not; the taking of the virginity must be savoured, like all true delights, with appreciation and in proper course. Meantime, he contented himself with arousing in Miss Smail certain sensations she had not known she possessed.

Nevertheless he was careful. Too swift and frequent an attempted journey to the realms of gold would result in the equally swift return of an outraged young woman to Mrs Udney's agency, looking for another situation. That would never do; *festina lente* must be the watchword, and he himself remained diverted, a pleasant change.

He decided to go up to London, leaving Miss Smail in suspense. Meantime, he set her, a trifle flustered, on her feet, himself still talking on about theorems; retrieved her spectacles from the floor where they had fallen, and blandly told her she might go.

"I shall not be here till next week," he said. "By all means borrow books; the maids will be in the library cleaning at times, no doubt." They never appeared when he was present, being instructed by Vance to remove themselves, their brushes and brooms, immediately his lordship should appear in the corridor. Ione approved of the practice, general as it was in upper circles, however inconvenient to the lower.

Miss Smail, persuaded by Lord Corbell's continuing unruffled demeanour that the whole thing had after all been in the nature of scientific experiment, tried not to feel disconcerted. In fact she was not entirely certain what had happened to her.

"You are improving my education as well as my daughter's," Corbell called out as she left the library. As he well knew, he was completing hers.

Chapter Six

Once in town, Corbell genuinely intended to follow the rest of certain possibilities he had already considered about the whereabouts of Etta. However, no combing of doubtful districts, court records or houses of correction revealed any knowledge of her, nor was she described among the list of unknown young persons who had thrown themselves in despair into the Thames.

As for Miss Smail, she had been communing with herself regarding the complete propriety of her own behaviour in the library before he left. For one thing, there had followed an agreeable sensation in a part of her physiology she had not fully realised she owned; and the realisation itself was clear evidence that she had, in Mrs Udney's words uttered to all her young ladies before their appointment, permitted undue familiarity from a gentleman, in this case a nobleman; but that made no difference. In fact, it would have been the same had Lord Corbell been an ordinary person; and there, in some fashion, lay the danger.

She knew what she must do. Joan was in the schoolroom, busy with prescribed arithmetic; her tongue was weaving back and forth in a manner one would normally have reproved, but Miss Smail had other occupations meantime. She found pen and paper, sat down and, while her pupil was still gainfully employed, wrote a cautious letter to Mrs Udney. It might mean leaving here, and the thought brought tears to Mercy's short-sighted eyes behind their spectacles; but to endanger one's soul was a greater risk than to part with undoubtedly agreeable employment.

She crept downstairs later on, when there was nobody about;

and left the letter on the tray provided for that purpose in the hall; it would be collected with the rest in the morning.

She was not to know that Corbell found it, having others of his own to send off after the brief absence in London. He saw the superscription, smiled, purloined the letter and, unforgiveably, thrust it in his inner waistcoat pocket. He read it later on in his dressing-room before going to bed as usual, unproductively, with Ione.

Lackmere, the 14th of November.

Honoured Madam

Forgive my presumption in writing to you, but I am somewhat disturbed. Lord Corbell, with whom you found me a situation in the early autumn, has begun to take what I feel are certain liberties of a kind concerning which I have no previous experience. In no other situation I have occupied has there been any question of them. I have always relied on my conscience and my morals, also on the fact that I unfailingly read a chapter of the Bible each night. [Corbell told himself she might at least have gained an inkling from certain portions of that volume.] *Can you, at this time of year, find me any other situation? I hesitate to leave my little charge, who is progressing under my care, but some other could perhaps instil into her what I am attempting, while forewarned of her father's habits, as I fear I was not.*

If I stay on for longer here I cannot, as you know, leave without a reference from Lord Corbell. An earlier exchange might preclude this necessity. I could, if that should transpire, still use the generous reference given me by the late Mr and Mrs Chalmers at Sutton Coldfield. I will, however, do nothing contrary to your advice. If you will kindly send this last as soon as is convenient to you, I will know what to do. Otherwise I tremble for what I know not. Pray aid me.

I remain, most honoured Madam, as always your very humble and obedient servant.

Mercy Belinda Smail.

Corbell happened to have retained the letter with which the celebrated Mrs Udney, who took a handsome percentage of her referees' earnings, had sent him confirmation, the contract of her referees of Miss Smail's added accomplishments, which included the use of the globes and a certain degree of elementary pianoforte instruction. It was easy enough to copy her writing, which like poor Mercy's was the precise neat copperplate expected of the downtrodden profession at present under siege. Corbell took devilish delight in composing a reply, and went up again to London for a further couple of days, keeping Miss Smail in predictable disquiet. He could transact some more business there in any case; also post the letter from the South Street box, which Mrs Udney would use and which was situated not far from his club.

Mrs Udney's Agency for Reliable Preceptresses and Female Tutors, the 17th of November. That had had to be risked in handwriting.

> *My dear Miss Smail,*
>
> *I am surprised that you of all persons should become tiresome. A man of Lord Corbell's distinction, position in the world and unblemished reputation in it – he has after all served several years on the bench – is unlikely to behave in any way which need, as you put it, disturb you. All employers have their eccentricities, especially gentlemen. It is advisable to humour these at the cost of departing from one's standards slightly for the time being. There is no other situation suitable to you at present – all are full – and I cannot undertake to find you one in future without a detailed written character from Lord Corbell himself. I strongly advise you to put up with his ways. His influence may well promote you, his displeasure might equally well degrade you to an extent that could make it impossible to find you further employment. Be prudent, but not unapproachable.*

She remained Miss Smail's affectionate mentor, Gertrude Udney.

It was exactly the kind of letter the old bitch might have written. He watched, with some amusement, its progressive effects on Miss Smail following his return.

He began, after that, to behave like a very eccentric employer indeed.

*　　*　　*　　*

At times he thought unbearably of Yolande, and his father's overriding physical need. Possibly he resembled him. Yolande's little successor, if one could call her that, had a brain, granted narrow, and a body, granted flat. He still could not see rhyme or reason for his own equally overriding desire for her. There was something about her that he wanted to conquer, but could not name it. Any of the maidservants could supply him with greater satisfaction; but he wanted Miss Smail, perhaps on only one occasion. It was the achievement that mattered, not its continuance.

There were certain things he had from life since losing Yolande, who had meant more than life itself. He'd coveted the Newmarket greys, and regretted losing them; he'd wanted The Ghluin and peace, and had lost both. He'd wanted a Daimler and a male heir. Miss Smail was unlikely to provide him with the latter. Perhaps success with her would lead to success with Ione. It was the only faint trace of logic about the situation. He pursued it.

While he was away, Corbell had in any case perfected a plan whereby Miss Smail might be ensnared to her undoing. He would show her the Roman tiles. If they achieved nothing else they would at least reveal to her why gentlemen were different. In her circumscribed life it was possible she did not yet know.

On return, he went down and again, savoured their perverted beauty. He had by now cleaned and maintained them over many years of deepening interest. He could understand why they had shocked Papa. The owner of the Romano-British villa which first stood here had had eclectic tastes and must have travelled, possibly with the army. The presiding god present was not Jove but Anubis, ironically confused with Mercury by many civilisations; but Mercury was male, Anubis sexless like many Egyptian deities. (The same could almost be said of Miss Smail.) It remained to be seen how she would respond to the sea-god Poseidon in his phallic guise of Athenon, to Phallus himself, to Isis and Osiris coupling to make Horus in their mother's womb, Eros rising unclad from the bed of Psyche. To hasten what might after all prove a lesser consummation Corbell rebuilt the black altar, heaving the marble blocks again in place before the Anubis tile.

Anubis aided Horus in weighing the hearts of the dead, it was supposed. The dog-god's head regarded him now sideways, the

154

white of one eye glinting in the light of the lantern. Candles must be lit ready for Miss Smail, and a brazier to warm her. Was it too much to hope that, overcome with sudden knowledge, she would submit to being blindfolded and immolated on the altar, in other words deflowered there? Down here, any sounds would not be heard in the house. He would bring the governess down by the steep inner stairs, and lock the door behind them both.

Invited, she came willingly enough, having had her erudition appealed to. He was convinced, he told her, that she would be able to help him decipher certain symbols. They might even be Sumerian. Miss Smail would not admit to being uncertain which civilisation that had been, but was flattered to be asked. She preceded Corbell, guided carefully, down the steep narrow flight, and heard him turn the key in the lock above. The sound disquieted her.

"We will go out again by the further door, past the general's memorial. You have not yet seen that."

Miss Smail was reassured, but only for moments. The images on the floor were all too clear. It was improper to have come. She gripped her hands together, and tried to keep control of the situation. "You should perhaps become an initiate, and prostrate yourself before Anubis," he suggested. Miss Smail bridled in the way only a registered preceptress can.

"I will do no such thing for any heathen god, Lord Corbell. I think that I should return upstairs."

Her face bore a red patch on either cheek. She had become a pillar of righteousness. The challenge spurred him and he made her remember his lameness. "Do not ask me to climb up again; I am not as lithe as yourself. If you have seen enough, we will go out by the vault."

He ushered her up the further steps, unfastening the door. Near at hand the general's white marble tomb reared, and Miss Smail paused to admire something she understood and approved of more than those dreadfully shocking classical tiles. The list of the third Lord Corbell's victories was most impressive.

She turned to ask the fifth lord a question about these, and found his face suddenly cold with rage. He did not reply, merely grasped her arm and dragged her past the adjoining tomb, which was low-set and which Miss Smail's short sight did not make out as that of Jocosa Corbell.

A deep outrage had flooded him, remembering. This tomb could be the only place where his father had first held down Yolande. He could hear her running footsteps yet, and sense her shock and sorrow. This little inferior creature need not detain him longer than was needed to take her in the folly, and have done with it.

He contrived to keep his voice civil. "I should like, as I stated earlier, to make a pencil sketch of your hands. Joan is out riding till supper; we have time." He explained that he kept his drawing-things in what had been a summerhouse she must have passed often on walks with Joan. "I keep it locked because of poachers. It has a roof of pine-cones." He was beginning to recover his calm. They walked on and out into the spring sunshine.

"Why, the primroses are out," remarked Miss Smail agreeably.

Thrumhead, pinhead; she enumerated them both. Every item could be used for improving the mind. She recalled walks in this direction with Joan, when the trees were bare and not, as now, commencing to bud. They had gone up as far as the pit, which was covered over with wicked thorns, leafless by then. They made the radius and diameter difficult to ascertain, and one understood that the exact depth was unknown. It was the kind of challenge that interested Miss Smail. No tremor of futurity assailed her. One thing she recalled from that walk; the mentally defective young man who carried baggage had come past with a grey-haired woman. He had seen her and as before, had come over and kissed her cheek. "Come away, Jemmy," had said the woman, who was Agnes Tesson. Miss Smail had, again, not recoiled. One remained charitable to afflicted persons.

Corbell led her towards the folly, and again turned the key. He begged her to be seated on the broad slatted bench which abutted from the wall, and to permit him to arrange her skirts. He hadn't taken time to close the door.

"Oh, pray – it was to be a pencil sketch –"

"Young ladies like you deserve better things than a pencil."

Her hands scrabbled helplessly on the slats of the bench, then, conveniently, she swooned.

He proceeded, thinking she might well come to herself without realising that anything out of the ordinary had happened. "My dear Miss Smail, I fear you fainted as I was arranging your skirts for the sketch. I was obliged to unlace your bodice to try to revive you."

Two pitiful halfpence had been the reward of that. He bit them gently. She smelled of soap. Otherwise he had swiftly demolished what was left of point O; the virginity, as surmised earlier, had been no more than a cobweb. After that, trouble began. Miss Smail was sparsely endowed, and making his way up her was like trying to force shot of too high a calibre into a small-bore rifle. However, he was determined to complete the business once and for all; there was no point in stopping halfway.

He thrust determinedly. She was still unconscious, but had begun to make small sheeplike sounds, whether of pain or pleasure was uncertain. Baa, baa, little white ewe. She would have a sore little tail tonight, he admitted; perhaps the only proof of initiation she would ever experience.

Having achieved her, he was unaware of any emotion even at the gentle, initial sliding open of the untried womb. He extended himself fully in her, taking time to rest on his laurels. It had hardly been a struggle worthy of anyone. He stared at the halfpence, pink-tipped like daisy petals above the pulled-down chemise. He supposed he ought to lace her up again.

A shadow darkened the open doorway; Joan, with both fists full of primroses. She was staring, with lips parted. It turned out later that the third Punch had cast a shoe. Corbell cursed, and felt himself ejaculate. It came with the pent-up force of a released, confined torrent. He withdrew, but of necessity had left a good deal in Miss Smail. Fastening himself, he made ready to hurry after Joan; she'd turned and gone off, leaving the dropped primroses wilting on the ground. "Tidy yourself," he snapped at the governess. She was coming to, and couldn't have seen Joan. He could perceive the child's figure in the distance, long habit trailing on the ground instead of over her arm.

On second thoughts Corbell decided not to overtake her; there was nothing usefully to be said. However, the prospect of a pregnant Miss Smail was not to be thought of. He must see Peggy Vance without delay about dosing her. It happened with the maids, he believed, first thing in the morning.

He remembered, too late, that the vicar was invited to dinner tonight and had sent word that his wife had a migraine. Ione had said they'd best have that dreary governess down; three was an impossible number. He regretted the inconvenience to Miss Smail, and went straight to find the housekeeper.

There had been a time, as a boy, when he'd resented the way

157

she knew about everything. Now, it was a relief. "I'll hold her nose first thing," was all she said. "It'll put matters right. You'll have to give her the day off tomorrow."

She was wearing an expression he couldn't read; it might have been one of triumph. Servants – and Peggy was after all a servant – resented governesses by tradition, as he already knew.

Miss Smail sent to ask if she might be excused attendance at dinner; she felt unwell. "Tell her she must certainly attend," said Ione inexorably. "She may go upstairs with Miss Joan after she has been down for sugared almonds." This was a habit when they had guests, supposed to teach Joan the ways of polite verbal exchange. It was seldom a success; the child merely stared and said nothing. Now, Miss Smail put in an appearance, having no option; her nose and eyes were red, as though she had been crying, and she concealed with some courage a certain difficulty in walking. Corbell, guilt-ridden, poured her a glass of madeira. Ione was talking to the vicar, and took no more notice of Miss Smail than she ever did.

The dinner was neither a success nor a failure, as Dr Ferris was as usual so pleased with the sound of his own voice that nobody else need say much. Miss Smail pecked at her food and ate very little. Joan was sent for in due course, but on returning upstairs did not take her governess's hand. Miss Smail lurched slightly as they made their exit.

"You should not have given her as much wine," said Ione. "Those persons aren't used to it."

She herself withdrew shortly, leaving Corbell with the vicar for an unconscionable time. He was glad he'd caught Vance before dinner. Tomorrow he would take Joan in the Daimler, with Peggy Vance joining them after administering the black dose. They were to pick up the pony, which was to be shod at the smithy. It would pass the time and keep Joan well away while Miss Smail would be unavailable, and he might also come to terms with his daughter again. She had undoubtedly seen everything.

Miss Smail spent a wretched night, with hurt still evident in the part of her body she hadn't known she possessed. She only remembered being left, improperly exposed, in the folly while Lord Corbell, evidently again angry, went away. She had made her way back to the house and upstairs somehow. Then there had been the dreadful dinner party, before which she had begun to feel increasingly unwell. Since, she had reflected on the growing eccentricity of this particular employer.

At last she fell into a light sleep, only to be awaked by a sudden inability to breathe. Her nose was being held. Accordingly her mouth fell open, to admit a large spoon whose liquid contents were most unpalatable. Miss Smail spluttered indignantly. Vance the housekeeper's blurred figure stood there, still wearing its frilled nightcap and shawl. Vance put out a hand and manipulated Miss Smail's throat, making the stuff go down.

"Swallow the lot, Miss, or there'll be a second spoonful. You've been a bad girl. The dose will settle things. You're to take the day off. Miss Joan's going out in the motor." Peggy didn't add that she was invited as well. It was better for Miss to think she was still on the premises, keeping an eye.

She picked up the bottle of black liquid and the spoon and departed, not heeding the governess's protests that she had no right to be treated like this, she'd complain to Lord Corbell. Peggy turned at the door.

"It's his lordship's orders that you were to be given it. Stay in your room today, and use the pot." There wouldn't be time to go along repeatedly to the blue-flowered lavatory. She didn't explain further, but left Miss Smail to find out the dire truth. Very soon she would have to leave her bed to obey the sudden, unpredictable and repetitive urgings of nature. They should leave her insides quite clear.

What bewildered and angered Miss Smail more than anything was having been called a bad girl. In fact it was what Vance normally said to servants in such circumstances, and had slipped out.

Vance herself went to put in her false teeth, and dress. Everything so far was satisfactory. Now his lordship had opened up Miss Smail it should soon be possible, on the face of things, to let Jemmy prove himself on Miss when she was sedated. My lord could take the blame for what it was hoped might happen after that. As it was, Jemmy by custom sat through household prayers gazing at the governess as though he was her dog. He had begun

159

to think of her as his sweetheart. Peggy had put the word into his head herself, repeating it till he understood it.

"She's your sweetheart, eh, Jemmy?"

"Yes. Sweetheart. Give."

"Not quite yet, dear. Perhaps soon."

It all needed careful supervision. One difficulty was Miss Joan.

Walshe had walked the pony already to the smithy. Joan sat in the Daimler in silence. Peggy on the other hand talked volubly, which was a relief as it tided over awkwardness. Unfortunately her growing deafness had to compete with the purring engine. She appeared to be filled with discreet triumph at having successfully dosed Miss Smail.

"Didn't want to swallow it, of course, but I held her nose first and then rubbed her throat. Told her she was a bad girl, then remembered who she was. Anyway, she got it down inside her, the black draught, I saw to that. She's making close company with the pot, up and down, back and forth. I can hear it through the wall."

He frowned at her to stop the unwary talk; Joan likewise, whether or not she understood, could not have failed to hear. The visit to the smithy, however, went off well, Joan taking an interest in Punch's fate as the fire burned cherry-red. "It hurts him, I expect," she ventured.

"Not for long." At least they'd spoken. Riding Punch back again proudly with his new shoe, she'd forget everything else.

So he thought, but one morning shortly after, going downstairs to the post-tray, he perceived his daughter in her riding-habit.

"Should you not be at lessons?" he asked. He had not again encountered Miss Smail.

"I don't like them any more."

He forbore to ask more for the time and let her go; then sent for the governess. When she arrived, he was seated behind the walnut desk busied with papers. He did not look up.

"Joan is out on her pony when she should not be. Why do you permit it? You are left in full charge of her; why is she not with you?"

"She will no longer obey me. I should like you, Lord Corbell, to look at her exercise book. For some time she has been wilful and pert, and I gave her fifty lines of her own choice to write out as a punishment. Pray examine them." Her voice was even; nothing untoward might have happened, then or earlier.

He opened the slim jotter, flicking idly through the pages. He could see the steady advancement Joan had made at the beginning; her scrawl had gradually changed to a fairly legible hand. *Reason and precision.* By now, it was somewhat too readable. In deadly clear characters, over and over again, could at last be seen *Miss Smail was a bad Girl and had her Nose held and had to run to the Pott all day.*

He looked up; the governess was as white as linen. "I am sorry," Corbell said. "You must whip her."

"I – I could not. I have always been averse to the very thought of physical punishment, especially for girls." He could not, in fact, picture the little starfish hands as wielding any vindictive strength, and said:

"Then I will do so. She must certainly be punished. You may bring her to me when she returns from her ride."

She brought Joan, having induced her to change into a plain dress. Corbell duly caned his daughter, who caterwauled predictably. He let Joan go at last, aware of certain schoolmasterish stirrings in himself. The governess, trembling like a leaf, was about to follow her pupil. "Wait," said Corbell. He took Miss Smail by the elbow and guided her firmly to the window-seat.

To himself as he had become, he was justified. Miss Smail was available, could no longer be entirely unaware of what might happen, and her knees had quite evidently turned, conveniently, to water. He told himself he would be prudent on this occasion. There would in any case be little likelihood of Joan's return.

Miss Smail began to make small sounds of protest and alarm. "Oh, pray – oh, no, no, not any more – that servant with the spoon – I – I could not, not again – if you knew – Oh, no – no, no, ah, no, pray, oh, pray –"

Peggy's enforced dose, with its unspeakable results; the uncontrollable, unpredictable spurtings of black liquid lasting half the morning, seemed to remain more vividly in Miss Smail's mind now than the prospect of further assaults upon her honour. He laughed, reassured her, and proceeded, gripping her sticks of thighs one in each hand to draw them apart. He could feel the sparse flesh yield hesitantly at last beneath the cotton columns. He made clear to her again that the dreaded spoonful of liquid had been a regrettable, but necessary, precaution, as they had been interrupted on the former occasion. "Leave matters to me," he told her. "You need have no further fear. Lie still."

It was, after all, what he might have said last time, and, he now resolved, would say again at others. Miss Smail brought him physical release by her very inadequacies. He went on to satisfy his requirements.

He watched her stumble off in the end, his brief need met without compromising her. He resolved to ask Walshe, who must surely use them in his assignations with the cook, to procure him a condom wallet.

Still later, it occurred to him that if this situation with her governess were to continue, Joan must properly be sent elsewhere. However, she was not intelligent enough to benefit greatly from school, and would be shy with other children. While he thought over the alternatives, providence intervened in the form of an invitation from Cousin Mildred Sissington. Might dear little Joan, who she had heard resembled herself when she was young, visit her in the north? They had never met, and she herself was growing old and would be glad of young company for a time.

Corbell hesitated only briefly. He had been unwilling to allow Joan anywhere near Alfred Sissington, for good reasons and remembering Etta; but the old lady would keep an eye, and in any case Alfred seldom visited his mother now she was no longer a source of ready cash. Neither Corbell himself nor Ione, truth to tell, had much affection for Joan; and Cousin Mildred would welcome the chance of moulding a young girl in the pattern expected to be achieved by an earlier generation; samplers, jam-making, domestic duties. The stay could, in fact, be induced to prolong itself indefinitely; and as for Miss Smail, any explanation of her continued residence could be produced simply by telling the truth, namely that she was helping him in the library.

Part V

Chapter One

Ione maintained her furred and rustling entrance to church on Sundays, progressing up the aisle to the Corbell pew, acknowledging the social and sartorial attention of alerted and nodding upper-crust heads. Nobody dressed as well as Lady Corbell, and her appearance was always eagerly scanned. Today she wore a dark fur toque on her piled golden hair, with a matching pelisse and muff and below that, a loose straight-cut coat of lilac grosgrain to disguise the fact that her condition would shortly become evident.

Corbell would have permitted Walshe or Fred to drive her in the Daimler, but Ione preferred not to appear in the everlasting dust-coat, plain hat and motoring veil such a state of affairs made necessary. As it was, she was able to enhance the pew alone. The maids and, thankfully, that governess attended house prayers; she wouldn't have wanted such a frump beside her. The carriage and bays had been brought out for her sole glory, and had meantime taken their place with the rest outside, in proper order on the circle of raked gravel which surrounded the building, and which was flanked by a dark old yew tree and several graves. Once their betters were inside, the hierarchy of coachmen, from the Lord Lieutenant's down, kept an eye on the horses and quietly placed bets, by way of Fred, on the outcome of Tuesday's races. Otherwise they didn't admit him to their circle; he was rumoured to have been married to that randy sister of Lord Corbell's, who'd disappeared. It unclassed him, and the matter no longer interested anybody.

The eventual departure, in strict precedence, from the gravel circle when the service was over gave the opportunity to the waiting great ones to foregather while their equipages drew up for them beyond the lych-gate. Valuable county gossip could, meantime, be exchanged and invitations issued informally. The vicar's wife, whose remembered migraine at the time of the annual Lackmere dinner had turned out to mean only one more pending inmate of the already overflowing vicarage – as the coarser among the congregation put it, Mrs Ferris rattled 'em out yearly, you could see the steps and stairs in the vicarage pew – wanted a private word with Lady Corbell. It concerned the new curate, who had assisted today for the second time but was still very nervous. He had had a personal disaster which had ended in a severe breakdown, and had been sent here by the Bishop on, as it were, a trial run. Would Lady Corbell, if it was not inconvenient, be kind enough to invite him to tea one day? It would give him confidence.

"By all means, and you must come also," said Ione, who liked company; croquet parties could only take place in fine weather. They arranged a suitable day, and her ladyship was then seen to dispose her lilac skirts in the by now waiting carriage, with Fred's small form obsequiously holding open the door. The vicar's wife gazed enviously after the shining creation as it drove off. A small coachman and a tall parlourmaid – Lady Corbell had both – were everyone's ambition. She herself would never attain either. She turned to marshal her subdued children, and they walked in an obedient crocodile back to cold luncheon at the vicarage. The vicar, and the nervous Mr Chillingfold, would follow by themselves.

Joan had departed, taken to London by Peggy and handed over there to Lady Sissington's faithful Scottish companion, Miss McVey. It was hoped that Punch the pony might follow when matters had become settled.

Now that his daughter was no longer next door at nights, and Walshe having obliged promptly with a condom wallet from his existing stock, Corbell felt doubly free to visit Miss Smail's room. On the first such occasion he ascended the stairs with the usual difficulty, taking his time and under no illusion that he could fail to be heard. He found the governess seated upright in bed, spectacles on her nose, reading her nightly passage of the Bible. She raised her eyes and stared at him reproachfully.

"Please –"

"My dear Miss Smail, you are continuing to be paid a salary without a pupil. Permit me to instruct you instead, and at the same time oblige me." He made no mention of any future reference which might be required of him. There should be no need.

He took the Bible firmly from her, and removed her spectacles. She made no further resistance, and presently the remembered creaking began. It was odd to be so close to it. "Oh, pray, the servants," murmured Miss Smail. Vance slept next door. She didn't like the housekeeper overhearing everything.

"I employ them as well as yourself." The sound of the knocking, creaking bed would be familiar to the older ones; only his lordship, fucking the governess. It was expected.

Bitter memory rose, and was downed. By now, he was stretching Miss Smail's inner parts satisfactorily; and the condom's reassuring fit enabled him to make her further acquaintance. He elicited certain phenomena which surprised him; her limbs ceased to be rigid, becoming pliable as bluebell stems trodden in a dark wood; and subsequently there began to come from deep within her a further sound, like a nest of disturbed dormice. Their muted squealings conveyed Miss Smail's genteel ecstasy; she had become a little mated female animal, a member, at last, of the unaffected human race. He had achieved as much in her, and congratulated himself. He would continue to visit her, not merely for her benefit in such ways. In addition, he had become aware in himself of a commendable flow of semen.

In course of his subsequent visits, this happened regularly. It occurred to him at last that this was the purpose of Miss Smail in her present aspect. In the language of Newmarket, she was a teaser; a little mare of no pedigree, set on to rouse the stallion before putting him to the waiting brood-mare.

It was therefore his clear duty, after the preliminary canter with Miss Smail, to rise from her just before the dormice would have commenced to squeal had he continued in her. He would then hasten downstairs as best he might, untying the condom as he went, and make a connubial visit to Ione. She, disturbed from sleep, was at first equally disturbed by his briskness; perhaps he'd seen his doctor.

167

As for Miss Smail, she had once been overcome by a rushing sweetness within herself, making her a stranger to her daily drab existence. If only Lord Corbell wouldn't go away so soon, it might happen again.

Corbell found the situation diverting. Reason, precision and mathematics might play their indirect part in fashioning him a legitimate male heir. By no means now would he neglect to visit Miss Smail increasingly. By day, when she came down pale and wan with lack of sleep, he took no notice, merely telling her coldly to get on with the indexing. At this she still proved excellent, neat and accurate. The library was beginning to assume a reliable aspect. He never praised her, nor addressed her without need. Their other relations remained strictly nocturnal. Miss Smail must by no means be encouraged to think of herself as an *éminence grise*. Her most useful position was still sitting upright.

From the world outside a faint breath of scandal had already wafted to Lackmere, not this time concerning Alfred, Lord Sissington more than somewhat. The clergyman whose wife Alfred had seduced, and whose uncle was a bishop, had suffered a breakdown after the annulment, feeling foolish. The bishop, anxious as bishops are to do his best for all concerned, asked Corbell if, in the circumstances, the unhappy young man might take up a temporary charge in the village church till something else could be thought of. Dr Ferris was in line for promotion to dean.

Corbell, glad enough to be of help, had agreed, and Ione asked the young unfortunate to luncheon after witnessing his extreme nervousness in church. He was only in his thirties, was said to be an erudite person, and his experiences, or lack of them, must have been deflating. Corbell, seeing him for the first time, decided that he resembled a stick of celery which has grown flaccid with lack of use. It could have been easy to foresee his incompetence as anyone's husband.

He himself was feeling triumphant in such ways. The day before yesterday, Ione had informed him crossly that she was pregnant. "You might have been more considerate," she put it. "As it is, it'll happen just about the time of the Ladies' Open tennis championship, and as for the Lieutenant's garden party, by then I'll look like a filled sack. I don't suppose I shall be able to attend."

He had kissed her, genuinely delighted at the news, and had proceeded to lay down rules for her welfare. She mustn't lace herself, must wear loose clothes, and must no longer drive in the Daimler along bumpy roads. "Gentle walks," he said. "Miss Smail will accompany you." It occurred to him that at that rate, he must cease to render Miss Smail's legs unable to support her. He would naturally cease to visit her in the immediate aftermath of this news.

However, Ione, whose mouth had drooped at the prospect of no more drives to church, when she collected the only gossip there was, rebelled at the prospect of gentle walks with Miss Smail. "If I have to look at that frump every day, I'll miscarry."

Anxious to oblige her in every way, he selected one of the maids to accompany her. Flo had been in employment here for a long time, and seemed reliable and unassuming. Vance had no objection to her absences on Ione's walks.

In fact, Vance was jubilant. His lordship seemed to have abandoned Miss Smail. In addition, now her ladyship was in the condition long hoped for, his lordship arranged to see to business in town. He would be away for several days.

Vance proceeded with her own long-planned arrangements which directly involved Miss Smail.

Peggy Vance, in course of her training as lady's maid, had had to learn about douches and clysters, as they were known then; now, they called them enemas. There were varieties of treatment by means of these. Herbal and other contents were inserted per anum and received back again by tube into a bucket or other receptacle. It had once been the duty of a lady's maid to administer clysters in public, even at court. Under the concealment of the wide skirts worn at Versailles under the Grand Monarque, they were often needed; the formalities of etiquette did not leave time, in a twenty-four-hour day, to relieve the bowels naturally.

Vance had given enemas frequently to Anna Corbell in her invalid days, if the bedpan proved a discouragement; and to Miss Etta in her randy ones. The full punishment of that last, when caught, had been a douche, a whipping, and a black enema, in that order, held down by maids for all three. She'd been left limp as a rag doll, howling and unbearably thirsty, Miss Etta, but it still hadn't cured her.

h

There would be no need for such elaboration with Miss Smail. Now that his lordship hadn't been with her for some time there would be no need either for a prior black enema. Miss knew its results already as given by mouth like the servants, the latter method being less trouble to prepare. What Peggy intended to do, and had in fact already started the evening before, was to slip a tasteless sedative into the governess's suppertime cocoa. Its effects would last long enough for her to be able to give a stronger one to the unconscious young woman in early morning, warmed to blood heat and mixed with Epsom salts. These, besides doing their expected duty, also dried out the wall of the womb and made it receptive to spermatic fluid, which clung longer than usual. It had happened to royalty and resulted in the birth of a princess nine months to the day. All this was stored in Vance's retentive memory. Nothing was giving way except her hearing.

She would both hear and see Jemmy, brought down in the cart by Agnes at half past nine. He would be brought straight upstairs, having been told he might have his sweetheart provided he didn't sing. Otherwise, with Miss Smail's spectacles kept prudently from her, it might as well be his lordship. The governess, unlike Peggy, wasn't informed of when he came and went.

Jemmy Tesson had mostly been happiest left to himself. He was aware of the cruel laughter of the world when he had tried to be like others, and could understand words he couldn't say. By now, he liked to be left with things which didn't mock and point. Animals trusted him and were never shy with him. At times he used to be allowed to help down at the home farm, scratching the backs of the brown sitting hens which would stand up then and let him take the warm eggs from under them, and put the logs in a basket to take up to the house. There had been a friendly little goat which used to walk with him, and he sang his tuneless song to her and when she was in the near distance, in the field, she would know he was coming and would bleat. After she was mated she would let him milk her, and mix the milk in pails to feed the calves when they left their mothers. He liked to visit the pigs, and scratch their backs as well, and carry swill to them and watch the big placid sows lying suckling their young. There were a great many piglets, but he couldn't count. Best of all was haymaking,

170

when his strong body mowed the long grass with a scythe so that it lay sweet-smelling till it dried, then Jemmy would take a hayfork with the rest and help to toss the dry hay into a great beehive stack, to be used later on as fodder for the horses.

He felt one with the rest then, but it was spoilt. One day he had been busy gathering and tossing, when a high supercilious voice came which wasn't one of their own.

"I wouldn't trust it with a hayfork, personally." It was the boy with orange hair, on a pony. He was staying with Master Ed. The scornful blue eyes raked Jemmy as though he saw an insect.

It was the boy who'd called out "Daftie! Daftie," long ago, one day at the lake. His name was Alf. Peg had come and rescued Jemmy from him then, and Master Ed had spoken up for him, but he'd been already crying. He didn't cry now, but flung down the hayfork and ran off, back to the cottages. He didn't go back. The farmer found somebody else to help him.

Once Peg had taken him with her to a wedding. They'd kept to the back, but Jemmy watched the bride come in dressed up and heard the groom, one of the footmen who wasn't a member of the sect, make his vows. One phrase stayed with Jemmy, he didn't know why. *With my body I thee worship.* For a long time he didn't know what it meant, but liked the sound of the words. Then he set eyes on his little sweetheart and knew he could worship her with his body. He wanted it more than anything. At household prayers he used to gaze at her, sitting there in her plain dress with her head bent. He knew she was an innocent like himself. They were different from the rest. At first sight he had kissed her. After that he only saw her at prayers, among other people. Now, it was to be as though there was nobody in the world but himself and her. Peg said so. He would like to kiss his sweetheart a great deal and hold her, and let the great flood from deep within him pour into her, richly and long. It would make them one. It was worship offered with his body and his heart. He was so happy already he knew he'd sing almost without meaning to. They had promised, Ag and Peg, that it should happen tomorrow. He could be happy thinking of it, and of making his sweetheart happy as well.

Miss Smail proved to have a small tight anus. Vance warmed the metal nozzle of the tube in her hands before inserting it.

171

Thereafter everything went according to plan. In a way, pumping in the enema made her feel like some man, having his will of Miss Smail. The behaviour of Jemmy might be one variable, as Miss herself might have put it had she known what was going on. Jemmy hadn't, despite the nightly games with himself under the cottage blanket, actually used his endowments before.

Vance heard them come presently, and arrive upstairs. Jemmy wasn't singing meantime. They went into her room while she remained in Miss Smail's, having prepared her, drained of all fluids and weak as a shrimp, and laid her ready on the bed.

Jemmy appeared, led by Agnes and lacking his trousers and shoes. The erection was already thrusting beneath his shirt. He went straight to the bed, climbed on Miss Smail and began kissing her repeatedly. The sight of a waiting sheelah, the ancient open invitation to fertility, would not be lost on any man. Soon his busy buttocks satisfied both his waiting grandmothers. Miss Smail's eyes remained almost closed.

However, what she was experiencing must be pleasant. She began to make little sighing yielding sounds, while Jemmy kissed and thrust. Presently he lay on in her. He was full of love, and wanted to give all he could to the beloved. Miss Smail began a gratifying moaning. Peggy looked behind her at the door. Nobody was about; the servants were all busy at allotted tasks downstairs.

When they lifted Jemmy away at last he couldn't help breaking out into his happy tuneless song. Perhaps for once it didn't matter. Agnes saw him dress and took him out again, the cart trundled off, and Vance brought a jug of snow-water from the ice-house to place beside Miss Smail when she should wake up. That wouldn't be till afternoon. Vance had already tidied and dried her, smoothing the bed and pulling up the covers. If Miss asked anything on coming to, she would be told she'd had a turn. Supper would be brought to her in bed. All of it had gone off very well, and could do so again more than once till his lordship's reappearance. By then, there should be signs one way or the other, and time would have ceased to mean much to Miss Smail. No doubt she was used to it all when his lordship really visited her.

Miss Smail came to herself aware of violent thirst. She saw the jug of water by the bed, seized it, filled the tumbler and drank.

She drank and drank again till the jug was empty. Soon she wanted to pass water, and tried to climb out of bed. Her legs were so unaccountably weak she subsided on her knees to the floor. The door opened and Vance stood there, with a bedpan. She might almost have been waiting with it on purpose.

"Get back into bed, Miss. I'll put this under you."

Miss Smail struggled between dignity and obedience. The latter would be incorrect, a betrayal of her profession. However, she urgently needed to empty herself of what she'd drunk. Having a bedpan slid under her and held in place by the housekeeper was degrading, but it would have been unthinkable to wet the floor before managing to get to the commode. Back in bed, she felt Vance pull up her nightdress, slide the pan under, then the warm flood came despite everything, bringing relief. Vance then dried her and eased away the pan, thereafter removing it.

The whole experience had been mortifying. What was worse, it happened again next day, and the day after that.

Vance, an expression of mild triumph on her face, continued to rinse out the bedpan in the blue-flowered lavatory. Miss Smail had piddled today without difficulty as usual. Everything could continue as it ought.

As the days passed Miss Smail tried not to drink as much water when she came to, but the raging thirst wouldn't allow her to help it. Something was very much the matter with her, and all Vance would say was that she was still having her turns. She'd never had turns before. By degrees it seemed as if Vance directed the whole of her life, wiping, drying and feeding her like a child, and carrying the pan, and trays of nourishing food, in and out. She didn't seem to need any bowel movements. It must be part of whatever was wrong.

Fortunately Lord Corbell came in a great deal. His visits were the only anchor to reality. Miss Smail wished she could find her spectacles. She couldn't seem to see him properly, but everything else went on exactly the same.

Vance was disturbed some days later by two sets of instructions; one from Lord Corbell sent by hand, to say he would return on Thursday, briefly to spend a night at home before journeying across to Ireland for a couple of weeks. He had to select a new factor personally. In the circumstances he hoped she would prepare, at short notice, a dinner for the senior judiciary on Thursday evening, to wind up temporary business till he was again available. As for her ladyship, she sent up a note to say she expected Miss Smail's company to take tea downstairs on Thursday afternoon at half past four, as the vicar's wife and the new curate were invited.

Vance set about giving orders to the cook and Walshe about dinner and wine for the judges and magistrates. It was probable her ladyship would want a tray sent to her room, it being a gentlemen's occasion. As for Miss, she'd have to be given a rest from the night sedative as well as the stronger one early tomorrow, and from Jemmy, leaving her steady enough on her legs to walk down to tea. It was unlikely his lordship would fail to go up to her after they'd all left. That meant more rinsing out, next day after he'd finally gone, and everything inside already maybe disturbed.

At least Miss could be allowed a bowel movement of her own tomorrow. There seemed to be a great deal of planning about the whole business.

As regarded business in general, Corbell had, during his visit to town, at last found news of Etta.

Chapter Two

While in London, as he occasionally did, he visited an exhibition of paintings. This one was in a gallery on a side street, and represented artists not in the main body of Pre-Raphaelitism, as they called it, but on its fringe. He stared at second-rate Guineveres and doubtfully drowning Ophelias, almost went away, then was arrested by the sight of a small water-colour hanging by itself. It was a portrait of Etta.

There was no doubt about it. The green eyes stared out at him like the remembered malachite of Jocosa's. Etta was posing as a Madonna, with a child on her knee. The child had dark hair; its face was turned towards its mother. Moreover, about Etta's thin neck hung the amber locket he had given her on her marriage to Fred and which had once belonged to Yolande.

It was as though they had known he would come, had waited to convey this message to him. His brain whirled; time and recent happenings faded. The lake water was again about him, a ghost in his arms. His seed had entered her, draining him; there had been the wedding next day, and no sign of Etta; then she had gone with Sissington, left him, and vanished into mystery, till now.

He noted, numbly, certain things. She wore the kind of gown she always had, loose uncorseted clothes such as these pseudo-mediaevalists favoured. He found himself examining the catalogue. The painting was not for sale. The artist's name was Harrigan. Corbell, who kept up more or less with events in the world of art, had never heard of him; yet he painted with precision. Corbell went to the porter's desk and asked for

175

Harrigan's direction. He was told it was in the Mile End Road.

"He's a potter, sir, as a rule; don't paint often," the man explained helpfully. He added that that Morris firm used a lot of Harrigan's stuff, decorating it themselves later on in Hammersmith.

Corbell took a hackney, which drove him down into mean streets, the air thick with yellow-green fog from the river. Presently it cleared, and he found himself confronted by rows of tenements, their ugliness almost redeemed by soot. Had Etta come here? Had she had the foresight, the intelligence, to become an artist's model? It was perhaps the one thing for which he had unwittingly trained her; besides, granted, one other.

Etta had never handled money; how had she contrived after leaving Sissington? That portrait had shown a boy perhaps four years old, but it might have been painted a year or two back. A sullen thought came to Corbell that perhaps the child was not his son; he himself was, after all, Etta's half-brother, there might be a resemblance from further back. He would know nothing till he saw Harrigan, and found out the age of the picture and the whereabouts of Etta. Where was she? How was she? Would she come back to Lackmere, and if so how the devil was he to cope with Ione confronted by her with such a boy? Miss Smail, for the present, no longer mattered; he had almost forgotten that affair, or decided whether or not it would continue.

He instructed the driver to wait and rasped the outer knocker at a lopsided door. Excitement rose in him; Etta herself might open it. What would she look like by now? One of these painters had immortalised a red-haired shop girl, creating from her Beatrice and the Blessed Damozel before she died of tuberculosis and laudanum. Lives ended. His own would end.

Nobody answered the door, and he found that it pushed open easily. Beyond was a passage, and at the end a half-glimpsed square of unkept grass. A side door, one of three, said HARRIGAN in laid-on paint. Presently a bearded thick-set man answered Edmund's knock, surveying him in surly fashion. He wore a potter's slop and his fingernails were rimmed with dried clay.

"You couldn't have come at a worse time," he said. "We're firing. Keep stoking, Ed. Don't stop for anything."

At the back of the room was a brick kiln, with fire showing bright inside its base and a squatting dark-haired child tending it.

176

Corbell caught sight of the child's profile and decided he must be about Joan's age; was this his own son? Whether so or not, the child didn't turn his head.

"Come in, for God's sake, and shut the door," said the potter. "Draughts kill the temperature at once." He led the way in; the room was lined with shelves, on which reposed various plain fired glazed pots and greenware. Once the door was shut Harrigan became more affable.

"Where is my sister?" Corbell asked him without delay; the potter was evidently a man of few words, and answered accordingly.

"Etta? She's dead, I'm afraid. She died a year ago. Her lungs went, I suppose, like Lizzie Siddal's. I dare say you're Eddie. She spoke your name sometimes; it was one of the few words she used. I always had a notion you'd come here sooner or later."

He wiped his hands on his clay-stained slop, then went and took down a honey-glazed urn from the shelves. "That's her, or all that's left," he explained briefly; all of his talk remained brief, his mind being as usual on the firing. "I burned her body in the kiln, as she'd have wanted. The law don't allow it, but she was happy enough here. Used to help me wedge the clay while she had the strength, then after that she'd lie and watch. Ed's good with that and the firing. He's a help to me, eh, Ed?"

The boy shrugged. He had shown no interest in Corbell's arrival, being totally occupied with feeding sticks of charcoal into the aperture. Once he spat sideways, like a man.

"Where did you find them?" Corbell asked. That Etta should be dead seemed in some way unimportant. She was still about, in whatever way.

"Found her huddled in a doorway in Islington, on the point of giving birth to this 'un," Harrigan said. "He, Ed, was born here. Wouldn't know where else to go, would you, Ed?"

The urchin again shrugged, still intent on the firing. Corbell could think of nothing to say. The fire roared upwards. There was a metal pipe leading out to the grass whereby the fumes no doubt escaped. "We have a seam of ball clay here, as well as an artesian well," Harrigan explained. "It's on the line of the breweries, good water, gravel base. Morris sends across his cart to take away my stuff and decorate it. I don't believe in decorating, it's the shape that should matter, but he pays." The small mud-coloured eyes returned to the urn. "She said, like, to give you the ashes when you came, and said 'Lake'. She knew you'd come, and here you are. Will you take them? There's a package, as well."

Later Corbell opened the package which had been handed him. It contained the amber locket, gleaming as he remembered, lying still in its chain. The sight aroused more emotion than had the urn with its silent content of ashes.

"The lid's sealed with wax, in case you want to tip the whole thing into the water. Otherwise you can empty 'em out and use the vase. She wouldn't mind which. She made a good model, Etta did. I won't sell that painting to anyone; don't do 'em often, like this occupation best. Keep up the sticks, Ed, do."

A grasp of the situation seemed to strike him suddenly. "You want to take him?" he asked, nodding towards the boy. "I'll miss him."

Ed spoke up then for the first time. "I ain't goin'," he announced, in the accents of the Mile End Road. He had still not looked round. Edmund left his own direction, tossed Ed a guinea, which the child bit distrustfully, then made his way back to the waiting hackney, seated thereafter with Etta's ashes on his knees and Yolande's amber locket against his heart. If anything should happen to Harrigan, Ed at least knew where to come. Corbell found himself trembling now it was over.

Next day, he returned home; and placed the urn, meantime, near the pipe organ, now seldom played. It was like Etta not to have wanted a funeral. He would wait a little, look at the urn now and again, and think of her ashes. Perhaps they had something still to say, some message for him; but for the time, there was only silence, as there had been for long from Jocosa. Could one spirit indeed occupy the bodies of two young women, separated by as many generations?

None of it was the kind of question he could answer. No doubt Miss Mercy Smail, with her respect for scientific fact as opposed to myth, could give him information out of her little prim pink mouth, her spinster's brain, perhaps even the part recently achieved. He would return to her at leisure, feasibly by now in the guise of Galatea. It seemed unlikely, but he himself was an unlikely Pygmalion.

Chapter Three

Chillingfold the curate, whose shattered nerves were beginning to recover from his marital experiences, had begun to make well-intentioned visits to Lady Corbell while she was unable to be driven to church. The visits took place conveniently at tea-time. On this occasion Ione had decided to have that governess down, as she herself had run out of things to say and the vicar's wife, as she now remembered, was no longer here but, by now, a dean's lady, like herself awaiting confinement.

Miss Smail appeared, looking indefinably less frumpish than usual. She'd even begun to develop some sort of figure. No doubt it was with being properly fed. Ione poured tea out of the large silver Georgian pot, saw her guests settled in talking about some matter they evidently both understood, and herself surreptitiously reached for the covered muffin-dish. She was frustrated in her intentions by Corbell, who had suddenly come in. He didn't take tea as a rule, and she hadn't known he was back.

"No, my dear, none of those for you; remember what the doctor said." He gave her large white hand an affectionate slap, took the covered dish firmly out of her reach and passed it to the guests. Ione's mouth drooped. Mr Chillingfold rose in courtesy to greet his unexpected host, and was told to sit down again. Corbell, a grotesque shape against the light from the window, drained his teacup standing.

"You were discussing, as I overheard when I came in, the power of a pair to form a series. That sounds remarkably like human life."

Nobody laughed, because nobody present had humour except himself. Despite her lack of it he found his need for Miss Smail clamouring in him. She had acquired attraction by some means. He could see little breasts swelling beneath the stuff of her bodice, thrusting outwards, like buds about to open, above the level of the unnecessary stays. Even the lines of her mouth had softened in some manner and her hair looked less dull. He felt jealous of the etiolated parson, who was again leaning towards her. Corbell overrode manners and said, "Miss Smail, now that you have finished tea I should be grateful if you would attend me in the library. I have a task for you which is fairly urgent."

She rose, flushing a little, said goodbye to Mr Chillingfold, and went. Corbell remained to make it clear that Miss Smail helped him with indexing in the absence of her pupil, his daughter. He then turned and limped after her. Ione, her thin fair eyebrows raised, told herself that had it been anyone but those two, one might have suspected a little affair. She poured more tea, in silence, for the curate.

Corbell came on Miss Smail standing uncertainly in the middle of the library floor. He put both hands round her waist, lifted her bodily and laid her along the window-seat, thereafter indulging in a brief exercise of *droit de seigneur*. "You may expect me again later tonight," he told her. He must go down to ascertain the quality of tonight's wine, meantime, for the judiciary. He was anxious that they be impressed, and had instructed Walshe to bring out the last of the second lord's port, long covered with cobwebs in the cellar. Galatea should be ready after it was drunk. He would be in a state to pay her closer attention by then.

He went out, having for some reason explained himself more than was his custom. Miss Smail pulled down her skirts in slight resentment. She would have liked to see Mr Chillingfold leave. They had taken to one another and shared an interest in subjects such as the Binomial Theorem. In course of more recent proceedings, she had heard him drive off on the gravel below. Her sect didn't permit her to attend church, and Lady Corbell, in any case, disliked anyone sharing the carriage.

Miss Smail was also disturbed by the reversion in Lord Corbell's manner. Lately he had been tender, considerate and loving, kissing her often when he came to her in bed. Now, lately on the library window-seat, he'd again been curt and had merely made use of her. She began to consider, once again, a letter she'd received from Mrs Udney while his lordship was away. It had mentioned a pending vacancy for a lady instructress in pure mathematics at one of the new colleges which were opening for women. It was exactly the kind of thing that ought to suit her, and once would have.

Outside, carriages were already beginning to arrive for the dinner, and lamps had been lit. Elderly male occupants were emerging one by one, for their equipages to be driven on to the stables. There would be a large number present, Miss Smail surmised. It meant she wouldn't be able to get to sleep till the small hours, waiting for Lord Corbell to come upstairs.

The weather had turned humid for the time of year, and after the curate had gone and the tea-things were removed by the coveted tall parlourmaid, Ione sought out Vance to complain about the discomforts of her state. She'd stopped being sick, but was beginning to feel languid and in need of diversion.

Vance was busy with preparations for the dinner, and hadn't time for her ladyship except to say that a tray would be sent in separately. "You got on all right when you had Miss Joan," she said. "The first is always the worst, and it's a long time yet," and she went on counting the silver.

Ugh, thought Ione. Cousin Mildred was welcome to Joan. She'd written recently to say the little creature was behaving very well, doing exactly as she was told – she was too dull not to – and that Alfred had been up, and seemed very fond indeed of the child; he'd bought her chocolates and liked to play with her. Tears rose in Ione's eyes, thinking of Alfred, whom she would never cease to love. She still thought of him as he'd been behind the palms in the ballroom, the time he'd proposed.

Corbell had decided not to inform his cousins of Ione's condition. There was no harm in letting mother and son think they'd got hold of the heiress. His chief task now was to guard Ione's health. There would be no connubial visits meantime. After tonight, he must catch an early train for the Irish ferry. Once there, business might be protracted for some time. He looked forward, accordingly, to spending the rest of tonight, after dinner, with Miss Smail.

The dinner was a success, the food excellent, the wine, as he knew, well chosen. He told himself he was one of those persons who are not made drowsy or inefficient by wine, and therefore drank a great deal. It seemed an eternity till the last guest finished his legal reminiscences and drove off. At last Corbell climbed the familiar stairs, in undoubted fettle. The afternoon's brief coupling had spurred him on; who was it who'd said drinking aroused desire and diminished performance? Probably Shakespeare, who after all didn't know everything. He, Corbell, fifth lord, was about to give the performance of his life. Galatea's resident nymph should come out of hiding. He himself would get some sleep tomorrow on the train.

Next day, after breakfast, Corbell caught his early train, likewise the connection from London to Holyhead. On both occasions he had the compartment to himself, which gratified him.

He wanted to savour memory from the night before. He still felt like a boar in rut. He stretched his uneven legs out in front of him, recalling the absent governess as a Cranach Venus or Eve, narrow white limbs yielding passively. Her cunt, seen at last fully when he'd pulled off her nightdress in course of proceedings, had been a light-brown isosceles triangle with its base facing upwards. Close coitus had revealed geometric truth; male and female together made a six-point star.

Her breasts were like two little apples not yet ripe. He had handled and mouthed them like a starved child gobbling blancmange. Her own mouth had transformed itself as he had once hoped it might; a pursed little prune no longer, but instead a pinkly tumescent sea-anemone, opening ready to emit fronds or else admit a man's tongue. Oh, he'd taught her.

He'd forgotten to tie on the condom, and it didn't signify. It was seldom that he had bulled a woman to capacity; never with Ione, perhaps that time with Etta in the lake. He no longer thought of Miss Smail as undesirable to be made pregnant. Increasingly he liked to think of her as swelling up like a little pear, unable to leave Lackmere in the autumn or at any time in the foreseeable future. He had mastered her, causing her dormice to clamour till they squealed. He had been unwilling to leave by dawn, but rose from her of necessity at last, agreeably sated. Yet there remained something about her which eluded him, had done from the beginning. He promised himself that he would think, over the next three weeks, what it might be; he had to be away for that length of time to complete the business which had brought him here in the first place. Once home again, he would solve the mystery of Miss Smail once and for all.

The tides were rough on the way to Rosslare, the old factor was waiting with horses, and on landing Corbell deliberately set aside thoughts of his clamorous concubine.

Now, in Ireland, it was raining. He must make himself concentrate on selecting the right replacement to have charge of the tenants here. Several applicants would be making an appearance over the next few days, and the wrong choice would mean having to travel to this damp green country a second time. He liked, here and at Lackmere, to be recognised as a good landlord.

The horses jogged along the potholed roads, the boat which had brought him turned back in a heavy sea, and geese grazed in the passing fields, fattening on the grass. Corbell's need faded to the back of his mind, watching them.

Chapter Four

Miss Smail had slept longer than usual, and when she tried to get out of bed it was to discover two things; on trying to gain the washstand, her legs had their increasingly customary, and agreeable, weakness after such a night as had just been spent. Secondly, she was naked.

This discovery – she remembered now he'd pulled her nightdress right off – had the effect of mild shock. Miss Smail's awareness of her own body, like Yolande's in her childhood, had been ritually forbidden. Both, before the occasional bath at convent and charity-school, had been handed a comprehensive sheet of striped ticking with a hemmed hole for the head. Undressing thereafter took place unseen within it. Having climbed into the bath the folds were draped on either side, allowing for a secret ritual of cleansing, emergence, drying and dressing, all unseen. The daily habits of dressing and undressing were likewise self-censored. No doubt the resulting lack of knowledge had continued in Miss Smail; unlike Yolande, she lacked an interest in life, merely confining herself to what she already understood. This was in its nature impersonal, the cool objective world of truth from numbers.

It occurred to her now that she had two breasts, both of which Lord Corbell had found interesting. Their circumference was equal. She put a hand under each, lifting them tentatively. This brought a reminder of what she'd felt at intervals during the previous night, between which there had been, more than once, the inexplicable sensation of being borne on a cloud of bliss. Miss

Smail stood for moments, aware of herself, for the first and last time, as an object of desire.

There was a sound at the door and Vance stood there. Miss Smail realised that she was in an improper state to be beheld, standing like this with her nightgown crumpled on the floor nearby. Her training did not desert her. "Kindly knock before you enter," she said. Mrs Udney had always warned her young ladies not to let servants get above themselves.

"I was going to say your breakfast's cold long ago. If you don't want it, I'll take the tray."

"You may leave it, meantime." She was hungry, now she thought of it.

Vance suddenly began to move towards her. Set her up, the little bitch! Talking like that, after all night with his lordship and half the house hearing. Everything might have to be done again, beginning with a douche.

Peggy forgot Miss Smail's superior profession. She seized the governess by her inconsiderable pigtail, forced her down into a kneeling position against the bed, and resolutely smacked her bottom till it was as red as a tomato. Miss Smail, in astonishment as well as pain, began to howl, then collected herself, though tears still pursued one another down her cheeks.

"How dare you – you have no right – I will tell Lord Corbell –"

"I've known his lordship a deal longer than you, Miss, though seemingly not so well. He'll believe me of the two of us. Get something on and eat your breakfast if you're going to. If the coffee's cold I can't help it."

She went out, knowing she'd forgotten her place. There was enough to do cleaning up after that dinner, and helping Walshe cradle back the few remaining encrusted bottles of the second lord's port they'd left. After all that, Jemmy would have to be brought down again, whether Miss knew his lordship was off to Ireland or not. Events were crowding in too fast, others not fast enough. Looking at that governess it still hadn't been possible to tell whether or not she'd started anything, or if so by whom. For the first time in her life, Peggy began to wonder if she hadn't taken on more than she could properly manage.

The folly in the woods had been left unlocked lately so that Ione, on her prescribed gentle walks with Holy Flo, might pause to rest there if she felt inclined. Her husband's drawings were kept inside in a folder, and paintings stacked against the wall or on an easel. Poachers wouldn't be interested, and neither was she.

There was only one thing that interested Ione and occupied her every waking thought since it had happened. One day, while walking past the pit up to the wicket, a spanking cabriolet with its hood drawn back had stopped in passing on the road. Inside, holding the reins with Eileen Penhaligon, in a ravishing new driving-dress of grey and persimmon beside him, sat Alfie.

He wasn't, of course, able to abandon charge of the sole horse in order to come down and clasp her, Ione, in his arms. Otherwise, as the expression in his unforgotten blue eyes made clear, he would undoubtedly have done so. How little he had changed! Did he remember that the last time they'd met, actually met, they'd been engaged? Time had dragged since then. She wasn't wearing anything as up-to-the-minute as Eileen, but at least her condition hadn't begun to show yet under the light loose coat. Eileen herself had jumped down in her impulsive way, and kissed Ione's cheek, leaving a scent of frangipani.

"My dearest Ione, it's been an age. How are you? Would you like to come on a little drive? We could all perhaps squeeze in."

There was nothing she would have liked more, and she could have killed Flo, who spoke up out of place and said her ladyship wasn't supposed to drive at present. Later, Ione gave the girl the rough side of her tongue, as it was known. Flo replied reasonably that if her ladyship lost the baby as early she, Flo, would have her backside flayed again by Mrs Vance, and once had been enough.

One didn't hobnob with the servants, and Ione made no reply. However, she persisted, with faith and hope, in going up to the wicket daily. A letter then arrived from Eileen, saying among other things that Alfred had to make a long stay in Wiltshire and wouldn't be about, and she hoped everything was as it ought to be with dearest Ione, and if not to be sure to let them know at The Towers. Ione suspected, rightly, that Eileen regarded Alfie as her own property these days and had probably arranged the Wiltshire visit on purpose. She lapsed into what she supposed was called laissez-faire, and failed to remark on the subsequent behaviour of Holy Flo or even to notice that when, that time, she herself had been talking briefly with Eileen on the road, Alfred had closed one eye to Flo in a most suggestive manner.

In other words Alfred was nowhere near Wiltshire, and out of many so chosen, found out smartly that Holy Flo, as rumoured, had the hottest tail in three counties. She would slip out after supper by the side door once it was dark, they would meet in the folly and share unholy delights. Flo was an expert at managing not to be caught, but Alfred used such occasions also to learn more; from where he sat or lay, it was possible to watch a good deal that went on inside Lackmere once it was lit up at night. He was still uncertain to what use such knowledge might be put, but to such as Alfred, Lord Sissington, nothing of the kind is ever wasted.

He also took time to reflect that Ione had put on a good deal of weight. If she wasn't allowed to drive, perhaps Joan wouldn't inherit the money after all. Otherwise the ensuing sixth lord would still be himself. The knowledge fortified him.

He and Eileen laughed together about the Wiltshire fib. Damp devotion wasn't required in the circumstances, and during the week he himself was safely in town.

Chapter Five

Miss Smail, meantime, having washed in cold water, felt her resolve, both physical and moral, strengthen. She was well aware that the whole situation had gone far beyond what Mrs Udney would have described as permissible, even allowing for the eccentricities of employers. The worst of it was that she herself had known this sweet tide of giving. That in itself, in the view of such persons as had brought her up, would be sinful, because pleasure was so. It had not been a constituent of the charity-school. What they would think there of last night's doings with Lord Corbell, Mercy blushed to imagine. Perhaps Mrs Vance had been less impertinent than one supposed.

In the nature of things, only one person could give her advice, and that was the young clergyman she had met for the first time yesterday. They had known an instant sympathy of soul. It was after all his calling to give advice to persons such as herself. That he might disapprove of what she had to relate was possible, but at least he would tell her, in return, what she ought to do. If she should apply for the mathematical lectureship he would tell her so. The strangeness of what was happening to her body bewildered her, and as this was a day when Lord Corbell would be in town, she was free to do as she liked.

The road lay two miles or so beyond the little rear gate where she'd often walked with Joan. Having ignored the cold breakfast, Miss Smail gladly ate provided lunch, and afterwards set out. The roundabout walk avoided exit at the lodge, and she preferred her journey to be private. On the way she asked herself what she wanted to say. Perhaps it would be best to begin by asking Mr Chillingfold to question her.

She walked firmly on, and the woods closed about her. She was feeling better now, after a rest and some food, though it was still inadvisable to sit down.

Two hours later she staggered back, bonnet lopsided, skirts crumpled, tears running down her face behind the spectacles. Amazingly, she realised she was still clutching her reticule; there hadn't been time to defend herself. A strange man in a bowler, with orange hair and a dyed moustache, had been hanging about in the woods near the gate. It was evident from some distance that he had been drinking spirits, and she had tried to evade him, but he blocked her way.

What happened next was horrid. "You're Corbell's little shoppin'-basket, eh? Joanie told me. She tells me all kinds of things. You were a bad girl with Crip in the folly, eh? Be one again," and he had, disgustingly, put both arms round Miss Smail and had begun to give her smacking kisses. Then his pouched blue eyes – he must have been handsome once – had grown ugly. "Crip took my girl, so I'm takin' his, for what it's worth," he said, then to Miss Smail's horror and indignation, threw her down on her back in the moss. Thereafter, Corbell's musings on the efficacy or otherwise of condoms were rendered irrelevant.

Afterwards – it was not possible to reflect till afterwards, back in her own room – she recalled what else he'd said, after using her for a long time. It was useless to struggle or cry out; nobody heard. The smug, triumphant voice of Angel Alf sounded again in her ears.

"What happens when little governesses get big bellies? What happens then, eh? He does it with men as well, you know. He did it with the groom. His sister told me."

He must have kept her on her back for almost an hour. Miss Smail began to realise that there was a great deal she didn't know.

Had she known also, the unfortunate Mr Chillingfold was still thinking of her. He had even ventured to write, trusting Miss Smail would overlook any precipitancy, inviting her to attend a little parish soirée. He was most anxious to improve their further acquaintance, especially regarding the matters they had briefly discussed.

Corbell had pocketed the letter before departing, and wrote from Ireland to the bishop of the diocese. Mr Chillingfold should certainly be removed elsewhere; his state of mind caused him to pester young women.

When next heard of, the unlucky young man had been transferred to Essex, in charge of a young men's hostel.

Walshe had chanced to perceive the encounter between Miss Smail and Lord Alfred; he was in the habit of keeping an eye up among the back woods on Saturdays, looking out for poachers in their free time. That he did not interrupt proceedings was due to an inbuilt awareness of his proper station. Lord Alfred was, after all, their own lordship's cousin, whatever one might think of him privately.

However, his delay in telling Peggy Vance, which in the ordinary way he would have done at once, was due to an unforeseen circumstance, the death of his maternal uncle, a ghillie on a Highland estate. It was incumbent to travel up for the funeral, an enjoyable affair preceded by a wake. It was, in fact, more than a week, his lordship being still away on business, till Walshe was able to inform Peggy, who held up her hands and said she'd always known that Miss Smail wasn't what she seemed. Walshe demurred, recalling Lord Alfred's overheard remark about little governesses. Miss Smail hadn't asked for it.

"Looks like he's trying to put the blame on our lordship," said Walshe. "We could prove he's in Ireland."

Vance looked grim. It was too late now for the black enema, it'd have to be the douche as well. There mustn't be any little bastards running about with faces like Miss Smail and hair like Lord Alfred. After she'd seen about Miss, it would all have to begin with Jemmy over again, and he was getting out of control.

"She shouldn't have been up in the woods in the first place," she said; what else did they go for except men? Miss Smail must have got into the way of it, lacking his lordship. Nevertheless, she would bring back Jemmy.

"Whyever she went there, she didn't expect him. He was on her before you could whistle, pore little bitch." Walshe never showed emotion and his face remained a mask. It was the sign of a good butler.

Walshe had, in fact, a clear memory of what Miss Smail looked like with her skirts flung up. Her thin splayed legs had been in cotton columns, and both hands had clutched her reticule like a raft of salvation. He himself had withdrawn out of tact before she staggered off. Lord Alf had called something after her that didn't impress.

Peggy clucked her tongue. If Angel Alf was hanging about at the wicket, it meant he was waiting for the maids or else for her ladyship. "Put in a good word to Sir Toby's coachman," she told Walshe who knew everybody. That way, it would reach Sir Toby himself. Alf might not be as welcome a guest at The Towers in future. As for their own lordship, she'd have seen both ways to Miss Smail before *he* got back.

She marched into the governess's room early on the following morning with all equipment, and without ceremony pulled down the covers. Miss Smail woke to indignation.

"I must protest at this constant invasion of my privacy. How dare you?"

"You're a bad young woman, that's how I dare. Waiting till his lordship goes off, then going up to that Lord Alfred in the woods. You don't want a baby, do you? That's why I'm here. They'd blame his lordship, and you'd end in a ditch."

She added that if Miss Smail made a nuisance of herself, she'd get Flo and May to hold her down. "Otherwise you'll do as I say, and it'll be needed more than once."

Miss Smail, frightened, had to admit that she didn't want a baby. Further situations would be quite unobtainable. The thought of having Flo and May to hold her down was intolerable. Weeping with outrage, she had to submit to the douche and enema. Her humiliation was complete.

Afterwards Vance went away and then returned with hot milk and something in it. Whatever it was made Miss Smail go off to sleep and continue in that or in a drowsy state, the length of which she was unable to calculate. Lord Corbell visited her often. At least, she thought so.

Angel Alf was savouring the sweets of revenge. Waiting about for Holy Flo on her day off had produced, instead, the governess. It was more than he could have hoped for. He had filled the puny bitch with enough to father the twelve tribes of Israel, if tits that size would let her conceive. Crip fancied himself as a Justice of the Peace, and such persons didn't get the governess in the family way. He, Sissington, had seized her dab of a nose to force her mouth open, as well as her legs. Crip's little shopping-basket had become a writhing mewling bagpipe, stopped at two orifices. It was better than the Etruscan flute. She was well-trodden ground already. He hadn't let himself go to such an extent since Chillingfold's wife in the organ loft at Newbury, or come to that Etta at the Ship and Bladebone. Thinking about dearest Ione in Crip's bed had no doubt started it. but she was running to fat when last seen, though still an armful.

Revenge. Crip had ill-treated him at school, jealous because Cousin Henry preferred him as heir. Crip wouldn't whack him or let them do It, even on the first Lackmere visit. Crip had horsewhipped him in front of Etta, later forbidding him the premises that would one day be his. Crip had taken away Ione out of spite and used her as a brood-mare. At least there had been only Joan till now as a result, and Joan was in his power. Soon, she'd be old enough to seduce. It would be a fitting way of paying Crip back. Crip had a mind as crooked as his body. To reply in kind with the governess had been fitting, for the time.

Jemmy was no longer happy. His sweetheart wasn't the same. Something had happened to her, and Jemmy didn't want any more to do it to her in bed. He had tried to say he wouldn't go down, but Peg had given him something that left him unable to help it. It was like a driving fire, not kindly. He felt himself hurting and stretching her, thrusting too hard and too long, making her cry. It wasn't the way it had been between them, and Peg stood over him and drove him on. Twice now she'd whipped him, to make him want it. That had had to be risked in her own room, as his stinging buttocks wouldn't travel in the cart. They'd cried together later while they were made to do it, he and his sweetheart. Jemmy wanted to take her away to where they could be private. There was nowhere; somebody guarded him always. They continued to make him need it, and his huge parts ploughed her. The two of them weren't innocent together any more.

*   *   *   *

In Ireland, Corbell received a letter from Sir Toby Penhaligon. It said nothing about Alf, but related the discovery of certain interesting letters from Calais which might well be of benefit to the business. If Corbell could help him decipher them, he would make it worth his while. Could he stay a night or two at The Towers on his way home?

Corbell immediately thought of Miss Smail. Her precision could decipher anything. He wrote to accept Sir Toby's invitation. The Towers stood within easy distance of Lackmere.

A second witness than Walshe had seen, quite separately, the governess laid down beneath Lord Sissington. Holy Flo had been the reason why he was there at all. It was her day off, and he'd promised her, as usual, a little ride round the premises, with a bit of fun beneath the hood of Sir Toby's two-wheeler while he, Alf, kept the reins safely looped over his wrist. After that Flo could be dropped off where her absent-minded old aunt had a cottage, and never knew whether or not to expect her on days off.

Flo was incensed at the sight of the governess receiving, whether she liked it or not, Alf's favours instead of herself. It was a waste of what he was good at. It was best to take herself off, and she did so without being noticed and said nothing to anybody. However, the sight had reminded her that she wanted to be near Lord Alf without fail, and no more waiting about in draughts and the dark hoping he'd turn up. If only there was a place at The Towers, she'd like to be there instead of at Lackmere, with old Vance prying and dosing. On her next free day, Flo dressed in her best and sauntered along there, asking the lodge-keeper if they could use a good worker with a sound reference. She hadn't brought it with her, she said, but would ask.

The sequel, not long before Alfred received his *congé* from Sir Toby, was that Flo was to be found sweeping out The Towers' guest corridor, having seen a good deal of the goings-on. Between Friday and Monday each week Lord Alfred was up there, leaving various bedrooms early. He couldn't escape Flo, busy with her broom. Twice he obliged in a cupboard, but in a hurried fashion. Truth to tell he had been getting sick of Flo anyway and had had

193

enough to keep him busy all night with the guests. One day he tenderly handed Flo an envelope sealed on the back with red wax and the imprint of his crest, from his signet ring. He said he wanted to see much more of Flo at his own place in London, and to hand the letter to Mrs Spicer, his housekeeper, whose name was on the envelope with an address in St. James's.

He gave Flo the fare and, believing every word, she packed her things and left The Towers without notice. She had never been to London before and found the tall houses grander than anything. Lord Alfred's proved to be one in a row where they all looked the same, except that his had a sign hanging out in the light wind, with a coffee-pot on it. The streets were full of more people than Flo had ever seen in her life, all dressed differently, and the air was full of cries of ribbons for sale and the rumbling of carriage-wheels on the cobbles. She'd have to get used to the noise.

Mrs Spicer opened the door in her frilled cap and black apron. She looked Flo up and down, then took the letter. Reading it she made out *Flo is a hard worker I can recommend personally. For God's sake get her off me. Yours ever, Alf.*

Mrs Spicer smiled. "Come in, dearie. You'll need a change of dress for working here."

Flo was given a glass of wine. Shortly a gentleman came in upstairs. He wasn't Lord Alfred, as she could just see through the haze caused by the wine. After that there were several gentlemen, all very well-mannered. It took some time for Flo to realise that she might not be seeing Lord Alf quite yet, perhaps never again. It was no good flouncing out; the young ladies weren't allowed back on the street till they had begun to earn their keep, and by that time they'd got used to it. In its way it was like Mrs Udney's Bureau, with a percentage taken, and you could earn extra money if you wanted to, by offering for the whipping-parlour on the third floor. At first the thought of that reminded Flo of Vance and that she might as well have stayed where she was. However, it was worth it to have money to spend. She was let out by then, and after all the occupation suited her much better than sweeping somebody else's corridor while they had all the fun. The food wasn't too bad either. Once or twice she sent a note to her aunt to say she was in a good place, but didn't give any address. On the whole, she forgave Lord Alf.

*   *   *   *

Peggy had decided to give Jemmy and Miss Smail a rest. Not only was Jemmy becoming violent and most unlike himself, and might even be a danger to Agnes up at the cottage, but the powders she herself was giving him were expensive, having come from India. Miss Smail was looking peaked, which might mean they'd done their job. His lordship would be back soon, and there must be no awkward encounters. Altogether Vance stopped the powders and enemas and sedatives, and told the governess to get dressed and take a little walk for the sake of fresh air. Miss Smail demurred, afraid of meeting Lord Alfred again.

"He won't be at The Towers this time of the week. In any case have the sense to keep away from the wicket."

Miss Smail went off, wordlessly, in her plain bonnet and dun clothes. She had become obedient, like one of the servants. Vance couldn't spare anyone to go with her. There was a good deal to be done pending his lordship's return. A household grew slack in the absence of its master. As for her ladyship, she no longer went for walks, preferring to save up appearances for clerical visits. There was a new clergyman nobody knew much about. The one they'd had before, who'd succumbed to his nerves and often came to tea, had left wherever he was and, had become like the fourth lord, preaching straight out of his head and going where he liked. He must be feeling more confident.

Corbell was no snob, and liked old Toby Penhaligon despite his occasional crashing vulgarities. He made no bones about his origins, having as a boy blacked boots outside a certain hotel in Albemarle Street. So successful was he at it that the mirror-bright results aroused curiosity in the minds of the mighty. Young Toby didn't tell them his mother made the polish from a recipe of her own; he pretended it was the secret one used by Beau Brummell containing champagne among other ingredients. The Prince Regent would have given his ears for the entire recipe, or receipt as it was known then; and he, Toby, had sworn not to divulge it. He didn't explain how he happened to know it, but the results spoke for themselves. When he had made enough in tips he began to sell the polish in tins labelled Penhaligon's Special, but making no written claims.

The sales paid off, and after Toby's mother had died in well-earned comfort he took an assistant who couldn't speak or write. Such things happen to the fortunate, and over the years Toby became an extremely rich man, investing shrewdly and taking an informed interest in the Turf. In this way he met the Prince of Wales, soon lent him money, and was able to marry a much younger wife with the right connections. Some thought Penhaligon Towers an excrescence in red sandstone, with its pepper-pot turrets obtruding violently on the landscape, but nobody refused Eileen Penhaligon's invitations. Sir Toby, as he had become, was proud of his house, his wife and their two small sons, following whose arrival he let Eileen do as she liked. Corbell, reflecting on all this over the excellent dinner provided in his host's private wing, told himself he would allow the same freedom to Ione if only she would deliver the goods, as Sir Toby himself would have put it. They appeared to be safely on the way. Corbell had sent word to Vance of his whereabouts without going into detail as to why he was here.

The sight of Sir Toby's purchase, certain letters found in France, had at first disappointed him; the paper was cheap and the ink faded to brown. On further examination his French couldn't immediately cope. It appeared that the contents had been deliberately obscured. "It's an acrostic," he said suddenly.

"Knew you had somethin' above the ears. Bought it from a feller who said he got it in Calais. Tried to blackmail me, sayin' they contain the real Brummell receipt and I'd been tradin' all these years on a fib. I didn't bat an eyelid. I've never put any such claim on the tins." He closed one eye. He had told the man that the way to treat a blackmailer, if that was what he thought himself, was to expose him, and that he'd tell the police. "That scared him," Sir Toby said. In the end the man had parted with the letters for much less than he'd asked, having signed an affidavit to the effect that there was no copy. "By now, it don't matter to me one way or the other about boot polish – I make enough all ways – but the tale's interestin'. If as you say they've disguised it so's it can't be read by any Tom, Dick or Harry, it might make a luxury item, at that."

He lit a cigar, Corbell having declined one. The fragrance filled the room. "Can't endure these cigarettes," Sir Toby remarked. "Smell of burnt paper."

"Brummell died mad," said Corbell. "He'd revolutionised English dress, however."

"Fled to Calais, deep in debt, after fallin' out with Prinny. Sponged on his friends in England for years, but couldn't come home. Last sane thing he did was to send a snuff-box to King George IV, as he'd then become, when he passed through Calais on his way to Hanover. The box was said to contain a letter askin' the King to receive him. Prinny wouldn't, but sent back the box with a £100 note in it. He was sorry for Brummell because he was wearin' a black stock, which in the old days he'd said should never be done by any gentleman as it proved he couldn't pay for laundry. Later Prinny made Brummell consul at Caen to give him somethin' to live on. It wasn't much of an appointment, but better than nothin'. Poor Brummell died soon, however, in the Calais madhouse."

"This letter says the snuff-box had contained something more when Brummell sent it to the King, but that it was stolen before it reached him. It may have been the secret recipe."

"Which is in the acrostic, eh?"

"I can make nothing of that, but I know someone who might." He thought again of Miss Smail. He had allowed desire for her body to occlude the possibilities of her mind. If she found the answer to what was clearly a money-making concern, he'd buy her a pair of silk stockings.

"What will you call this new brand, if we decipher the recipe? Penhaligon Particular would conjure up the era."

"And we could charge all hell for it. Stay for a day or two, Corbell," said Sir Toby, looking suddenly lonely. "Eileen's expectin' guests for the Friday to Monday. They's a giddy lot here now."

The guests would be cavorting in the upper corridor. He needn't meet them. He wanted a closer look at these letters, from early in the century, and to give them as soon as possible to Miss Smail.

Corbell stayed at The Towers for two nights, with little Lady Penhaligon flitting in and out like a friendly robin while she made ready in the main part of the house for the accustomed Friday to Monday guests. The fashionably notorious guest corridor upstairs, with its myriad rooms inviting sin at night by arrangement below the pepper-pots, was part of the *mores* of the

Prince of Wales's set, to which the Penhaligons almost, but not yet quite, belonged. Guests should have included this time again, Eileen informed Corbell brightly, a cousin of his, Lord Sissington, who was of course most amusing. Her husband and he had met at Goodwood some years ago now. However, he couldn't come this time, such a pity.

Sir Toby closed one eye.

"Want it," said Jemmy.

He was always fretful on Sundays, when he wasn't allowed it, Agnes thought; but this wasn't the sabbath. She was baking griddle cakes on the fire and didn't turn her head. "I can't take you down today, Jemmy, and that's that." She couldn't explain why, which was that Peggy had said his lordship was coming back and Jemmy must be kept out of the way meantime. It was easier said than done. He kept saying, "Want it, want it," and if thwarted could take one of his fits. The door was hooked up and he couldn't get out unless she let him, but she was beginning to be almost afraid of being left with him alone. He was big and strong now, and knew his own needs. He hadn't the wit to push up the hook for himself.

Agnes was affected with sudden weariness. It had been going on long enough by now for what Peggy wanted to happen if it was going to. If not, she herself couldn't spend her life waiting to take Jemmy up and down in the cart and watching what he did when he got there. It didn't, when you thought of it, matter as much as all that if the Tessons came to an end. Everyone did, and what were they now but cottage folk and servants? They would never own the manor or be grand folk again.

Agnes wiped a stray lock of grey hair from her forehead and straightened from bending over the cakes. They'd burn if she left them, and in a minute or two they'd be ready, good and fresh. She went to the door and undid the hook.

"Go out if you want." Peggy would prevent his getting into the house or upstairs. She couldn't spend her own life helping matters. She'd done her best, bringing up little Margaret and marrying her to George. It was God's will what had happened. Perhaps this notion of Peggy's was displeasing to God.

Jemmy had already slouched out. He was singing. He would

find his sweetheart. The trees swallowed him, with their long shadows darkening the moss. He would like to lay her down on it, the green moss. It would make them a soft bed, and he would kiss her and do it to her there for a long time, and they would be happy again.

Corbell had been driven from The Towers in the small cabriolet, with the Calais papers in his pocket for Miss Smail. However, he did not go straight to the house. The back road was more direct, and he wanted to avoid waiting correspondence and tiresome talk. Also, a painting he had made of the west front of Lackmere should be dry in the folly by now and ready for varnishing. Meantime, he was free to enjoy his woods and the turning trees. He directed the driver not to wait. He would return to The Towers tonight in his own carriage, having with hope obtained the answer to the acrostic to take back with him.

He limped in the direction of the folly, using his cane; and shortly perceived the slight figure of Miss Smail herself, appreciating the autumn colours in her dun dress and bonnet. He resolved to give her the papers to decipher later on. Meantime, he hadn't had her for three weeks.

He made towards her and grasped her by the arm. She started slightly. Corbell led her into the folly. The nostalgic scent of pine cones and varnish rose, left from the summer's sun.

He brought out the papers and wasting no time, opened Miss Smail's bodice and stuffed the envelope well down behind her stays. He didn't close her up again, intending to enjoy the little apples presently. "I want you to decipher that," he told her. "It is a French acrostic. You have studied French, I assume?"

"I was taught it with water-colours and the pianoforte, as an extra subject." She could not, evidently, think of anything except in terms of her profession. He wondered, listening to the flat little voice, why she was essential to him, and felt the need rise.

"Have it ready by the evening if you can. There is a French dictionary on the shelves if you require it." His voice was growing thick. "Get your drawers off. I want to see your cunt."

Miss Smail submissively untied her tapes and let the drawers fall. She tried to retrieve and fold them tidily. "Leave that," he told her. "Lie down on the bench."

He needed bodily relief, and took it. Miss Smail's bonnet had already become a trifle displaced when it occurred to Corbell that not all was as he'd left it. "By God, I'll thrash the skin off your bottom and legs," he said suddenly. "Who was, it? How often? Where?"

She was as wide as a canal. It could only have been one of the servants; nobody else had access to her. He himself had given her a hot little tail, that was it, then had stayed away too long. A session with the crop from the tackroom would teach her a lesson, and Peggy must dose her again. It had been like leaving a little bitch in heat to wander in the open. He felt angry and betrayed.

Miss Smail had begun to snivel. "Only you – only you, the other day again, oh –" It had been like they were now, only she hadn't been able to see clearly without her spectacles. His dark head had bobbed above her then as now, his weight crushing her as always. So often she'd felt like a small plain moth spread on a board, his strong pin thrusting in her to fasten her down. Now, he was angry, and she didn't understand why.

"You lying little bitch, I've been out of the country these three weeks."

"Oh, no – oh, no –" It didn't make sense. He must have found out what had happened up at the wicket, and was blaming her, but it hadn't been her fault. Vance had cleared everything out, had said his lordship must never, never know and that she'd feel the flat of her hand again if she said a word to anybody. Vance's applied hand had quenched several stirrings of independent thought in Miss Smail over the last weeks. By now, she was a drilled, obedient puppet, lacking spirit or will. Lord Corbell was going to thrash her, and she was very much afraid. She began, fearfully, to blurt out the truth as far as she knew it.

"Oh, pray – there was a strange man up at the wicket, and it was not my fault, I don't know who he was, and he –"

"Did he do this to you?" It would be a poacher. There was constant trouble with them, though not of this sort. He ought to have the wicket barred, the pit closed over. The little fool. "Did you go to Peggy? Did she clear you out?" Whoever it was had taken time to widen her. Vance would at least have seen to it that she wasn't pregnant. She was still speaking, the governess, babbling excuses for herself. What, he asked, had she been doing up at the wicket?

"I – I wanted to consult the curate and did not want to go down by the lodge. Oh, pray, do not make me remember any more – it was horrid – but now –"

"The curate does not have the wherewithal to be worth consulting. In any case I have had him sent elsewhere."

The bishop had replied to him in Ireland accordingly. Corbell withdrew, still angry; and having risen from her, turned to face other anger.

Jemmy's face remained a mask as always, but his dark Tesson eyes flashed fire. His hands came up and grasped Corbell by the throat. He found himself trying to make certain sounds. Master Ed had been doing it to his, Jemmy's, sweetheart. He was going to kill him.

Corbell felt the blood thundering in his head, the world swimming round. He recalled defending himself at school; instead of trying to dislodge the fiercely squeezing hands he shot out a strong left, hitting his assailant's jaw. Then he kicked out with his short leg at the other's testicles. Jemmy collapsed, screaming, to the ground. Corbell reached for his cane and began to thrash the contorted shape, continuing till it was nothing more than a whimpering object lacking humanity. He himself felt foolish with his trousers round his ankles; it added to his fury. He'd forgotten Miss Smail, and when he turned round she had gone. She hadn't screamed.

Corbell glanced briefly at Jemmy, who was beginning one of his fits; twitching, eyes rolling upwards in his head with the whites showing, and foam gathering at the edges of his mouth. It would be fortunate if this encounter finished him.

Corbell tidied himself, took the cane and proceeded to follow Miss Smail, then remembered last time, here, with Joan; it had been pointless to mention the matter. The governess would undoubtedly raise the alarm at the house; there was no need to wait.

He picked up his painting, which had fallen from its easel to the ground in the struggle. It wouldn't be the same again. His throat felt stiff and sore already, and he'd grazed his hand. He regretted dismissing Sir Toby's driver; otherwise he could have returned straight to The Towers. As it was, he hoped Miss Smail would have the presence of mind to deal with the acrostic. Other matters regarding her did not, meantime, coalesce; it was unlikely that Jemmy would have been permitted intimacies with her.

201

Miss Smail had been already frightened at the prospect of chastisement, and was doubly so at the sight of two men fighting who greatly resembled one another. She was not in a state to put two and two together, but took time to feel regret that Vance's afflicted grandson had seen her bared. He'd always been respectful.

Unable to bear watching longer, she rose and fled to the house. The first person she encountered was Walshe, on duty in the hall. She blurted out her take to his impassive face.

"They're fighting – Lord Corbell and Jemmy – up at the folly –"

"You should return upstairs, Miss. I will see what can be done."

He was like a wooden figure, she thought. Butlers had to be like that. It was only on regaining her room and the small swing mirror that she realised he'd seen her with her bodice open. She blushed; that was improper. She hoped Lord Corbell wouldn't hurt poor Jemmy too much. She fastened her bodice with uncertain fingers, feeling less conspicuous with it closed.

She had heard Corbell himself arrive when she was halfway up. His voice was cold and even, different from the thick breathing he emitted when within her. It was as though he was two people.

"Mrs Vance's grandson will have to be sent to a place of confinement. He has just tried to assault Miss Smail. I was in time to prevent it."

She wanted to cry out, to deny it, to say what had really happened. She saw them fetch Vance from downstairs, hurrying out bareheaded in her apron. Later she returned red-eyed, but by that time Miss Smail didn't see her. She had gone to lie down, exhausted and trembling; and slept. Through her sleep she heard a carriage drive off. It was Corbell, gone to make arrangements about the death certificate. Everyone had known these fits would kill Jemmy in the end. Peggy had managed to be with him when it happened.

Peggy had run fast up to the folly. The contorted thing on the ground had once been Jemmy. He was still twitching. She knelt and took him in her arms.

"It doesn't matter, Jemmy darling. Let Peg hold you. It doesn't matter. It doesn't –"

The sad eyes, wide open, rolled upwards. They held tears. The fit was over. He spoke clearly, as though the damage to his brain had healed.

"Ed does it to her," he said, then died. She had known he was dying even in the fading light, which wouldn't show his eyes glazing over. She held him for instants, then let go. The doctor would have to come, to sign a paper and say he'd died in his fits. Her trained eye caught sight of some white object lying on the floor in the folly. She rose, and picked up Miss Smail's drawers. Vance rolled them up absently and stuffed them in the pocket of her apron. They could go to the laundry. She knew now what had happened.

If there was a God, Miss Smail was carrying Jemmy's child. It mustn't be lost. She stayed by the body till she saw them come with lanterns. By then it was quite dark.

Miss Smail heard a carriage drive away. Remembering the envelope his lordship had left with her, she fished in her stays and retrieved it. It was her clear duty to decipher it tonight as he'd asked.

With undeviating devotion to duty, Miss Smail set about the task by lamplight. She found the acrostic perfectly simple. Unaware that to keep the answer to herself could make her an extremely rich woman, she stole down to the library and wrote out the answer in her neat copperplate hand, thereafter leaving it under the malachite paperweight. She then went to bed.

Corbell returned in the small hours, after fetching the doctor to Jemmy. He read and pocketed the solved acrostic, returning thereafter to Sir Toby by carriage. The pair of them celebrated till dawn with some excellent brandy the Prince Regent would not have scorned.

Corbell downed his conscience. Lackmere was in mourning, but The Towers needn't be, and neither was he. He would have to travel home to supervise funeral arrangements tomorrow, and listen to whatever the doctor had had to say. It needn't involve him otherwise.

Miss Smail, not anxious for a further visit from Lord Corbell, found it difficult to sleep. The calming effect on her nerves brought about by solving the acrostic had left her, and by now she

203

was in a state of increasing uncertainty.

She had heard Lord Corbell's carriage drive off after his remarks in the hall, then return, then go away a third time. She had stolen down to the library to see if the acrostic was still there; it had gone. The mystery of his comings and goings baffled her. If as he said he had been out of the country for three weeks, she herself must have spent some time in a feverish state; what Vance called her turns. She had never previously been given to them, had always known the time and the date precisely. Now, the changing colours in the woods today had told her it was autumn. More time by far must have gone by than she knew. She had had fevered dreams, illusions, been given Vance's constant cures and medication; and yet tonight, she had seen a man fight his shadow. That had been real. She hoped Walshe had been as good as his words and had helped Jemmy, left badly hurt at the folly. She wasn't clear why he had attacked Lord Corbell. A great deal went on at Lackmere that she didn't know about.

Remembering Walshe, she remembered also that he had seen her in a state of partial undress. Worse, she'd left her drawers on the floor of the folly. She must go up and retrieve them as soon as possible. She only had one spare pair, and in any case it wouldn't do for them to be found.

On the other hand she didn't want to walk up there alone again. What had happened to Jemmy she didn't know, and the earlier unpleasantness up at the wicket proved it wasn't safe to go unescorted. She had never had to think of such things before; plain and self-effacing, nobody had ever noticed her. The world of mathematics had been her refuge, and only Mr Chillingfold, who had been sent away unkindly by Lord Corbell, had shared it. There was nobody left now to whom she could turn. Vance made her afraid.

In any case Vance didn't seem to be about. No doubt she was up at the cottages with Jemmy. The house was quite silent; now it was nearing morning there was usually a quiet awareness of movements from the servants, cleaning and weeping and lighting the fires. Everything had to be ready, and they themselves out of the way, before their betters woke up and came out. Miss Smail no longer felt like one of their betters, or like anybody, even herself.

It was past dawn, and she rose and dressed miserably. She was hungry; now she thought of it, with all the stir yesterday they hadn't sent up any supper. Miss Smail opened her Bible and read a portion of the Book of Joshua to pass the time till breakfast, but today even the trumpets bringing down the walls of Jericho had a flat uninspiring note. Miss Smail rose from her chair and drank some water from the ewer. No breakfast appeared, and in the end she ventured to go and knock on Vance's door. There was no reply. Certainly nothing was as usual. Miss Smail resolved to go down to the kitchens and look for some food.

There was still no sign of anybody, but a single presence blocked her way; Walshe, in his shirt-sleeves. Deliberately making herself forget his improper sight of her yesterday evening, she asked if she might have something to eat. Everybody seemed to be elsewhere.

"I can bring you a bit of bread and cold meat. They're all up at poor Jemmy's wake. I'm waiting here in case his lordship comes back from The Towers, and needs shaving and that." He added that Lord Corbell had gone to fetch the doctor to Jemmy last night, but he'd already died in one of his fits. Mrs Vance had been with him.

The news hit Miss Smail like a blow in the stomach. If Jemmy had died in a fit, Lord Corbell had brought it on with his cane. She wouldn't say anything. She waited till Walshe returned with the bread and meat on a plate, and a cup of yesterday's milk from the farm. He couldn't make coffee, he explained, none of the fires being lit.

She began to eat and drink hungrily, but Walshe seemed inclined to talk. "We won't be hearing Jemmy's snatch of song again," he remarked. "He used to make it when he was happy with himself, instead of talking, which he couldn't."

Miss Smail found herself visited by sudden dire certainty. She'd heard the song only once, a tuneless note, after loving-kindness and a rain of kisses that weren't Lord Corbell's way as a rule. Afterwards, after the nastiness at the wicket, it had become like they'd been at first, hard usage of her, then rising too soon.

An awareness of what had been done to her was becoming clear in her mind. It had started when she saw the two men fight, looking like each other. The reason for what might have happened was, however, not clear, and without reason there could be no certainty. Miss Smail clung to this resolution with the shreds of

205

her sanity. Nevertheless, Lord Corbell, by his own admission, had been away three weeks.

Miss Smail suddenly slid to the ground in a dead faint. The food remained half-eaten on the table.

There are two things a man can do when a young woman faints in his sole company. One is to revive her. Walshe did the other. The cook wasn't available till Thursday for natural reasons, and he had a lot saved up. Having achieved matters in some haste lest anybody return too soon, he got off the governess again, put back her clothes the way they'd been, fastened himself and made off. Their two lordships could take the blame if he'd left more in Miss than intended. As for Jemmy – oh, he'd heard him come and go – he was dead, and that was that.

Presently, from the kitchens, he heard Miss Smail get up and go out, evidently having noticed nothing out of the ordinary. Walshe took a piece of the cold meat she hadn't touched, and ate it himself. It wasn't certain when anyone would be back, or his lordship either; a wake could go on for days. Sam at the cottages would have made the coffin already. It was his own plain duty to wait here for his lordship. He'd best light the kitchen fire to boil some water for when they all came back. He'd been on the way to do it when he'd been interrupted by that Miss Smail.

Chapter Six

Miss Smail had got up from the floor, aware that she must have taken one of her turns. Her legs were shaky, as they had not been when she came downstairs. The thought of climbing up again was unwelcome. She remembered that she ought to go to the folly to ensure that her drawers had been removed, or else to retrieve them. There was food still left on the table, but she didn't feel like eating. She set out, gradually recovering as she walked. It was a grey day, and might rain.

The way up was deserted, and having ensured that the folly had been cleared of signs of her presence, the governess saw a grey-haired figure come in sight. It was Agnes Tesson, whom Miss Smail had seen now and again at household prayers. Her own presence seemed to be anticipated.

"Peggy Vance sent me to fetch you. She wants you to see him before they close the coffin. Beautiful he looks, the way he ought to have been."

The cottage was full of people, in the way those who have ignored the living come together unfailingly in time less for the death than for the funeral. Many who had jeered at Jemmy and excluded him were present, heads bowed, part of the accepted community. Vance sat at the coffin's head without expression, and did not look up.

"So you're here," she said.

Miss Smail looked down. It was the first time she had seen a dead person and the way the flesh smooths out over the bones. Jemmy, now his dark eyes were closed, had a distinct resemblance to the general when young. A bruise had darkened the right side of his jaw. Otherwise he seemed peaceful, even smiling. Miss Smail, obeying an urge she didn't recognise, reached out one small hand and touched his cheek. It was cold and hard, like set wax. Wherever he was now, perhaps he knew she'd touched him. Her hand fell to her side. Rain was beginning its muffled patter on the thatch of the roof. Vance suddenly spoke, with her eyes still fixed on Jemmy's face.

"You'd best wait and come back with me in the cart. The road will be wet."

"I should prefer to walk." She had a sudden dislike of being near Vance, a desire to get away.

"No, you'll wait for the cart. They're closing him now. We won't stay."

She stood up, a tall woman with dead eyes. The rest started to leave, and Sam, the man who'd made the coffin, lifted on the lid. Vance turned away and shepherded Miss Smail out to the cart. Miss Smail obeyed, again a cipher. The others, Agnes among them, stood and watched the cart go off.

It trundled down the path between the woods. Miss Smail didn't ask about her drawers. Instead she said timidly, out of the silence, that Jemmy had looked very much like the general.

"That's not surprising. He was his grandson. It don't matter who knows now."

Too much was happening at once, and too much information poured into her ears in the jolting open cart, with the rain increasing in strength even among the sheltering trees and soaking her thin clothes as she sat. It left Miss Smail shivering and confused about the history of the Tessons and Corbells, even poor Maria Tesson's curse on all of the name. As far as she could understand it, both Lord Corbell and Jemmy had been part Tesson from Jocosa, and surprisingly from Vance herself, who had borne a daughter to the general. At that rate everybody was accursed; Lord Corbell with his twisted spine, Jemmy with his damaged brain, the unknown Etta with her deafness. "What this heir will be that her ladyship expects to bear his lordship now, time will tell," said Peggy in a tone that boded no good.

Miss Smail was made aware, for the first time, that Lord and Lady Corbell were expecting a child. That meant that she herself was, as Vance had once said, a bad young woman. Again, she hadn't asked for it. She felt herself overcome by a deep and penetrating tiredness. All she wanted was to be left alone. She hoped Lord Corbell wouldn't come back tonight, or that if so he wouldn't come upstairs.

"If he's back, you'll give him what he wants," said Peggy firmly. It was becoming essential, with the confusion over Lord Alfred, that their own lordship should assume fatherhood of any child there might be. Miss Smail was beginning to snivel, as Vance called it, and to say again she didn't want it. "I'm tired, and he says he'll beat me because of the man at the gate. I had to tell him because he knew I'd been with someone else." She began to whimper. Vance had earlier promised punishment once again if she said anything at all. The person she'd formerly been would not have put up with any of it. What had become of her, where had she really been, during the times she couldn't clearly remember? What was to happen now? The future, when she thought of it, was full of fear. Mrs Udney wouldn't take back a bad young woman.

Miss Smail did not return upstairs after entering the house. She went into the smaller drawing room, the one where Lord Corbell had first interviewed her. She stared at the pale ruined blur of her own reflection in the cracked mirror. It was the face of a lost soul. She mustn't stay here. Lord Corbell had lied about Jemmy after killing him. She would have that on her mind for the rest of her life, and the sight of Jemmy's dead face in his coffin. There was evil here, and she'd shared in it. She must leave without a reference, before Lord Corbell returned.

She gripped her reticule, which as always accompanied her. There was enough money in it to take the post-chaise to London. Once there, she would appeal to Mrs Udney. Her former situation had provided her with enough references. She didn't care what she took; there would surely be something available. The main thing was to leave in time not to miss the post-coach, and she must walk the length of the path to the lodge. If they questioned her there, she would say she had been urgently called away.

Rising, lips set firmly, she went out. It was still raining, and by the time she reached the gates she would perhaps be soaked if it worsened; but perhaps it would cease. Miss Smail wrapped her cloak about her with the reticule secured; it contained money, a handkerchief and a comb. She could buy other necessaries; she hadn't spent much, living here.

The lake was grey, with little spatterings of raindrops on its surface. Miss Smail walked on, seeing them worsen. The rain grew worse, and it became necessary to shelter under a tree. By now, there was danger of having missed the post-coach; but she wouldn't go back. Somebody, the new clergyman at church who didn't know her, would surely shelter her for the night. He might know where Mr Chillingfold had gone. A faint ray of hope reached Miss Smail, growing soaked beneath her tree; a wind had risen, driving in the rain. It was growing dark early. She huddled within her wet clothing. Whether or not it had been a mistake to come, she wouldn't go back. It was a matter of principle. She had forgotten her principles lately, and deserved to suffer for it. To be cold and wet was not a matter of life and death; she'd dry out in the coach, or the vicarage. She didn't know where that was, but would ask.

Time passed. The rain was pelting down. To enter the post-coach looking like a drowned rat wouldn't do. Even the vicar might hesitate to admit her, or his servant if he had one. She knew very little about such people. Somebody had said Mr Chillingfold had become a lay preacher. He would certainly help her in some way if only she could reach him. He might be nearer than London.

A flash of lightning came, and terrified her. Others had been struck by it beneath trees. The rain was coming down in sheets, and thunder pealed. Miss Smail had to admit that she didn't know what to do. She stood there, shivering and frightened. The path was in deep puddles, and to walk was itself hardly possible now. In fact, it had become impossible to do anything but stay where she was. The danger was that they might come looking for her, but that was unlikely until the rain had stopped. She must simply be patient, and move on when it could be done. Dark was, however, about to fall, and the storm was wild. It wasn't what she was used to.

Suddenly she heard the distant lodge gates clang; a carriage was approaching, its lamps already lit. The blaze blinded Miss Smail for instants, and she shielded her eyes. The puddles splashed as the horse's hooves disturbed them, spurting up water and making her already wet skirts sodden; they clung against her knees. She hoped the carriage would pass by, as it was going towards Lackmere; but it drew up. The near door opened and Lord Corbell's arm reached out, and pulled her in. It was useless to resist; the lamps had outlined her, shrinking against the bole of the tree. There was no escape now, none. He'd been drinking spirits; his hands explored her bodice and slid up under her skirts. The driver started up again and the carriage splashed on. In the far distance, there were lights in Lackmere windows. The rain was slackening, too late.

Corbell had returned from a short journey in a brittle temper. The digging of poor Jemmy's grave had revived an antique quarrel over boundaries, and he had had to drive to reassure the cheeseparing old owner of the abutting acres that any trespass would be paid for. Corbell had more than once offered to buy the whole adjoining field, as the present cemetery was overcrowded and when his own time came, the vault being full, there might be no room for a fitting tomb. After a tiresome cent-per-cent discussion, his host had surprisingly produced some excellent brandy. The genial afterglow had still been with him when, driving home, the carriage-lights had picked out the figure of his little whore, cowering beneath a tree. No doubt she was there for an assignation which hadn't been kept owing to the weather. He resolved to show her who was best at it, and pulled her in. Exploring Point O, he concluded she'd been at it already; the man, whichever servant it had been, had gone.

Droit de seigneur took place again. She couldn't help it, couldn't get away. She heard her own moaning begin, drowned by the ruthless drumming of rain on the carriage roof and the rhythmic clop-clop of the bay's hooves among the puddles. For that reason the driver was taking the lake path slowly. It had never seemed as long. The yellow lamps jogged against the fading daylight. At last they outlined the portico. Miss Smail by then was almost too exhausted to climb out. She made her way uncertainly up the few steps, not knowing how she'd face the stairs. The rain had soaked her to the skin, and she began to shiver. Hands grasped her and half-carried her upstairs. She hadn't known Vance was back. The burial must be over.

Vance had decided to give Miss a warm hip-bath; she seemed chilled to the bone. It would have to be done quickly; his lordship would be up after he'd dined. She saw Miss to her room, and had the maids, returning by now, hasten to bring up cans of water warmed by Walshe's lighted fire. Miss Smail, having been undressed, crouched naked in the bath, while Vance poured warm water over her, rubbed her down and then dried her with fresh towels before putting her in a clean dry nightdress and into bed. She tried to persuade herself that there was a slight darkening of the nipples, an early sign; but it wasn't certain.

The bath was removed. Miss Smail lay in bed, frightened of the prospect of Lord Corbell's uneven footsteps. He'd said he was going to thrash her. Vance had gone, and there was nobody left to help or explain. She didn't want to be disturbed. She wanted to sleep.

Corbell had left the driver to take in his baggage. He had mounted the box and himself drove the carriage along to the stables. He used up some of his anger by rubbing the bay horse down, then went to the tackroom to select the crop. She'd been at it again today while he was elsewhere; that had continued to be evident. He would dine, then go up. He thrust the crop in his pocket, having divested himself of his coat. He returned to the house, fingering the unyielding leather. Miss Smail wouldn't find it as easy to lie down under a man tomorrow.

Corbell went in to dinner as he was; Ione dined in her room these days. The crop jutted from his pocket inconveniently and while eating, he removed it, placing it beside him and grasping it again when he came out. He looked forward to chastising Miss Smail. Afterwards, he'd take her again. The adage of a woman, a dog and a walnut tree might apply.

However, Peggy was sitting in the chair below the general's portrait. She rose, her tall figure in black mourning.

"You're not going to use that on her." She hadn't failed to see the crop. Something of the kind might be expected. She stood with the general behind her, an ally. Corbell recalled that she must have known his grandfather.

"She couldn't help any of it," Vance said. "I want a word with your lordship."

She had made up lies, based on what she had found out about Holy Flo before she'd left. That Lord Alfred had forced Miss Smail to meet him up at the wicket weekly. He'd made her come with him, on carriage-rides, and scared her into letting him make use of her. If she didn't he said he would tell the agency she let Corbell visit her in bed. That would mean she would never get another situation. It was a weak story, but better than letting his lordship know about Jemmy; she herself might lose her place if that came out. "She'd be afraid to tell you if she's pregnant; it's either his or your own," Vance finished. "He would try to give her a child on purpose, to lower your name in the county. She's too innocent to know what's happened; that sort know nothing. I've rinsed her out for both of you, and that's as much as I can do. Let her stay on upstairs; she needn't be seen, and I can have it adopted at the farms."

"Are you certain there is a child?" he asked. His anger had evaporated. Repeated experiences with Alfred would no doubt have widened her. As for earlier today, God knew. Between them, he and Alf might have given her a taste for it. One way and another, Miss Smail was not to blame; but a child of Alfred Sissington's should not continue at Lackmere after the birth.

He had only too much reason to remember Sissington already. On returning to Sir Toby with the triumphant solving of the acrostic riddle by Miss Smail, the old entrepreneur had said, "Clever little woman," but looked grave.

"There's bad news there, Corbell, I'm afraid. My coachman tells me your cousin Alfred laid down the governess some time ago at your rear gate, and did her wrong when she wasn't willing. My man was informed by your man Walshe, who saw it happen. I've sent word across here that if Lord Alf is on the premises, he's to go. He can take the small carriage and leave it to be collected at the station. I had a bit of a tantrum from Eileen, who's fond of him and he entertains the guests; but she knows I'm in charge here when it comes to it. He won't show his face again at The Towers; can't have that kind of thing, whatever else goes on."

Corbell had left, with the promise that a contract would be drawn up regarding Penhaligon Particular. Sir Toby added that they should give the young woman some money. "No, I pay her a salary and she takes her orders," said Corbell. The idea of an independent Miss Smail was distasteful. In spite of what had happened, he was relieved that it had been Alfred then and later, and not some stranger.

He questioned Walshe, who was evasive; no, he hadn't liked to intervene, being his lordship's cousin. No, he didn't know anything else that had happened, or if it had. Corbell didn't question Peggy again. After dinner he took a lamp and went upstairs.

Miss Smail was lying in bed, her head turned away. Corbell set down the lamp and pulled down the covers, then lifted her nightdress up to her shoulders, leaving her exposed. He took the lamp and examined her abdomen and breasts, without touching her. Her mouth drooped, fearfully; she was expecting to be beaten. He heard himself speak, coldly.

"I understand that you may be with child by my cousin Sissington. If that is the case, you may stay here till you have recovered from the birth; it will be taken away and fostered elsewhere. You will then be given a reference in order to return to your former profession. Most women in your position are less fortunate."

He was staring at her naked pussy, tempted; but heard her voice, in a whisper like a child's.

"No, please – not now, not again, I'm tired."

He flung back the covers, picked up the lamp and went out; his uneven gait caused shadows to dance crazily on the walls. Left again in darkness, Miss Smail turned on her side and drew up her knees in the foetal position, and slept. She hadn't troubled to pull down her nightdress. It didn't seem to matter any more.

Corbell was still not physically satisfied; the time in the coach had been too short. It occurred to him that Ione's pregnancy was sufficiently advanced by now to permit of a small marital foray. He made his way down to the master bedroom, finding the way almost unfamiliar.

Ione was in bed, but not alone. Rising from her, in disarray at sight of him, was Fred.

*   *   *   *

214

Corbell was unaware of the persistence of any sensation except sight. Ione's mouth had fallen open in what appeared to be a soundless scream. A shutter then closed in Corbell's mind. He was aware thereafter of swimming in the lake, its cool benison cleansing him from some unremembered and appalling experience. He had no idea of how he had come to be there, no memory of taking off his clothes. Naked as the primal Adam, he breasted the water with strong strokes, hearing the new, laboured breaths that had come lately, no longer as when he was young. Nevertheless this was his loved element, making him equal to other men, perhaps more powerful. It was natural that he should find himself here now: but why?

While swimming, he noticed curiously that the knuckles of both his hands were grazed and bleeding. He had no recollection of having struck anything or anyone.

He came out at last, found his robe lying in the boathouse and put it on. It was night, but Corbell knew his way blindfold. The stars were in any case bright enough, with no moon. It was like the time he had come out early to the frozen lake at Christmas and had seen the white ghost on the opposite side which might or might not be Jocosa.

That had been long ago. He tried to bring himself back to the present. He still could not recall what had happened, but there came to him by then a faint recollection of unpleasantness, the smell of horse and human sweat, straw, manure, great fear. He began to shiver, and thought of solace, but for some forgotten reason was unwilling by now to go to Ione. He made his way inside, and upstairs to the governess's room.

It seemed some time since he had climbed the attic stairs, and he took them slowly; but the swim had strengthened him. He came to the familiar door and opened it, closing it again silently after him.

Miss Smail was after all asleep, lying on her side, her head tucked down among the covers, her knees drawn up in the position no doubt occupied in the unimaginable womb. She was breathing audibly, almost snoring. The sound amused him; evidence of the fallibility of all women when taken unawares. Miss Smail would no longer be expecting him up here by now, so late. He drew down the covers carefully; and beheld a miracle.

The moon had not yet risen, but the stars were bright enough

215

to reveal Miss Smail's single unsuspected and incomparable beauty, seen for the first time where the skimpy nightgown had in some way rucked itself up, perhaps in sleep. Her small round pearly buttocks were perfect, irresistible. He gazed on them with a kind of wonder, a growing and inevitable desire. At the same time he thought how innocent she still was despite him, unaware of this very asset, the charity-school authorities undoubtedly having failed to provide two full-length mirrors. He recalled Yolande's having told him of being made to undress in girlhood beneath provided covering to have a bath, left unaware of her own white body; and Miss Smail had certainly never been permitted to know, by reflection or any other means, that from the back she was as beautiful as Psyche. Recalling that Cupid had not, after all, been known to avail himself of this aspect, Corbell quietly, easing his twisted body upon her, climbed in.

She stirred a little, then as he entered her from the back began to cry out in desolation and pain, face pressed hard against the pillow.

"Lie still," Corbell heard himself murmur, too greatly enchanted to say more than made it clear that this way, he needn't use the condom. That this should be Galatea after all, in the guise of Ganymede, furthered his delight. He understood now why he had felt so unaccountable an attraction. He was reassured as well as transported.

Miss Smail, still face down, had begun to emit small whimpering sounds like a betrayed puppy. It had been necessary to adjust her limbs, and he did so as if by habit. The familiar creaking of the bed began, and he told himself he didn't care who heard, Peggy or any other. This was paradise, and solaced him for whatever it was he could not immediately recall. He was Jupiter, king of the gods, the white bull, the proud eagle; with Ganymede, his chosen boy; his boy-girl. The blessed catharsis, the free release of seed up into her, came. Miss Smail was crying out by now in an ecstasy she herself did not understand; a harsh unaccustomed sound, while her buttocks at last responded quivering to the sudden attack of a wet god, Poseidon, come from the sea. Her shocked mind could not entirely grasp what had happened. Corbell knew he would never willingly return to her in any other way. This, for the third time in his life, was fulfilment.

Elation was still with him when he rose at last and left her. The

216

stars had gone and daylight would soon break; he wanted to extend his lightness, his joy, in some fashion. He covered up the owner of the pearly pates, having used her till she was flaccid; and went out of the room and downstairs. Down, ever down he must go, limping to the cellar, the place of his earlier discovery, the Roman pavement itself, to give thanks to the heathen gods. His short limb seemed to aid him as if it were grown the equal of the other, or else perhaps he had come to be one of them, the gods; Hephaestus, lame Vulcan, married to Venus for her punishment in having refused to submit to great Jupiter, but he himself was Jupiter now, or had lately been so all night, in the attic room. He would light a black candle to his newfound Ganymede among the phallic tiles, flat images of Ishtar, Anubis, every god but the God of his father, and Horus' eye. He heard his own laughter; then, when he reached the cellar at last, the blood went back to his heart in cold shock at the sight that lay on the tiles themselves.

Fred was lying there, dead. His neck had been broken; the head lay awry, its features punched till they were almost unrecognisable. The blood on the faceless remains had dried by now, the gaping mouth emitting a blackened tongue. Fred's enormous parts protruded beyond his breeches, as happens with hanged men. He was already stiffening. There was a halter about his neck, the one from the stables. Corbell could remember, now, taking it down from its place. He could remember, now in part, most things. All this could only have been done by himself. There came again a transient recollection of certain smells, chiefly that of fear. It rose strongly, to the added memory of the condemned man's whining.

The body must be concealed; but where? Had he thought of it already, killing coldly, having duly planned the tomb?

There were tombs in plenty nearby. Whatever was to be done must be done at once, before the servants were about first thing in the morning.

From where it hung, Corbell took down the heavy vault key. He ascended the further steps, opened the door at the passage end, and surveyed the rows of identical stone lids. Inside were coffins of varying sizes; his mind worked coldly and clearly now. His mother's would be small. He owned Anna Corbell little enough in life. She could shield him from arrest, unwittingly, after death.

He took the lighted lamp he had brought to the cellar and

k

placed it at the top of the steps, where it would shed light on both places. Then he took Fred's inconsiderable weight by the scruff. He dragged it along like a dead dog, a sack of coals. The body was not yet totally stiff. Corbell laid it down, heaved the lid off the destined tomb – desperation made him strong enough – and bestowed the corpse, like pliable packing, in the space left between coffin-end and retaining stone wall. Then he replaced the lid, having taken little heed of the coffin or its earlier contents. His mother Anna, inside, would long ago have shrivelled against her bird's bones. Fred he had left in the foetal position, head against folded knees. It was like the barrow-burials from early times. He would think no more of it; if anyone asked for Fred, he had gone about his own business.

Corbell went out, locking the vault and taking the lamp with him. He looked for traces; there were none, except a small dark patch of blood on the tiled floor. Corbell spat, and rubbed it with his hand till it was gone. Then he extinguished the lamp, replaced it and went back upstairs. He found himself in Ione's room, directed by an impulse which was still not clear to him. He remembered that he had in some way felt deep anger and betrayal regarding her.

She was lying in bed, white-faced with terror, her mouth loose, a fool's. "What have you done with him?" she whispered. "Where is he?"

He guessed then what must have happened. He still could not recall it clearly to mind. "The child," he heard himself say aloud. "Is the child mine?"

She began to snivel. "That's all you care about, making your heir. You accustomed me to all of that, then left me alone as if I hadn't any feelings. You've never tried to understand me, never cared for me. You only married me to spite Alfred; oh, I know." Her mouth drooped petulantly, Fred perhaps already forgotten. He had, after all, been only a servant. Corbell could not have been expected to allow him to remain after the discovery.

"Is it my son who will be born, or not? How long has this been continuing?"

She didn't answer. He went to the bed and stood over her, thrusting both hands beneath the covers to feel her belly. A child lay in there; he had no means of telling exactly when it should be born. He remembered the crop. It needn't remain idle. He

218

threatened her as he had threatened his little concubine. Both were whores. "If that proves a bastard you'll pay, expensively and long. I will not, however, touch you till after the birth."

It occurred to him that the late tiger had after all had many opportunities with her; driving her earlier to church alone, exchanging horse-tips often; Corbell knew she indulged in them, as he paid the bills; and in his own turn had indulged her by appearing to notice nothing. He had spoilt her from the beginning, he told himself. He remembered that he hadn't answered her about the fate of Fred, and did so now; it was all she need know. "He has been dismissed," he told her. "You will not see him again."

"Go away. Leave me. Send for Vance or my maid. I feel ill."

"That is nobody's fault but your own." He was, however, disturbed lest she miscarry. "In future a servant will stay always with you," he said, not adding that she was too untrustworthy to be left alone. He would instruct Vance, when she returned, say her ladyship's nerves were being afflicted by her state and that she required constant company. Peggy would, as always, obey unquestioningly. He would leave her with Ione during the day, and at nights would return to his dressing-room, which he should never have left. Nobody would ask about Fred; he had kept to himself, apart, evidently, from this.

Chapter Seven

By then, it was morning. Corbell ordered breakfast to be sent to him in the library, and that otherwise he was not to be disturbed. He was angry when Miss Smail – it seemed another life since she had become Ganymede – nevertheless came quietly in, dressed for outdoors. If she hoped to take advantage of last night's situation, he was not in the mood for it. "Go to your own concerns," he told her, as if he addressed a stranger. She stood there, adamant; she had never looked as plain. She was wearing a bonnet and cape, and he noticed that she carried her ark-shaped hamper.

"I will not detain you long, Lord Corbell. I want to say that I am leaving. What happened last night I will no longer tolerate. It is what Abraham refused to the men of Sodom, and they were destroyed by God."

"Where do you expect to go?" he asked, lifted almost into levity out of his former mood. She wouldn't get past the lodge on foot; they would ask questions, and inform him before allowing her to leave. It was, however, probable that she knew, only too well, the back entry to Lackmere through the woods.

"I am going to seek the protection of the new clergyman in the village. I have not met him, but it does not signify. It is his Christian duty to protect me. I will tell him what has occurred, and trust that he can find me some situation." Her voice faltered.

He envisaged her probable fate as a housekeeper or, just possibly, village schoolmistress, and his own reputation in shreds.

That should not happen. He felt relief; at first he had thought she referred to Fred's murder, then realised she could not know of it. He felt a steely resolve harden in him. He knew very well what to do with Miss Smail.

"The vicar owes me his living," he told her. "He will call you a brazen hussy and show you the door."

It was not strictly true; and the pompous new man had not been here long enough to be transferred on his own intervention, like the bishop's erstwhile nephew-in-law. The laughter of madness began to rise in Corbell. He reached out and took Miss Smail by the wrist, causing her to lay down the hamper. Her face whitened; her mouth, which had regained its prim contours, loosened in the way which had frequently edified him. She had begun to tremble, and turn from white to red.

Corbell had already decided that swift action was the only answer. "Come," he told her, and led her, almost unresisting, to the organ room. He had seldom used her here. This was the bed on which his father had lain with Yolande. He didn't like to be reminded of it; but why allow memory to deter him now? The dead were alive only in recollection.

He loosened the strings of Miss Smail's bonnet and removed it; its presence was pretentious in the circumstances. Then, without pity or hesitation, he tore her gown from neck to navel, the strength of both hands destroying bodice, stays and chemise.

Miss Smail sobbed aloud; it was her only gown. His face had become a demon's, thick brows knitted, eyes bloodshot and glaring. She wondered if he was quite sane. "That will be a sight to intrigue the vicar, will it not?" she heard him say. The gown, lacking support, subsided limply to the floor.

He flung her on the bed face down, tearing the tapes of her drawers and peeling them away to expose her bottom, bared among tumbled linen. Incredibly, after last night her little rear portal was still stubborn. He began to spank her, holding her down with his left hand. A red mist descended, and he had no memory of what happened next. He came to himself with an awareness that someone was scratching at the door. It proved to be Walshe, with a telegram on a tray.

"Thought I should bring this up, m'lord. It's just come."

Corbell shut the door behind himself, tore open the yellow envelope and read the contents. Walshe remained poker-faced, giving no sign, like the good servant he was, of the tantalising glimpse he'd had when the door opened a crack; Miss, arse bare and smacked red as a rose, lying quiet, face down across the bed. It went to show you never knew. Well, he wouldn't say a word either, except to Peggy. He heard his lordship say he must leave immediately for town.

"Harness the trap," said Corbell. "Before that, find Vance and tell her Miss Smail has torn her gown, and must be found another."

Walshe inclined his head, without expression. Consideration was always a feature of his lordship. Vance had resumed her duties now, after the burial.

On being found and told, Vance said none of her ladyship's cast-offs would serve; they'd be like boats on that one. "The only thing would be Miss Etta's grey flannel," she said. "That will have to do for the time."

They stared at each other, but neither spoke. Walshe went off to get ready the trap in time for his lordship's train.

On the journey, Corbell allowed the shock of the words he had lately read to sink into his mind, exhausted as it was by the happenings, one way and another, of the last few hours. *BE AT CLUB TOMORROW, WEDNESDAY, I SAW WHAT HAPPENED*, they read. It seemed unlikely that they could refer to anything but Fred's murder.

There was also the matter of Ione. He had already arranged for Peggy to sit constantly with her. Delayed shock might have adverse effects even on the passive heap of flesh she appeared to have become. Perhaps he should have treated her differently from the beginning. He felt layers of responsibility build up in his mind. The first requirement was to deal with Alfred. Whatever he had seen, enough money would settle him; a regular allowance, to cease if he broke his word.

At the surface of his mind, Corbell recalled Peggy's telling him she'd already found Miss Smail a gown.

Sissington appeared at the club, settling himself gracefully in one of its armchairs. By now he resembled a sleek and confident tomcat, despite the pouches beneath the eyes. His moustache, waxed gallantly, had been touched up with too-dark dye. Otherwise he was as usual, and seemed neither to recall the circumstances of their last meeting nor the one before.

The porter hovered, as porters do. Sissington ordered whisky for himself and his host, to be put, as Corbell correctly surmised, on his account and not his cousin's. He endured the situation as part of a chronic tensing of every faculty, a universal caution. "State your business," he said coldly, at the same time turning the delivered glass to savour the aroma of a fine malt. To fortify oneself was advisable in one way, though not another. He must be wary of any slip of the tongue.

Alfred, on the other hand, began to talk as though he had already imbibed. His eyes gleamed with triumph above their pouches.

"I've seen Lackmere often again despite you, old boy," he began affably, as though they had parted on the best of terms. "Bumped into Toby Penhaligon at Goodwood one year, and we both backed a good 'un. He asked me down, and since then I've been, you know, once or twice. I haven't been lucky enough to meet Ione."

That was unsurprising; Corbell had resolved from the beginning that Ione should never visit the Towers, among Eileen's giddy company, unescorted by himself. The geraniums masked a good deal of going-on. "They do a damn' fine breakfast," Sissington continued. "Afterwards I used to tend to take a little carriage-exercise in old Toby's two-wheeler, and in the nature of things pass by your wicket.

"One day I thought I'd look in; why not? After all the place will be mine eventually, unless poor Ione gives you a boy even now." He looked up and down at Corbell's deformity, as though it extended to his private parts. "Pleasant to see the old woods again, and the folly; and there was your little governess, trippin' up towards me. I'd heard about her from Eileen P. Sent her away – the governess, I mean –" he snickered – "well and truly fucked, old boy. She was ripe for it, I can tell you. Sang for her supper third or fourth time up, forget which. Those open drawers are an invitation."

He leaned back in the club armchair, sipping the malt with a companionable grin that showed teeth not quite what they had been, despite the dentist. Corbell overcame a desire to smash his face in. He must first find out why they were here at all. He wouldn't have been brought as far to listen to what Alfred had done to Mercy Smail. Nevertheless it was ugly. He heard Alfred still talking on suavely, his voice slurring slightly; obviously he had fortified himself for this occasion earlier.

"That little piece is as narrow as a quill pen till anyone starts investigatin'. You'd been up her more than somewhat y'self, Crip, I'd say; twisted, it might be the Grand Union Canal. Stuffed her like a goose all the same, four times right up. Ran off like one in the end; couldn't seem to get her legs back together, ha, ha. Tell you what to do, old boy; try turnin' her on a spit, plenty of bastin'. Fold up her legs against her and truss them tight closed, then stitch her up. Put in the long spike, you know, then a quarter-hour's turnin' her over a hot fire, and she's good and ready." He leered companionably.

Corbell remained silent.

"Any news of Etta, old boy?" Sissington continued. "Gave *her* what she needed as well, for as long as she'd stay under me. Didn't want to think of you with Ione, truth to tell. Still don't."

He remained sober enough not to give away the fact that he had indeed had a glimpse of Ione one day in the woods while awaiting Flo. He'd heard the babbling sounds of a woman's ecstasy, and had ventured forward to watch Ione and Fred, at it together in the parked Daimler, half hidden by trees. It was risking a good deal to do it in the grounds; Crip sometimes walked as far. The sight after so long, and the current activity, of his erstwhile betrothed had moved Angel Alf not at all; she was running to fat. Typically, he had put the situation at the back of his mind for future use. He had thought at the time that there would certainly be murder if Crip found out. Well, it had happened; and now the crooked devil was here, in front of him. The sensation of power was pleasant, remembering the horse-whip.

As for Corbell, now hearing the true story about Mercy Smail, he was filled with a pervasive anger. There seemed no part of what he valued, or now realised that he had, left unsullied by Alfred; Etta, the inheritance, and now, evidently, this. He let the chaos of his thoughts harden; he would give no information whatever to this scoundrel regarding Etta, not even the fact that she was dead. It was unlikely that such as Lord Sissington would ever encounter Harrigan the potter, let alone Ed, stoking charcoal. As for the governess, he would deal with her on return, Vance or

224

no Vance, pregnancy or none.

He ordered more whisky to induce the other to go on talking before he fell into an inebriate's silence. Presently the reason for his own summons came out, as foreseen.

"I saw you, Crip, you see," the other remarked coyly. "I saw you string up that poor bloody tiger of yours, then later shove him in a tomb in the vault. You shouldn't have carried a lantern. Its light shows a long way."

He had drunk a good deal, he said, one night after a local visit – no, it wasn't to The Towers – and had come back hoping to see Ione or, who knew, little goosey might have passed by. He didn't mention Flo.

"Suppose I must have gone to sleep in that folly of yours. There was nobody about, and when I woke it was dark. I could see what happened from there, the first time; then waited, because I knew you'd be back after swimmin'; couldn't leave the poor bugger like that on the tiled floor. It was worth the wait, Crip." The grin widened, becoming a comic Greek mask. "It's taken a day or two to send for you, because I had to write it all down in detail, and put the writin' where it's safe. You can rely on me not to send it to the police if you do as I say. You want to know what I say, eh? If you don't, it's bad for you; and all I need do is wait till they hang you on a silk rope, then everything's mine."

He reverted to the matter of Fred, saying he had seen Corbell frog-march him to the tack-room. "You behaved then somewhat urgently, Crip, old boy. You didn't horsewhip him, as is your habit if you remember." His eyes were cold. "Whatever the poor devil had done, he paid. You knocked him about most shockin'ly; didn't seem able to stand up for himself. Then you took down some tack, put it round his neck and hanged him, jerking, till he was dead. I think you went somewhat beyond your limits as Justice of the Peace, old boy.

"After that you took the body to the cellar, I suppose through that door. I could see nothing more, and waited; there was no hurry for me, but a good deal for you. I knew you had to dispose of the body before morning."

Sissington smiled, this time with closed lips. "I found a place where I could see better," he said. "I went back to the little folly, where one can wait in a certain warmth; it gets cold by night, as you no doubt know. I waited a long time, Crip, but I didn't sleep.

In the end I saw a lamp or candle come at last into the vault; and I saw other things. I saw you lift the lid off a tomb, put the body in and replace the stone lid. I can tell the police where to look. You don't want them, do you, Crip? You would rather listen to the conditions I shall make, eh?"

Corbell was fingering his third glass, but knew he had kept his wits about him. It had occurred to him, while listening to Alfred's conditions, that neither he nor his mother yet knew of Ione's pregnancy. It was the kind of thing, in any case, Cousin Mildred's generation only mentioned in hushed whispers if at all. As for Miss Smail, it no longer mattered.

Sissington had gone on talking. "According to the entail, and by right – you should never have married – y'know the Corbell title and estate will, as I say, one day be mine. The fortune is, however, yours to dispose of. I assume it will go to your only daughter, with a jointure for Ione."

Corbell remained silent. It was his strength, and Alfred's weakness that he had drunk too much. He was announcing now that as soon as she was old enough, he himself must marry Joan. "Meantime, she must be brought up by my mother in the north."

"A hostage," Corbell put in evenly.

"A hostage, dear boy. She will be kindly treated. She will learn to think of me as her future husband. There must, naturally, be an allowance made for her upkeep."

The amount he named was sizeable. Corbell had expected worse. Everything, of course, must be signed up. "On the return of your document," Corbell stated quietly.

"Of course, old boy, of course. There is nothing personal in all this. You can be assured of my silence as long as, er, the allowance continues to be paid."

"It will be paid as long as you remain silent." On this note they parted. Corbell did not dine downstairs. He was aware of a sudden weakness of body and mind, a surge of revulsion. It again included Mercy Smail.

Despite the urgency of what must now be done with Fred's body, Corbell stayed in town that night. He was in no state, without a rest elsewhere, to deal with the general situation awaiting him at Lackmere. It was pointless to remind himself that it only remained for Ione to give birth to a son of whom he was undoubtedly the father. How was he to tell?

226

He thrust down any recollection of, let alone desire for, Miss Smail. The revelation direct from Alfred had diminished her value. The matter need not affect him. He dismissed all thoughts of her, lay on the club bed and ate and drank whatever they sent up, trying to deal logically with what must next be done.

He would take the morning train, and on reaching home would work quickly to checkmate Alfred. There was the pending, and unavoidable, visit of his parents-in-law to deal with. Lady Leonora had been present at Joan's birth, and naturally wanted to be at this one: and as Pussy last year, during a game of baccarat, had taken a seizure and was by now childish, to bring him also. The prospect was inconvenient but, thankfully, brief. It was only that everything seemed to be happening at once.

Chapter Eight

When Corbell returned he dealt savagely with waiting mail, ordered a collation to be sent up to the library as he would not go down to luncheon, and set himself grimly to deal with other business till it should be dark enough to carry out his perfected plans regarding the second disposal of Fred's body. He surveyed his own role as accomplished criminal, and found that it left him devoid of feeling. He then became aware of a presence standing humbly before his desk; Miss Smail.

He had not sent for her, had not even taken time to remember her. It became apparent that she was wearing Etta's gown. It had been shortened at sleeves and hem, giving the governess a clownish appearance. He stared at her as though she were a stranger. She was saying something; Mrs Udney had written earlier: might she have a reference?

Of all disturbances this was the most inconvenient, almost laughable in its irrelevance to his plans. He reminded himself that this was the first time he had encountered her since being fully informed of her intimacy with Sissington. *Stuffed like a goose.* It made a fool of her and of himself. From Alfred's relation of events, either of them might well have impregnated her, just as Peggy had stated. Were the reference she now demanded to secure her another situation, the prospect would be welcome enough unless she began swelling up, in which case the blame would be laid on himself. His reputation as a magistrate, a pillar of the community and of morality, would vanish overnight. No, Miss Smail must remain for the time. He made her a deadly reply.

228

"My dear Miss Smail, the only position you are fit to occupy is, evidently, the horizontal. I am informed that you freely lay down under my cousin Sissington in the woods at the back gate and elsewhere. As I do not intend to share premises with him, you will continue to oblige me in a way I have already shown you. Meantime, you may go. You will not see Lord Sissington again."

"I – I did not – oh, he overcame me all of a sudden. I had not foreseen it. I told you I did not know who he was."

"What were you doing up there? Few go as far without a reason."

Her hesitant reply sounded guilt-ridden. "I – I already told you I was anxious to talk with Mr Chillingfold, the young clergyman who came to tea."

Her voice had sunk to a whisper. That way round? The vicarage was in the other direction. He laughed bitterly. The little whore! She'd been with Alfred again since, no doubt.

"It would have done you no good to lift your skirt for Chillingfold. His marriage was annulled, one sign that he was unable to carry out the duties of a husband." He looked her up and down. "You had best put him out of your mind," he told her. "In any case, as you know, he has been sent away."

"That – that was not why I –" She stood there, mouthing inanities, contrary to her usual precision. It was evident that he believed nothing she said, that he had no respect for her. She whitened, turned, and made her way out. The disappearing sight of Etta's grey gown reminded him, for the first time, of a ghost. He downed the sensation of unease, and returned to contemplation of what must be done with what now remained of Fred's body, finally to conceal it. That must happen, without fail, tonight.

Chapter Nine

Miss Smail earlier, while her employer was still away, had contrived to receive a letter from Mrs Udney. It was reproachful, implying that an answer should have been sent to earlier correspondence. This statement bemused Miss Smail: perhaps the posts had been at fault.

A vacancy, the letter stated, would again shortly occur in a post which required considerable ability in mathematics, theoretical and applied. The person lately chosen had not given satisfaction. By now, there would be a number of applicants, but Miss Smail might perhaps be included if she took the trouble to reply on this occasion. Appearance was important, as an interview would be necessary with the governors of the establishment in question, a socially sought-after school for young ladies who might be expected, these days, to go on to higher things, perhaps even in time including a contemplated college, for women only, at Oxford. A high degree of competence, and of character, was expected, and immediately necessary, as went without saying, an explicit reference from Miss Smail's present employer. Mrs Udney implied that Lord Corbell's title might tip the scales.

Mercy looked down at herself in the late Etta Corbell's old flannel gown. Lord Corbell, on the day of his departure, had rendered the other almost past mending. Miss Smail ventured to ask Mrs Vance, whom she was by now fearful of approaching, if it could be ready soon. "There isn't time at present, with her ladyship's condition and my having to keep an eye," replied Peggy sharply. To speak of such things to a young unmarried female would not in the usual way have been proper, but this one knew more than she thought she did.

Peggy felt distinct triumph at the fright Miss looked in the grey flannel. As Walshe had put it in his earthy fashion, that skirt always had pulled up too easy. The plainness of the garment had in some way set off Miss Etta, but it didn't do anything for Miss Smail. In fact, it made her look like one of the women Peggy recalled seeing, in course of her day-long marriage with Josiah, being herded like cattle on to a grim transport ship at Portsmouth, to be sent to Botany Bay. Convicts, they'd been. Miss Smail looked like one now. Perhaps when his lordship next set eyes on her, he'd have second thoughts. Tearing the other gown in two like that, and all the rest!

However, there had been recent encouragement. Miss had been heard being sick into the blue-flowered lavatory. Mercy by then had stopped thinking of torn gowns. That her ladyship was in a certain condition must mean that Lord Corbell still acted as a husband to her. That state of things should not be surprising, yet Miss Smail felt miserable and betrayed. She knew nothing of biology, and by now the distinctions between right and wrong had become blurred. She had accused Lord Corbell of acting like the men of Sodom because she knew the story of Abraham very well. Also, what he did to her in other ways had brought, now and then, a sweet flooding of joy through her body. All the same, her upbringing told hers anything of the kind was bound to be sinful. Perhaps her own punishment had been the horrid experience with the man at the gate, and Vance's humiliating treatment afterwards. Altogether a side of the world she had never imagined was being made manifest to Mercy Smail. She felt lost in a dark forest, out of sight of the sun.

The best thing to do was to sit down and write to Mrs Udney. Miss Smail did so in her neat handwriting, not permitting the feeling of having been abandoned to overcome her again until the letter was finished. It said she had not heard earlier, and would gladly apply for so interesting a situation, but sadly had had an accident to her gown. Lord Corbell was away at present, but as soon as he returned she would send on the reference. She then sat staring at her ink-stained finger, and admitted to herself that she did not truly want to apply. Such a post would once have meant everything in the world; her talents were exactly suited to it. Now, all she longed for was to set eyes on Lord Corbell again. She would, of course, ask for the reference. To receive it would, however, break her heart.

As it happened, he sent her away terrified, insulted, tearful, bewildered and thankfully blind as to the future. There was one small comfort. He had insisted that she stay.

Fred was disposed of this time in a spot unperceived by anyone. It was the deep chalk-pit where from time immemorial, rubbish had been thrown when the earlier house-privies became full, or bonfires failed to destroy some inconvenient matter. The pit was still hidden by encroaching brambles and was far enough from the house to be known to few except, by now, no doubt, Miss Smail and Joan, who had been known to pass it on occasion during their improving botanical walks to acquire specific knowledge of *rubus fruticosus*. Joan would not be passing by the pit again for a long time, if ever. Miss Smail could, if necessary, be further subdued. If the Pusey-Pounds remarked on her presence and Joan's absence, he would imply that their granddaughter was on a short visit only to her second cousin Mildred Sissington. Lies came easily now.

He instructed Walshe to make a search for poachers, and himself took out a gun. It was, however, unlikely that Sissington would show himself again now his demands had been met; a large sum of money had been paid over before Corbell left town. With no sneaking presence probable in the wood, Corbell made his preparations, telling Walshe he himself would take the night watch and, if necessary, bring any culprit to justice.

There was a tarpaulin in the boathouse, and Corbell went down as he often did, retrieved it and rolled it up. He then carried it back towards the house, leaving the little boat rocking in the shadows, untenanted. Corbell remembered the time he had found Sissington in there, coupled with Etta. Her ashes remained in the organ room but must be rested soon in the lake. Would her arm, or green-eyed Jocosa's, one day reach for him and drag him down? That kind of fancy was his no longer. He was a living stone, without a heart, without feelings of any kind; a murderer.

He had put on old clothes, the jacket he wore for shooting; there were dried bloodstains about the cuffs from long-dead pheasants. He disliked the sport and remembered how he seldom indulged in it except on the rare occasions when there were guests in season. He fortified himself now with brandy, likewise not a customary habit since his marriage-night; drew on thick leather gloves, and went down to the cleansed Roman pavement.

This was where Fred had lain. The images on the tiles stared up, lucid as far as their nature would allow. There was no smell except for that of the spirits on his own breath; he asked some power or other for strength to carry out what he now had to do.

The vault keys hung as they had done since he had bestowed Fred's body earlier. That it would no longer be fresh was more than probable, and the faint stench of corruption met Corbell even as he opened the vault door and neared his mother's tomb. He spread out the tarpaulin on the stone floor, heaved aside the lid, and scooped what had once been Fred from where it lay, not looking at it directly, holding his breath meantime. He folded up the corners of the tarpaulin to cover what lay within, then looked for any traces of the late occupant remaining in the open tomb. Something moved; a crawling maggot. Corbell crushed the thing between gloved fingers, searched for more but found none. No doubt they inhabited the removed body itself.

He replaced the stone lid, leaving everything apparently as it had been. The ensuing burden was light enough, as he already knew. He carried it to the outer door, using the corners of the containing tarpaulin. It was late evening, not yet night; he had arranged the time for when a lantern should not yet be initially necessary, yet when it should soon grow dark enough to remain unseen. As it was, he knew every step of the way, in darkness and light.

The chalk pit lay among the further trees. Like other parts of Lackmere it might well have been there since Roman times or earlier. Corbell thrust aside the concealing brambles with his free foot and tipped what was left of the dead man down, shaking the tarpaulin free of maggots. Thorns caught at the unspeakable thing, meantime delaying its fall. Edmund brought out a knife he always carried in his pocket, and cut at them till they gave way. The body slid downwards, to what depth could not be certain; that of the pit was itself unknown. It might tunnel on beneath the earth, towards the lake or the sea itself, fifteen miles distant. Whichever was the case, the thing was done. Corbell closed and replaced the knife, and left Fred's second grave.

What was he himself now? Cuckold, cripple, murderer; no more than those? Circumstances determined what a man became. *The fault, dear Brutus* . . . but that supposition had been wrong. He himself had, since before his birth, been other than what he might have become had he been born straight like others. After Yolande came it hadn't mattered, but listening to his father with her had destroyed both innocence and hope. By now, he was a stone, who could feel nothing.

The leather gloves stank. He would cleanse them and the tarpaulin in the lake. Deep in the water, Jocosa lay; he hoped she would excuse him. He stripped off the gloves and cleansed them along with the tarpaulin at the water's edge. By the time he had finished he was drenched in sweat. He replaced the gloves, with water running off still, in the boat to dry, then undressed himself and went in, swimming till he felt free of what he had earlier striven not directly to touch.

The coldness of the water dispelled the fumes of brandy in his brain, although without its aid he might well not have been able to bring himself to do what he had. Hair plastered down on his head, body still wet, he emerged at last, took his clothes and waded back to shore. He had put the jacket across his shoulders for warmth.

Returned to the house, he found himself trembling, less with cold than with recollection. He downed more brandy in strong gulps, remembering again how the fourth lord had had as much to say against the drinking of spirits as concerning fornication. A lost soul was a lost soul, nonetheless, and he might as well reap the benefits while they were available to him.

All that was, that might be, should be, had already been. Corbell made his way to his room, dried his hair, donned his brocade robe and went in to see how Ione fared. She was asleep, breathing heavily; by now her bulk began to swell the bedclothes. A maid, put there by Peggy, slept as usual on the pallet. Ione was watched by night and by day, as he had ordered. Corbell returned to his dressing-room, and slept.

For some days it seemed incredible that nothing had been remarked by anyone. He had expected repercussions, and began to find it difficult to concentrate. He turned to the only diversion he had except reading; Miss Smail. She had never, after all, been a person for whom he had feeling. He could use her unfeelingly, and care nothing. He could use her as regularly as before, but differently; until the onset of, perhaps, two labours instead of one. From Miss Smail's point of view it would make no difference to the outcome. It should, in fact, suit her better.

Part VI

Chapter One

Miss Smail was enduring her afternoon spanking. She was uncertain why it had to proceed, as she hadn't done anything lately to merit it. Hitherto her tear-filled eyes had usually focussed on the vibrating malachite paperweight on Lord Corbell's desk, across which she was as a rule placed; but today that and what followed was happening on the bed in the organ room. The reason was that although Lord Corbell was now consistently using her from the back, she was steadily filling up at the front, and by now it was less inconvenient to lean her increased girth against the yielding covers. Vance said not to trouble, it was all in the course of nature, and here was a good warm soapy enema to take away anything nasty. The enema was comforting, high up in her afterwards. She had stopped asking questions about anything. At the desk, her legs had ended by kicking back in a kind of ecstasy, hampered only by the new flannel drawers, which had subsided round her ankles.

That had been a favour, as her others had been ripped beyond mending. Lord Corbell had been dismissive. "You know damned well you don't need any drawers." However, Miss Smail had protested piteously that the attics were draughty in winter. Four pairs had accordingly been extracted from Lady Corbell's charity-bundles. They were unworn, of good quality, and had been purchased some years previously by an elderly donor after the brief fashion of a let-down rear flap, for the relief of nature, had prevailed about the time of Waterloo.

Undoing the two requisite buttons afforded Corbell an instant's glimpse of paradise, but Miss Smail herself required stimulating thereafter out of a certain residual coyness. He found that by the time he had chastised her peerless globes to the colour of the Penhaligon geraniums, she was tumescent, which made entry easier. Otherwise he had no emotions on the subject except that by now, with Alfred's child or else his own growing heavy in her, the walnut desk was no longer properly receptive. Also, Ione's parents were to arrive shortly for the birth of the heir, and as Pussy by now was evidently childlike he might wander into the library at any moment. Here, at least, was private.

He told Miss Smail she might go, not assisting her to do up the buttons. Her drab departure went unnoticed by him; he had gone out to the bookshelves to look up a quotation which eluded him. It was from *Othello*. He found it, and sat staring at its relevance.

> *The Anthropopagi, and men whose heads*
> *Do grow beneath their shoulders.*

Charlemagne, one understood, had believed that men living north of the Baltic had the heads of dogs. Perhaps Anubis had penetrated as far. Corbell put back the book. The indexing was finished, and Miss Smail seldom now came downstairs unless sent for.

He recalled that Etta's ashes were still on the organ-room mantelpiece, and had witnessed his recent act. He ought to sink them in the lake.

The Pusey-Pounds arrived. Later, having changed for dinner, Corbell led his mother-in-law in, but apart from her too-bright chatter there was nothing much to say, and between courses Ione appeared to fall into a doze. In the end everybody ate in silence, which suited the host as his mind was elsewhere.

He had recently sent Joan the amber locket for her birthday. It was after all as much hers as anyone's. He felt tears prick his eyes still, remembering its two last owners. In those days, he could feel affection even after love was dead. When had he changed to what he had by now become? He had no feeling for his wife, none for his little catamite upstairs, none yet for the heir about to be born, who might after all be his own. Rather than concern himself with

240

a safe birth he found himself considering coldly how to deal with Cousin Mildred, who would certainly see any announcement in the papers. Alfred would be less certain of the value of his bride, but there was still the money paid; and possibly Cousin Mildred had in any case grown fond of Joan by now, and would keep her in the north. It would be inconvenient, to say the least, if the girl were returned to Lackmere.

He returned his own attention to his parents-in-law. Although like all the human race they had aged with the passing years, Lady Leonora had lost her harried look; she enjoyed life in Cannes on Corbell's secure allowance, made direct to herself. Pussy, however, was a pitiable sight, having been forced to abandon his reason for living except for the few recent halcyon days outside Paris, when he had expensively renewed his youth at Longchamps. Otherwise, bent at the knee and bleary in the eye, he appeared to know nobody including his daughter and son-in-law, and mumbled incessantly to himself about forgotten odds at twenty to one. Ione herself kept clapping her hands to her stomach as if the pains were about to begin, but somehow they never did. It began to look as if the Pusey-Pounds' stay would have to be longer than had been assumed. The labour did not seem imminent, and Pussy at least had to be entertained if he was not to be left wandering about the premises. Lady Leonora naturally wanted to be with her daughter, which freed Vance for renewed care of Miss Smail. It therefore fell to Corbell, much against his inclinations, to help to pass his father-in-law's time. The best thing to do with Pussy, lacking a racecourse, was to take him carriage-driving.

"Where's Fred?" was the first inconvenient question, with a different coachman seated in front.

"Gone away." It sounded like a fox. Pussy mumbled that it was a pity, they wouldn't get another like Fred in a hurry. He began once again to relate the late jockey's unsurpassed performances at Newmarket. "Knew exactly what he was doin'."

Corbell, to take his mind off the subject, suggested that they should take the day to look at Ely Cathedral. When its shape reared in the near distance above the flat land, old Pusey-Pound showed surprising knowledge about the early education there of Edward the Confessor. "Turned out a damned fine huntsman, whatever else they said. His mother used to send buckets of elvers

l

to the monks. Never see elvers now. Fine food."

A small crowd had collected outside when they returned from the soaring nave, and a lay preacher was holding them spellbound. To his slight shock, Corbell recognised none other than Mr Chillingfold. He had, of course, heard about the latter's secession, and rather admired it. The celery-stick had filled out, and appeared prosperous in a dark and well-fitting suit of clothes. They kept the carriage waiting to listen for a minute or two. As a preacher Chillingfold was mellifluous, and seemed to convince himself as well as his audience. It was, Corbell thought, like listening to Papa once more. At the end everybody broke out into a psalm, and following that a basket was passed round for collection. Corbell, mindful of his own coat of arms, managed to make his way to the preacher and invite him to join them for late luncheon at an inn. He could not be entirely certain what had impelled him, but over moderate stewed beef and dumplings found himself inviting Mr Chillingfold to come and take a service at Lackmere. His own erstwhile part in ridding the local church of him as curate remained unstressed; it was doubtful if the man knew of it.

"My wife is very shortly expecting our child. If you could come before then at your convenience, it would be elevating."

Certainly it would divert Lady Leonora, a torpid Ione, and the assembled household. There was also the matter of Miss Smail. Corbell heard the preacher enquire for her, and his own deadly reply.

"I fear she has been compromised by my cousin Sissington, along with several undiscriminating women. She will remain at Lackmere till it is decided what is to become of her. I have no wish to turn her out on the roads, as many employers would do."

Mr Chillingfold was silent. "Elvers," Pussy broke in. "Nobody knows now what the word means. Baby eels, tasty when fried. Some saint told the monks here they looked like eels when fornicatin', and that's why the place is called Ely." He grinned, revealing teeth still surprisingly his own. On this embarrassed note – it was well seen the old gentleman was beyond comprehension of what he'd said – they parted, having arranged a provisional date for Chillingfold's Lackmere house-service. Corbell told himself again it would please Ione. It would also, as he knew quite well, thoroughly discredit Miss Smail. Whoever was responsible, even the grey flannel was beginning to bulge noticeably.

Chillingfold departed in a state of profound shock. The experiences of his marriage had scarred him, and having set eyes on Miss Smail he had carried her in his memory as pure, unsullied and acquainted only with such matters as appealed to his intelligence. She had, in fact, cast soothing balm over his estimate of women. Now, like his former wife, she had succumbed to Sissington. It was like Eve with the serpent – the eel, Ely – he shrank into himself, and knew that, this time, he would never emerge. He must seek some form of refuge which would shelter him from the necessity of considering, or ever being considered by, females. It could not happen at once; he must ponder the requirements, take advice in the right quarters, weigh the pros and cons. First, he couldn't prevent himself from going to Lackmere as arranged, even if it proved to be his last extempore sermon, the unforeseen prompting of the Spirit that had also come to the fourth Lord Corbell. That unhappy man had taken his own life, lacking his woman. He, Marcus Chillingfold, would use such prompting in the service of God. There must be no more fleeting affections. He must try to resemble St. Augustine. The time to start was now.

Corbell still saw no need to stint himself of his Ganymede, even though Vance told him the governess was by now becoming visibly pregnant. "It's either your lordship's fault or else Lord Alf's," she put it. She seemed to keep insisting on the matter. He admitted to himself, recalling sundry leaked condoms, that he might perhaps after all be involved. The possibility left him without feeling. He reflected that when he had first set eyes on her, her mouth had reminded him of a little tight pink anus. Now, he was loosening both. She was nothing now but a rag doll, to be manipulated.

He told himself he was her benefactor. She was still being paid, housed and fed; other such young women would have been given their instant dismissal. The adoption of the child when it was born he would leave to Vance, and Miss Smail by then could go; he would have his son by Ione.

He was being troubled at nights by a recurrent dream. In it he was buggering the child Etta, and she was laughing. He admitted to himself openly now that he must have wanted it with her. His anger spilled out unreasonably on Miss Smail accordingly. The harder he used her, the more, in his own mind, he avenged Etta and punished Sissington. He knew the notion was by no means logical. Etta was dead, and Alfred was, had always been, oblivious to the need for any kind of punishment even when he'd justifiably horsewhipped him. A complete lack of any moral sense must be a convenience. He was losing, almost deliberately, any he himself had ever possessed.

Obstetric results not even yet being manifest regarding Ione, it began to look as if the Pusey-Pounds' stay would have to be prolonged after Mr Chillingfold's arranged visit, which would take place shortly. Ione, roused briefly out of her torpor, had seized the opportunity to make it a small social occasion, followed by lunch.

The guests began to arrive, Lady Penhaligon in a black hat trimmed with gulls' feathers; she looked like a seabird about to take off. Corbell greeted her and Chillingfold, with whom he sat, as was customary, on the dais in the hall. The general's portrait looked down on Ione, who lay by now on Anna's transported chaise-longue, herself looking, if one had to be uncharitable, like a Middle White about to farrow. The household filed in with clean hands, caps and collars. Miss Smail sent a request to be excused.

Corbell remained pitiless, and sent up one of the maids to tell her that if Lady Corbell could make the effort to be present, so could she, and that they would delay the commencement of prayers till her arrival.

While waiting, the ladies talked politely among themselves. Ione noticed that the Lord Lieutenant's wife was wearing the new S-shape, a feat she herself might hope to achieve once this unspeakable prospect was over. She did not feel at all well and by now, regretted asking company. The guests, who had not been aware how near her time their hostess was, civilly hoped that it was not inconvenient to have accepted. Lady Leonora sat on her daughter's left, Pussy, mumbling happily aloud, beyond that. A vacant chair had been left for the governess. Mr Chillingfold stared at his open Bible.

A pause ensued, and Corbell's Ganymede, his she-minion in grey flannel, at last came in. She was walking by now in the faintly compensatory, backward-tilting way of gravid women. Her mouth had loosened by habit. Corbell watched Chillingfold turn to ice.

Miss Smail disposed her much-assailed backside gingerly on the chair. Her eyes sought Chillingfold in desperation; he would not look at her. She was shrinking and uncertain in the public eye. That she was, by now, what Charles II used to describe as a ship in full sail was not very evident beneath the all-embracing grey flannel except for those with eyes to see. Only her walk betrayed it.

The prayers commenced. It had been expected that there might be something said about the fruitful wife. Instead, almost despite himself, the disillusioned Chillingfold found the terrible words of the Epistle to the Romans thundering out of him, clearly and irrevocably.

A sound disturbed the moment's astonished silence in the hall, broken only by Pussy's incessant *sotto voce*. The governess had burst out sobbing, had risen, stumbled off and out of the hall. The Lord Lieutenant's wife raised her eyebrows beneath her elaborate hat. Ione's close-set gaze surveyed her spouse with increased distaste, and equally increased awareness. It was grotesque to picture Corbell and that creature together, but it had happened, evidently. The servants did not turn their heads, being too well trained and in any case aware of the situation. Presently the invited company went in to luncheon. Miss Smail would have been excluded in any case.

"Extraordinary young woman," remarked the Lieutenant's wife. No one else commented, and Corbell ventured to remark that Miss Smail had become somewhat hysterical since the departure of her charge, which among other reasons made her post uncertain.

"You will, of course, give her notice now," remarked Ione, toying with her soup but eating nothing. Later it became apparent that the waters had burst, but being well-bred she gave no sign till it was time for the guests to walk out on the terrace, when she admitted she didn't feel quite up to joining them.

The company having departed, Ione gave birth upstairs, after an easy labour, to a large healthy boy. Vance wrapped him in swaddlings after his nose and mouth had been cleansed, and once his grandparents had briefly seen him took him downstairs again to show to her master.

Corbell knew at once that the child was Fred's. It had Fred's ears, always an unmistakeable sign. All its life it would resemble Fred. Corbell accordingly decided that the life must be short. He was a murderer already, his soul, accordingly, damned; this new-born creature would feel no more discomfort than at the drowning of a kitten.

"Give it back," said Vance.

He returned her the wrapped child. She smothered it swiftly, as his father had smothered Anna; pressing the covers against its nose and mouth till it had ceased to breathe. Then she said to Corbell, "You may tell her ladyship, when she's in a state to be told, that the baby has been taken to be cared for, as it may not thrive."

The faded eyes surveyed him with triumph which bewildered him. "Shall I insert a stillbirth in the gazettes?" he asked. He was taking her advice, like an initiate in evil. She'd saved him from infanticide, at least.

"Leave it for a day or two. It won't be longer. I know what I know."

Later, when she had recovered enough to take a little broth, Corbell visited his wife. Ione's eyes were filled with the usual dislike. He told her the baby had been sent to be cared for, as its health was uncertain.

"It was alive," she said. "I heard it cry."

Suddenly her face twisted into ugliness. "Don't ever touch me again," she said. "Don't ever touch me again."

They had recommended, in any case, that she have no more children. He turned and left. There was, after all, nothing to say. He must rely on whatever it was Vance knew.

Following all of that, it was time to deal finally, and as it turned out forever, with Miss Smail.

She came when sent for, wearing her cloak over her gown. He realised that it was a long time since he had looked at her except from the rear. He remained coldly angry. She had narrowly avoided making a fool of him in public, only his quickness of response over her supposed tantrums concerning Joan's absence having saved him. He handed his Ganymede a bag of money and an envelope.

"That will be enough to maintain you until you find another situation. I have written an adequate reference for you to give to Mrs Udney or some other, containing acceptable reasons for your early departure." There was, in fact, enough to maintain her till the birth, whenever it was; you couldn't tell from looking at her now, in the grey gown and cloak. She could leave the result on the doorstep of Fred's orphanage, he decided. He was unable to summon up any feelings.

"You have ruined me, and now you are sending me away."

She spoke quietly, and he replied evenly enough.

"Far from ruining you, I have widened your experience, Miss Smail. You have cause to be grateful to me, I assure you. Pack your things, and I will instruct Walshe to drive you to the station."

He had picked up the malachite paperweight, and was examining its unique opacity. Something he heard her say then made him look up at her; she was regarding him for the first time clearly, behind eyelids still red with weeping. He had not before noted the colour of her eyes. They were like the water of the lake on a clear day.

"You must know I love you," she said. "I would not otherwise have permitted certain things of which I had no previous awareness." Her voice trembled at the end, and she fell silent.

Love? It had no part in him or he in it; he must insult her out of it. He heard himself answer her with deadly accuracy. He used obscene and unpardonable language she would never forget. As had happened in her own induced transports, words came out of him that he hadn't known he knew. Love? It was buried in Yolande's grave. He would not even remember Yolande at this moment. Having said it all, and more than all, he shouldered his way past the former governess out of the room. If he were to remain, pity for her might weaken him. In passing he had a last glimpse of her face, grown suddenly white and formless, an idiot's. He took himself elsewhere, and heard her steps running, running away. She'd regained the use of her legs, at least. Corbell gave the grin he had that could resemble a demon's. The devil, after all, remained his master.

There was no room left in the vault for yet another tomb, and as the dead baby's coffin was small Corbell presently surveyed the existing tombs with a view to interring it in one of them, as was done in Westminster Abbey itself and sundry monasteries; he remembered seeing, on his travels, one where every few hundred years, the former occupants' bones were emptied out into the local river and fresh corpses, as it were, installed in their vacated places. His method now would be less drastic; he would simply have the small coffin laid at the foot of a larger, within the containing stone.

Memories of what had had to happen with Fred's body pursued him, and he avoided Anna's grave. The other which might yield room, at the foot of the already present coffin, was Jocosa's. He had them lift away her stone, then demanded to be left to himself. He wanted to see what death had made of her; to be truthful with himself, had always wanted it. If one believed tales of vampires, she might be incorrupt; those, like saints, seemed to avoid decay. In any case the vault was dry.

He unfastened the hasps, lifted the lid, and looked down on her. For instants he drew back in horror.

It was still recognisable as a human face, although the fine skin had shrunk long ago against the skull. Jocosa's dark hair had grown since death, and lay about her. Her eyes were open, but with the glazed dry appearance of one long dead; their green colour could still be ascertained.

What repelled him was the severed nose. That had taken place in life, the mediaeval punishment for harlots. The dry septa curled inwards. Jocosa Corbell had never, Peggy had it from her mother, been seen again without a thick veil.

"By God, she paid," her grandson said aloud, hearing his voice echo in the vault. He had been about to replace the lid over the ruined face when a gleam of metal, by her side in the coffin, caught the light from the raised lantern he held.

He reached in, against her rigid body, and drew it out. It was a sword; the lost sword that had failed to be drawn at Waterloo. The memory of his own searches in the attic, hoping to find it in boyhood, came. He would have been beaten wherever he found it. General Lord Corbell had elected to lay it beside his dead wife; an atonement? A symbol of undying vengeance? Nobody now would ever know.

Corbell surveyed the sword after taking it out to the light of the

248

day. There were marks of corruption on the long blade here and there. He would clean it himself, and hang it below the general's portrait, in its scabbard again at last. He had replaced the lid of Jocosa's coffin and told those outside that the tombs were, after all, full.

The child's remains must be buried in a new grave, possibly in the churchyard field. It would mean having this consecrated in any case, which in turn meant waiting until the diocesan bishop had leisure for the appointment.

Meanwhile the baby's coffin, already constructed, could remain on the floor of the vault. Corbell locked the door, and left it. There were other matters to consider for the time.

He cleaned the sword till it was again bright and shining, and limped up to the further attics for the first time in many years. The scabbard was where he had long ago replaced it, in the trunk with the disturbed white-and-silver dress. It had seemed incomplete beneath the general's portrait. Nothing seemed to have changed since his father had caned him for discovering the musical-box. Now, everything fell into place.

He took the scabbard downstairs, had it polished with saddle soap and placed where the sheathed sword could be hung once more against the wall beneath his grandfather's portrait. He balanced the sword in place himself, with no other person present; and addressed the stern portrayed face aloud.

"She caused you to abandon your sword, and you left it in her coffin. Now I have returned it to you, and she has paid by death, will you and she rest in peace and allow me the same?"

There was no answer; had he expected one? At last he turned away from the portrait and the sword, and gazed out at the lake. It was grey today, with rain, as once long ago when he had climbed to the attics as a child, hoping to please his father; and had instead found that which so greatly displeased, and had led to the coming of Yolande. Was he the man who had once been that child? Did he care now for anyone, except perhaps old Peggy? He told himself that he did not, no doubt could not, now.

Miss Smail had run away fast from recollection, even from geometric truth, which had shattered. She had left behind her spectacles, and could see only blurred objects lacking them; tree-

249

trunks at last, rearing grey and sudden so that she knocked against them as she went; twigs and branches strewn across missed paths, tripping her up painfully. Twice she struggled from her knees and hurried on, grazed and bruised, with a twisted ankle. She must reach the pit, and end her life. It was impossible to continue. The agony in her mind was extending to her body, which had begun to be separately invaded by a fierce, unfamiliar pain. It didn't leave her as she ran, acquiring a kind of rhythm, as if a force not her own was thrusting down in her. She wanted to be rid of it, to become herself again in order to die. She must plunge straight down into the depths alone, knowing nothing more. The pain, however, became so bad that she couldn't overlook or overcome it by wanting to be done with it and with everything. It encompassed her.

Reaching the pit's edge at last she collapsed once again, on her knees. She gave birth kneeling, howling like an animal; then stretched out to grope towards the welcoming edge of death. Now that the pain had subsided she clutched at the sharp thorns of the brambles for secondary hurt to come to her relief. The torment of the other had left her weak; her head would no longer support itself and she felt the scarifying of her face as it fell against the sharpness. She closed her eyes in an illogical fear of being blinded.

She was no longer herself in any way. She was no longer anyone.

Her heart, the heart he hadn't wanted, began an uneven fluttering. Its strings began to wrench like a wrongly used instrument. The instrument stopped playing, and Miss Smail lay still. She hadn't had to go down to seek death; it had come for her. The child kicked weakly among her skirts. Miss Smail herself would have been the last to approve of the disorder. She had never fully understood everything that had happened, till now.

Walshe had been instructed to have the trap ready to take Miss Smail to the railway station to catch her train. However, she did not appear, and after waiting for some time – he himself would be relieved enough to see the last of her – sent for Vance. By now, the morning train would have gone.

"She's not in her room," said Vance, who had come down still in her apron, but with a shawl flung on. She had been with her ladyship all night, Pusey-Pound having taken a mild seizure, so his wife was with him. "Turn the trap round," said Peggy now. "We're going up to the woods."

She sat with her strong hands clenched in her apron, face and body tense. She didn't talk, and Walshe knew better than to make her. As they approached the trees he thought he heard a faint mewling sound. Vance, getting deaf, hadn't heard it, but in any case told him to stop.

"Wait here with the pony," she said. He watched her go, and walk upwards to the pit, her tall figure still visible among the bare trees. She was a strange woman, and made him uncomfortable with her habit of knowing everything.

Reaching the pit, Vance saw what she had expected to see, except that she was looking at a dead woman. Miss Smail's body was stretched out at the pit's edge, her hands reaching towards it, clutching at the brambles. Her face was hidden. Vance stood still for seconds, recalling the tale in the Book of Judges where a concubine was thrown overnight to the sons of Belial, and was found dead in the morning, with her hands stretched out on the threshold of the house where her lord was. Lord Corbell was in his library at present, and didn't want to be disturbed.

There was a slight movement among Miss Smail's skirts. Vance knelt down and brought out a tiny premature baby, a boy. He was still attached, and warm. She felt in her apron for scissors, and cut the cord. Taking off her shawl she held the child upside down and slapped him to make him cry, then cleansed his nostrils and mouth with the full folds of her apron before wrapping him in the shawl and laying him aside. He had dark hair. Vance turned to the dead mother.

Miss Smail had fulfilled her destiny and outlived her usefulness. She'd meant to go down the pit; well, it should happen. She was light, and easy to drag and shove down. Vance waited to be sure the disturbance of the brambles had subsided, then picked up the shawl, inspected the baby again and returned with him to the trap.

"Found him in the woods," was all she said. Walshe knew it was all he'd better say as well. He'd seen and heard nothing, after all, but the child's newborn cry.

251

Chapter Two

Corbell recalled Peggy Vance coming to him to say Miss Smail was still not to be found. "My lord, Walshe waited with the carriage at your order, to take Miss to the station, he said, but she didn't come out. Her things are in her room, not packed, and she seems nowhere in the house. We thought maybe you'd changed your mind, but that I'd best ask. There's only the later train left."

"Tell them to look in the grounds," he said. He himself took his cane and, stiffly, set out. He stared at the lake, wondering if she was in it. If she had chosen his father's way out of life, she would be found sooner or later. Otherwise there was the chalk pit. He avoided walking up as far. There might be a lingering odour there still.

By nightfall there was still no sign, no word. Vance by then had brought a baby in to the nursery. It lay in the cradle, wearing a little white cap that covered its ears. It seemed to be thriving. Her ladyship, of course, hadn't milk to feed it, so it was taken up to the cottages again once seen. Ione, still in bed but recovering, thought the police should be informed about Miss Smail. Corbell replied testily that he didn't want trouble. "I paid her her salary. She can look after herself, no doubt." He was hiding disquiet.

Ione was triumphant. "The money's still lying on the chest of drawers in her room, Vance says, and her spectacles are somewhere. I think you ought to make enquiries." She was beginning to enjoy her promised freedom now there was an heir. Soon she would be up and about. She'd get them to drive her to The Towers to see Eileen; he'd never allowed her to go there alone.

Lady Leonora had not been present at the actual birth because of the state of poor Pussy, who wouldn't be with them long. However, he knew he had a grandson. In passing, Vance had shown them both the first baby in its wrappings, and Pussy opened one eye, looked, said, "She slept with Fred," and relapsed into pleased desuetude. Lady Leonora slapped his hand gently.

"Mortimer, you must never, never speak so again." The bundle with large ears had been taken to Corbell. "Promise me to keep silent."

Pussy didn't have to; he had quietly passed to a celestial Derby in which all horses won. If it had to happen, it couldn't have been more convenient.

Arrangements for the funeral occupied everyone's attention for some days. Miss Smail's matter was then resurrected by a letter from Mrs Udney of the bureau, saying she hadn't received her proportion of Miss Smail's salary or any explanation of why not. She reminded Lord Corbell that an agreement had been signed, and that the matter was actionable.

After that, with his father-in-law safely buried, Corbell sent for the police.

He had no opinion of the parish constable, who was often drunk. However, a man from London came, Mrs Udney evidently having made further complaint. Corbell interviewed him in the library.

"Miss Smail came to you with excellent references, I believe, Lord Corbell. It seems extraordinary that she should have vanished, as would appear to be evident. Can you think of any possible reason?"

The sharp eyes raked him. They would see, Corbell knew, only a middle-aged man with a respected reputation in the county. He kept calm, saying not too little or too much; let them extract what they required, if they could. He said Miss Smail had seemed to him a sensible young woman, more than competent to fill her position, in fact rather too much so for his daughter, who was not very clever. He smiled.

The detective's gimlet gaze never left his face. "Where is your daughter now, Lord Corbell?"

"In the north, with a relation, Lady Sissington. It was decided by my wife and myself that Joan would benefit from a sojourn with her."

"Is it possible that Miss Smail had gone to join her?"

"Certainly not without my knowledge. My cousin would have informed me of the fact of her arrival. She would, in fact, have resented it; she objects to the higher education of women, and will instruct Joan in domestic matters and in polite manners, as hers, despite everything, remained somewhat gauche."

He continued to smile, not too broadly; he reminded himself of the time, long ago, when he had told some enquirer Etta took fits. "So there would have been no question of the governess's accompanying her," surmised the detective. "Why then did you keep Miss Smail on?"

"Because we were uncertain of the length of my daughter's stay. My cousin is no longer young, and might well have sent Joan back soon. We might then have had to make do with a less well qualified governess than Miss Smail."

"Did your daughter and Miss Smail deal well together? Was there affection between them?"

"In moderation. Joan liked to ride her pony better than anything." He thought vaguely of the third Punch, still out at grass, no doubt, in the north.

"Then why, Lord Corbell, did you write out a reference for Miss Smail?" said the detective with sudden sharpness, pouncing like a hawk. "It was found, you know, on her table among her possessions, such as those were."

Corbell studied his fingers; the man no doubt thought he had him trapped, but he replied quickly. "I have not liked to say it," he murmured, "but I had reason to complain of a certain aspect of Miss Smail's conduct. It was partly for that reason that I sent my daughter away."

"What was that aspect, Lord Corbell? I should be grateful for the whole truth."

"A certain over-familiarity with my groom, whom I dismissed some time ago." He was deliberately telling lies; Fred and Miss Smail were dead, he was alive. *Sauve qui peut.*

"Is it possible that Miss Smail may have joined him wherever he has gone?"

"Anything is possible. I was not well enough acquainted with Miss Smail entirely to follow the workings of her mind. As far as I knew, her talents were for mathematics and botany." He was leading the other away from the deliberate earlier suggestion; a vision came to him of the chalk pit. If she was found down there, if they both were, it would look like a double suicide, undertaken separately. It might serve, or else might not. He waited in silence.

"It is odd that she left her money behind, let alone her spectacles. I am told she could not see a yard without them." He had already questioned the servants.

"Possibly it was pride. Women take strange fancies."

"Yet the groom would not be of the education or the class to support her as she was accustomed. Have you no idea of his present whereabouts, Lord Corbell?"

"None. I sent him packing. I had complaints of the kind about him earlier." He remembered Mhairi; if needed, that could be ascertained, though it was long ago and would be distasteful.

"It is possible that she has made away with herself," said the detective. "The obvious place would be the lake."

"Drag it if you wish, but in that case respect what you may find at the bottom."

The detective looked at him as though he were slightly mad. No doubt it was the oddest case on which he had yet been sent. The police force in question was moderately recent.

"The body will float in a few days, in that case," he said carefully, "unless she has weighted herself with stones, in which event it may take longer, or else not appear at all." He began to discourse on the already familiar gases of decomposition, and had obviously passed his examinations thoroughly; he was still fairly young and did not, evidently, know the details of the fourth lord's death. "She may, however, be lying injured, in which case – in any case – we have a trained pack of bloodhounds. If Miss Smail is anywhere to be found, they will find her."

Later, Corbell gave Miss Smail's small worn cotton glove, to start the scent. "I trust their baying will not disturb my wife, who is in a delicate state of health," he remembered to add.

The detective promised that the noise would diminish soon.

The hounds proved to have names like other dogs, and large sad faces. They set out on the trail and as promised, did not take long. It led them straight to the chalk-pit. Mercy Smail's body was dredged up, its clothes torn and the face bruised with contusions made during the fall. Her neck was broken. "That ain't all," said the sergeant, who had gone with the bloodhounds. There was another body down there, he added, in a more advanced state of decomposition; a man's. The thing to do now was to identify both, then wait for the pathologist's report. Corbell, explaining the baying of the hounds to Ione, found himself cool as snow. He had had no doubt whatever that Mercy Smail was dead. It was possible that he would have to use his wits both before and after the pathology report became available.

Neither of the dead persons having any known next-of-kin, Corbell had the task of identifying them. The deliquescent heap that had been Fred was only recognisable by its teeth and ears. Corbell turned away, sick; and saw the other sheet turned down to reveal Miss Smail.

Her face was discoloured, and lacerated with brambles and stones, the head lying at a queer angle. The skin was slightly bloated by contact with water, and he found his mind distance itself from the sight of her to conjecture as to whether or not the lake's source ran through the base of the pit. If so, the former's grey existence was omnipresent, unavoidable. The governess's mouth had relaxed in death, the eyes were closed tightly, perhaps in a final terror of being blinded by thorns. He turned away, saying evenly, "Yes, that is Miss Mercy Smail. I will see that the agency which sent her to me for employment is informed. She has no relatives, as you are aware."

They had drawn the sheet back over her face, and he limped out of the mortuary into the fresh air, away from the smell of formalin and from the other gruesome thing which had once been Fred.

The police returned once the pathology report had become available. Of the two, it had been easier to investigate Miss Smail. "I have to say the governess was not intact, and had lately given birth to a child."

"The groom's. I had not mentioned the matter, as the child is dead."

"Not to mince words, Lord Corbell, she'd been buggered as well, not seldom. There were traces of semen in her back passage, some of it fresh. The other corpse, as you saw for yourself, wasn't." He failed to add that the pathologist had said he'd never seen anal stretching like it.

"Perhaps that is the reason why she threw herself down,"

256

remarked Corbell. "I cannot imagine anyone hereabouts who would do such a thing, however."

Mercy Smail; blundering out of the house after his brutal dismissal; stumbling, running, myopic, blind with tears, towards oblivion, away from the intolerable memory of what he had said, of how he had used and abused her. Corbell closed his eyes for instants, then opened them to find the detective regarding him curiously.

"You and your wife are on good terms, Lord Corbell?"

"Excellent. She has just given birth, successfully, to my son. I find your question impertinent." It was best to grow a trifle heavy.

"We have to investigate all possibilities. Where were you on the night before Miss Smail disappeared?"

"The time of her disappearance seems uncertain. Occasionally I swim in the lake in evenings. I probably did so then. Any of my servants will verify that matter if they happen to have noticed it, but being used to my habits they may not have done so."

"We will enquire. After your swim, where did you go?"

"To my bed, of course. I do not at present share Lady Corbell's because of her recent condition. At any other time she would have witnessed the fact." He decided to stress his aristocrat's privileges with this fellow; his own unblemished reputation with the county, his standing as a Justice of the Peace; even a slight innuendo that if matters went too far, he was in a position to set on foot certain trouble in London.

"So there are no witnesses to the fact that you did not go up to Miss Smail in her attic room and commit an unnatural act with her?" the detective persisted.

"My dear sir, I had boyhood experience of those attic beds, as I slept in one. They creak. Had such an occurrence taken place the entire household would have known. Again, I find your question impertinent and irrelevant. I must ask you to be as expeditious as you can; I have a meeting to attend locally."

This happened to be true; also, it would be worth any servant's place to recall the creaking of beds at any time. The man left, and it was not till later, from Peggy, that Corbell heard the details of the finding, at last, of Fred. A wayward bloodhound called Scally, who always went a trifle off scent, had gone first to the locked vault door and been enticed away, as everyone knew there were only coffins inside to attract him. After once again sniffing firmly back at the locked door, Scally had been taken away despite himself to the rest, then sniffed again with interest at the chalk pit, baying, after poor Miss Smail's body had been lifted out, badly scratched as it was with thorns. "But for him they might not have found Fred, him being well under. Who'd have thought it? I'd have that pit covered over, my lord, if I was you; a wonder there hasn't been more accidents."

It had been a piece of luck to bring in Fred to his story. The devil was helping his own, after all. When the police had finally gone Corbell went to the decanter and poured himself one brandy, then another. Over the days that followed he drank increasingly, and did not visit Ione.

Meantime, he received a deadly little congratulatory note from Alfred Sissington, regarding his handling of the whole question of bodies in the pit. It had been impossible to keep the matter out of the papers, but names had been suppressed.

It was unlikely Alfred would attempt further blackmail now, Corbell decided, that he had virtual custody of Joan. He himself did not reply to the letter. It was also, by now, his word against Sissington's regarding earlier happenings with Fred; he had long since cleared away all traces. To treat the whole matter as a cock-and-bull story, if need arose, was the answer. He again assured himself that his standing in the county would bolster his position: and Alfred was still being paid.

If he had known, Peggy Vance had saved the day for him in general. Questioned further by the police after the voluntary appearance of the Penhaligons' coachman, who made a statement, they interviewed Peggy regarding the late Miss Smail.

Peggy wasn't going to let his lordship get the blame for anything. The dead were dead, and she stated firmly that that governess hadn't been all she ought to be, waiting about for men at the back gate on her day off. In fact, though it wasn't spoken of, she'd had a baby by that Fred. She could show them the corpse.

She led them, heavy-footed, down to the vault and watched them open the little coffin. The baby had not yet begun to decompose beyond recognition of its ears. Otherwise, it might have been that Lord Alfred's. His lordship here didn't permit him to enter the premises, but he came in. Everyone knew Miss Smail had lifted her skirt to him as well.

As a result, the London branch sought out Lord Sissington. He denied knowing anything about either death. Yes, he'd picked up the little governess once, he remembered; she'd been a hot little piece, asking for it. Yes, he'd laid her; that wasn't against the law, was it, if the girl was willing? No, he hadn't done anything to make her kill herself.

"Ask my cousin Corbell," he said smoothly. He had no evidence as to how far Crip was involved in the death, but making trouble for him was second nature.

They had to let him go, asking him to remain available meantime. He'd seen the man Fred down at Lackmere in old days once or twice, he said, that was all.

The police were discussing the matter of alcohol in the blood, and how it had been too late this time to test for it in the earlier case. "I'll swear it was the old devil buggered her, whatever he says, but there's no way of proving it," said the detective regretfully. There would only be trouble at the top if any attempt of the kind was made. It was better to leave the nobs to their consciences, if they had any, which at times seemed doubtful.

Chapter Three

Corbell could think of no remedy for his state of mind. That last should have contained guilt, if not grief, at Mercy Smail's death, and did not. All he felt, and knew it, was a certain triumph at having avoided embarrassment with the police. He was not even particularly aware of his own physical needs. Ione wouldn't let him near her by now in any case. About again, he was aware of her close-set gaze; its expression made him uncomfortable.

The baby Peggy had brought in – whether Ione suspected what had happened or not he never knew – was to be christened Claud, after the general. By now he was feeding placidly from the wet-nurse, still wearing a little bonnet over his ears. The birth had been announced in the papers, and letters of congratulation began to arrive by the next few posts, together with others of commiseration over Pussy's death. As for that tiresome governess, it was assumed she had been got rid of.

Several funerals followed at Lackmere. The two suicides, spoken of as such by now everywhere, were buried together outside the churchyard field, and the baby with them, as it was doubtfully a Christian soul. The significant funeral was Pussy's, and a surprising number of old racing friends turned up and, later, visited Fred's grave. Pussy was, of course, respectably contained within the churchyard wall. Lady Leonora, in her black veil, said she preferred not to go back to Cannes; bridge at Harrogate was comparatively restful, if Lord Corbell agreed. She added that it was so suitable that the two lovers, Fred and the governess, should lie together in death as in life. In its way it was like Abélard and Héloïse. Lady Leonora had always prided herself on a smattering of information regarding all subjects a civilised person should know.

After she had gone, and after the funerals were over, Ione spoke up, her eyes like ice. "You killed Fred, didn't you? I knew you would. He never looked near that governess."

He made no answer. From the cold place at the back of his mind where facts lay, one raised its head. A wife could not give evidence against her husband. No doubt Ione knew that as well.

It was a long time since Corbell again ventured to swim, though he gazed often at the lake. He consoled himself these days by returning to his studio, having effaced all memories there of Mercy Smail; had the police found sketches of her they might not have given up so easily. He had burnt the sketches, watching with relief as the unforgotten starfish hands curled up and darkened forever into unidentifiable ash.

Thinking of ash, of death, made him draw the Corbell Strumpet as he had seen her portrayed for himself before her last portrait was destroyed. When the face was finished it so resembled Etta's that he added a gold crown. He contrived what was almost a facsimile of Harrigan's portrait of Etta and her son as the Christ Child, face turned away; Ed's face had been turned also, watching the kiln firing, so Corbell had never seen it. He would like to meet Ed again. Etta's face and dark hair, and the green eyes, looked out from above the formal folds of the gown he now drew, her hands clasping the child's tree-straight body.

This was his son. It was incredible that the unforgotten coupling in the lake should have failed to result in conception. Sissington's brief possession of Etta after the wedding had been brief; she'd run off, he'd said as much.

Corbell found himself thinking of Ed more and more. He would be almost a man now, with a potter's grip. He had dark hair; what were his features?

*   *   *   *

Time passed. Lady Leonora expired in course of a rubber at Harrogate. It was the way she'd have wanted to go, Ione said. She herself showed no emotion at the death, any more than at her father's. Corbell decided that she lacked intelligence. It suited him to proceed with the plan building up in his mind. There seemed nothing to prevent it, barring any refusal of the man Harrigan and Ed to part with each other.

He wrote, but there was no reply. He determined to pursue the matter in person. After all, he would be remembered as a stranger who had interrupted a firing.

Other events detained him meantime.

Corbell was disturbed when Walshe came one day to give in his notice and ask for a reference. The excuse he gave was that the cook was pestering him to marry her, and he wasn't the marrying kind.

"She's been pestering you for years. Why not think of it? You'd be well fed in your old age." It would come to the same thing; there must be some other reason.

"Naow. I want to see a bit o' the world, Australia and that."

"So that's it. Digging for opals is hard work, they tell me, and so is panning for gold. You're not young enough. You're older than I am." He could remember the slightly older boy at the knife-grinding machine years ago, telling him what fornication meant. If Walshe went, he himself would have to hire a valet, coachman and butler, and the cook might take the notion to leave.

"She won't," Walshe assured him. "She's settled in."

He seemed adamant, and Corbell unwillingly wrote him a reference for years of varied and useful service. He would miss Walshe, with his everlasting poker face and his reliable way with confidences. Corbell disliked the idea of strangers, being convinced that everything changed except himself.

Walshe went off with the reference and a determination to make himself scarce as soon as it was expedient to do so. The baby heir resembled nobody more than Miss Smail, except that his hands weren't the shape of her neat little starfish, but surprisingly spreading like his own, hands that could turn to anything. Also, the child's hair, now it had grown in, was the colour of the late governess's cunt. The situation might not be spotted or guessed at if he, Tom Walshe, got away fast. He wouldn't be panning for gold, but knew where he intended making for; Devil's Island, Van Diemen's Land, lately Tasmania. He wouldn't be found among the poor devils shut in cells down near the beach, where they often hanged themselves. He'd be up among the newcome nobs, one of the first to become a gentleman's gentleman; paid what money he liked, having been in service with an English lord. The new nobs had their carriages and their coachbuilders, and needed shaving as it should be done, and their wives would want their hair curled and the lice picked out of it. He hadn't any illusions. The reference apart, he'd see to it that his lordship didn't find him easily. As for the old women at the cottages, Vance and Ag Tesson, they could go on being crazy about the boy they thought was Jemmy's; he knew all about *that*. As it was, they saw more of Master Claud now he was running about on his thin legs than her ladyship did, but that was the same as had happened with Miss Joan. The upper crust didn't care the snap of its fingers for its children, which might often mean they were really somebody else's.

Corbell, in fact, could summon up very little affection for Claud, mostly out of disquiet lest Ione note the likeness to Miss Smail. For that reason he let the little fellow spend his time up at the cottages, in the care of old Agnes Tesson. Peggy went up a great deal, and seemed to dote on him. If enough time passed, those who remembered Miss Smail would be few. She was forgotten already except for her name on a tombstone, alongside Fred's.

This he knew was the final insult to her. He went down alone one day once the stone was up. Frederick Corbell and Mercy Belinda Smail had both been in service at Lackmere; the year of their deaths was the same. That was all anyone need know, whatever they surmised.

"You say you loved me," he said aloud. "I loved once, and can never love again. I drove you to your death, and now have dishonoured you. If your love is strong enough to be glad you have saved me from a silken rope, so be it." He turned away.

During the ensuing weeks he found out what his own payment must be; perhaps from shock, he was impotent. It mattered little, except for his continued resolve that Sissington should not inherit.

For that reason alone, little Claud as an heir would not do. Peggy's rinses might have failed in either instance; the child might be his own or Alfred's. His premature birth made it difficult to be certain.

An heir of his own blood was essential. There was only one source now; the boy he had seen in Etta's portrait, then later on, stoking the potter's kiln in the Mile End Road. The more he thought of it, the more essential Ed's part in the plan became. Gradually the idea of what must be done took shape in his mind.

He wrote to Harrigan again, demanding that Ed be sent to him. If the man made difficulty, enough money would settle the matter. After that, Corbell knew what to do.

PART VII

Chapter One

Again Corbell had written to Harrigan without reply, and was considering going up to town; the man might have moved, or have died: it should not be impossible to trace Ed, by now without doubt a trained potter. Meantime, Corbell went out among his tenants still, in the way his father had used to do; dealing with complaints, threatening a husband who had beaten his wife, arranging for slates to be replaced or thatch to be repaired; seeing one very old woman admitted into the cottage hospital as she had no family left. He was thorough about such things; she hadn't been alone for long.

Returning home, with duty done, to be informed that a young gentleman was waiting for him in the study, he felt irritated. He wanted to relieve himself and have a bath before dinner. Swimming had reluctantly been given up this year on the advice of his doctor.

When an edition of himself as he used to be, but straight as a sapling, rose at last from the study chair, the years rolled away. "I'm Ed," stated that personage unnecessarily.

Corbell continued to stare. It was the first time he had seen the boy face to face, and his eyes were grey with black fringed lashes; Yolande's eyes, with laughter at the back of them. Whoever had been his father – and Corbell had never been in much doubt that that last night of all in the lake with Etta could have hardly failed to conceive a child – this was Yolande's grandson.

Corbell reached out a hand and touched him. Ed was real. Had he said he would never love again? He loved Ed at sight.

It turned out, when Ed had wolfed down a meal and become ready to talk, that Harrigan had got married to a widow who owned four pubs "and she didn't want me around." He fished out a flat wrapped package from his jacket, which was worn at the elbows. "Didn't want this either. Harrigan said to bring it to yer. It's of me and my ma."

Corbell opened it, staring down. There was the portrait he'd seen of Etta and the boy, which had enabled him to trace Harrigan the first time and find out what had become of Etta herself. He stared at it so long that Ed had at last wiped his mouth with his sleeve and stood up. "I needed that," he said. "Can I get a job here, guv?"

Corbell smiled, and did not reply. He sent for Vance to put fresh sheets on the bed in the upper spare room, and to see that Master Ed had a hot bath and was given a clean shirt or two. Life, which he had thought was finished, had begun.

"It is a family resemblance," he assured Ione, who said nothing. "You will recall my half-sister Etta. You met her briefly before our wedding."

"At that rate he's your cousin Alfred's son. She went off with him."

He had not even had to say it to her.

One of the first things Corbell did was to take Ed down to the lake. They went to the boathouse, where the little boat had been kept caulked and watertight as ever. Corbell climbed in, and would have taken the oars, but Ed seized them. "I can row," he boasted. "Ever heard of the Thames?"

It turned out that he had often swum in the Thames as well; if you knew where to go, certain of the reaches were clean at high tide. "Me and Harrigan used to swim. He said he used to take Ma. She was good at it. I don't remember."

They rowed out to the centre. Ed stripped off his clothes and made ready to dive in. Seeing once again that white, white flesh, Corbell felt time roll back and further back, till he was a boy again. Sun-warmed flesh, briefly glimpsed above white muslin in a garden heavy with roses: Yolande, that time his father came home.

He had noted Ed's royal parts. This was surely his son, the link between past and present; Jocosa, Yolande, Etta, himself, all who knew the lake.

Ed had intercepted his glance. "You can if you like," he said. "Harrigan used to. That's why his old woman wanted me out past the door."

The first time Harrigan had done it to him, he said, was while Ma's ashes were cooling in the kiln. He'd said it would take their minds off things. After that they'd made a habit of it.

Anyway, Harrigan said Ed had to earn his keep. Later on, he'd done it back to Harrigan as well. "That was why his old woman wanted me out of the way," Ed said again. "Maybe he wrote to you?"

"No. I wrote to him. What about girls?" He found the matter left him without feeling.

Ed shrugged. "Well, there they are if you wants 'em. I don't mind which."

There was one more thing to be done; to dispose of Etta's ashes now the time had come. They had been a link with Yolande. Now, he had Ed. Corbell limped to the organ room in the very early day, took the urn down and placed it in the boat. He would sink the contents in Ed's company.

They rowed out together, and came to the place where long ago his father had made him dispose of forbidden beauty, broken shards of silver, the last remaining portrait of a green-eyed girl with dark hair. Was Jocosa waiting now for Etta to join her, the two made one?

He said no prayer, being still a disciple of Anubis. The god would weigh Etta's heart. He cast the urn down into the waiting water, watching it career, spiralling a little. Then he unfastened the green enamel eye fob from his watch-chain and sent it down after the urn. The Corbell Strumpet had both eyes again with which to regard her granddaughter.

Ed had said nothing and taken no part. Corbell watched him dive into the water and swim like a seal. The silver arcs and ripples about his twisting merman's form brought the older man a deep contentment. His son, conceived in this very place, must not yet know of his own identity. It was part of the plan that he should not.

Sissington had always been afraid of water. This boy had never been got by him.

269

From then on, there seemed no limits to Ed's kingdom. Within weeks, three of the maidservants had been duly dosed by Peggy, whose hand and eye were still unerring in such ways. Ione, noticing at last that she seemed constantly surrounded by red-eyed young serving-women, broke her rule of no hobnobbing and asked a little between-maid what was the matter with her. The girl sobbed out that it was that Ed; he'd done it before you knew where you were.

Ione, outraged, then spoke to Peggy, only to be told that his lordship let Ed do as he liked. It wasn't her place to say anything.

"Well, *I* shall say something," replied Ione, She duly complained to her husband, who laughed.

"They're bound to blame Ed, because he's young and handsome. It may be anyone, and they don't dare speak up."

"Whoever it is, I don't like that boy; he's common, I can't think why you spend so much time in his company."

"Console yourself; he will be sent to a finishing establishment shortly. After all, as Alfred's son, he deserves to be made into a gentleman."

He left her with her induced thoughts.

There was an expensive establishment north of Hyde Park, where young males of all sorts were rendered fit to enter polite society. In spite of Ed's ribald comments about having to be made posh, Corbell entered him there; it was colloquially known as the Sow's Ear, and taught among other things boxing, fencing, clay pigeon shooting, correct ballroom dancing and etiquette, riding in the Row, and the proper use of the English language. Ed could already imitate the toffs with praiseworthy ease, but Corbell insisted that he take the course seriously. He himself used frequently to travel up to town and stay at his club; taking a hackney over early in the morning for the pride of watching Ed, among grocers' sons and others anxious to be turned into young gentlemen, rise to the trot with ease; he was quick and apt to learn.

Corbell often took him to music-halls and other places which might interest him. Once out driving, they passed a pub Ed said was one of Ma Harrigan's. "Let's get out," he said. Corbell was unwilling, but could think of no reason to refuse. He dismissed the driver and paid him. They went into an old-fashioned bar, with lettered mirrors and a thin-faced barman. No, Mr and Mrs Harrigan were in Brighton for a few days. "Come up and see the prints," said Ed, downing a pint. "They're worth something."

They were upstairs, and turned out to be mostly about Prinny; from gilded youth to stout middle age, increasingly cruel; showing him at last dressed as a woman in a straw hat, his enormous belly uplifted to form a bosom. Corbell reflected on the cruelty of his upbringing by a father who lacked understanding. He limped downstairs at last.

"You've taken a long time," said Ed. "Let's have dinner here."

They had dinner, not badly served and cooked, then decided to stay the night. The room had striped wallpaper and a pair of engravings, not as interesting as the prints. Corbell wondered if Harrigan would sell him the set; he would perhaps write.

Ed was still undressing when Corbell lay in bed. There was a glass on a tray near the wall, with a jug of water. Ed poured some out and instead of drinking it, balanced the half-full tumbler on his extended penis. He was laughing. Corbell suddenly felt tears rise. Here was Etta's flesh and Yolande's; he had earlier denied himself in the boat on the lake. Now, he wept openly, desirously. "Want it?" said Ed.

"No. I have something else I want you to do."

Corbell explained his plan. Ed was incredulous, his grey eyes wide.

"The old girl? She wouldn't ever. She doesn't like me, says I'm common. Maybe she's right. Gimme a wild oat or two just for a bit, do."

Corbell promised him his wild oats. They appeared to consist of going down to the village at nights to drink with other young men. However, the rumour of an affair with a young woman came soon enough. Corbell pawed Ed like a woman himself, begging for it to stop. His jealousy gnawed at him; a harsh echo to the long-ago envy of poor Mercy's clergyman. He surveyed himself as he was, without enthusiasm. Ed was standing with his thumbs in his waistcoat, grinning. He was well aware of his own value.

"You said I was to get experience; well, I'm getting it. Nothing serious, don't fret." It was Dolly, he said, up at the pub; she was a tart, though particular. He described certain of her aspects.

Corbell decided with cold deliberation to bring on Ione if Ed wanted a woman. She had been forced to live like a nun since the

271

last birth, never touched by himself, watched day and night by Peggy or other servants. In nature, the plan should work.

Ed had revealed a talent with motors. Ione would enjoy little drives in the Daimler, driven by the young man she believed to be Alfred's son. Dislike in a woman often turned to attraction. He instructed her to put on her dust-coat and veil, and watched them drive off. He had for some time told the lodge-keeper to say her ladyship was not receiving; the days must hang heavy on Ione's hands.

It was after the third drive that Ed, returning her ladyship and encountering Corbell in the hall, put up both thumbs and closed one eye. Afterwards he explained that they'd parked in a convenient clump of trees. It might have been the same clump used, for the same purpose, long ago by Fred.

"She don't 'arf ask for it," Ed began to say, as Fred had once done at The Ghluin. By then it didn't matter where it happened; soon, as the weather worsened, a favourite place was the late Anna Corbell's chaise-longue, with a fire lit. Eventually a carpenter had to be called in to repair it, as it had unaccountably broken across the middle. "We does things proper," said Ed. "I have her in the Daimler after church, anyway. It ought to do the trick." He knew very well what was wanted.

Corbell now slept in his dressing-room, less deprived than diverted to hear the silent opening of the door from the passage that led to Ione's bed. Ed's sliding in was professionally soundless. It occurred to Corbell, listening thereafter to the fashioning of his grandson, that he had never till now heard Ione's transports, kept behind bitten lips now lest he hear. With himself, she had continued to resemble the Parthenon. Now, she was Juno, with the impudent young Ixion who had ended up by falling, long and hard, back to earth and had ended up tied to a wheel in Hades. He, Corbell, was Jove, listening not with godlike jealousy but with objective entertainment.

Ed would report to him frequently. "Funny thing, she calls me Alfie when we're at it, then Ed when we ain't. Who was Alfie?"

Corbell did not inform him; he would never have heard of, or encountered, Sissington. The question of his own paternity did not appear to trouble the young man; he took life as it came. All the same he was growing restive.

"When's this foreign tour coming off?" he asked one day,

adding that even the parish bull got put out to grass. He yawned, remembering to put a hand up in front of his mouth.

"As soon as you've done your job. There's no proof yet."

Proof was forthcoming shortly. One evening at dinner Ione admitted she didn't feel like eating anything. "You may not have noticed I haven't been my usual colour for some time. You don't notice much about me. I waited to be certain before telling you, although there is absolutely nothing you can do. The law – oh, I'm not a fool – says you're the father of any child I may bear. I'll see to it you don't kill this one. I'll have witnesses in the room, and won't let it out of my sight."

Corbell did not reply, and drank his coffee. He hadn't been certain that she knew about the earlier situations.

"Well?" Ione asked. His silence had disconcerted her. Ed was absent, probably in the village. That was why she'd chosen the occasion; she'd known her state for some time, and was filled with a pleasant sense of vengeance. Ed was Alfred's son. The whole thing was poetic justice. After everything she'd endured, Corbell deserved it. She had expected rage, however, and felt cheated.

"I wish you a happy delivery," was all he said. He rose then and went slowly out; she heard his uneven footsteps dragging away.

Chapter Two

Now Ed was in control of events, Corbell felt able to proceed with plans he had some time had in mind for young Claud, now aged six. Given that the boy might have inherited his mother's intellect, he was prepared to send him to a good school and later, if he showed promise, to Cambridge except for one factor. As there was a possibility that the father was not himself but Sissington, Corbell wanted to ensure that under no circumstances should Claud marry. It was an echo of his own father's attitude to himself, as he wryly recognised.

There was one haven open to Claud which had not been considered for him; it would allow gifts to develop and a vocation to be encouraged. Claud must accordingly be received into Yolande's religion. It was said that if a boy was taught by Jesuits from the age of seven, he was theirs for life. High office would be available to Claud in the Catholic Church, and celibacy would be enjoined in any priestly office. It was a way of ensuring a living for the child which would remove him from the vicinity of Lackmere.

He knew Claud would have to receive instruction, and was uncertain how to go about this. By now, Yolande's harsh prioress aunt must be dead. He wrote to the convent, whose direction had been found among the fourth lord's papers. Feeling as if he was offering the infant Samuel to the Temple for life, Corbell phrased his letter carefully. He was in charge, he said, of a child whom he would pay to have educated at a Jesuit school, being himself outside the faith. He mentioned his late stepmother, Yolande Lady

Corbell. Writing her name gave him a churning at the heart.

The reply came in the neat handwriting of the present prioress. If Lord Corbell would care, by arrangement, to call with the little boy, and consult their chaplain, he would find that everything required would be made available. The prioress added that one very old member of their community remembered Lady Corbell as a child among them, and that she was still prayed for regularly.

It was a strange feeling to limp up the steep hill between laurels, as El Capitano must have done long ago with a child beside him, exactly Claud's age. He was less well acquainted with Claud than the cottage women were, and the little fellow's speech was theirs and manifestly local. That would need correction.

They found themselves outside the great door with its closed grille. They grated a pin of the old type, and saw the wood inner panel slide open. A portress in a meticulously laundered veil led them in silence along well-polished passages smelling of beeswax. Reaching the prioress's parlour, a further grille opened in the wall beyond. A pleasant high-coloured woman of perhaps forty, seated and with an attendant nun behind, greeted them from behind it. Corbell wondered if she had known Yolande, but didn't ask. Nuns looked younger than they were. The prioress greeted them both and suggested that Claud might like to visit Sister Vincent, who had a telescope. He went out with the portress, and Corbell was told he might now discuss matters in private with the chaplain, who expected them.

"His name is Father Chillingfold."

Corbell reflected in silence on the nature of coincidence. He hadn't heard of the preacher's conversion, which must, to allow for training and ordination, have taken place about the time of Mercy's death. No doubt that had impelled him to it. Possibly he had been given this relatively undemanding appointment because of his nervous disposition and his history. That this should have been considered by the authorities boded well for Claud's future.

Chillingfold entered, in a black soutane. Neither wasted time in formalities. His face was thinner, resembling his earlier self. "The boy concerning whom I should like to ask you to make arrangements is unaware of his parentage. He is the son of Mercy Smail and Alfred Sissington."

He had determined to treat the possibility as truth. If Chillingfold felt any emotion, he showed none. The prioress's grille had closed quietly, leaving them together. When Claud was returned after arrangements had been completed the priest treated him as any other child. "What did you see through the telescope?" he asked. Claud's prim little face became animated.

"Nothing much, because it's daytime. At night you can see the stars and the planets. Sister Vincent is a hundred years old."

"You may leave him safely," said Father Chillingfold. He would instruct Mercy's son and arrange for him to be christened. After that the Jesuits should teach him. He himself hadn't been acceptable for so long and rigorous a special training. He was content here meantime.

Corbell left money with them, and promised to pay all costs. He went out to where silver birches reared on the hill, with poppies bright at this holiday season and no young lady pupils in sight. The young Yolande had once sat here alone with her lesson-books. As at that time below the high Alpine villages, he felt close to her. He made his way slowly back to his waiting carriage, leaning on his cane.

Telling Vance was less easy, although officially Claud was his son. She rounded on him, not so deaf now that she didn't understand Master Claud had been sent away to school.

"Taking him away as young. He hasn't lost his milk-teeth yet."

"He is not too young to start to be educated according to his station." By the time Claud's future was decided one way or the other, Peggy would be no longer with them. Her faded eyes blazed fire.

"He's the last of the Tessons. If you didn't know before, you should know now. My Jemmy was his father. The blood is as old as the Conquest. See to it that he knows when he's old enough. *I* know what's going on with her ladyship."

He had always resented the fact that she knew too much. The widening of poor Mercy's parts was at last explained, also Jemmy's sudden attack on him at the folly. The best answer was silence, and the hope that Ione and Ed would have a son whose blood was his own.

*   *   *   *

276

Corbell arranged a trip to Italy for Ed and a friend from the Sow's Ear. It would renew one's own memories when Ed came back. Rome, Tuscany, Pompeii; the equivalent of the Grand Tour of old days. He made Ed promise to talk Sow's Ear English and not that of the Mile End Road, and arranged sizeable banker's drafts in different locations.

It would be necessary, now, to keep an eye on Ione, who, judging from certain recent sounds and signs, had developed, at least for the time being, the sexual appetites of a later Roman empress. It was kept from her as long as possible that Ed was going away, and after breaking the news, which she took with unexpected calmness, Corbell himself accompanied her constantly, still sleeping in his dressing-room at nights with the door open. He tired easily these days, and was therefore often present when occasional company visited Ione. In this way he heard the Lord Lieutenant's wife say brightly about the coming baby, "It's so splendid for you both, after the last poor little boy being so delicate he has to be sent to be specially cared for." A random harvest had sprung up, evidently, about Claud.

When she had gone the silence was so heavy he had to go out of the room for relief. Once he would have plunged to find it in the lake. Now, he could only look forward to Ed's return, to watch him swimming again, his muscles rippling beneath the tanned white skin. He hadn't written, and Ione seemed less plaintive about his absence than might have been foreseen. However, no other man, young or old, was allowed to come near her. Corbell and Peggy took turns to keep watch.

He tried despite everything to devote himself to Ione, playing two-handed whist with her in the evenings, though she did not seem to have inherited her mother's flair with cards. As for her erstwhile passion for backing horses, it was given no chance. On fine days, there was the croquet lawn; but increasingly Ione refused to invite women friends to play, saying as time passed that she couldn't show herself now, she looked, again, like a filled sack. Corbell therefore made himself drive her about the grounds in the motor, aware that he could by no means replace Ed even had he wanted to. She complained constantly of discomfort, and one day he flared out at her for being, at that rate, too idle to walk.

"At least you have two great strong legs of equal length. You underrate your own good fortune."

"Oh, you're always hard on me. You've never liked me. You should have let me marry Alfred, as I longed to."

Always Alfred. No doubt she saw the latter still as she remembered him, behind the potted palms at the ball where he'd proposed. By now he was a middle-aged roué, in debt right and left. Corbell had the consideration not to say so, drove home and left Ione again with her memories. No doubt she had consoled herself with the thought that she was carrying Alfred's grandchild. He himself would be the last to disillusion her.

Engaged in the pointless games of cards, only half aware of the petulant, thickening woman opposite, Corbell would reflect on the state of things if this birth did not come to term. The doctor had earlier advised no more children, though Ione was not yet forty. He, Corbell, knew it was his own need for Ed which had forced matters; as it was, he missed the boy intolerably. Grotesque alternatives circled in his mind; Ed was by law the son of the fourth lord's daughter Etta and her husband Fred. Nobody knew Joan was Ed's half-sister. He himself was already deep in crime. If something went wrong at this birth, he would insist that Joan be returned to him. On Ed's return he would accustom them to one another's company. Alfred could do less harm than before. It was a long time now since Fred's murder; the evidence by this time would prove very little, and the blackmail could cease. Payments might, after all, have been made to allow his cousin and potential heir to keep up his position in society.

The possibilities grew. As things might soon stand, a marriage between his own daughter and the fourth lord's grandson would rival any claim of Sissington's except as regarded the entail; and the law could argue over that till the Day of Judgment. Alfred after all had small means of combating any such decision except with sums provided by Corbell himself.

It diverted him to play with the situation, while Ione's large white hand inevitably chose the wrong card. Of all things, fate had not deprived him, Corbell, of money. Everything he touched seemed to turn to gold except for what he wanted most. How long it seemed since Ed had gone away!

Nevertheless his conscience would still prevent such an outcome. The law was an ass, no doubt. The metaphor was not apt. He had seen donkeys in Spain, patient, maltreated, adaptable yet stubborn, enduring all things. Ancient tribal law had stigmatised

278

incest because inbreeding would lead to the weakening of the tribe; but in the present case it would be better by far for Joan to marry Ed than the degenerate Sissington, whose father in his unreformed days had been known as the Palomino Stud. In any case if Ione gave safe birth to Ed's son, nothing need be altered.

Altogether Corbell felt restless, and for the first time since Ed's departure made his way out to the boathouse, rowing out to the centre where Etta-Jocosa lay. Perhaps after all, long ago, he should have copied his father, filled his pockets with stones and made the lake, once his refuge and delight, his grave. Sissington could have married Ione, inherited, lived here as he would; and yet, the thought was intolerable.

Once, to forget it, he Corbell, would have stripped and plunged in over the boat's edge, swimming till his mind was clear. Now, his breaths came too quickly even with the effort of rowing out as far. He was old, and would soon die.

He must have slept, there in the boat. He had a dream, and in it saw Yolande. She was wearing her white dress.

"Edmund, Edmund, do not sin any more. You have destroyed life, destroyed love. Soon again you will see the amber locket, and then, my darling, you will die. After that there will be a long time of darkness, but I will continue to pray for you as always. In the end the light will come, and we will meet again."

He awoke to find himself cold and stiff, hunched over the oars. It was growing dark, and he had not the strength to row back to the boathouse. He took the boat to the near edge, cast anchor and climbed out. He had the feeling that this might be his last time on the beloved water.

It wouldn't be long now, Yolande had said. He need endure very little more before the long darkness. That meant he would see the amber locket soon. He remembered he'd sent it to Joan. That must mean Joan was coming back. There might be love between her and Ed. He didn't know what she looked like now, his daughter. Love. He'd denied it to her, to Mercy Smail, to Etta, Ione and Claud.

There was nothing to do now but wait. He loved Ed, at least. He must live till he saw Ed's grey eyes again.

Ed was not a good correspondent, and the time passed slowly. As with other young men, he wouldn't come back till his money was spent. He scrawled a line at last to say he and Tot, the other boy from the Sow's Ear, had visited Pompeii and liked it better than anywhere. That had been three weeks ago. Ione was in her sixth month. She had said surprisingly little about Ed's long time away. It was almost as though she'd forgotten him. She had ceased to show herself in company, keeping mostly to her room, with Peggy, old now, nearby.

The two experienced travellers returned in due course, browned with the Italian sun. Ed had grown in confidence, never having greatly lacked it; he seemed broader in the shoulders, more of a man. Corbell found himself unable to keep his hands off this son, caressing him as though he had been a woman or child. He listened to the stories of their travels as though they had been the Arabian Nights. Part of it was lies, he knew. Ed was an accomplished liar. He only grinned when he was caught out. He had no morals whatever; it was part of his attraction.

Corbell tried to forget his own tiredness and to take on a new lease of life. Ed was home; that was all that mattered. Ed was home.

Shortly news of another kind announced itself in the papers, but Corbell happened to miss the advertisement. Lady Sissington, Alfred's long-suffering mother, had died unexpectedly in the north. He would normally have attended the funeral, but didn't want to leave now Ed was home.

Chapter Three

One day Corbell stopped on his way across the hall to look up at the general's portrait. He hadn't done so for years, merely taking its presence for granted in passing. Now, again, it was strange to see his own head on a straight body. The portrait's presence, in its bright coat and medals, had always dominated Lackmere. Now, with the restored sword hanging below in its scabbard, the general himself should be, to all intents, fully present. Corbell wondered what his grandfather would think of events before and since the fourth lord's death. The stern heavy-browed face gave away nothing.

He became aware of dragging footsteps, and turned to see old Peggy Vance. She used a stick now to get about, like himself. She stood there beside him and looked up. Her hair was white long ago, her dark eyes opaque, her hearing gone. She wouldn't hear the resonance of what she said next. Like all the deaf, she spoke out on a harsh note, triumphantly.

"He did it to me on the master bed, the general, before he died. Margaret was his, and Jemmy was Margaret's, and Claud was Jemmy's, a Tesson, by that Miss Smail. I saw to it. It was long ago, but I haven't forgotten. You were wrong to bring back the sword, Master Edmund. The general meant it to stay where he'd put it. You haven't brought fortune on yourself by anything you've done."

"Did you know where the sword was?" he asked, close in her ear. At the same time he told himself Claud could equally well be his own. Peggy's black draught didn't always work, and neither, as all men knew, did condoms. That first time in the folly could itself have sired Claud. He might have been born at term or else before it. Nobody knew now. The main thing was that Ione mustn't hear. He tried to draw Peggy back to her ground floor room with its shelves full of nostrums whose labels she could no longer see.

"Oh, I guessed. I didn't need to ask. I can remember seeing his lady in a thick veil, in the state her ladyship's in now, in the tower. She was sitting with her hands idle, looking out at the lake. I was with my Ma. Ma knew everything about most that went on, but she was wrong about me, and never said so, never said she was wrong."

She was getting childish, he decided. She had been here, after all, longer than he could remember. Lackmere wouldn't be the same when she had gone. It was possible that he himself would go first, a close run between them.

He saw her slowly back to her room. The master bed with its black velvet and its gold baskets had seen many things. There was no reason why it shouldn't have seen that. By now, it didn't matter, and the last Tesson, if that was what he was, had been provided for and judging from report, was doing well.

Rome hadn't impressed them, Ed was saying; all them statues and churches. He and Tot – Tothill was staying for a few days – preferred Pompeii, as stated. That volcano hadn't been the end of everything. There were the secret clubs still, places women weren't allowed into. There had been a giant phallus at the top of a flight of stairs. He, Ed, could beat it any day. They'd been admitted at last into the painted chamber and, on giving assurances, to the club where men whipped each other. "Sets you up a treat," said Ed, reverting to the Mile End Road in the way he had when moved to enthusiasm. He said he'd brought something home from there to use. "If you liked, we could do it all three on them Roman tiles. It's what they used to do to each other."

He had already drawn out from his baggage a long vicious object and stood holding it, with the archaic smile of the Apollo of Veii. It was the Pompeian club whip.

*   *   *   *

The brazier had been lit in the cellar, where nothing had changed from long ago. Ed lit the paired black candles bought then. They had all three stripped, Corbell among them. He would not in the ordinary way have exposed his twisted body, but he could deny Ed nothing. The sight of Tothill's repelled him slightly; it was weedy, the parts small. Ed's father turned with relief and pride to his son's splendid nakedness. He saw Ed take the whip and flex its length. Patient on his tile, the dog-god Anubis waited, ready to weigh the hearts of the dead. Death? Nobody was dead except Cousin Mildred. *Poor little fellow, what a tragedy.* He'd outlasted her, when all was said.

Ed began to whip him and Tothill; shoulders, legs, buttocks. The visitor started to laugh and dance with a high girlish sound. Corbell stood still at first, enduring, then felt rejuvenated. The stinging pain made him young and potent again.

He began unevenly to dance, aware that for the first time since Mercy's death, he was having an erection. Like the rest he laughed out loud while the blood streamed from him. Ecstasy overcame him. He cradled his restored penis in his hands, calling out, "O my son! O my son!"

Time had rolled back; he was a young man, capering in a cellar. Etta, Etta would enter, the scapegoat; and this time he would lie with her from the back. *My sister, my bride.* She had given him Ed, after all. Ed whipped on, like Papa had once been used to do. Corbell was laughing wildly still, calling out the word itself. "Papa! Papa! Papa!"

He heard Ed answer, mockingly. "Papa! Papa! Papa!" Ed had always been fairly certain; why otherwise had the old boy taken such a fancy to him?

"My turn," Corbell called out, breathless, bleeding and flogged. There were sects who did this to the extent of madness still.

He tried to seize the whip, but Ed evaded him with a master's flick. "Kneel," he ordered. Corbell knelt obediently on the Anubis tile. He felt Ed come and straddle him, then enter. This was the ultimate ecstasy, the final damnation. The black candles flared. The fifth lord, kneeling on the dog-headed tile, raised his head and bayed at the probable moon.

There came another sound then; a woman's scream.

They fell apart. Ione was standing behind the black altar on the

283

stairs, hands clutching her distended body beneath the nightgown and shawl. Her mouth was a black, open void. She screamed on, using words he hadn't known she knew.

"That's what you do, you filthy devils. He's *your* son. I should have known. Don't touch me again, either of you. Peggy. . . Peggy, she's ill . . ."

The last word trailed away in a renewed scream; she had gone into premature labour. The child shot out of her precipitately, hitting the tiles with its head. It was a girl, with marmalade hair.

Corbell's first thought was that she must have slept with Sissington. It could not have happened, however; she'd been watched constantly, by him and by Ed. Ed. Sissington's son, who had lately possessed him. Corbell was filled with self-disgust. He heard a young man speak, someone with no business here.

"I've cut the cord. Help me to get her upstairs, the pair of you."

She was heavy, a dead weight. The child lay kicking, astonishingly alive. Corbell helped to lift Ione's weight and somehow, they got her upstairs. Peggy had had a seizure; it turned out that that was why she'd come in search of them. The baby lived.

He didn't want to see Ed again. He sent money to tell both young men they might go off wherever they chose, except here. That was all.

Lady Corbell must have had some kind of shock, the doctor said. The pregnancy had been proceeding normally. As it was, the little girl had a strong physique to have survived so sudden a birth. The situation must be accepted that there could be no more children.

Peggy recovered partly. She would never again be able to speak clearly. As it was, she'd said everything to him she had to say. He went to her, seating himself in the chair by her bed and holding her flaccid hand. It was wrinkled, the hand of the very old. She tried to smile.

It would be useless to try to atone to Ione now. She had never liked him, by this time loathed him, and had reason. She wouldn't see him, but the nurse said she'd managed to keep down a little broth, and should recover.

Corbell asked himself if he was at fault for having prevented her marriage to Alfred in the first place. What did he know of love? So much had happened that shouldn't, and had failed to happen that should. If instead of avoiding Etta he had got a child on her who was Fred's nominal son, he would have been next heir. As it was, he'd driven Etta to the streets after leaving Sissington. That name recurred in every facet of his existence. He had withheld love from everyone except Yolande and Ed. He could feel none any more.

"My lord, forgive my coming in, but I thought this might be urgent."

The new butler – after all he had been here five years – had brought an envelope. It bore the superscription of a firm of Edinburgh lawyers. Corbell gently laid aside Peggy's hand to open it, did so, then frowned in disquiet.

The late Lady Sissington had left her considerable fortune to Joan Corbell. As she was still a minor it was the firm's duty to inform her father as her proper guardian.

His first thought was that he hadn't properly considered the implications of Cousin Mildred's death. His second was of Alfred's probable reaction. A once doting parent had no doubt surmised what Alfred would do with money; it would vanish. She must have become fond of Joan, and not have expected – nobody after all did expect – to die as suddenly as she had.

Corbell pictured the situation now. There was a companion, a Miss McVey, who no doubt chaperoned Joan. The funeral must have taken place before the will was read. He had been remiss in not keeping up with events, in allowing himself to be led away by the lures of Pompeii and Anubis. He rose. It was time to use an innovation Ione had persuaded him to have installed and whose presence Corbell detested; the telephone.

Silence beat between ringing sounds, himself and Scotland, then he heard the Scottish housekeeper's voice in answer to the bell. No, Miss McVey was no longer with them; after what she'd seen happening in the conservatory between his lordship and Miss Joan, she'd flung up her hands and departed for Caithness. As for his lordship, Lord Alfred had ordered Miss Joan's things packed, saying he was taking her south to her parents. The housekeeper's voice indicated that it wasn't before time. She herself was awaiting instructions as to what was to happen to the establishment. Most of the servants had left, but she had felt it her

n

duty to stay for the time being.

Corbell remembered, out of courtesy, to enquire about the details of Cousin Mildred's death. "Ready for church, she was, in the sealskin as usual, and the pearl earrings, and dropped like a stone, poor lady, in the hall on her way out to the motor." There had been a fair turnout at the funeral, with Lord Alfred hurrying north, no doubt with expectations. The housekeeper's sniff could be heard over the telephone. It hadn't been anticipated that Miss Joan would inherit everything; Miss McVey, for all her years of faithful service, might perhaps have expected something.

Corbell put down the receiver. There was nothing to do but wait for a day or two, then, if no news came, make discreet enquiries. Alfred Sissington would certainly have deflowered Joan as soon as he learned the terms of his mother's will. Now, the child – she was still under age – was in Alfred's possession, with all that implied. Corbell reproached himself. His own treatment of Joan had hardly been that of a father.

Tomorrow – it seemed to arrive like Nemesis – was the appointed day for household prayers. He had the feeling that his own death would occur soon enough not to see many more.

Chapter Four

Joan Corbell had been brought up with the kind of affection that consists of constant nagging, as a result of which she listened to very little that was said to her and lived her own inner life undisturbed. She had been carefully instructed in most of the arts necessary to make a good wife, and it was assumed from the beginning that Lord Alfred Sissington would become her husband when she was old enough. A silver-framed photograph of him, taken at the time he proposed to her mother, stood on Joan's dressing-table and was the first thing she saw on waking. She had not seen him personally for some years, and dimly remembered being bought chocolate and played with by the being in the photograph; a handsome, bright-whiskered and blue-eyed young man.

He became the object of her dreams, which were fairly constant as she had nothing much else to think about. She was not fond of reading, not apt with needlework, had learnt to make jam and cook and polish and dust, as Cousin Mildred believed that young wives should know what they were telling the servants to do by means of having done it themselves. Joan had obeyed passively, still dreaming of Alfred and of how she would make jam for him in exchange for the remembered chocolates. She had no imagination and clung to the things she knew.

In the past, neither of her parents having taken much interest in her, there were two things she remembered with affection. One was Punch the pony, whose arrival in Scotland Joan had greeted with such joy that Cousin Mildred became adverse, and reduced riding to a sparsely permitted minimum. When Punch died Joan almost broke her heart, but didn't say so; it was difficult to say anything of the kind, conversation not being encouraged in any case; young girls kept quiet, minding their manners.

The other thing, or person, she could have remembered with affection was Miss Smail. Miss Smail had brought out, as Cousin Mildred would have said, the best in Joan. However, the glimpse she'd had of Papa and Miss Smail together in the folly had disturbed her passive mind to an extent that made her actually dislike Miss Smail and, almost, Papa, especially after he'd caned her. Soon she had been sent off to Cousin Mildred for a little visit which had turned into a long one. As she grew up she began to resemble Cousin Mildred more than ever, until at last that lady, disillusioned as to the habits and reputation of her once adored angel of an only son, changed her will and left the money to Joan. This was more of a protest against the way things had turned out than foresight as to how they thereafter might. Cousin Mildred could not, naturally, predict that she would drop dead as suddenly as she had.

Joan had taken refuge over the years, since the death of Punch and when she could, in the privacy of the conservatory, which was large and contained mostly begonias, generally in flower. Joan would stare at the prim pink and red blossoms and think vaguely of making jam for Lord Alfred and looking after his linen when they were married. After Cousin Mildred's funeral, which she had not attended as women didn't, she went and sat there, unaware and uncaring that the will was being read, but recalling a brief glimpse at last of Lord Alfred in black as the chief mourner; she would hardly have known him. When he came into the conservatory, and made straight for her, Joan couldn't think what to say. He didn't look at all as one had expected from the photograph; his eyes were bloodshot and baggy, and his moustache was much too brown. However, he kissed her, and said how glad he was that he and his Joanie had met again at last, and of course they must be married at once now poor Mama was dead. He then took down her knickers. Joan didn't like to protest. She had been taught never to answer back. As a result, the one thing Cousin Mildred had refrained from teaching her about the duties of a wife was learned, too soon and without subtlety, among the begonias.

288

At the end Cousin Alfred kissed her again, his breath smelling of stale cigarette-smoke and whisky, and said how glad he was that Joanie was now truly his, and nothing would part them, and her things must be packed and he would take her south to her Papa and Mama, and he and she would be married.

Joan, used to the notion, didn't answer. She understood very little when the lawyer came in to tell her she was an heiress. She and Alfred journeyed south and on the way, shared three brass bedsteads in three successive hotels. Crip, his cousin was thinking, couldn't refuse the marriage now, and the sooner the better, as he'd tried to ensure. Joan was dull both in and out of bed. Some more money at last would, however, be welcome.

That was all Joan knew, except that she had remembered, before leaving, to put on the amber locket her father had sent her, saying it had been her step-grandmother's. It was pretty, and shone.

She hadn't taken the photograph in its silver frame. Somehow, she didn't feel like it. Reality was different. However, Joan had always been brought up to do as she was told.

They arrived at Lackmere just as the household had straggled in for a confused version of household prayers. Vance had been taken so ill this time she would certainly not recover, and the fifth Lord Corbell was carried in from the lake just in time to see the gleam of amber on a young girl's breast. Then he died.

The scene was stolen by Ione. Casting her vast form on Alfred's bosom, she cried, "Alfie! We can be married at last! Oh, if you knew what I've endured!"

Lord Alfred thought quickly. The widow's jointure would be considerable, and he'd already made sure of Joan. He let go of Joan and embraced Ione. The fifth lord's face was, meantime, covered with a sheet. If anyone noticed Joan's mouth open in a wail, they put it down to grief for her father.

Chapter Five

"So poor Joan Corbell was unable to greet her father again, after so long," said the new vicar of the combined parishes of Lackmere and Penhaligon. It was many years later, after two wars and much had happened afterwards, including the axing of the railways, which with the decline in agriculture made the region practically deserted except for summer tourists. All of the young had gone. "That was unfortunate."

"Maybe, or maybe not," said the colonel, who took the readings and with two other elderly parishioners played bridge with the vicar on Thursdays. The colonel had the advantage of a housekeeper whose mother had been in service at Lackmere as a girl and remembered certain happenings after the fifth lord's death. The colonel brushed up his superb white handlebar moustache with a forefinger. "Nobody seems to have thought much about Joan with the funeral baked meats coldly settin' forth the marriage tables. Ione and Sissington lost no time as soon as the fifth lord was buried, and set off for a Paris honeymoon. While they were away, who should reappear but Ed."

"For money, I suppose," said the vicar. He was no longer surprised at anything, having been retired, by reasons of age, from a hectic parish in the East End of London.

"Again, maybe or not," said the colonel, stacking the cards; the second couple were late. "He hung around Joan, chattin' her up. It isn't likely she interested him; what he'd come back for, at a guess, as soon as Corbell was dead, was to continue the affair with Ione. After all, she was a fine figure of a woman, and his

290

little daughter by her was still at Lackmere. The news of her remarriage must have shaken him. When they came back, Ed looked Alf over and decided he couldn't still be what he'd once been. From later evidence, Ione thought the same thing.

"All the same she wasn't goin' to have a great pole of a girl like Joan hangin' about Alf, which no doubt she did from habit. As for Sissington himself, he had this fixed idea that his descent, not poor Corbell's, should inherit the Lackmere title and estate. On his marriage with Ione he began it by callin' himself Sissington-Corbell.

"Well, Ione, who had her commercial side, said to Ed, her lover, that she'd pay him a bit to marry Joan and keep her out of Alf's way. Ed wasn't too keen to be landed with Joan, though by then he knew he wasn't her half-brother because of the marmalade baby they'd called Lilian. However, he decided it would do no harm, because at the same time Alf had paid him not to touch her. All that came out later at the inquest. Meantime, they were married, Joan bein' still in a kind of daze, and settled down, if you can call it that, in the coachhouse, which Ione had had refurbished.

"That might have been all right in its way, but for the results of what had opened among the begonias and the brass hotel bedsteads. Alf used to keep visitin' Joan anyway while Ed was out at the pub, sayin' to Ione he was goin' for a little stroll to smoke a cigar. He hadn't much hope of Ione's obligin' him with an heir by then, and Ed bein' his son, a supposed child of his and Joan's would have to do. After all, it was a family habit.

One day poor Joan came up to the house to see her mother, sayin' she felt sick. Emmie's ma remembers her trailin' in, lookin' like yesterday's forgotten laundry. Ione thought, if she thought at all, that any baby must be Ed's. She didn't like that."

The vicar stared down at the green baize table. The other couple were still late. "Go on," he said quietly.

"Well, Emmie's ma had stationed herself outside the door by then, as you'd expect, and saw and heard what happened. Ione was sittin' on the sofa with her head on Alf's shoulder, kittenish like, and by then Alf looked like a dilapidated ginger tom. Ione didn't much notice what Joan looked like or care why she'd come. She says, purrin' away, that she and Alfie are goin' to have a dear little baby, and Joan must come up to the house often and play with it.

291

"Joan didn't answer. She turned and walked straight past Emmie's mother out of the house, and down into the lake, knowin' she couldn't swim. Nobody noticed, any more than they'd ever noticed much she did. The body didn't float up at once, and by then was only identifiable by the amber locket the poor girl was wearin'. After the inquest – everythin' came out then – it was buried with her. Before that, Ed had found Alf Sissington and smashed his face to pulp. Then he went off to sea, sayin' he'd had enough, money or no money. He was never traced, and as for Alf, he wasn't seen about so much after that. Even Ione couldn't take to the look of him by then.

"When she did have the baby, it was a son, and the image of Ed."

"That would lead to a few complications."

"Not bloody half, savin' your cloth, Vicar. It led to an almighty lawsuit for the rights to the title of Claud, sixth lord, as opposed to the new arrival. By then, Claud was well up on the ladder of promotion at Rome, as he'd shown an uncanny flair for finance and was negotiatin' on behalf of the Vatican Bank. It didn't matter too much to him about the title, but the witnesses they called in were a variety, if you like. One was madam of a brothel in St. James's who swore she'd seen Sissington couplin' with the governess to produce Claud, and that old Peggy Vance, the housekeeper then, had changed the babies to try to fox the police about the governess's death.

"The governess's name was Mercy Belinda Smail. I have looked up the parish records to try to discover why she is buried under one stone with Frederick Corbell, as the only person of that name I can identify was married to the Honourable Henrietta Corbell, the fifth lord's half-sister.

"Well, there was gossip, fostered by old Peggy. She was an old devil, set on her own ancient line being replaced. They'd been the Tessons. You can still see their flat tombs on the ground in the older part of Lackmere vault. Peggy isn't buried there as there wasn't room. She's in the churchyard field. She died the same day as the fifth lord. They say she bore a daughter to the old general."

The general's portrait was by now in the library, upstairs with other Lackmere papers. His sword was kept separately under glass, with a small gold fob showing an enamel eye they'd found on draining the lake. It had been disentangled from other

292

unrecognisable and blackened silver shards. There had also been a honey-coloured urn, date last century, containing a white powder the contractors had unfortunately emptied out into the residual mud when their picks broke the urn.

"Here are the Pinkertons," said the colonel with relief; he was happiest over a game. A crunching outside on the gravel gave rise to the missing couple's appearance; they'd been delayed by a telephone call and couldn't ring up to explain.

"Never mind. You cut," said the colonel to the vicar. Bridge commenced, and halfway through the evening Emmie, bright and too cheerful in a flowered two-piece and over-blonde beehive, brought in a tray of malt whisky and four glasses. They paused and drank.

The vicar decided he was going to go further in the matter of the wrongly buried governess. She might well be the cause of certain hauntings reported more than once, and always taking the same nature; hurried footsteps, running towards the old pit which was long closed over by a grille, and leaving a feeling of horror, fear and pain. There was also the figure of a child in white standing at the further side of what had been the lake before it was drained for health reasons when the house had briefly been a retirement home and then, as the elderly inhabitants grew nervous and left, a rehabilitation venture for young offenders. That hadn't been a success either; one of them broke his leg on the slippery surface of what had become a football field, and sued the authorities for a sizeable sum. The estate was now derelict, except that the National Trust had taken charge of the Roman tiles and had denied entry to anyone under the age of eighteen. The vicar had already tried exorcism, at which he had been known for occasional success. It hadn't worked; the evil was there still. He would consult the bishop about having the governess's remains reburied separately.

"Wake up, Vicar," said the colonel. "It's your turn to deal."

The bishop proved not only helpful, but constructive. He suggested that, subject to the district council's approval, there seemed no reason why the lake should not be undammed and allowed to flood back, officially to encourage tourists to come in summer to the National Trust site of Roman tiles. The unofficial reason was that it might give the child ghost the chance to immerse herself once again in the water. Health reasons, however they had been put forward on behalf of the nervous occupants of the retirement home, no longer applied after further accidents on the resulting slippery surface. A sunken garden had been projected at the time, but nothing grew. There was no doubt that *lacù mare* had some connection with the sea, and the lost ashes trodden long since into the ground by doubtfully rehabilitated footballers might well be those of the missing Henrietta Corbell, who had no recorded grave. As for the governess, her reburial was the province of the bishop himself and the Home Office. He and they had no objection whatsoever.

The double ceremony was arranged with the minimum involvement of the media, although television cameras would record the mighty rushing back of waters for future viewing. The small party of elderly observers of the actual scene would prefer peace and quiet. The bishop, the vicar, the colonel, a representative of the council and another from the National Trust witnessed the turbulence. Across the stretch of grey resulting water a fourth figure watched from the outer door of the vault. He was brightly robed and sat in a wheelchair, which his uncharacteristic hands could operate with amazing speed. Cardinal Claud Walshe-Tesson had flown in from Rome yesterday, had stayed overnight at Vaughan House in London, and had been driven here early enough to perform a certain private ceremony. Inside the vault, as a rule closed to the public, reconsecration would ensure the continued rest of Jocosa, Anna, the fourth lord and Yolande. There had been no room for the fifth lord, who was buried in the field. However he did not appear to be a restless spirit.

Ione, who had died in an inebriates' home, had been cremated. So had Alfred, Lord Sissington-Corbell. The cardinal's rival for the sixth title had been killed, unmarried, at Ypres. The cardinal himself had no wish to revive the dispute and had quietly assumed the name Peggy Vance had assured him was his. In addition, he had by request adopted that of a former servant at Lackmere who had died many years ago in Tasmania, its richest inhabitant. He had left his money to Claud, his son. The cardinal had long given up any attempt to explain matters to himself, and nobody else now cared. He donated the money to good causes and adopted his benefactor's name as asked. He had come to his mother's reburial as a matter of primary importance. Injustice had undoubtedly been done to her.

Miss Smail's second grave had been dug ready nearby the fifth lord's, though not too near, as the vicar surmised this might lead to more hauntings. Both parties were entitled to their separate identity. The opening of the first grave was witnessed by Cardinal Walshe-Tesson among the rest, having been conveyed in the colonel's Land Rover. He trundled himself out of the back at the entrance to the cemetery field, hands actively wheeling, pebble-thick glasses glinting in the moderate sun. Some of those watching knew they were seeing, in extreme old age, the face of Mercy Smail. The cardinal must be almost a century old. His thin white hair blew sparsely beneath his cyclamen biretta. He wheeled himself forward to touch the small coffin as it was hoisted out of the grave. Fred's had been left still covered with earth.

The cardinal murmured a prayer in Latin, Bishop Lomax one in English. The vicar stood with head bowed. Somebody, probably the colonel, had left flowers on the new grave. It was duly filled and a small service held over it. A flat tombstone bearing Mercy's sole name would be installed later. Fred would receive another. There were beginning to be complaints from those who always complain about the eventual lopsidedness of vertical tombstones and their danger to the public safety.

Afterwards the vicar entertained everybody to lunch.

Over lunch, the talk was cheerful. The cardinal said he'd had a good flight and was returning to Rome at once, as there was urgent business. No doubt the urgency of business had kept him alive as long. While he was present the vicar ventured one query. What had become of His Eminence's sister Lilian?

"I can tell you," replied the colonel unexpectedly. "I married her."

When the astonished silence had subsided, he asked if the name of Tiger Lil meant anything. "It was her code name in the Resistance," he said. "She wasn't young by then. Our marriage broke up before the war, don't know why, one of those things, we continued fond of each other. She'd been sent to finishin' school in Paris as a girl, liked it and stayed on, speakin' French like a native. She became a dress designer, built up a famous business; nobody would have known that when she wasn't to be found, she was parachutin' over places like Czechoslovakia, takin' coded information and bringin' it back. They got her in the end." His eyes darkened. "They severed her right thumb at the wrist, so's she would never draw again. She used to keep that hand in a little white mitten. I wanted her to come back to me – I'd been with Monty at Alamein – but she said she wanted to become a nun, and became one in Perth, W.A. She'd dead now. When they cut off her hair she sent me a lock. It was still bright. I wore it under my battledress, like a talisman. That's all. Thought I'd mention it. There's some good in the family, after all. Excellent coffee, Vicar. You're a man of parts yourself."

He had seen, on Remembrance Sunday, a row of medals on the vicar's surplice. Everybody had something they kept to themselves.

The whole thing was kept discreetly out of the national press, although the cardinal's visit was recorded in the Catholic ones, and the local gazette made respectful mention of the matter now it was safely over. Renewed interest was naturally taken in the Roman pavement after the television broadcast. It was again cleaned, treated and advertised by the National Trust. Owing to its lascivious nature there were still queries as to whether or not young persons under the age of consent should be allowed entry.

However, forward-looking members of the committee decided that nothing was unknown, these days, to the young; and that the historic interest attached to colonial expansion of the Roman Empire, and the adoption of foreign gods, would be of value now history itself was, for the time being at any rate, off the curriculum as far as formal education went.

The long-neglected area – it had never recovered from Beeching's axing of the railways and the subsequent decline of agriculture under the EU – was given a mild promotional boost for next summer's bed-and-breakfast season, which farmers' wives had embraced now the most ancient settled occupation of man had gone the way of all flesh.

In other words, things were more or less as they had become expected to be, except for the departure of the ghosts. The child at the lakeside did not reappear, and the terrified footsteps were no longer heard hurrying towards the pit. As for the Corbell Curse, there were no Corbells left. It was therefore assumed that everybody once concerned now rested in peace.